The Love of Zion and Other Writings

Avraham Mapu
The Love of Zion
& other writings

TRANSLATED BY

Joseph Marymount

WITH AN INTRODUCTION BY

David Patterson

The Toby Press

The Love of Zion and Other Writings, 2006

The Toby Press LLC

POB 8531, New Milford, CT 06776-8531, USA
& POB 2455, London WIA 5WY, England
www.tobypress.com

Introduction copyright © 1964 by David Patterson,
revised 2005. Adapted from *Avraham Mapu: The Creator
of the Modern Hebrew Novel,* East and West Library,
Horovitz Publishing Company Ltd. London.

This revised edition uses English transliterations of Hebrew
words in the convention according to the SJE *Standard
Jewish Encyclopaedia,* Editor Dr Geoffrey Wigoder, 1992.

English translation copyright © 1919 Joseph Marymount.
Originally published as *The Sorrows of Naame* from the Hebrew
Ahavat Zion, National Book Publishers, New York 1919.

Translations of further selections of *The Guilt of Samaria*
and *The Hypocrite* copyright © 1964 David Patterson.

ISBN 159264 129 6, *paperback*

A CIP catalogue record for this title is available
from the British Library.

Printed and bound in the United States
by Thomson-Shore Inc., Michigan

Contents

Preface

The novels of Avraham Mapu may be regarded as the first productions of real merit in modern Hebrew literature, and they have exercised a powerful influence on its subsequent development and on the renaissance of Hebrew as a modern language. They are equally important for the impact which they made on the segregated Jewish communities in Eastern Europe in the second half of the nineteenth century.

The following introduction presents an outline of the author's background, followed by a brief biography and a serious literary appreciation of his work. It includes a representative selection of his writings in English translation. In this way it is hoped that the interested layman and the student of comparative literature may gain an insight into the quality of modern Hebrew writing and the development of Hebrew literature during the last hundred years.

David Patterson

Note

The following abbreviated titles appear in the text:

Mapu. Kol Kitevei Avraham Mapu (The Collected Writings of Avraham Mapu), Tel Aviv, 1950. All references to Mapu's works are drawn from this edition.

Klausner. J. Klausner, *Historiah Shel ha-Sifrut ha-Ivrit ha-Hadashah (History of Modern Hebrew Literature),* Vol. iii, second revised edition, Jerusalem, 1953.

The introduction has been adapted from Professor Patterson's *Avraham Mapu: The Creator of the Modern Hebrew Novel.* The advanced reader is advised to consult the original work, which features further sources and notes than the scope of this volume can offer.

Introduction

A century and a half have passed since Avraham Mapu published the very first Hebrew novel—incidentally, the first novel in a Biblical setting in any language—and at one stroke created a whole new realm in Hebrew letters. Since its original appearance in 1853, the scope of Hebrew literature has broadened beyond all recognition, and it now encompasses a rich variety of literary form, written in a far more complex and subtle idiom than that employed by Mapu. Technical experience and linguistic resources have so improved in the intervening years, while such elementary literary skills as characterization, plot-construction and the art of dialogue have meanwhile so developed, that Mapu's novels necessarily appear somewhat naïve and immature. Nevertheless, the creative artist who dares attempt some new and unfamiliar pattern needs imagination, courage, and tenacity of high order. Even when he accomplishes the rare feat of winning immediate recognition and acclaim, posterity alone can estimate the real significance and the validity of his experiment.

Of Mapu's three novels, his first, *The Love of Zion* remains the most significant. It broke fresh ground, opening up the prospect of a free and independent life to a people hopelessly cramped and fettered by political, social, and economic restrictions. For Mapu's contemporary public it depicted a new world. This achievement, as a pointer to Mapu's contribution as a novelist, deserves serious attention. As the great critic F. R. Leavis remarked in *The Great Tradition* (1948):

> ...it is well to start by distinguishing the few really great—the major novelists who count in the same way as the major poets, in the sense that they not only change the possibilities of the art for practitioners and readers, but that they are significant in terms of the human awareness they promote; awareness of the possibilities of life.

If this criterion has real validity, then *The Love of Zion* must bear the stamp of greatness. For not only did it create—not merely change—the possibilities for a Hebrew novel, but in addition it gave open expression to the mute longings and half-sensed groping of a whole people towards a fuller and richer life.

This study is devoted to a critical examination of the literary qualities of Avraham Mapu's three surviving novels—*The Love of Zion (Ahavat Zion), The Guilt of Samaria (Ashmat Shomeron)* and *The Hypocrite (Avit Tzavua).* Of a fourth novel, *The Visionaries (Hozei Hezyonot),* a small fragment of seven chapters is alone extant, so that only occasional reference has been made to that work, which reputedly comprised no less than ten whole parts. The disappearance of the manuscript spelled personal tragedy for its author; it must be regarded as an equally tragic loss for modern Hebrew literature.

Since the first moment of publication all three novels have proved firm favourites with the Hebrew reading public, a fact to which some ten editions of *The Guilt of Samaria* and *The Hypocrite,* and no less than fifteen editions of *The Love of Zion,* bear ample testimony. The latter, indeed, soon became the first "classic" in modern Hebrew literature, and has been translated into a wide variety of languages, including Russian, French, German, English, Arabic, Judaeo-Arabic, Judaeo-Persian, Ladino, and Yiddish.

Although *The Love of Zion* nowadays shares the fate common to so many classics in being relegated to historical courses, its influence on the course of Hebrew literature in the second half of the nineteenth century and even in the early part of the twentieth can scarcely be overestimated. A considerable proportion of the major Hebrew writers during the last one hundred years have readily admitted their indebtedness to Mapu's first novel, which for many served as the first introduction to the very concept of literature as such.

Two of the three novels under review, namely *The Love of Zion* and *The Guilt of Samaria,* are historical romances set in the ancient land of Israel in the period of the prophet Isaiah, and spanning the reigns of Kings Ahaz and Hezekiah in the southern kingdom of Judah. The third novel, *The Hypocrite,* is a tale of contemporary Jewish life in eastern Europe, in which the author attempts to outline the conflicts raging within his own society and suggest mild palliatives for some of its more obvious weaknesses. But although the historical romances are separated in time from the contemporary novel by no less than two and a half millennia, all three reflect an astonishing similarity of ideal and aspiration. All of them may be regarded as the progeny—in many respects, indeed, the consummation— of an intellectual ferment, to whose tenets Mapu remains, perhaps, the last wholly-committed adherent of real stature in Hebrew literature.

A People in Ferment

The intellectual ferment, which was destined to play a decisive role in subsequent Jewish history, arose as an expression of revolt against the physical and mental restrictions of the ghetto, first imposed in the middle of the sixteenth century and subsequently maintained for some two hundred and fifty harsh and bitter years. Effective opposition to the humiliations of such legal inferiority may be traced to the small but wealthy Jewish community in Berlin in the second half of the eighteenth century, at whose head stood the illustrious figure of Moses Mendelssohn. Stimulated by the impact of the humanitarian ideals emanating from France, and by a more tolerant attitude in certain influential sections of society, a movement grew up within German Jewry, whose object was the emancipation of the Jews and the amelioration of their material and cultural condition.

Modelled on the German *Aufklärung*, the Hebrew movement of enlightenment, known as *Haskalah*, attempted to provide a bridge in Jewish life from the medieval world of the ghetto to the modern world of Western Europe. As the first step, it advocated a reform in Jewish education calculated to facilitate Jewish participation in the broad stream of European culture by grafting secular elements to a syllabus hitherto entirely composed of traditional, religious studies. For the *Maskilim,* as the exponents of enlightenment were called, some understanding of European culture appeared to be an essential prerequisite in the long, hard struggle for emancipation.

Mere changes in the school curriculum, however, were clearly not enough. If the debasing effects of the ghetto were to be annulled, measures had to be sought to bolster the self-confidence of the Jewish people, restore its dignity, reawaken its emotional life, quicken its aesthetic sense and generally counteract the stultifying consequences of long isolation and confinement. A serious attempt to solve these very formidable problems became the primary concern of the exponents of *Haskalah.* In view of the limited resources at their disposal, however, the efforts of the *Maskilim* were largely concentrated upon the task of fostering a renewed interest in the Hebrew Bible, which could be made to serve many of their manifold purposes at one fell swoop. A realization of the glory of the national past might help to alleviate the degradation of the present; the pastoral and agricultural background and imagery of scripture might serve to re-establish the contact with nature which had been severed by centuries of ghetto life; the exalted poetry and sublime language of the Bible might similarly awaken dormant aesthetic feelings and encourage an interest in literature for its own sake.

The Hebrew of the Bible, then, was to become the main channel through which the Jewish people might be led towards the glittering vistas of European civilization. But in order to enjoy the fruits of European thought and letters it was first necessary to embark upon the laborious task of composing original works and translating a wide range of studies from various languages into Biblical Hebrew. This clumsy and somewhat artificial exercise largely determined the course of modern Hebrew literature for no less than a century, and is primarily responsible for the strange incompatibility of form and content which characterizes so much of the writing throughout that period. The process gave rise, however, to a number of praiseworthy, and indeed heroic, attempts to overcome the serious linguistic limitations which the pioneers of modern Hebrew literature deliberately imposed upon themselves. Of these, the novels of Avraham Mapu remain the most successful examples.

The *Maskilim,* however, were not content to rely upon Biblical Hebrew as the sole method for the attainment of their ends. In spite of bitter orthodox opposition, they enthusiastically advocated the study of foreign cultures and languages, particularly German, in order to provide a growing generation, hungry for secular knowledge, with the instruments necessary for its acquisition. With the repressed avidity of centuries, young Jews hastened to absorb the new learning. In the space of a few short years these eager students attempted to catapult themselves through a process of cultural development, which in Western Europe had evolved gradually and painfully over two and a half centuries. Small wonder, then, that the effects upon Jewish life were disastrous! In Germany, the path to secular knowledge soon became a high road to conversion. University education and legal equality were purchased wholesale at the price of Judaism. The new Hebrew, which had in most cases provided the first stepping-stone towards enlightenment, was discarded as soon as the student had acquired sufficient German for his needs. Had it been limited solely to Germany, modern Hebrew literature might have flourished for no more than two or three decades. Fortunately, however, seeds of the new movement were carried over to the much more fertile soil of Eastern Europe.

The partitions of Poland at the end of the eighteenth century had resulted in the incorporation of a large, well-populated area of Jewish settlement within the boundaries of the Russian Empire. In consequence, the policy of Russian nationalism fervently pursued by the Czarist administration in the nineteenth century came face to face with the spectacle of a numerous, compact, and undeniably alien element living just inside the country's western borders. This alien body clung tenaciously to its own distinctive religion, language, mannerisms, habits of food and dress, and constituted a self-contained, inbred and highly self-conscious society, with a widespread, esoteric system of education, and—from the viewpoint of the regime—of highly doubtful loyalties.

In seeking to neutralize this potentially hostile segment of the population, the government resorted sometimes to a policy of conciliation, but more frequently to one of ruthless oppression. During the long reign of Nicholas I (1825-55), the oppression worsened into a nightmare reign of terror, characterized by ferocious assaults on the economic and religious structure of Jewish life, and the introduction of a system of compulsory military service of twenty-five years' duration, with child recruits mercilessly pressed and kidnapped into pre-military training establishments. Few of these Cantonists, as they were called, were ever reunited with their families. The sorry plight of Russian Jewry was further aggravated by a remarkable natural increase in population throughout the nineteenth century, accompanied by a proportional increase in the difficulties of eking out even the meagrest of livelihoods. Grinding poverty became the all-pervading and most compelling factor in Jewish life. The scope of economic activity was so severely limited that a man with a barrel of herrings was considered a merchant!

The first ten years of the reign of Alexander II (1855-81), however, seemed to herald an era of reform. Juvenile conscription was finally abolished, a number of the more irksome economic restrictions were rescinded, while Jewish students were even allowed entry to the high schools and universities previously barred to them. This latter measure, which was aimed at the cultural integration of the Jewish population in place of the prior unsuccessful attempts at religious conversion, received the enthusiastic support of the growing band of *Maskilim*, the Jewish exponents of enlightenment.

The Hebrew renaissance in Germany, though but shortlived, had not vanished entirely without trace. Wandering scholars from the towns and villages of Eastern Europe, after making their way to Berlin or some other great centre of enlightenment in search of the new learning, had later returned to spread the ideas of *Haskalah* in the lands of their birth. To these *Maskilim* the government's educational proposals seemed a heaven-sent instrument for the reform of Jewish life as well as for the eventual acquisition of political and economic emancipation. Hence they embraced the cause of secular education with unabated zeal, urging Jewish youth to take immediate advantage of the new facilities.

The encouragement of secular education, however, excited the bitter antagonism of two powerful forces within the Jewish community—the orthodox Pietists and the Hasidim. Both these factions, long at war with each other, launched a combined attack upon the movement of *Haskalah,* in which they at once discerned an inherent threat to themselves. The exponents of *Haskalah,* for their part, eagerly responded to the challenge, attacking the rigidly restrictive traditional education, which regarded all branches of secular study as anathema. They denounced the narrowness and bigotry of a religious framework which attempted to isolate the community completely from the rapid developments of the outside world, while devoting the lion's share of its intellectual activity to interminable, hair-splitting arguments on the fine points of ritual theory and practice. Against the Hasidim they took up the cudgels even more readily. In its initial period the movement of Hasidism had represented a new flowering of spiritual activity. By the middle of the nineteenth century it had partly degenerated into a conglomeration of base superstitions and semi-magical practices under the stress of weaknesses inherent in the system—notably the unrestrained faith in the wonderworking Rebbes—which lent itself to exploitation and abuse, and which presented a blank wall to any attempts at mass enlightenment.

To this three-pronged contest, bitterly waged between the *Maskilim,* the Pietists and the Hasidim, a further complication was added, a phenomenon arising from the teachings of *Haskalah,* but distressingly unforeseen. The young people, who had responded readily and in growing numbers to the call of *Haskalah* for enlightenment, secular education and entrance to the universities, went a step further, and embarked upon a process of rapid assimilation to the majority culture. Once again the instrument of the Hebrew language, into which the *Maskilim* had so laboriously translated a copious number of foreign works on art, literature, and science, was used as a means of acquiring the secular knowledge necessary for entrance to a university, and promptly abandoned.

This had not been the intention of the *Maskilim* at all. For one of their chief aims had been to revive and fashion Hebrew into a suitable medium for the expression of the richness and beauty of life, whereas instead, they found themselves the unwitting abetters of a ceaseless process of complete estrangement from Judaism. The movement of *Haskalah* in Russia never successfully recovered from the shock, even though a similar fate had overtaken it in Germany some fifty years previously, and might not, therefore, have been entirely unexpected. Even during the last decades of the nineteenth century the *Maskilim* still raised the cry of enlightenment and education, although in ever more feeble measure, until finally the poet J. L. Gordon (1831-95), after a lifetime of struggle for the ideals of *Haskalah,* could only utter the despairing cry: "For whom do I toil . . .?"

Against this complex background the battle of *Haskalah* was fought, and, before the reaction of disillusionment, with a naïve confidence and an intense conviction of being in the right. In very great measure the *Maskilim* penetrated the unhealthy forces at work in the Jewish community, even though failing to recognize the immensity of the stresses and strains at work, so soon destined to bring about the cataclysmic changes in Jewish life which they proved powerless to prevent. Nor did they understand, until the damage had been done, the negative side of their own efforts, and their own contribution to the undermining of the communal unity—a breach which has never been repaired.

In the meantime, however, they set about reform with a fervent and missionary ardour, so that similar threads of polemic and tendentious writing—although coloured in accordance with the form of expression—may be discovered in the satires of Joseph Perl and Isaac Erter, in the poetry of Judah Leib Gordon, and in the novels of Avraham Mapu. In particular, Mapu's long novel of contemporary life, *The Hypocrite,* served as a pattern for the militant, social novel, which has occupied a dominant place in Hebrew literature for almost a century.

The peculiar merit of Mapu's novels thus lies in the fact that they may be regarded both as the consummation of the first major division in modern Hebrew literature, and equally as one of the important formative factors in its subsequent development. It is with the literary qualities responsible for so unusual a dual role that the following chapters are primarily concerned.

Avraham Mapu's Life and Work

No study of the role of Avraham Mapu in the development of modern Hebrew literature can fail to notice the striking contrast between the imaginative life displayed in his novels and the sheer drabness of the life of grinding and relentless poverty which was his personal fate. The narrow limits of his own physical horizons and the dull monotony of his daily routine serve only to emphasize the romantic fantasy which permeates his stories, and to underline the rich and exciting adventures encountered by so many of his characters almost at every turn. Indeed, there is an element of alchemy in Mapu's talent that serves to translate the dross of a humdrum and humiliating struggle for existence into a golden dream-world of excitement and romance. Certainly, few novelists could have emerged from a less promising environment.

Avraham ben Yekutiel Mapu was born in Slobodka, a suburb of the important Lithuanian city of Kovno, on the tenth of Teveth, 1808. The Jewish community, numbering some six hundred families, was miserably poor. The low, wooden houses flanking the unpaved streets each provided shelter for no less than four or five families, while hunger—as the growing child learned only too early—was the normal attending circumstance of life. Only the close ties of affection between the young Avraham and his parents could compensate, in some measure, for the poverty-stricken conditions of the home.

His father, Yekutiel, was considered one of the leading scholars of the town, and earned his living by teaching Hebrew. The teacher, or *Melamed,* ranked among the lowliest occupations in Jewish society—at least, as far as remuneration was concerned—and few were they who would resort to it while any other avenue of livelihood remained open. Suffice to say that the word "teacher" had none of the associations of dignity, or a certain social standing, which it carries at the present time. Lessons were usually given in the teacher's own home, the classroom coinciding with the living-room, and extended, even for the youngest, from dawn to dusk. The teacher was frequently a bitterly frustrated man, and often found a sadistic outlet for his anger in savage punishments meted out indiscriminately to his young charges. For the Jewish child life was all study and no play, and the anxieties normally associated with adulthood began to weigh upon him only too early.

Yekutiel, however, seems to have been a kindly, though ailing, man, and in spite of his straitened circumstances, succeeded in giving his son the prevailing Jewish education. Avraham's mother, Dinah, was a shrewd and pious woman, more capable than her gentle husband, and possessed of considerable strength of character which, on occasion, she was not afraid to exert on behalf of her son, when she disapproved of the company he was keeping. The young Avraham, though undernourished and weakly, was endowed with great intellectual ability. At the tender age of seven he joined the ranks of his father's advanced pupils, and at twelve he was considered fit to leave the *Heder* or elementary school, and continue his studies alone in the school of advanced studies known as the *Beit-ha-Midrash*. He had already earned the coveted title of *Illui,* reserved for child prodigies, and early in life he mastered much of the Talmudic learning of the day. Yet such were the teaching methods of that time, and so completely was the study of grammar neglected, that he was unable to compose two or three sentences in correct Hebrew—an unpromising beginning for a future novelist!

At fifteen he was introduced to the mysteries of Kabbalah by his father, who was himself engaged in its study. It is related that his imagination became so inflamed by the hidden and mystic doctrines, especially those known as practical Kabbalah, that he performed an experiment designed to make himself invisible, carefully following the prescribed incantations and rather gruesome directions. Convinced of success, he was bitterly chagrined at being greeted by a friend, while walking home "unseen." Although disappointed at the failure of his experiment, he attributed it to the fact that he had not yet reached the required degree of spiritual purity. However, this appears to have been his sole attempt to perform miracles.

In the year 1825, at the age of seventeen, he married the daughter of a well-to-do inhabitant of Kovno. In accordance with the accepted custom which favoured early marriage, but which afforded the parents complete freedom to arrange a betrothal without prior consultation with the principal parties concerned, he saw his bride for the first time on his wedding day. Their subsequent relationship was cordial, but never deep. Indeed, this first marriage seems to have exerted little influence upon him, especially since the young bridegroom was not at first required to earn a livelihood for his family. The father-in-law was normally expected to provide his daughter and her husband with a number of years of board and residence in his own house—a clause to that effect being usually inserted into the marriage contract. Hence after his marriage, Mapu moved to his father-in-law's house, and continued his studies there. While living in Kovno, he made the acquaintance of a certain Rabbi Eliezer, and under his influence began to frequent Hasidic circles, to which movement his interest in Kabbalah had provided a certain affinity. Neither his father nor mother was pleased at this development, but whereas his father acquiesced, either through tolerance or mere weakness, his more determined mother intervened personally, and removed her son from the group by force.

Even after his violent leave-taking from Hasidism, Mapu maintained his interest in Kabbalah, which occasioned a period of close contact with Elijah Ragoler, rabbi of his native Slobodka, who was also engaged in its study. Their relationship, however, proved fruitful for another reason. During his visits to his friend's house, Mapu discovered a copy of the Psalms with a Latin translation. This chance find was of great importance to Mapu's subsequent development; indeed, he was inclined to regard it as the foundation stone of his secular education. It aroused in him a desire to learn Latin, in which language he later became proficient, although he was forced to acquire it without the aid of a teacher, since the study of Latin was virtually unknown amongst the pious Jews of Eastern Europe. It has been suggested that his knowledge of Latin may have helped him considerably towards an understanding of the spirit of ancient times, and a comparison of the translation with the Hebrew original may well have caused him to examine the Bible with more detailed attention. Certainly from this time it is possible to trace a growing interest in languages, resulting in the study of French, German, and Russian, in all of which he achieved a fair measure of proficiency, in spite of the primitive methods of linguistic study, which were alone within his reach, and the hostile attitude to the learning of foreign languages prevailing in Orthodox circles.

The impoverishment of his father-in-law compelled Mapu to seek employment, and to begin the bitter struggle to maintain himself and his family which was to continue throughout his life. He therefore accepted an invitation to become tutor to the children of an innkeeper in a village near Kovno. The living-conditions which he experienced at the inn were even worse than those he had known in his own community. The smoke-filled room in which he gave instruction forced him to conduct the lessons sitting with his charges on the floor, where the atmosphere was slightly less polluted. A Catholic priest, who one day chanced upon him in this sorry posture, could not refrain from mocking the "Schoolmaster." Surprised, however, at Mapu's apt reply in Latin, the priest aided him towards a more thorough mastery of the language by lending him books from his own library. Mapu remained in the village not more than six months, but during that time, he may have imbibed that appreciation of country life which is so marked in his novels.

His next appointment was more congenial. In the year 1832 he was invited to become tutor to the children of a wealthy merchant in Georgenburg, a small town not far from Kovno. During the two or three years of his sojourn in Georgenburg, he left his wife and family in Slobodka, sending them the whole of his small salary. The separation from his family, however, was compensated in some measure by his introduction to contemporary Hebrew literature, which turned his thoughts towards the ideas of the movement of enlightenment, or *Haskalah,* then being propagated by its exponents, the *Maskilim.* Consequently, after his return to Kovno, where he again spent two or three years, he began to disseminate the ideas of *Haskalah* among the local youth, and acquired something of a reputation for his efforts. But his years of wandering were by no means over. About the year 1837/8 Mapu moved to Rossieny, this time together with his wife and family, and he remained there as a teacher for six or seven years.

Rossieny, at that time, had become a centre of *Haskalah* and within a short time Mapu occupied an honoured position among the enlightened. The happiness he experienced made him conceive a deep affection for the town, which he once described as "a city of wise men, who love their people and their holy language." Among the *Maskilim* he met in Rossieny, his most important relationship was with Shneur Sachs (1816-92), who combined a deep love of the Hebrew language with a profound interest in his nation's past. Although eight years his junior, Sachs influenced Mapu profoundly, and encouraged him—according to Mapu's own testimony—to concentrate on Hebrew and the ancient history of Israel.

The years in Rossieny were clouded only by financial worries, to escape from which Mapu petitioned the government for permission to open a school for girls, but without success. In 1844, however, he was appointed to a teaching post in the Hebrew school in Kovno, and returned there, leaving his wife and family in Rossieny. He was able to send for them the following year, but his wife died not long afterwards in 1846. Instead of improving his material position, he had worsened it. His salary was small, and all his efforts to obtain an additional post remained unrewarded. In 1847, therefore, he accepted the proposal of Judah Opatov to become tutor to his son, and moved to Vilna.

Although Vilna was the greatest centre of *Haskalah* in Lithuania, and Mapu became acquainted with such celebrities as Adam haCohen (1794-1878), Samuel Joseph Fünn (1818-91) and Kalman Schulman (1819-99), he appears, nevertheless, to have found the town no more congenial than the house of his employer. Opatov was a harsh and illiterate man, but possessed of great strength of character and prone to acts of violence. When Mapu informed him in 1848 that he had been appointed a teacher in the government school in Kovno, Opatov assaulted him physically and Mapu fled his house. Mapu never forgave the insult, and it may well be that he modelled the ignorant but successful boor, Gaal, who plays a leading part in *The Hypocrite*, on his former employer. In spite of his short stay in Vilna and his lack of affection for the *Maskilim* he met there, Mapu was doubtless influenced by the spirit prevailing amongst them. The Hebrew writers in Vilna were characterized by a tendency to Romanticism and a devotion to the Bible and the Hebrew language. His contact with them inclined Mapu in the same direction and formed a natural continuation of the influence first exerted by Shneur Sachs.

The teaching post at the government school proved permanent, and from the year 1848 Mapu resided in Kovno. After leading the life of a widower for several years he remarried in 1851. His second marriage was far more successful, and during the first ten years of his final sojourn in Kovno his slightly more favourable financial circumstances added to the happiness of his domestic life. This was the fruitful period of Mapu's literary productivity, and his fame as a novelist spread rapidly. One of the greatest moments of happiness in

the author's life occurred in 1857 on receiving the personal congratulations of Norov, the Russian Minister of Public Institutions. Mapu
was always deeply moved by the recollection of this signal honour,
and expressed his gratitude to the Russian minister in a poem inserted
in the introduction to his novel *The Visionaries.*

The happy years were not destined to continue. His wife
was afflicted with a long illness, which severely drained his limited
resources, already overtaxed by the heavy expenditures arising from
his publications. His troubles were increased by a growing persecution
on the part of the Pietists and the Hasidim, who bitterly opposed his
advocacy of enlightenment, and influenced the censors to delay or
even forbid his publications. Even without their hostile intervention
publication was difficult enough, and constituted a constant source
of irritation. Moreover, from 1860 onwards his own health began
to fail. His right hand was affected with palsy, and he was forced to
continue writing with his left. His time, too, was greatly curtailed
by the numbers of private lessons he was compelled to give in order
to supplement his income. In spite of every obstacle, however, his
literary activity continued unabated, as his ailing body strove to keep
pace with his fertile and tireless mind.

One pleasant incident served to ease the burden of his later
years. In the early part of the year 1861, Mapu received an invitation
from his brother, with whom he always maintained an affection-
ate relationship, to spend a few weeks in St Petersburg. The author
was delighted with the splendours of the great city, and particularly
enjoyed the opera he heard there, which in his characteristic *Melizah*
(smoothness) he referred to as "the song of players in the valley of
vision." He returned to Kovno refreshed in mind and body, the pleasant memories of his visit firmly embedded in his thoughts.

His happiness was short-lived. In 1863 his wife died, and he
was left alone. In a letter to A. Kaplan, dated 21st Tevet, 1864, he
expresses his wish to marry a third time, preferably a healthy woman
of about forty years of age, and mentions two women who have been
suggested as eligible. He dismisses them, however, on the ground that
one is ailing while the other has children. It is the pathetic revelation

of a sick and lonely man, anxious to be assured of some companionship in his remaining years. But in the end he remained a widower, continuing to write to the accompaniment of growing acclamation on the one hand, and increasing poverty and physical pain on the other. In 1866, the disease of his fingers returned in an even more acute form, so that every line he wrote became an agony. But he not only persevered with his writing, but even planned new novels, which were to outweigh his previous works.

Towards the end of the same year he contracted an additional illness, this time gall-stones, and his strength began to fail him. When his brother, in consequence, invited him to Paris in 1867, Mapu joyfully accepted his offer, meanwhile determining to undergo an operation in Koenigsberg *en route*. An ardent admirer of French literature and eager to sample the culture of the French capital, he set out with high hopes at the end of the year. But in Koenigsberg his physical condition deteriorated sharply, and he was unable to proceed. In spite of his weakness, his mind remained clear until the end, allowing him to continue with his work, and at the same time engage in literary discussion with the visitors to his sick-bed. He died on Yom Kippur, 1867.

Mapu's Creativity

The origins of Mapu's creativity may be traced to his early twenties. According to R. Brainin, the idea of his novel, *The Love of Zion*, was first born as far back as 1830, and several passages were written as early as 1831. Certainly, the long interval between the conception and final publication in 1853 indicates a slow and gradual development. The novel appears to have passed through three distinct stages. While the form of the first draft is not certain, it would seem to have been modelled on the allegorical dramas of Moses Hayyim Luzzatto. The influence of Shneur Sachs, however, directed Mapu's attention towards the Bible, and he chose the theme of Shulamit from the *Song of Songs*. But in its final form, *The Love of Zion* has retained no trace of Shulamit, and the hero and heroine are called Amnon and Tamar. It has been suggested that the work was complete in manuscript form in 1844, but that Mapu was so nervous of publishing it in case the reception should prove unfavourable that he continued to alter it from time to time. The novel was finally published in Vilna in 1853, some three years after its despatch to the censor.

The appearance of *The Love of Zion* was roundly acclaimed, and in the four years that followed its publication, no less than twelve hundred copies were sold—no mean achievement considering the small numbers of *Maskilim,* and in view of the almost universal poverty. Although Mapu himself complained bitterly that the story was read far more than it was bought, he felt sufficiently encouraged to embark upon further creations. Taking advantage of the more liberal spirit which marked the accession to the throne of Alexander II in 1855, Mapu chose a setting of contemporary Jewish life for his second work, *The Hypocrite*. This lengthy novel contained five parts, of which the first was published in Vilna in 1858, the second in 1861, and the third in 1864. A second edition containing all five parts appeared posthumously in Warsaw in 1869. Financial difficulties, and constant frustrations due to censorship, continually delayed publication, causing the author much needless irritation and worry. But the reception of each separate publication was no less enthusiastic than that which had greeted the appearance of *The Love of Zion,* although the small number of copies actually bought was once more quite disproportionate to the lavishness of the praise.

Simultaneously Mapu had been engaged on the composition of a third novel, *The Visionaries,* dealing with events in the time of the pseudo-Messiah, Shabbetai Zvi. This work was sent to the censor in 1858, together with the first two parts of *The Hypocrite.* The growing campaign of his enemies, however, brought pressure on the censors to forbid the publication of the work. Whereas the publication of *The Hypocrite* was subject only to irritating delays, *The Visionaries* was never allowed to appear in print in spite of all Mapu's frantic and repeated efforts. Worse still, the manuscript disappeared altogether—and was never recovered. To the end of his days Mapu's grief over this loss was inconsolable. Of this work, reported to have run into ten complete parts, only a fragment of seven chapters remains extant.

Sickened by the persecution which these controversial novels had engendered on the part of the fanatical Pietists and Hasidim, Mapu reverted to the Bible for the background of his fourth and last novel, *The Guilt of Samaria*. His great inventive capacity rarely allowed him to be engaged on a single production at any one time. The first part of *The Guilt of Samaria*, written simultaneously with the third part of *The Hypocrite*, was published in Vilna, in 1865. In the same year Mapu produced a second edition of *The Love of Zion*, an unusual but gratifying event within the lifetime of a Hebrew writer of that generation. The second part of *The Guilt of Samaria* appeared a year later (Vilna, 1866), when Mapu's health had already deteriorated due to the strain of such copious production.

In addition to his novels Mapu, a born teacher, published several textbooks designed to improve the clumsy educational methods of his day. Of the two such works, *Hanok Lana'ar* and *Der Hausfranzose*, which appeared in Vilna in 1859, the former outlines a new method for teaching the rudiments of Hebrew, based on the author's own experience, while the latter constitutes a primary textbook for the study of French. Written in German, but with Hebrew characters, it provides an interesting example of the efforts made by the exponents of *Haskalah* to widen the cultural interests of the community. In the introduction, written in Hebrew, Mapu poured out all the pent-up bitterness accumulated from the difficulties of publication, the small sales of his novels, and the fate of his beloved *The Visionaries*. He expressly states these factors as his reason for producing simple but helpful textbooks instead of working on further stories. His third production of this type was published in Koenigsberg in 1867, and bears the title *Amon Pedagog*. In this work he portrays his methods of teaching Hebrew. But even within the framework of a textbook his creative talent emerges in the form of a story, which he unfolds section by section as an illustration of the rules to be explained. This was the last publication before his death.

Throughout his life the author possessed a high opinion of the value of all forms of literature, but rated the imaginative story above any other literary genre. He was the first to conceive the idea of a novel in Hebrew, and courageously set about the task of creating it in the face of all difficulties. An appreciation of the measure of his success and an evaluation of his work will be attempted in the following pages. But perhaps the most moving tribute to his achievement is that engraved in three short Hebrew lines upon his gravestone:

> *Generations have passed and generations will come,*
> *But his writings will not be forgotten;*
> *And the purity of his art will always remain.*

Tales of Villainy and Romance

The task of creating an entirely new genre in Hebrew literature presented Mapu with a number of extremely thorny problems, all requiring immediate and simultaneous solution. Each of the many individual ingredients comprising a novel bristled with perplexing and unfamiliar difficulties. Form and treatment, style and language, characterization and dialogue all demanded the most careful and exacting consideration—in the absence of any prior Hebrew novel to serve as guide. In spite of its comparative brevity, it is scarcely surprising that the author laboured on the composition of his first, most highly cherished novel for more than twenty years. Yet, formidable though the various other difficulties of composition proved to be, the central problem of weaving a sustained and viable plot remained, perhaps, the most elusive. Admittedly, some of the themes might well be modelled on one or other of the variegated patterns of the European novel. On the other hand, not even in European languages had a novel as yet appeared which drew upon the Bible for its subject matter. The plots, moreover, were intended to serve a dual purpose. Not only was the author anxious to compose a romantic tale of heroism and adventure, but he was equally determined that his stories should serve as a means of propagating his own particular ideals. This uncomfortable fusion of didacticism and romance accounts, at least in part, for one of the least satisfying aspects of the stories.

Mapu's novels bear certain points of striking similarity. In spite of the differences of subject matter and treatment, all three employ the same principal elements of motivation—love and intrigue. The theme in each case depicts a struggle between the forces of good and evil. The former are represented by characters who are bound together by personal ties of affection and devotion to an ideal, which in the historical novels consists of a deep love of Zion, and in *The Hypocrite* a passion for enlightenment. The latter are embodied in individuals who are motivated primarily by the hope of personal gain, and who are prepared to go to any lengths to further their nefarious purposes. The interaction of these two sets of forces gives rise to a chain of complex developments, with the initiative principally on the side of the villains, who remain, until the final denouement, at least one step ahead of the heroes. The latter, indeed, display throughout an irritating naïveté, and triumph in the end—as triumph they must—far more by good luck than good management. They leave the impression of winning by a rather fortunate knockout, after having been severely outpointed.

Like Milton's Satan in the early books of *Paradise Lost,* it is the villains who—contrary, perhaps, to the author's intention—often command sympathy, and certainly arouse admiration for their daring and resource. The paragon of virtue may awaken respect, but some admixture of human weakness is required to win the wholehearted support of the reader.

For the modern reader, then, the plots of Mapu's novels contain only a secondary interest. Lacking in originality, depth and subtlety, they must yield pride of place to the style, the language, and the setting of the stories. For his own generation, however, the plots, and particularly the plots of the historical novels, constituted the most attractive and fascinating aspect of his work, both because this literary medium was hitherto unknown in Hebrew literature, and because of the quick excitement of adventure which stood out in dazzling contrast against the colourless fabric of his readers' own lives:

> Scarcely had he finished when a troop of horsemen came riding through the wood towards them brandishing their swords—young Ephraimite warriors in rich attire, and at their head a lovely maid, but fearsome to behold with flashing eyes and glowing cheeks. She sat astride an Egyptian horse, emboldened by the gay trappings on his neck, but made bolder still by virtue of his rider set for battle. Her long hair enfolded her firm neck, and she was clad in a loose garment of chequered gold, whose skirts floated as the wind caught them in her headlong gallop. And as she approached the field of tournament, one of the Ephraimite youths cried out: "Make way, make way for the pride and glory of Ephraim's warriors."

For a youth whose physical life was confined to the poverty and squalor of a village in the Pale of Settlement, and whose intellectual activity was harnessed to the machine of dry, Talmudic casuistry, Mapu opened up a new, refreshing world. The vivid descriptions of heroism and determined action, the free expression of emotion, and above all the colourful scenes of a people living unrestricted in its own land, inflamed the imagination of a generation starved of life and happiness. The novels were read in cellars and in attics, furtively and in stealth, and never without a quickening of emotion and the gleam of a new and unexpected hope. Above all, they taught a rising generation that life must be *felt* as well as understood. Indeed, the stimulus provided by the publication of Mapu's novels in arousing imaginative and emotional forces long congealed constitutes one of the most striking aspects of his achievement.

Yet, the very impact exerted by his stories piquantly serves to emphasize a major source of weakness in Mapu's plots. It is paradoxically strange that a power of imagination sufficiently vivid to conceive the urgent need for tales of exciting adventure and romance in Hebrew literature, and one which succeeds so well in conjuring up a convincing picture of ancient Israel, should revert time and again to the use of almost identical themes, and present a somewhat depressing similarity in the construction of the plots, and particularly in the employment of dramatic device.

Of the three novels, the plot of *The Love of Zion* is, perhaps, the most successful, by virtue of its comparative simplicity and unpretentiousness, although even here there is a tendency to run wild in the final stages. The brevity of the novel, however, exercises a salutary effect in limiting the complications of the plot, a factor further enhanced by the completely dominating theme of the love of Amnon and Tamar. Both of noble family, the hero and heroine are betrothed from the very womb! By a series of misfortunes, however, Amnon grows up as a shepherd, unaware of his heritage, while his rightful place is taken by the loathsome Azrikam, who also usurps his claim to Tamar. Azrikam's machinations are supported by the villainous Zimri, and several equally unscrupulous accomplices. By saving Tamar's life, Amnon wins her love, and the story pivots upon the wicked plots of the villains to alienate her devotion. So effective are their efforts that all seems lost, until a series of fortuitous coincidences unite the happy pair and restore Amnon to his rightful place. A sub-plot consists of the love of Teman, Tamar's brother, for Peninah, Amnon's sister, which is likewise dogged by misfortune until the inevitable happy ending. The plot is bolstered by mistaken identity, ominous dreams, attempted poisoning, arson, murder, and similar melodramatic devices. The romanticism is colourful and unashamed—and for the reader of more sophisticated tastes, absurdly naïve.

The pattern of events in *The Guilt of Samaria* is basically very similar. Although the main emphasis in this novel is on the historical background rather than the individual, nevertheless several love themes of central importance are simultaneously developed, accompanied by the inevitable series of disappointments and frustrations. The web of intrigue is frequently so bewildering and the much greater length of the novel allows complications to be introduced to such an extent that on several occasions Mapu is constrained to make use of rather tedious repetition to help his readers through the labyrinths of the plot.

E. M. Forster has remarked: "Every action or word in a plot ought to count; it ought to be economical and spare; even when complicated it should be organic and free from dead matter. It may be difficult or easy, it may and should contain mysteries, but it ought not to mislead." All too often the complications of Mapu's novels are both artificial and misleading. In *The Hypocrite,* for example, both Naaman and Eden are reported "dead" so frequently that the reader is in a constant state of irritating confusion.

The faults inherent in the plot-construction of *The Guilt of Samaria* are, indeed, even more conspicuous in *The Hypocrite.* Here the plot is far too thin for the exceeding length of the novel. At the end of the second part the author addresses the reader directly with the promise of even better things to come. The remark is significant because the story could easily have been wound up at this point, and has to be re-developed to extend over three additional, lengthy parts. The machinations and intrigues required to sustain the plot border on the fantastic, as a web of intrigue is spun to entangle the interwoven love themes which comprise the story.

Mapu's dramatic technique consists mainly of complicated love themes, intrigue, revenge, forgery, interception of letters, concealed identity, convenient deaths, and defamation of character. It also reveals a marked tendency on Mapu's part to develop his plots via the medium of conversation, so that it appears, at times, as if the action were unfolding in indirect speech. In *The Hypocrite* especially the conversation heavily outweighs the action, which contains neither sufficient variety nor conviction to sustain it. As a result, the many feeble passages inevitably undermine the reader's interest.

An ingredient common to all the stories is the frequent insertion of dreams and nightmares; dreams are frequently recounted or at least mentioned, very often comprising interesting digressions from the main course of events. In this respect Levi's nightmare in *The Hypocrite,* in which he witnesses his own death and subsequent torments, is particularly fine.

A further device, employed repeatedly in the stories, is the introduction of letters. They are used both for the advancement of the plot, and for purposes of description or reflection. Even in the historical novels their number is considerable, *The Love of Zion* containing six and *The Guilt of Samaria* five. They are treated as an everyday occurrence and occasion no surprise, in spite of the rare mention of letters in the Bible, and there almost always for state or other important correspondence. *The Hypocrite,* however, includes more than sixty letters, and contains features common to the class of epistolary novel exemplified by Richardson's *Pamela.*

Among the more attractive techniques which Mapu employs, the minor stories interspersed in the novels figure prominently. In spite of the naïve and rather crude construction of the overall plots, the handling of the minor themes is skilful and delicate. Uzziel's story, for example, bridges a difficult time gap in outlining the events prior to the opening of *The Guilt of Samaria.* Again the love story of Azriel and Shiphrah infuses an idyllic element into the rather sombre texture of *The Hypocrite.* The minor episodes often demonstrate a vitality not found in the overall plots. In the historical novels, particularly, they provide much swift and dramatic action. Mapu is at his best in presenting a series of vivid pictures with all the brevity and pungency of Biblical narrative, and from time to time displays genuine touches of dramatic skill. Tamar, for example, wildly excited at hearing her lover's voice after a long separation, and anxious to run out to meet him, cannot find the key to her room.

One additional feature deserves attention in *The Guilt of Samaria* and *The Hypocrite.* In the historical novel, characters from *The Love of Zion* are frequently mentioned and even re-introduced. The most notable example is the villain Zimri, who plays a leading part in both stories. Towards the end of *The Guilt of Samaria* he completely disappears from the stage. Mapu was faced with the difficulty of preserving him from the fate of his partners in crime, to fulfil his later adventures already described in *The Love of Zion*. Hepher, Bukkiah and Carmi escape retribution on similar grounds. But even in *The Hypocrite* frequent reference is made to *The Love of Zion*. The author was anxious to keep his first and most popular novel constantly before the public eye and lost no opportunity of stressing its worth.

The significance of Mapu's novels, however, stems less from the plots than from the glimpses they reveal of the life of two distinct eras. His strength lies in the sympathetic feeling for environment and atmosphere which permeates his stories. If it is the function of the novelist "...to reveal the hidden life at its source..." or if the power of the artist is "...to guess the unseen from the seen, to trace the implication of things, to judge the whole piece by the pattern, the condition of feeling life in general so completely that you are well on your way to knowing any particular corner of it..." then Mapu may be credited, at least, with having made an initial and not unimportant advance towards the fulfilment of that aim. For in *The Hypocrite* he has drawn a revealing, if limited, portrait of the life and values of his own society, while in the historical novels he has attempted to broaden and enrich the picture of a life presented by the Bible only in bare outline.

Ancient and Modern Settings

While the plots of Mapu's novels are distinguished neither by originality nor by variety, his portrayal of setting is of a very different calibre. In all three novels the setting not only serves as a framework for the plot, but frequently usurps the interest and casts its own radiance over the darker patches of the stories. The plots may wear too thin, the characters may sometimes appear shadowy and unsatisfying, but the setting succeeds in maintaining its freshness of appeal. It has a life and virility of its own, and forms the stem from which the other branches of the novel grow organically.

In the measure that great novelists completely sum up a period by an evaluation of the forces at work in the society they depict, Mapu's writings are distinguished by his ability to bring an epoch to life. Inferior in all other respects, his success in creating atmosphere in his historical novels gains him a place among the masters. The rich imagination of a true artist enabled him to crystallize the life and society of the Bible. The flimsiness of the materials at his disposal serves only to emphasize his achievement. From the books of Kings, Chronicles, and Isaiah it was possible to extract an historical background, echoes of the pattern of society, hints of dress and habits, but the spirit of life could be breathed only from his own nostrils.

A significant pointer to the resource which Mapu displayed in expanding the outline history of the Bible may be found in the list of characters preceding *The Guilt of Samaria*. The persons in the story are grouped according to families, and appended to the family of Zichri is the quotation:

> And Zichri, a mighty man of Ephraim, slew Maaseiah, the king's son, and Azrikam the governor of the house, and Elkanah that was next to the king. (2 Chronicles, xxviii.)

From this slender evidence, Mapu constructed one of the principal themes of his plot. Not only does Zichri become an important character in the story, but in addition Mapu endows the slaughtered Elkanah with two wives, Yehosheba and Noah, and two daughters, Kezia and Shulamit, of whom all but Noah play leading roles throughout the drama. The scattered references of the Bible, pregnant with possibilities, afforded the ingredients which Mapu required. His strong imagination caught them up, clothing the bare bones with flesh and blood. The generous treatment of such isolated fragments of stories explains the secret of Mapu's creative force.

Mapu's real strength lies in his power of description, particularly the description of nature. His portraits of the scenes and landscapes of the land of Israel are outstanding. Living in the totally different surroundings of Lithuania, Mapu accomplished the remarkable feat of conjuring up a vivid and convincing picture of a country he had never seen. Relying on his deep knowledge of the Hebrew Bible, which he exploited to the utmost, with perhaps the additional aid of a geographical work on Palestine by Jacob Kaplan, he visualized the hills and valleys, the towns and villages, with an uncanny accuracy. That he made mistakes in geography is hardly surprising. They may well be forgiven in the general completeness of the picture he presented. There can be no doubt that his novels stimulated in his readers a profound and detailed interest in the ancient homeland.

But Mapu did not confine himself to descriptions of the physical characteristics of the land of Israel. Even more significant is his portrayal of the pattern of life in Biblical times. The vital currents of life emerge in a succession of vivid and brilliant scenes—the joy of an abundant harvest; the thronging crowds in Jerusalem for the Feast of Tabernacles; the armed might and overweening pride of Nineveh. Moreover the frequent interspersion of customs and beliefs echoed from the Bible constantly infuses touches of authenticity into the narrative.

In *The Love of Zion* the historical atmosphere is more in evidence than the historical events, which merely form a framework for the love theme of Amnon and Tamar, without dominating the scene. The only historical sequence of major importance is the threatened invasion from Assyria.

Parallel with the historical background, a strong idyllic element runs through the story and pervades it with a sense of calm. Although a common ingredient of all Mapu's novels, in *The Love of Zion* it is particularly conspicuous. All three novels eulogize the delights of the simple, rustic life, and its superiority to the vice, bustle and restlessness of the city, in a manner worthy of Virgil's *Bucolics*. All three employ the idyllic device of soliloquy—in *The Hypocrite* it appears principally in letter form—for the expression of contemplative calm or the speaker's reaction to the beauties of nature. The nature portrayed is, of course, perpetually friendly, providing sustenance of itself, as seen through the eyes of the city-dweller, and not of the farmer, more familiar with its vicissitudes: nature, in short, as it appeared to the English romantic poets. And all three portray a highly stylized version of romantic love, undying and faithful, despite every adverse trick of fortune—a love, too, frequently engendered at first sight, and in most unlikely circumstances.

But whereas in the later novels the idyllic theme is a minor element, in *The Love of Zion* it is all-pervading, and lends its specific colouring to the whole novel. In *The Guilt of Samaria* and *The Hypocrite* far greater importance must be attached to the historical and contemporary scene respectively, as the background on which the plot is embroidered, and the characters introduced. In *The Love of Zion* the love of Amnon and Tamar is paramount, and the historical setting, important as it is, remains secondary. In both the later novels the canvas is broader, and *The Guilt of Samaria* contains an element of epic. *The Love of Zion,* on the other hand, is a microcosm, self-contained, and endowed with much of the sense of detachment and timelessness, so necessary for the idyll, which permeates, for example, Goethe's *Hermann und Dorothea.*

So strong is this pastoral, idyllic element that it finds expression in the oaths with which the characters pledge themselves. Naame swears Teman to secrecy with the words:

> ...I charge you by the roes, and by the hinds of the field...

Amnon invokes the sun to witness his undying love, and Tamar calls upon the moon. These pastoral scenes, which afford such scope for calm, imaginative description and rich imagery, and where the background is so subtly reminiscent of the early stories of the Patriarchs, represent some of the most effective of Mapu's pictures.

Whereas in *The Love of Zion* the historical background serves only as a framework for the loves and intrigues of the individual characters, in *The Guilt of Samaria* it assumes much greater significance. Although the threads of the plot are far more numerous and entangled than in the first novel, and the tortuous relationships of the individual characters continue to occupy the centre of the stage, two deeper and more vital dramas are simultaneously enacted in the wings. On the one hand the national rivalries of Judah and Samaria portray the dark struggle for supremacy which continues throughout the story. On the other hand there is a constant and no less bitter fight between the worship of Baal and the faithful belief in God. The heroes and villains pirouette upon the scene like puppets whose strings are jerked by giant hands in the shadows. And in the background, like a lurking tiger, there is the constant menace of Assyria, threatening desolation and captivity.

The historical background of *The Guilt of Samaria* encompasses the kingdoms of Judah and Samaria in the last days of the latter. Most of the action takes place prior to the greater part of the story of *The Love of Zion,* but later than the first two chapters of the former work. It provides a natural prelude to Mapu's first novel, although the product of a considerably later period of the author's literary activity. In consequence the construction is more mature. Several of the characters of *The Love of Zion* reappear at a more youthful stage of development in *The Guilt of Samaria,* a factor which presented some intricate problems of integration. As they are mainly villains, Mapu has to resist the temptation to kill them off! The period comprises the dark days of the reign of Ahaz in Judah, and the happier period following the ascension of the righteous Hezekiah. In Samaria the story outlines the licentiousness and unbounded pride which dominated the reigns of the kings Pekah and Hoshea and culminated in the final catastrophe of the fall of the northern kingdom. The action revolves about the lamentable hatred of the two kingdoms for each other, the disastrous battle in which Judah is vanquished and Jerusalem overrun and the disintegration of Samaria.

This broad background, which mirrors the ebb and flow of the tides of national fortune, adds an element of epic grandeur to *The Guilt of Samaria* not felt in the earlier novel. The interweaving of personal and national issues, the exploits of kings and nobles, the admixture of prophecy and sacrifice all contribute to produce this effect. The most successful episodes in the story completely supersede the individuals involved. They consist in the vivid scenes of prisoners being led into captivity, in the fine descriptions of the disastrous battle for Judah or in the jostling, insulting crowds that flock to the celebration at the sanctuary at Beth-El which forms a prelude to the disaster that befalls Samaria.

Unlike the calm setting of *The Love of Zion,* the kaleidoscopic background of *The Guilt of Samaria* pulsates with movement and violent action. But in this story, too, there are many passages of natural description. The opening chapter of the novel, which introduces the lone bandit, dwelling on a mountain crag, has all the wild atmosphere of Walter Scott's *Peveril of the Peak.* Equally effective are the descriptions of sunrise on the mountains of Lebanon and the portrayal of the fear and loneliness of a forest at night. Here Mapu demonstrates once more that his main strength lies in description rather than action, in setting rather than plot.

In contrast to the depth and richness of the setting of *The Guilt of Samaria,* that of *The Hypocrite* appears shallow and pale. In spite of the great length of his novel on contemporary life, and the broad canvas on which it is portrayed—the scene swings from Lithuania to Macedonia, Italy, Germany, England, and Palestine—the pattern of life is nowhere profound. It remains true that Mapu succeeded in depicting the society with which he was familiar in considerable detail. But the life of that society was so hampered and restricted that its motivating forces appear comparatively trivial and petty. In place of human sacrifice and the worship of Baal, the evils to be overcome are hypocrisy and slander. In place of the disastrous, internecine strife between two kingdoms, both faced with complete destruction, the antagonism consists of wordy warfare between orthodox and reform factions. The heroes are falsely accused of eating ritually unclean food or selling ritually unclean wine. Evil consists in the interception of letters or the forging of credentials. The pettiness of the issues reflects the shallowness of the life.

Mapu has etched a detailed picture of Jewish life in a small Lithuanian town in the last century. The novel constitutes an evaluation of what men lived by, their ideas and beliefs, their public and private relationships. It contains a veritable store-house of current folklore, superstition and local custom, including, for example, such medical practices as remedial blood-letting from the hand, or visiting the graves of pious men in cases of sickness. More importantly, the story depicts the bitter conflicts which divided the community into hostile factions, in particular the growing antagonism between the older generation, desperately anxious to preserve a rigidly traditional framework, and the younger generation thirsting after secular knowledge, frequently to the detriment of its loyalty to Judaism and the Hebrew language. These conflicts, which served only to accelerate the powerful forces of disintegration within Jewish life, were soon destined to result in revolutionary consequences of the utmost importance for subsequent Jewish history. The delineation of a social background already in flux is indicative of Mapu's grasp of the problems of his own society.

In spite of the blatant melodrama and complex machinations of the plot, Mapu regarded his novel as a vehicle for serious social criticism. He was especially concerned with the inferiority of woman's status, and his heroines illustrate the changing relationship between the sexes in their striving for an adequate education and their hostility towards the accepted practice of arranged marriages irrespective of their own wishes. Again, he was scathingly critical of a mental climate which demanded that Jews should deliberately remain in ignorance even of the language of the country in which they lived, let alone of foreign languages, while at the same time blindly accepting what Mapu considered to be the irrational superstitions of the Hasidic sect. That he described a world which has utterly disappeared only adds to the importance of the novel. It is significant, too, that the contemporary setting served as a model for Mapu's immediate successors almost without exception.

His power of description, moreover, is as vivid here as elsewhere, whether in the atmosphere of poverty and despair that pervades Yeruham's household, or in the overnight company of a wayside inn, or in the delightful scenes contained in the letters from the Holy Land which rival the natural description found in the historical novels and form a connecting link between all his works. In *The Hypocrite* Mapu's skilful handling of the setting is once more in evidence. It suffers by comparison because the life portrayed is so shabby and drab. But that life represented Mapu's own world, and its portrayal serves only to emphasize the power of an imagination which could escape from it so utterly and reconstruct the world of the Bible with such colour and such conviction.

Studies in Black and White

In spite of the differences in setting, chronology and subject matter, which sharply distinguish Mapu's historical romances from his contemporary social novel, an examination of the role of the characters reveals in either case the same twin features. On the one hand, they represent little more than personifications of good or evil qualities, without depth or complexity. While their adventures may excite amazement, their personalities offer few occasions even for surprise. The subtle mystery which veils the innermost thoughts of the living person, the factor of unexpected reaction is almost entirely lacking. With few exceptions the whole personality is revealed to the reader, but rather as a pencil sketch than a portrait in oils. On the other hand the characters frequently appear to fulfil the part of observers, in which capacity they reflect the author's views on various aspects of society. In the manner of the Greek chorus they stand aside, approving or disapproving, but themselves taking little part in the main stream of action.

Both these phenomena stem from the tendentious nature of Mapu's writings, and both are precedented in Hebrew literature. Mapu was familiar with the allegorical personification of virtue and vice, which appears in the dramas of Moses Hayyim Luzzatto (1707-1747) and especially in his final drama *La-Yesharim Tehillah* (Praise to the Righteous). Here the characters bear such names as Yosher (Righteousness), Emet (Truth), Tarmit (Falsehood) and Hamon (Populace), and roughly correspond with the personifications known as "Humours" in English literature of the seventeenth century. The people in Mapu's novels are, of course, more developed, and they are presented not as allegorical figures but real persons. They remain, nevertheless, more symbolic representations than individual personalities. Nor can it be a coincidence in *The Love of Zion* that the real name of the malignant yet foolish Azrikam is Nabal (Degenerate), while the tavern-owner is appropriately dubbed Carmi (from *Kerem,* Vineyard). Many such traces of personification occur throughout Mapu's novels. In *The Hypocrite* such names as Zadok (Righteous), Gaal (Nausea), Ahituv (Brother to Good), and Ahira (Brother to Evil) are clear examples of this tendency.

Again the role of onlooker or *Zofeh* occupies an important place in the literature of *Haskalah*. The device stems from the picaresque story, whose object is "…to take a central figure through a succession of scenes, introduce a great number of characters, and thus build up a picture of society." In medieval Hebrew literature the great exponent of the picaresque story is Al-Harizi (1165-1225), whose most important work *Tahkemoni* is an imitation of the *Maqamas* of the Arabic writer Al-Hariri (1054-1121). In European literature similar tendencies may be discerned in the epistolary fiction composed in the style of both Montesquieu's *Persian Letters* and Richardson's *Pamela.* The exponents of *Haskalah* adopted the framework, but used it polemically. In the two works *Megalleh Temirin* (The Revealer of Secrets) and *Bohan Zaddik* (The Touchstone of the Righteous) Joseph Perl (1773-1839) employs this method to pour ridicule on the Hasidim and to suggest remedies for the plight of Galician Jewry. A similar social motive characterizes *Ha-Zofeh le-Beit-Yisrael* (The Watchman of the House of Israel) by Isaac Erter (1792-1851), in which the emphasis on the observer is incorporated in the title. This work, published posthumously, comprises a collection of articles and sketches, of which perhaps the most effective is the picaresque fantasy *Gilgul Nefesh* (Transmigration of the Soul). The device affords wide scope for the satirist and reformer.

The suitability of the letter for reflections on and criticism of the state of society is adequately demonstrated by Goldsmith's *Citizen of the World.* Similarly, the large number of letters in *The Hypocrite* provides a convenient medium for the expression of Mapu's ideas. The character who composes the letter is able to advocate reform and reveal the evils of society, while himself remaining little more than a shadow.

Didactic elements are largely responsible for the weakness of Mapu's characterizations. Tendentious writing is not conducive to the broadest views; on the contrary it is apt to ignore the mixture of virtue and vice which comprises human character. The heroes in Mapu's novels embody the ideals of *Haskalah,* while the villains personify their antithesis. Didactically this method contains one great advantage, for the reader can entertain no doubts of the final supremacy of right over wrong. Artistically, however, it is less successfull, as the virtues and vices portrayed are congenital, the bad characters are fundamentally, if uncomfortably, incorrigible. Thus the death-bed repentance of so many of Mapu's villains is artificial and unconvincing. On the other hand the exaggerated morality of most of the heroes has a tendency to cloy. Both extremes serve only to emphasize the naïveté of the characterizations. In this respect Mapu's technique does not develop and in all three novels the pattern remains the same.

The merits of Mapu's creations must be sought, then, not as individual personalities, but rather in the possibilities of character which he presents. The writers of *Haskalah* were faced with a formidable obstacle in using the great figures of the Bible as heroes in their own works. They are portrayed so much better in the original form of the Bible itself. In both *The Love of Zion* and *The Guilt of Samaria* Mapu's heroes are "Biblical men," but not historical figures. He painted a new Jew, not a product of the diaspora but native to the soil of ancient Israel. Within the limits imposed by the idealization described above this new creation is vigorous and fresh, and presents a healthy contrast to the stunted characters of contemporary Hebrew prose of the time. The general treatment of the latter has been summarized by S. Halkin in *Modern Hebrew Literature* as follows:

To sum up, *Haskalah* prose aspires to the same ideal Jew as does the poetry. But *Haskalah* poetry celebrates this ideal character as if he already existed. The prose treatment of the theme, by contrast, is sadly sober, even embittered by the realization of the great distance between the Jew as he is and the Jew as he should be.

The Biblical setting of the historical novels allowed Mapu to escape the dilemma. He was able to portray the Jew as he should be by depicting the ideal Jew as he was.

Mapu does, however, introduce Biblical figures side by side with his own creations, perhaps following the example of Alexandre Dumas in *Les Trois Mousquetaires,* in which historical figures appear together with the author's inventions. In *The Love of Zion* Isaiah and King Hezekiah appear in person during the Assyrian attack on Jerusalem. In *The Guilt of Samaria* Ahaz, Hezekiah, Isaiah, and Micah are introduced quite frequently. Ahaz is even described as being in love with Miriam, one of the heroines! Mapu undoubtedly exercised considerable daring in introducing prophetic figures and making them perform upon his stage. Although the prophets add little to the plot, and although Mapu wisely refrains from any attempt at detailed description, they help to establish authenticity of atmosphere and their speeches embody the ideals for which the heroes strive.

Of the two broad classes into which the characters may be divided, the villains are the more convincing. In spite of the exaggeration inherent in the author's method, they have a quality of realism and vitality largely lacking in the heroes. They are ruthless, resourceful and cunning, outwitting their opponents at almost every turn. When they enter the scene the stories quicken pace. Mapu has endowed his principal villains Zimri, Omri, and Zadok, with a malignancy akin to that of Iago.

Just as the villains tend to be more convincing than the heroes, the female characters are more skilfully portrayed than their male counterparts. Throughout his stories Mapu displays a delicate feeling for womanly emotion. All his young heroines are faithful, devoted and compassionate, while remaining spirited and independent. In *The Hypocrite* Elisheva represents Mapu's ideal conception of the new Jewish woman, devoted to her people, faith, and language, but nevertheless determined to pursue her education and live a full and cultured life. She presents a sympathetic but courageous figure, personifying Mapu's desire to foster the emancipation of the Jewish woman and raise her dignity and status. Even more successful are the portraits of the more matronly Miriam and Yehosheba in *The Guilt of Samaria*. Refined, wealthy, and mellowed by suffering, they reflect a maturity and understanding rare in Mapu's characterizations. Expressive of Miriam's generous nature is her gracious consent to her husband's proposal to take the unhappy Yehosheba into his home as a second wife.

But the heroines, too, have their wicked counterparts. The Amazon-like Keturah and her daughter, Reumah, clad in armour and breathing fire gallop on and off the stage. Reminiscent of Camilla in Virgil's *Aeneid,* these warlike women, terrible and cruel, present a strange, new spectacle in Hebrew literature. The scenes in which Daniel accepts Reumah's challenge to single combat are among the finest of all three novels. In *The Hypocrite* female villainy is represented by Zaphnath. Lascivious, deceitful, and fickle, she, too, is a character of flesh and blood, although the attempt to describe her womanly wiles sometimes finds the author a little out of his depth.

It is perhaps ironical that the least convincing characterizations in Mapu's novels are those which lay closest to his heart. The new generation of enlightened young men, symbolized in *The Hypocrite* by Naaman, Hogeh, and Ahituv, are colourless and unreal. In these young *Maskilim* Mapu strove to find the saviours of the Jewish people and the harbingers of a new and better life. But they are too abstract and indeterminate, too far removed from purposive or concerted action to be of great significance. Indeed, the harsh conditions of Jewish life allowed little real scope for the activities of the *Maskilim.* The idea of Zionism, which was later to serve as a focal point for young idealists and provide a fruitful avenue for constructive work, had not yet been crystallized. In spite of all Mapu's efforts the heroes of *The Hypocrite* remain pale shadows, the unreal visions of a vanished world.

A Neo-Biblical Style

Of the many influences exerted upon Hebrew literature by the rise of *Haskalah* in Germany during the last decades of the eighteenth century, its effect upon the literary style adopted by the majority of Hebrew authors for almost a hundred years proved most decisive. In attempting to reform the system of Jewish education as a prerequisite to any real participation in the broader life of western Europe, the exponents of enlightenment staunchly advocated the cultivation of more highly refined modes of expression as an essential step towards a higher level of aesthetic appreciation. This latter goal, it was believed, would also result in an improvement of ethical standards, in accordance with current concepts of the close connection existing between ethics and aesthetics. To that end the *Maskilim* deliberately opted for a return to Biblical Hebrew in place of the somewhat crude and crabbed style of Rabbinical composition then generally in vogue.

By emphasizing the superiority of the language of the Bible, and particularly its sublime poetry, the advocates of *Haskalah* hoped to develop the aesthetic sense regarded as so necessary for Jewish regeneration, and at the same time—with the aid of Biblical imagery and metaphor—help to rekindle the interest in nature which had been crushed by generations of ghetto life. They believed, moreover, that a renewed study of the Bible would foster a sympathetic appreciation of a more heroic age in Jewish history with all its emphasis on political freedom—an important psychological factor in the struggle for emancipation. As a champion of the ideals of *Haskalah,* Avraham Mapu proved so devout an adherent of its literary creed that he may well be regarded as its most consummate exponent.

The style of Mapu's novels, therefore, is of necessity preconditioned. Its source lies in the self-imposed limitation of modelling his work primarily upon the style and language of the Bible. In the absence of any prior Hebrew novel to influence his choice of style, the predilection of the exponents of *Haskalah* for the purity of Biblical Hebrew inevitably determined his medium. Moreover, it is reasonable to concede that many of the elements essential for his creations were to be found in the Bible. The books of Prophets, Psalms, and Job provided the materials for natural description; the Song of Songs furnished him with the raw materials of romantic love; the books of Samuel and Kings afforded a simple but powerful model for narrative, while the point of view of the Bible with its clear-cut distinction between right and wrong, good and evil, provided the mould from which the "black and white" characters might be cast. Upon these basic elements Mapu directed the powerful beam of his imagination, harnessed to a highly developed faculty for creating historical atmosphere, and a most sensitive feeling for language. These are the raw ingredients of Mapu's novels to which he adhered with remarkable fidelity.

For his reading public, too, the adoption of such a method possessed an immediate advantage. Familiarity with the content, language, and style of the Bible provided a natural bridge to this new, literary domain. The transition was so natural, the framework so well remembered, that to many *The Love of Zion* appeared almost as an extension of the Bible itself, and young lovers began to call each other "Amnon" and "Tamar." It is unquestionable that his delightful use of Biblical language must have been one of the chief reasons for the popularity of his novels—his readers would have felt so much at home! Moreover, the consistent employment of Biblical language provides a large measure of artistic unity, which prevails in spite of the weakness and intricacies of the plots. The very first paragraph of *The Love of Zion* strikes the keynote, and the reader is at once transported into a Biblical setting, comparable to that of the Bible itself. The climate is convincing and the enchantment real:

> In the days of Ahaz, king of Judah, there lived
> in Jerusalem a man whose name was Yoram, the son of

Abiezer a nobleman in Judah and captain of the host. He was possessed of fields and vineyards in Carmel and Sharon, and flocks of sheep and herds of cattle in Bethlehem, which is in Judah. And he was rich in gold and silver with fine and stately palaces. And he had two wives, the name of one was Haggit, the daughter of Ira, and the name of the other was Naame. And Yoram loved Naame exceedingly, for she was comely. But Haggit, her adversary, envied her and vexed her sore, for Haggit had two sons, while Naame was without child. But Naame was pleasing both to look upon and in her ways. So Yoram gave her a dwelling for herself, that Haggit, her adversary, might not afflict her.

But the premise that the linguistic foundations of *The Love of Zion*, *The Guilt of Samaria,* and in great measure *The Hypocrite* are Biblical is in itself a striking reflection of Mapu's creative powers. The initial problems facing the author in this choice of medium were as difficult as they were obvious. How could Biblical language adequately satisfy the very different demands of the novel? How could words and phrases, sanctified by religion and made authoritative by thousands of years of tradition, be adapted to a secular and fictitious context? Finally—and perhaps most seriously of all—how could such usage fail to suffer by comparison with the unassailable grandeur of the original? Each formidable in itself, the three problems together formed a seemingly insuperable obstacle.

The strength of Biblical narrative lies, moreover, in the brevity of the stories. Its adaptation for the purposes of a full-length novel confronted the author with the very serious problem of maintaining the interest over long periods in a medium especially suited to conciseness of expression. Mapu was compelled to paint atmosphere and create detail while using a Biblical style which concentrates only on essentials. The sublimity of Biblical narrative arises from the restraint displayed at moments of great dramatic tension. At such moments, when an explanation might destroy the entire effect, a terse phrase can arouse the deepest emotion. Such is the force of Abraham's answer when Isaac seeks the victim for sacrifice. Herein lies the poignancy of the description of the dead concubine with her hands upon the threshold. The imagination is inflamed to the point of outrage, yet in the first example the Hebrew uses six words and in the second example three.

The Bible story is characterized by a hardness of outline, by a rigid economy of expression, by a relentless exposition of consecutive facts, with almost no attempt at psychological analysis or philosophic speculation which may serve as motivation. Thus the early life of Moses to the time of his selection for the divine mission is sketched in a few, brief pictures. The significant facts are singled out and hammered home. All extraneous detail is ignored, or left to the reader to supply. The Bible story is a narrative of events arranged in their time sequence. It is a skeleton narrative that bites into the imagination to supply the flesh and blood, and therein lies its strength.

But as E. M. Forster has observed: "...there...seems something else in life beside time, something which may conveniently be called 'value,' something which is measured not by minutes or hours, but by intensity ...And what the entire novel does—if it is a good novel—is to include the life by values as well...." And again: "...but observe already how that other life—the life by value—presses against the novel from all sides, how it is ready to fill and indeed distort it, offering it people, plots, fantasies, views of the universe, anything except this constant 'and then...and then...'." As a novelist Mapu had to supply those very elements of 'value' which Biblical narrative is so careful to omit, while at the same time using a medium of expression which derives its force from such omission. It is hardly surprising that he sometimes fails badly; it is all the more surprising that he has achieved so large a measure of success.

Mapu's answer to these problems consisted of a direct attack upon his material, without reservation and without apology. The Bible in its entirety became grist for the mill of his invention. Complete appropriation was followed by analysis and refashioning. The ingredients remained, but the treatment was varied at need. With the dangers of plagiarism and parody confronting him at every step, Mapu succeeded in threading his way to the height of originality. That he has had no successors, in spite of the popularity of his novels, is ample testimony of the difficulties that beset the way.

The authenticity of the Biblical scene, which forms the background of both Mapu's historical novels, is engendered by this constant and thoroughgoing employment of the characteristics of Biblical language. There is, indeed, an interpenetration of Biblical idiom which forges between these novels and the Bible a link so genuine and so organic that it is not without reason that they have been described as a new commentary on the Bible. From the Biblical language stems the Biblical quality of setting, atmosphere, dialogue—and hence characters—and even to some extent action.

Mapu appears to have been so steeped in the language of the Bible that he thought in it and lived it—as though he had inherited the mould of thought of its ancient authors.

The fundamental mechanics of Mapu's prose constitute a fusion of elements of both the prose and poetry of the Hebrew Bible. From the prose he adopted the "Waw Consecutive"—the phenomenon of Hebrew grammar that determines the swift-moving action, the relentless consecutiveness and the subtle colouring of Biblical narrative. From the prose, too, he derived the terseness of outline, the bare yet rhythmic statement, the simple but significant phrase, and, above all, the economy of expression that, stripped of all unnecessary adornment and sometimes tantalizing in its austerity, can yet, with a few vivid strokes, sum up a whole period or—what is still more difficult—convincingly span a long passage of time. Thus the boyhood and youth of Azrikam, during which the evil growth of his character gradually festers through long years, is depicted in the single vivid sentence:

And Azrikam grew up in Yoram's house like a malignant thorn.

But from the richer language of Biblical poetry he derived the materials necessary to bridge the gap between story and novel. The poetry of the Bible provided the pithy phrase, the forceful parallel, the penetrating contrast, and more especially the richness of imagery. Therein lay the sources of natural description, ethical inspiration and idyllic love. In short it contained the living word, the key to conviction and reality. The very choice of Biblical theme and setting threatened at once both artificiality and imitation. Only by a fusion of the language of both poetry and prose could Mapu create a medium sufficiently flexible to overcome the difficulties inherent in his task. It is this which gives the singing cadence and lyric texture to his prose. But only a careful examination can reveal the thoroughness, the painstaking selection and combination of phrase, which underlies the apparent simplicity and the smooth current of his writing:

> So Daniel was left alone with Joach, who stood wrapped in thought with eyes fixed upon the smoke rising from the incense above the groves, while ideas welled up from the depths of his heart: I gaze at the earth beneath my feet, and raise my eyes to the heavens. I ask of you, great luminaries—sun, moon and stars: Who summoned you from the dark void? Who created you from nothing and set you there? You move along eternal paths, resting neither by day nor by night, but revolving ever more. If, then, you are gods, why do you not rest?

It is true that Mapu, no less than other exponents of *Haskalah,* was obsessed by the principle of adherence to *Melizah,* a concept which lays great emphasis on the choice and arrangement of words and phrases. At its best the term represents the sensitive selection of an apt and colourful image, particularly when drawn from the Bible. But it is an attitude to language which only too easily declines into high-flown and euphuistic expressions, sometimes bordering on the fantastic. All too frequently it is characterized by a mediocrity of subject matter swaddled in inflated and over-ambitious phraseology. For its adherents, however, *Melizah* symbolized 'good taste,' suggesting a highly developed, aesthetic approach to life.

As an illustration of the fine balance which time and again retains the flavour of the Bible, and which immediately arouses associations in the mind of the perceptive reader, a few examples may suffice. In her revulsion at the thought of an approaching union with the loathsome Azrikam, whose very presence she cannot bear, Tamar utters the half-prayer:

> "May He, who puts an end to darkness, put an end to Azrikam's love for me."

Again, when Teman, while admitting the obscurity of Amnon's birth, nevertheless defends his beauty, wisdom and strength, Azrikam adapts a phrase from Amos into a biting retort:

> These three I can forgive him—Azrikam answered—but for the fourth, his learned tongue, I will not turn away the punishment.

Both phrases evoke an immediate response as of something long-remembered, while fitting subtly into the framework of correct context. Indeed, a great part of the charm of Mapu's style is that the mind of the reader well versed in the Hebrew Bible—just as the "Soul" in Plato's "Theory of Ideas"— seems little by little to remember and recognize scenes once perfectly familiar.

Frequently, moreover, a passage from the Bible is interpolated with slight modification, wherein the rhythmic parallelism adds an additional emphasis or poignancy to some moment of deep emotional stress. Stricken with pain and despair at what she considers unspeakable baseness in Amnon, Tamar bursts out:

> "I cry unto the mountains, Cover me; and to the hills, Fall on me."

On the other hand Mapu can employ the same device with equal facility to summarize background and create atmosphere, coining a parallel phrase scarcely distinguishable from the Bible itself. Thus he portrays a political background so corrupted that the righteous are forced to seek safety in concealment and flight with the words:

> Righteousness dwelt only in the forest, and Faith in caves.

No less effective than the constantly recurring parallelism is the frequent use of contrast, which performs the same function of terse summarization, as, for example, when Uzziel expresses the bitter hopelessness of his position in the phrase:

> "Lo! My grief is close at hand, but help is far away."

The examples cited above constitute a few of the innumerable phrases modelled on the Bible, and the many idiomatic devices by means of which Mapu succeeds in creating the Biblical framework and colouring of his historical novels.

The extreme limitations of Biblical language naturally compelled Mapu to rely greatly on the *Hapax legomena* (a word or form that occurs only once in the recorded corpus of a given language) and on the rare words and combinations of words which appear in the Bible. He frequently modified the form of the word or phrase to suit his own context, sometimes colouring the adaptation with a new shade of meaning. In this respect, however, his approach was generally cautious, calculated to ensure the aptness of any fresh connotation. On numerous occasions, however, Mapu became the inevitable, if unconscious, victim of his own educational background. His deep and wide-ranging familiarity with the vast corpus of post-Biblical literature frequently impelled him to introduce words and phrases endowed with shades of meaning not found in the Bible, but firmly established in the later strata of the language. Other words, again, are employed with a connotation deriving from their usage in Yiddish—Mapu's own vernacular. Frequently, moreover, resort is made to vocabulary which does not occur in the language of the Bible at all.

A parallel linguistic problem is reflected in another facet of Mapu's style. His writing shows a remarkable fondness for particular phrases, which he employs constantly. The frequency of these phrases, which recur time after time throughout his novels, inevitably arrests the reader's attention. This phenomenon is partly due to Mapu's preference for *Melizah*. More importantly, however, it provides one of the clearest illustrations of the limitations of language at his disposal, which compelled him to resort repeatedly to the same expression. The problem is felt elsewhere. Purist as he was, Mapu was yet compelled to expand his linguistic resources more deliberately in the composition of *The Hypocrite* in order to find terminology suitable for the problems of contemporary life, for which Biblical Hebrew proved to be a clumsy and inadequate medium.

In view of the arguments propounded above it must be stressed at this stage that *The Love of Zion* and *The Guilt of Samaria* are historical novels, but not Biblical novels. Mapu drew widely on the Bible for his style, language, and setting, and these Biblical elements are fundamental in both novels. The fusion is so complete that from it arises the feeling of organic growth from the parent source. But the stories are not mere imitations of the Bible. No attempt has been made to expand either one or several of the Bible stories into novel-form. Nor can the prose, in spite of its Biblical elements, be equated with any particular sections of the Bible. Indeed, a careful analysis of Mapu's style reveals many syntactical idiosyncrasies, frequently resulting in types of sentence-structure unknown to Biblical Hebrew. Mapu's works depict the life and times of the Bible, and breathe much of its spirit, yet they remain unmistakably original creations.

Thus it is that by virtue of its evenness of style and its unity of artistry *The Love of Zion* represents the most complete creation of all Mapu's novels. In *The Guilt of Samaria* he delved far more deeply into Biblical history, and the work is far more mature in the dramatic construction, the delineation of background and the realism of the evil forces embodied. In *The Hypocrite* the contemporary scene is depicted in broad aspect, and an attempt is made to sum up the life and values of the author's own world. But the very length and scope of these two novels throw up their faults into sharper relief. The course of the narrative is not even, frequently the interest flags badly, there is much doleful repetition, and very weak, flat passages occur where the theme is stretched too thin. These faults are inherent in the style. The effectiveness of the chosen medium varies inversely with the length of the novel. *The Love of Zion* is sufficiently short and concentrated to justify the use of a Biblical style. As the length and complexity of the succeeding novels develop, the inadequacy of such a style becomes increasingly apparent.

In Search of a Vernacular

Of all the difficulties with which the novelist is confronted, and which vary according to the nature of his theme and approach, the central problem of convincing dialogue remains constant; the living word constitutes an indispensable instrument.

   The raw materials for the novel encompass almost the entire range of life itself, some part of which the novelist is always attempting to portray. But just as human speech is the underlying principle in all the manifestations of society, without which group life as a whole is inconceivable, so dialogue is the pivot about which the complex ingredients and relationships of the novel revolve. A novel, then, will be true to life and convincing in direct proportion to the sense of reality and conviction apparent in the dialogue. For whereas in real life the individual character creates and moulds his utterance, in the novel, by a reverse process, it is the dialogue which creates and moulds the characters. If the dialogue is natural and alive, the characters will follow suit. But if the dialogue is stilted and artificial, no descriptive power of the writer, however great, will bring the characters to life.

   For the author writing in a living language the acquisition of the materials for dialogue presents no great problem; he has only to use his ears—even if the process demands eavesdropping on the conversation of chambermaids through a hole in the floorboards, as practised so successfully by the dramatist J. M. Synge. In his daily life and at every turn he is confronted with the unbounded richness and variety of human expression, which he may adopt, modify or imitate at will. For Mapu the problem was very different and far more difficult. He set out to write novels in a language which had not been used in common speech for tens of centuries. The language had indeed maintained an unbroken literary tradition of vast extent. But even this literature was mainly concerned with religious, legal, or legendary material, to the comparative neglect of matters more closely related to everyday conversation. In the virtual absence of a spoken idiom from which he might draw inspiration, this task must be regarded almost as a *creatio ex nihilo,* and represents one of Mapu's major contributions to the development both of Hebrew literature and of the very conception that Hebrew might be revived as a spoken language. Even to the present generation, long familiar with the phenomenon of Hebrew as a natural and accepted instrument of daily speech, Mapu's success is impressive if somewhat quaint. To Mapu's contemporaries and near contemporaries the effect must have been startling, and the significance of the achievement clear. It would be unfair to expect that at one fell swoop Mapu should forge an instrument sufficiently flexible to portray the infinite variety of expression required by the novelist to suit every conceivable time and situation. Mapu, clearly, could do no more than pave the way. The criterion for criticism in this instance must be that he succeeded at all—that the dialogue was actually written.

But Mapu was faced with an added difficulty. As his specific aim was to create a novel in the language of the Bible, he was compelled to renounce the characteristic language of subsequent strata of Hebrew literature, which would have rendered him invaluable assistance in the formation of dialogue. As if the difficulty of creating a living idiom from a literary language were not enough, he had in addition to confine himself to one section of that literature, a section, moreover, whose vocabulary is limited in the extreme. Within the framework of this literature—the primary source upon which Mapu could draw—the passages couched in the form of conversation comprise a comparatively small proportion of the whole. Yet from these flimsy materials Mapu succeeded in constructing the dialogue of two entire novels, together with by far the greater part of a third.

Interspersed in the Bible there are, of course, elements of dialogue full of the freshness and spontaneity of living speech, such as the conversations in the Book of Ruth or those between God and Satan in the Book of Job or the scene in which Solomon is confronted by two women, each claiming to be the mother of a child. It has, indeed, been pointed out that Mapu was the first to make full use of these elements, which were invaluable by virtue of their scarcity, and which had to be exploited to the maximum. But apart from these primary sources the Bible contains numerous secondary sources of dialogue, that is material which, although not in the actual form of conversation, can be adapted to dialogue quite naturally and with little alteration. Elements of dialogue lurk beneath the surface of the numerous stories of the narrative books. They may be sought in God's injunctions to the Israelites and in the passionate outbursts of the later prophets. One feels them in the soliloquies of the Psalms and, in didactic form, in the concise epigrams of the Book of Proverbs. The emotions of sadness may be expressed in the words of the Book of Lamentations, and the intimate love conversations arise naturally from the language of the Song of Songs. Again a tertiary—or even less direct—source of material for dialogue may be discerned in the natural description embodied in the Bible, which is found in sufficient quantity in the Latter Prophets, in the Psalms, and in Job to form the basis for the more imaginative and descriptive elements of dialogue.

But in the final analysis the sum total of all the possible materials for dialogue which can be derived from the various strata of the Bible, even by a master of that medium, remains sadly meagre compared to the resources which the novelist, writing in a living idiom, has constantly at his disposal. With *The Hypocrite* the limits of

Biblical dialogue are finally reached. In this novel, which is approximately five times the length of *The Love of Zion* and which depicts the life of his own period, Mapu was compelled to face the inadequacy of his chosen medium. The Biblical flavour of the dialogue is manifestly unsuitable for a novel of contemporary life. A similar phenomenon, indeed, appears in H. Melville's great novel *Moby Dick,* in which some of Captain Ahab's inspired utterances are highly reminiscent of the language of the prophets. But Melville introduces this type of language only sporadically and deliberately, when he feels the medium of contemporary prose inadequate for the emotions to be expressed, while his other characters meanwhile converse in a familiar idiom. Moreover, Biblical terminology is clearly deficient for many of the conversational themes engendered by the problems of modern life which find expression in *The Hypocrite.* In any case Mapu felt himself compelled to break fresh ground and to introduce into his conversation some of the language of later strata of Hebrew literature, and even traces of Aramaic phrases, a device which Mendele Mocher Sefarim (1836-1917) was later to develop so successfully into a comparatively racy and highly colloquial form of dialogue.

It must, then, be conceded *a priori* that the greater part of the dialogue is stilted and artificial, and that despite Mapu's heroic efforts to hammer out his material into pliable form, the direct speech only too frequently lacks vitality. This defect is enhanced by a tendency—found commonly in Biblical Hebrew, and not unknown even in Modern Hebrew—to couch polite conversation in the oblique form. The stilted nature of much of the incidental dialogue may be illustrated from the first meeting of Amnon and Yedidiah, the father of Tamar, whose life has been saved by Amnon's bravery:

> And Yedidiah raised his eyes and said: "Is your name Amnon?"
> And the youth said to him: "Amnon is the name of your servant."
> "Are you the one that saved Tamar, my daughter, from the savage lion?"—Yedidiah asked him further.

"The Lord was pleased to strengthen the hand of
your servant"—Amnon answered with modest grace.

"May the Lord bless you, my son!"—Yedidiah
said—"And you will be an honourable man in Zion.
Behold! I am in your debt for this deed, and I shall
reward you accordingly."

Closely connected with this latter problem is the manner of introducing direct speech. For the novelist in a modern European language there is a great choice of words for introducing a statement, question or reply, which obviates the monotony of a constantly recurring use of the verbs "say," "ask" and "answer." In the absence of any such wide range in the Bible, however, Mapu was limited to a very small selection of suitable verbs, a liability which naturally becomes more pronounced where the dialogue consists of brief statement and reply, and the words appear with a proportionate frequency.

The extreme limitation of such verbs and their monotonous repetition throughout the length of three novels constitute a serious defect in Mapu's style. They provide one of the most striking instances of the difficulties involved in the adaptation of the materials of the Bible to the construction of a modern novel. For whereas simplicity and repetition of form are characteristic of the Biblical narrative, and indeed accentuate its forcefulness and appeal, they are totally unsuited to the vastly different canvas of the novel, which demands far greater flexibility and variety. This defect is pathetically obvious and must be admitted even while recognizing the greatness of Mapu's feat in creating dialogue and the large measure of success which he achieved in the attempt. Nevertheless, there can be little doubt that Mapu's novels, both by virtue of their own merit, and through the great influence which they exerted on subsequent Hebrew novelists, helped in no small measure to prepare the ground for the extraordinary revival of Hebrew as a spoken language, which Mapu had, himself, so dramatically prophesied.

Guide and Moralist

Although in so many respects a revolutionary in the realm of Hebrew literature from the point of view of the form, setting, and conception of his novels, Mapu was too much a child of his generation to remain aloof from its missionary spirit. On the contrary he felt himself a conscious champion of the cause of *Haskalah,* and the ideals of that movement, as reflected in the cultural, religious, social, and economic struggles of the time, are inextricably embedded in the body of his writings.

The principal ideas, which comprise the element of didacticism in Mapu's novels, and which roughly correspond with the main aims of the movement of *Haskalah,* may be divided into five categories:

1. The glorification of the Jewish past.
2. The encouragement of a discriminating use of the Hebrew language with an attendant refinement of taste.
3. The dissemination of knowledge and enlightenment.
4. The inculcation of a lofty, ethical attitude to life.
5. The improvement of the social and economic position of the Jewish people.

These several aspects, however, are not treated as separate themes, but rather interwoven one with the other to such an extent that the aims appear synonymous and mutually dependent.

The glorification of the Jewish past is, of course, inherent in the very conception of the two historical novels, and embodied in the name *The Love of Zion.* Although couched in very different form, these two novels have much in common with the productions of *Hokmat Yisrael,* or *Jewish Science,* which did so much to restore the national pride of the Jewish people. But apart from their historical interest, these stories contained a living message for Mapu's own generation. The full, free life of the individual and the national independence, so clearly portrayed in these novels, as well as the healthy and organic connection with the soil, presented such a striking contrast to the harsh reality and meagre existence of contemporary life, that his readers could not but have been awakened to a longing for better things and to the need to break the fetters of gradual decay which enveloped the Jewish community.

It is clearly an exaggeration to portray Mapu as a creator of the Zionist movement, a fact which S. L. Zitron has pointed out. But there can be no doubt that the influence exerted by these novels and the deep longings they aroused helped to prepare a mental climate suitable for the growth of the Zionist idea. It may be doubted whether Mapu's personal conception of a physical return to Palestine went beyond the traditional idea expressed by the ageing Obadiah:

> But be sure of this, that Zion's paths are in my heart, and that as soon as my money is returned, I shall take my staff in my hand and journey to the holy city; for who is there, or what is there, to keep me here?

What is more certain, however, is that his stories represent a symbolic, indeed prophetic, call for national revival, and as such have exercised a profound influence on subsequent generations of young readers.

Mapu's love of the Hebrew language was equalled only by his earnest desire to foster its widespread use among his own contemporaries and to raise the aesthetic level of publications in that medium. His motives for writing in Hebrew and his choice of the imaginative story—which he refers to as *Hazon* (a vision)—are described in the introduction to the third part of *The Hypocrite* and the introduction to *The Visionaries*. With the publication of his novels in Hebrew, Mapu hoped to attract the young generation to a deeper attachment to that language, and thereby counteract the tendency towards assimilation so conspicuous among the Jewish communities of France and Germany. In addition he believed that by stirring their imagination and widening their mental horizons he would encourage the youth to seek learning and wisdom. Mapu felt deeply the pressing need to raise the general level of taste, and the emphasis on *Tub Ta'am* (good taste) is maintained constantly throughout his writings, sometimes under the name *Leshon-Limmudim* or *Zahot* or *Melizah*, although the latter term is also used—generally together with the word *Mashal*, as in Proverbs, i. 6—in the sense of a penetrating understanding.

On the other hand the orthodox opponents of *Haskalah*, for whom even the study of Hebrew grammar was anathema, are characterized in Mapu's novels by their utter disregard for the refinements of language as in the case of Hamul:

> And apart from his Talmud, which he had studied
> since childhood, he knew nothing, but despised *Melizah*
> and *Zahot* and *Leshon-Limmudim*, which he regarded
> as vile words and wasted study.

To Mapu fine speech and fine character are almost synonymous and the heroes throughout the novel display a due regard for wisdom and the beauties and subtleties of language. Amnon, for example, is praised with the words:

> For beyond all riches he preferred to understand
> *Mashal* and *Melizah*....

The clearest example of Mapu's crusade for the refinement of Hebrew appears, of course, in his own use of the language in his novels, but an additional spur to the development or taste can be felt in the discussions on literature and literary criticism which he portrays inside the framework of *The Hypocrite*.

Closely connected with the call for the refinement of language is Mapu's constant plea for the dissemination of knowledge and enlightenment. Indeed, apart from its intrinsic value, the former concept is regarded as the instrument of the latter. No less than the "Age of Reason" in France and the "Enlightenment" in Germany of the previous century, the movement of *Haskalah* believed that the spread of the ideas of reason and understanding would eradicate the evils of society and advance the cause of civilization. In consequence the need for popular enlightenment was regarded as a matter of paramount importance, towards which every effort should be expended. Hence, too, the constant stress on the importance of learning foreign languages—an occupation regarded by the orthodox as anathema. All the virtues required for the new type of being, whose every action would be guided by reason, were embodied in the ideal figure of the *Maskil.* As the spearhead of the attack on the forces of darkness and ignorance, the *Maskil* would eventually conquer with the weapons of wisdom, moral superiority, and good taste in spite of all the harm perpetrated by foolishness and superstitious prejudice. The concept is stressed continually in Mapu's writings:

> Even if fools hide themselves in gloom and desolation, the wise man will gradually lighten our darkness....

The bad characters, on the other hand, are conspicuous by their hatred of these qualities:

> ...But his greatest fault was his complete hatred of knowledge and understanding, of all *Melizah, Zahot* and *Leshon-Limmudim....*

Typical of the philosophy Mapu is endeavouring to expound is Amnon's reward for saving Tamar from the lion's jaws. He asks for and is granted an education, while Yedidiah exhorts his instructors:

> ...Take of your spirit upon him, and give him good counsel, that he may understand *Mashal, Melizah* and *Zahot,* and know the Lord.

As a life-long pedagogue, Mapu could not refrain from emphasizing this lesson repeatedly.

One of the keynotes sounded throughout the novels is the constant stress on a lofty, ethical approach to life, which is again closely associated with refinement of language:

> Behold, *Melizah* and morality were twin-born
> from the beginning of time....

Moral and religious sentiments—modelled on the prophetic books and Wisdom Literature of the Bible, and in the historical novels actually uttered by Biblical prophets—occupy a prominent place in all three stories. They all end happily with a generous reward for the good characters and the shameful exposure and punishment of the villains, who, moreover, regularly repent.

Throughout the novels a constant barrage is directed against fraud, deceit, and especially hypocrisy, which is made the central target for Mapu's scorn, and which in *The Hypocrite* is treated as a principal theme, incorporated in the very title. In this novel it is closely associated with forgery, also an integral element in the plot. It is of interest, however, that neither the frequent interception of letters, nor the constant reading of correspondence addressed to other persons, nor the practice of listening to a conversation behind closed doors is censured despite their contravention of Jewish ethics. This fact constitutes a further illustration of the dubious morality even of some of the good characters, which has been pointed out, and hardly accords with the stress Mapu lays on the importance of good deeds as well as piety:

> And yet I have known men who occupy them-
> selves with ethics all day, and from too much contem-
> plation of ethics they do not see their fellow-men for
> looking at the heavens....

Wretchedly poor all his life and himself a victim of the crushing poverty in which the Jews of eastern Europe lived, Mapu could hardly refrain from suggesting improvements in the social and economic conditions of his people.

Frequently, too, the story serves as a forum for his ideas on education, wherein he forcefully portrays the bad effects of harsh and exclusive book-learning, so widely practised by the Pietists, and advocates his own use of more gentle methods. The barbaric practice of burning secular books is censured severely, while the underhand methods of the traditional match-maker, quite indifferent to the happiness of the young couples whose marriages he is so anxious to arrange, receive a due share of satire. A further reform, strongly advocated, is the emancipation of woman. Elisheva is the representative of the new type of woman, independent, cultured, demanding equality of education with her male counterpart. It is significant, too, that Mapu stresses her interest in handicrafts as a field of creative and aesthetic expression. His advocacy of economic and social reform, however, is generally moderate and restrained in comparison to the bitter polemics which abound in the novels of his successors, who frequently resort to cutting satire and biting irony for the propagation of their views. But for the most part Mapu points his lesson in good faith, on the one hand fighting to preserve the finer elements of Jewish tradition, and on the other indicating the new values to be adopted in a changing world.

Mapu's Contribution to Hebrew Literature

An evaluation of Mapu's contribution to Hebrew literature involves some consideration of his own debt to previous writers both in Hebrew and in European languages. His celebrity is firmly based on precedence. He was the first to create a Hebrew novel, and thereby paved the way for the emergence of this important branch of modern Hebrew literature. But many of the component features of his novels, and particularly the mechanics of his plots, were derived from a number of sources. Mapu's originality lay in the overall conception of his works, and in the skilful adaptation of his material. That his inventive capacity was limited is demonstrated both by his frequent

borrowing of dramatic devices and by the many repetitions and simi-
larities which occur throughout his novels.

The influence of the Bible on Mapu's works is most conspicuous in the setting, style, and language of the historical novels,
and extends in less measure to *The Hypocrite*. It constitutes the primary source of Mapu's inspiration. Due regard, however, must be
given to the importance of the Hebrew poets Moses Hayyim Luzzatto
and Naphtali Herz Wessely (1725-1805), both of whom Mapu held in
high esteem. The influence of the latter is less specific, being apparent in tendencies rather than in detail, and stems principally from his
magnum opus *Shirei-Tif'eret*. This work comprises a long epic poem,
dealing with Moses and the Exodus from Egypt, and modelled on the
Messias of the German poet G. F. Klopstock (1724-1803). Although
the poem is no longer rated very highly, it was loudly acclaimed by
the poet's own generation, and Wessely was considered for a time the
leading poet of the day.

Wessely introduced new forms into Hebrew poetry which were
followed by Hebrew poets for more than sixty years, and which may
be discerned in the songs interspersed by Mapu in his own novels.
Mapu, however, displayed little poetic inspiration. His poems are
clumsy and wooden, written in a halting rhythm, and with a scan-
sion often imperfect. They represent one of the least convincing elements of his stories, and provide an interesting example of a literary
climate which fostered the composition of Hebrew poetry almost as
a duty regardless of any lack of poetic talent on the part of the writer.
Moreover, the poems in the historical novels are quite anachronistic
in form. Their European metre and rhyme are quite foreign to the
poetry of the Bible. In this respect Mapu was, perhaps, influenced
by Bulwer Lytton's *The Last Days of Pompeii*, in which many songs
in European form are introduced anachronistically into an historical
framework, and with which Mapu may have been familiar in its German or French translation. In any case the phenomenon of "Biblical"
songs in modern rhythm was sufficiently common in Hebrew drama
to be acceptable, while a fondness for lyric poetry, particularly that of
the French, German and English romantic movements in literature, is

evident in the second period of *Haskalah*—a tendency best exemplified by Mapu's contemporary, Micah Joseph Lebensohn (1825-52). But an experiment of this nature can prove successful only in the hands of a genuine poet, and Mapu's complete lack of self-criticism with regard to his poetic compositions sadly undermines the effect.

Wessely's influence on the novelist, however, consists of idea rather than form. The poem *Shirei-Tif'eret* focused attention upon the Bible as source material for modern literary composition. The influence of Wessely stems also from another source. The poet was a champion of the movement of enlightenment. A series of letters addressed to various Jewish communities was later collected in book form under the title *Diverei-Shalom ve-Emet.* In these letters Wessely advocated reforms in the Jewish educational system calculated to widen its scope and introduce secular knowledge. In regarding the expansion of the Jewish curriculum of studies as a prime essential for the amelioration of the social and economic position of the Jews, Wessely helped to establish the principles of *Haskalah,* and his ideas are echoed in Mapu's novels, particularly *The Hypocrite.*

The influence of Moses Hayyim Luzzatto is more direct, and traces of it are discernible in the plots, dramatic devices, background, and ideas common to both authors. The process is most in evidence in *The Love of Zion,* in which novel elements from Luzzatto's allegorical dramas *Migdal 'Oz* and *La-Yesharim Tehillah* have been freely adopted. From the latter Mapu utilized the device of the betrothal of babies.

The lucid Hebrew, which Luzzatto employs with such skill and dexterity, and which infuses a spirit of freshness and life into the dramas, is reminiscent of Mapu's own lyrical prose. It would seem that a strong tie of sympathy existed between the minds of the mystic, Luzzatto, and the romantic dreamer, Mapu.

There is reason to believe that Mapu may also have been influenced by a group of Hebrew dramatists writing in Germany in the early nineteenth century. Although almost all these writers have vanished into oblivion, Professor Rabin has demonstrated the part they once played in the literature of the *Haskalah*. Apart from an interesting attempt by I. B. Bing of Würzburg to create a Hebrew slang, a number of other writers connected with Breslau composed several romantic plays on Biblical and post-Biblical themes, apparently inspired directly or indirectly by Joseph Ephrati, the author of a popular drama devoted to the reign of King Saul entitled *Melukat Sha'ul* (Vienna, 1794). Their foremost representative, David Zamoscz, composed, apart from a Biblical drama, two realistic plays devoted to the problems of contemporary German-Jewish society. As social themes were destined to become predominant in Hebrew literature from the sixties of the nineteenth century onwards, Zamoscz may be regarded as something of a pioneer. These playwrights may well have influenced Mapu not only in his historical novels—the drinking scenes in Carmi's inn provide, perhaps, a case in point—but also in his social novel, which played so important a role in directing the attention of modern Hebrew literature towards the compelling problems of contemporary Jewish life.

Among the writers of Hebrew prose whose influence may be discerned in Mapu's novels, due regard should be paid to Joseph Perl and Isaac Erter. As exponents of *Haskalah* in Galicia, these writers poured forth their satires against the social evils of their time in quasi-novel form. Mapu was able to profit by their example in the technique of story-telling, and they provided a precedent for the melodramatic and farfetched incidents to which Mapu was so prone.

Turning to writers in European languages, Mapu seems to have been influenced principally by the French romantic novelists, the elder Dumas and Eugène Sue. The notion originated from a letter received by R. Brainin from Dr L. Mapu, the author's son, stating that his father was influenced by the French romantic writers, particularly Victor Hugo, Dumas-Père and Eugène Sue. Moreover Brainin asserts, on the authority of D. Z. Bramson, a close acquaintance of Mapu's youth, that the latter considered Sue to be the foremost exponent of the art of the novel. It is true that Mapu strongly opposed the translation of Sue's novels into Hebrew. But the reason may well be, as A. Sha'anan suggests, that this antagonism stemmed from Mapu's knowledge that his own novel, *The Love of Zion*, owed much to Sue's *Mystères de Paris*, whose publication lowered the value of the originality of his novel in his own eyes. Certainly Mapu experienced pangs of jealousy at the immediate success of K. Schulman's translation, and the financial gain which the translator enjoyed.

The influence of Dumas-Père is largely external. From him Mapu learned the art of creating atmosphere, and of clothing his plots in a romantic-historical mantle.

The influence of Eugène Sue, on the other hand, is more clearly discernible in the aim of Mapu's novels, particularly that of *The Hypocrite*. The *Mystères de Paris* was primarily considered a militant social novel, and in common with *The Hypocrite* it presents a social purpose within a romantic setting. Both novels aim to portray existing social evils, and suggest reform. But whereas Sue depicts an economic struggle between the upper and lower strata of Paris society, Mapu outlines an ideological conflict between the old and new generations inside the Jewish community. A further similarity between *Mystères de Paris* and *The Hypocrite* lies in the complexities of the plots, which abound with melodrama, conspiracy, and timely coincidence.

In the light of the various factors outlined above, it may be seen that Mapu's creative power must not be sought in the form of his novels. The structure, the dramatic technique, and the characterizations all lean heavily on previous writers, and all display grave weaknesses and limitations. From a technical standpoint Mapu resembles a clumsy apprentice rather than a finished craftsman. He never mastered the art of weaving a convincing plot, and his inability to sustain interest over long periods is particularly evident in his more lengthy novels. Nevertheless, Mapu's writings are stamped with a freshness and originality which more than atone for all his borrowings and limitations, and display an element of genius.

❧

Mapu's main contribution to Hebrew literature appears in the overall conception of his works. He possessed an imagination and descriptive power that could bring dry bones to life. In his historical novels he made the Bible live and endowed a remote period in history with a vividness and freshness of appeal such as no commentary or explanation can offer. His greatness consisted not so much in the intrinsic value of his writings as in the possibilities that he revealed, which placed him at the head of a new literary epoch. His strength lay in the portrayal of setting, in the smoothness of his style, in his mastery of Biblical language. He clearly indicated that the Hebrew language might eventually be forged into an adequate medium of expression and adapted to serve the manifold needs of modern life. And above all he gave vent to the free expression of emotion, transfusing a somewhat dry and intellectual literature with the feelings of heroism and love. His novels provided an emotional stimulus to generations of young readers, fostering a pride in the national past and focusing attention upon the Holy Land. Hence, their influence on the Jewish national movement from which Zionism later emerged constitutes an important factor in modern Jewish history.

His importance is almost equally in evidence in another direction. The ideas on social and educational reform, expounded in *The Hypocrite,* helped to set a fashion among the Hebrew writers who followed him. The influence of the elements of realism in his novel of contemporary life may be traced in the writings of P. Smolenskin (1842-85), J. L. Gordon, R. A. Braudes (1851-1902), M. D. Brandstätter (1844-1928) and Mendele Mocher Sefarim, who developed the positivist and social aspects of their work still further. Indeed, the realist novel depicting the problems of contemporary society has continued to occupy the dominant position in Hebrew literature to the present day. It is of interest, however, that none of the major novelists who succeeded Mapu attempted to imitate his strict Biblical style. Little by little they began to follow Mapu's own advice in utilizing the linguistic resources of later strata of Hebrew literature. Either they lacked Mapu's facility and mastery of the language of the Bible, or they felt that his three novels had exhausted the possibilities of that medium, and sought a richer and more flexible instrument of language. But in any case, the clumsiness of Biblical Hebrew as a means of depicting the complex phenomena of the modern world became increasingly apparent as the range of subject matter depicted in the Hebrew novel widened.

The Love of Zion

Translated by Joseph Marymount

Translator's Dedication

To the tender memory of my beloved wife Rose, whose solicitous care and love I so grievously miss as the years pass along; whose loss, during my own convalescence, left me groping in the infinities of spiritual aspiration, where I found the only solace and comfort, in the long hours of darkness and grief, through my love of the classical Hebrew of which this translation is a part; and to my dear children, whose unselfish devotion and innumerable instances of self-sacrifice made this work possible, and especially my daughter Charlotte, who still in her teens, was my loyal emanuensis, my lovable and invaluable companion throughout the trying period of those days, I affectionately dedicate my book.

—Joseph Marymount, 1919

Chapter one

During the reign of Ahaz, the King of Judah, there lived in Jerusalem Yoram, a warrior, who, by mighty deeds of arms, had attained the proud position of Commanding General of the armies of Ahaz.

Though Ahaz, the King, was an idolater, a worshiper of false gods, Yoram was a firm believer and devout worshiper of the one true God, omnipotent, all seeing, the God of Israel, and God had blessed him with abundance of earthly possessions. His lands extended from Carmel to Sharon, yea, and even to Bethlehem, Judah. His sheep and cattle grazed in vast numbers over the verdant and luxuriant vales and hillsides of that territory. His vineyards smiled in abundance and were the most productive of that favoured land. His coffers were filled with gold, and priceless jewels were stored in the vault of his treasury.

Yoram had two wives: Haggit, daughter of Ira, was his first wife and she bore him two children; his second wife was the beautiful Naame, and although she had borne no children, Yoram loved her the better. Observing this, Haggit's heart was seized with hatred, resentment, and jealousy, and she sought every opportunity to insult and humiliate the gentle Naame. Yoram, therefore, according to the custom of his time, determined to build and maintain a separate household, over which Naame should reign as mistress.

Now, there lived in Jerusalem at that time a money-lender named Josifat, whose consuming passion was the acquisition of great wealth. Under the garb of piety beat a heart of cruel avarice. The first in the Holy Temple, he was the last to linger in the articulate prayer. His offerings were the costliest, and so, in the estimation of many, he was regarded as a pious, God-fearing man. Yet those who were unfortunate and indebted to him were mercilessly deprived of their possessions by process of law, and the ear of the court inclined to Josifat's plaint, because of his reputation for sanctity. This Josifat had an only son, whose name was Matan.

Ira, the father of Haggit, was at enmity with Josifat, because of a dispute in which they had become involved over the boundary line of a fertile piece of land, and Josifat, by his consummate shrewdness, sought to overcome Ira.

Much as Ira hated Josifat because of his rapacity, so much in opposite and inflamed degree did Matan, the money-lender's son, love Haggit, the daughter of Ira. Haggit was at that time in the full bloom of her maidenhood, and Matan, in the ardor of his love, determined to woo and win her in spite of the enmity existing between their parents.

One day, while paying court to Haggit, Matan said to her, "My father is very old, his days are numbered. Upon his death, if you but give me hope, I shall return all of what he took from your father and, in addition, the adjoining property, which I, as his only son and heir, shall inherit." Haggit, thinking that her father would regain his possessions through her assent, pledged herself to Matan, although at the time she was secretly engaged to Yoram, with her father's knowledge and consent.

Soon after this Josifat died, and Matan became the possessor of his father's wealth. One can easily imagine the number of Josifat's victims who crowded around Matan and clamored for restitution of his ill-gotten gains; but Matan had inherited his father's miserly nature and refused to listen to their pleadings.

Matan's love for Haggit would not allow him any rest, for she had promised to become his wife when he had entered into possession of his father's estate, and the time had now come. So Matan hastened to Ira, the father of Haggit, and said, "Now that I am absolute owner of all my father's wealth, I will restore to you the lands which he took from you, and I will also repay you all that you lost during the time that you were deprived of their revenue. Even more than this shall I bestow, if you will give me the hand of your daughter Haggit, whom I dearly love."

And Ira replied, "Your father robbed the poor, oppressed and afflicted the unfortunate, and the curses of many whom he wronged will fall upon you. How can I give my daughter in marriage to a man who is loved by none, whose soul is stigmatized with a hereditary curse? On one condition only shall I give my consent to your marriage with Haggit; that condition is that you return to everyone whom your father defrauded all that by right belongs to them, and thus, by restitution, redeem yourself in the eyes of the people."

"You set a high price upon the hand of your daughter," replied Matan, "but so great is my love for her that I cheerfully agree and accept the conditions you impose."

Then said Ira, "When the time for mourning for your father shall have ceased, I shall give my daughter Haggit to you in marriage."

Matan, highly pleased with Ira's promise, and self-satisfied with his own magnanimity, returned home in joyful humour, to fulfill without delay the requirements demanded of him by the father of Haggit. Accordingly, Matan summoned to his house that evening all the people aggrieved, and in the presence of trustworthy witnesses said to them: "For many years you were at variance with my father; against his shrewdness you could do nothing in the courts. Then you came to me, and I, also, was deaf to your pleadings and would not harken to you. I knew you would be helpless in court and in every contest I would come forth victor. Now, however, I am moved to righteous impulse, and out of the goodness of my heart I shall here restore what you have been seeking for years without avail, for 'Know ye that I am a God-fearing man.'" And the entire assembly blessed him and the remainder of the evening was spent in feasting and rejoicing until the hour of separation and return to their homes.

The entire community was astonished at Matan's beneficence and magnanimity, and he became the hero of the day.

When Matan went to the home of Ira for his promised bride, she was no longer there. "Where is Haggit?" he excitedly exclaimed.

"Ashamed am I to be the bearer of ill news to you," said Ira, "but I must tell you that Haggit had fallen in love with Yoram, the great dignitary. Of this, Matan, I knew nothing, but so it is; she is even now married to him."

Then Matan realized that father and daughter had conspired against him and that, too, he was powerless to undo the good he had already done. Intensely angry and revengeful though he was, he controlled his emotions and said, "It is God's will that Haggit should be the wife of Yoram, and I do not regret the good I have done through your advice. I have started in the path of righteousness and from it I do not intend to depart. The cloak of charity which I have donned, I shall never discard. May it please God that your daughter find peace and happiness in her husband's home; my heart will rejoice to see her ever happy."

And Ira, clasping Matan's hand, said: "Therefore the righteous shall praise thee and will proclaim thy deeds in public. Now, if you wish to show your kindness and chivalry still further, come with me to the house of Yoram, and tell him and my daughter that you have forgiven them for the evil they did you, for without your forgiveness their happiness would never be complete."

So Matan, with smiling face, accompanied Ira to Yoram's house, and extended to Yoram and Haggit his forgiveness and congratulations. Then Yoram, overpowered with so much unselfishness and goodness, said to Matan, "I see in your face the reflection of the Divine; therefore let us be true friends." And from that time, Matan and Yoram were bosom friends, even as brothers; but in the depths of Matan's heart there dwelt an evil purpose, the smoldering fire of fierce revenge, when opportunity should arise to leap into consuming flame.

Chapter two

Hananeel, a nobleman, of the Tribe of Ephraim, living in Samaria, came, according to the Mosaic Law, to Jerusalem during the Feast of the Tabernacles. He brought with him his daughter Tirzah, a maiden of seventeen, who was so beautiful that all the young noblemen who beheld her fell in love with her at first sight. Among her admirers was Yedidiah, the philanthropist, a descendant from the Kings of Judah, Minister of Finance and worshiper of one true God, of kindred soul to Yoram in righteousness and justice to the King, and so a bosom friend of Yoram. Yedidiah gave a ball in honour of Hananeel and his daughter Tirzah, and to this ball he invited his closest friend, General Yoram, and his wives, and all the students of the Theological School, which he maintained, and many others of his friends. While the ball was in progress, Yedidiah said to Hananeel, "Zion is the home of everything beautiful; therefore, let your daughter be one of her beauties and bloom like a rose on the hills of Zion."

Hananeel made answer, "She will bloom if she is planted in a garden which is fed with the dew from Heaven."

"Let me be the garden for your daughter," said Yedidiah, "for the fear of the Lord is like the dew from Heaven to me, and even great riches God did not withhold from me."

"For a whole year the most noble among the Ephraimites have been asking for the hand of my daughter in marriage, but she despises them and their riches. She says, 'Ephraim is corrupt; they are idolaters. Therefore, I hate them and will have none of them. I wish to marry a man of Judah and a resident of Jerusalem.' It is for this reason I brought my daughter here to give her to him whom she may choose. So speak yourself to the damsel, and if she selects you I will bless you both in the name of the Lord."

Thereupon, Yedidiah went to Tirzah and said to her, "Tell me, fair lady, how do you like Zion and her people?"

"Zion is like the Garden of Eden to me, its people like unto angels," replied Tirzah.

"Your words make me feel proud that I am a resident of Jerusalem," said Yedidiah.

"Indeed, all residents might be proud if they were all like you," replied Tirzah.

"I am gratified to have found such favour in your sight. I wish only to find such favour in the heart of her I love," said Yedidiah.

"May that heart be blessed by God," murmured Tirzah.

"May you, fair lady, be the one so blessed by God and me," said Yedidiah.

"Be you the messenger to my father for me, and what he will tell you shall reveal my heart's best wish."

And while they were talking together, Hananeel approached and said, "If you, daughter, will listen to my advice, he who stands beside thee is the one I would wish to find favour in your sight. He is in the prime of manhood, a man of honour, and one who dwells in the fear of the Lord."

And Yedidiah laughed and said, "Your daughter does not see me in that light; she sees me as an angel."

"Therefore," said Hananeel, "let me also be like an angel who comes in the name of God to unite your hearts and bless you in the presence of God who dwells in Zion."

And Tirzah said to Yedidiah, "I find you to be the only one, and so I wish to be to you, and on that condition I will be yours."

Yedidiah answering said, "You and you only shall be my love, and no other shall ever come between us." With these words they were betrothed and soon after married.

Hananeel stayed with his children a whole year, and his heart rejoiced to see his daughter happy in Zion and to witness how she was so dearly loved by her husband. At the close of the year of Hananeel's stay in Zion, the Philistines invaded the lower part of northern Judah and occupied the cities and villages of their territory, and Yoram was summoned to active service, and ordered to prepare to lead his army to active war with the Philistines. At the same time his wife, Haggit, bore a third son to him, and he called him Azrikam, which means "God shall help him to subdue his enemies." Haggit's maid, Hella, wife of Yoram's butler, also bore a son, whom they named Nabal. Haggit commanded Hella to give her own child to the other servants to raise, while to her was entrusted the rearing of Azrikam. Uchon, Hella's husband, was much dissatisfied and resented this arrangement, but remained silent.

Naame, Yoram's second wife, was about to become a mother, and so also was Tirzah, wife of Yedidiah.

Yoram called Yedidiah to his summer home, which was situated on the Mount of Olives, and said to him, "I leave tomorrow for the impending war. No one can forecast the future or lift the veil that conceals the unknown. Who can tell that I shall ever return safely to my home and loved ones? Therefore, let us make a covenant, which shall extend even to our children: If I shall fall in war or be taken captive by the enemy, you shall be a father to my house and the guardian of my children. You shall appoint overseers for my estates according to your best judgement. I shall only stipulate that you shall not remove Sisry, one of the theological scholars, who looks after my lands near Carmel, nor his older brother Avicha, for they are God-fearing people and relations of my wife, Naame. Furthermore, if our wives, Naame and Tirzah, should bear one a son, the other a daughter, they shall be betrothed, and, when their time shall come, be united as man and wife, because Naame and Tirzah love each other even as you and I, and we can live in the fond hope that that love may be perpetuated in succeeding generations. The crops from the lands of Carmel shall supply food for the Theological students, and on every holiday there shall be set a table to accomodate four hundred poor widows and orphans, as it has been my habit and custom to do; and finally, to you, my friend, I give this summer palace as a parting gift to you and yours forever."

Then Yedidiah answered and said, "Highly as I value this beautiful palace as a gift, it is the generous impulse which prompts its bestowal by you upon me that I prize more highly. In the palace I shall dwell, if only to be reminded of your princely generosity. Here is my ring; put it on the forefinger of your right hand, and it shall be a pledge of our everlasting friendship. And if it be God's will to bring you back to us, we will offer thanksgiving to Him, and we and all our households will rejoice together in this beautiful summer palace." With tears in their eyes, they embraced each other and parted.

Early next morning, Yoram called his wives and his children and blessed them. He blessed his wives, and, in Naame's parting embrace, wept most bitterly. Then at the head of his assembled army he marched to war with the Philistines.

After these events had transpired, Tirzah gave birth to a daughter, and Yedidiah caller her Tamar. Hananeel, her grandfather, had a ring made, in which his name and Tamar's were engraved. He gave it to his daughter Tirzah, saying, "This ring shall be a testimonial that Tamar shall be an equal heir with my children to all my wealth, and she shall wear this ring when she becomes older." Hananeel stayed another month in Zion, and after blessing his children, returned to his home in Samaria.

Soon after Yoram's departure, the sad tidings were brought to his home that he had fallen captive into the hands of the Philistines, and his wife, Naame, cried bitterly without ceasing. Haggit, seeing the grief of her rival, rejoiced over the captivity of her husband and cried aloud, "Now shall Naame be exalted above me nevermore! I and I alone shall be mistress of Yoram's house!" And so she was; her rule over the servants was arbitrary and absolute, punishing them unmercifully if they did not please her. Naame was indifferent to all that was passing around her, immersed only in the waters of the grief that overflowed constantly upon her bruised heart. Uchon, the butler, suffered constantly at the sight of the indignities daily inflicted upon his wife, Hella, at the hands of her mistress, Haggit, and his mind was engaged in gloomy and harrowing thoughts of vengeance and retribution.

Chapter three

When Justice Matan discovered that Yoram did not entrust him with the care and guardianship of his household, he became jealous of Yedidiah, and his hatred towards Yoram grew to such intensity that his captivity filled him with gladness and elation. "The time is now at hand," said he, communing with himself, "to revenge myself of Yoram for all my past wrongs." He frequently visited Yoram's house to comfort Naame and Haggit, but in his heart he rejoiced to see Haggit living as a widow, yearning for her husband. On one occasion, as he entered Haggit's home, he found her in terrible wrath, beating her servant, Hella. Upon seeing Matan she refrained and said, "Mark my trouble! I appointed this slave to be nurse for my son, Azrikam, and leaving this room for a moment, I learned upon my return that she had gone to the servants' quarters, there to nurse her own son, the miserable wretch!" Uchon, who was present, saw the insults put upon his wife, and wept; then turning to Matan said, "Be you the judge! I have seen my poor child left alone in his cradle, crying continually, with none of the servants to care for him, so I called my wife that she might nurse him. Was there anything wrong in that action? If there is, I alone am to blame; let me and not my wife be punished."

At these words, Haggit, like an enraged tigress, sprang and roared at him, "You low, miserable slave! Who wants you here to stay in my employ? And did not my husband try to free you, but you said, 'I love my master, my wife and my child, and do not wish to be freed.' If you do not wish to be punished by me now and at all times, you had better bear the bitterness of your lot in silence."

Matan heard all that passed between them but made no comment, while in his wicked heart he said, "I will kindle a fire in Uchon's heart that will blaze into fiercest vengeance, and make him a willing tool to accomplish my own designs for long deferred revenge." And so he bade Uchon to come to his home that night.

When Uchon came to Matan's house, he said, "You have seen the wrongs I have had to endure from my mistress. Judge me and advise me how to escape from the hands of this woman."

And Matan answered and said, "Does not your wrath burn like fire? Turn it on the dwellings of your master, Yoram; burn his house and all its inmates, and so gratify your hatred on the woman for all the wicked things she has done to you and yours."

Uchon's eyes flamed with murderous light, and he said, "Do you speak in earnest or are you merely jesting?"

"Oh, you ignorant fool," said Matan, "would I laugh at such a poor wretch, burdened with so many insults and afflicted with such degradations as you?"

"But, why should the noble Naame suffer for Haggit's indignities?" answered Uchon.

"Listen, and follow my advice," said Matan. "Put fire to the house of Haggit and also to that of her servants. Save only the wife and son, whom you will call Azrikam. Yedidiah, nor even his wife who never saw the child, will not recognize the one from the other, they being of the same age. Naame's house you shall spare, so that suspicion will fall upon her, for everyone is aware of the bitter hatred which exists between the two wives. This tragedy will compel Naame to flee from the wrath of Haggit's relatives, and no one will be left of thy master's house. Then your son, who will then be known as Azrikam, will be heir to all of Yoram's lands. Your son's wealth shall be your reward for your work; mine shall be the treasures which Yoram hid in a secret vault, to me personally known and of which I have the key. I shall send two shrewd and reliable men, Hepher and Bukkiah, to get them and deposit them in my house, and so repay myself for the money and lands I returned to my father's creditors. You can depend upon the men I have named. They are considered pious and estimable men, upon whom suspicion will never fall."

Uchon's heart beat with exultation and joy at the scheme proposed, and he said, "Never was such a plot conceived in hell or purgatory."

"Do not be afraid," said Matan. "Come again and I will direct and instruct you in all that will be necessary for you to do." Uchon came, and he and Matan worked out the details of their infamous plot. Concerning the exchange of the children, they decided not even Hepher or Bukkiah should know.

No better night for the consummation of the crime could have been selected by the conspirators. The darkness was dense, the fog so thick that one could scarcely see a hand's space in front of him. All was silent in the house of Yoram, and Uchon emptied the secret vault of his master. Hepher and Bukkiah carried the treasure to the house of Justice Matan and then hid it in the cave. Uchon took his son from the servants' quarters and barred the doors from the outside; Hella did likewise to the house of her mistress, Haggit. Then Uchon put fire to the four corners of the house and the flames leaped to the skies. When Uchon saw that the flames had completely surrounded the house, he ran to the innocent Naame's house, and, with hands outstretched, his voice arose in fearful lamentation, "Oh, Mistress, a fire is consuming Yoram's dwellings, and none is there to save the inmates and all must perish! My wife, Hella, sprang through a window with the infant Azrikam, son of Haggit, while Haggit and her other two children the flames overcame, and all are lost, lost, lost! Woe, woe is me, for my son also was burned to death in the servants' quarters!"

While they were talking, Hepher and Bukkiah passed Naame's house and said one to the other, "See you, it was Naame's jealousy that was the cause of this awful calamity."

A cold shiver of fear shook Naame's frame, and she cried despairingly, saying, "Some evil doer hath done this, and falsely accuses me of setting fire to Yoram's dwellings! Oh, woe is me! Where shall I go?"

And Uchon said to her, "Disguise yourself in men's clothes and run away, ere the relatives of Haggit arrive and seek revenge for Haggit's death."

Naame, as suggested and advised by Uchon, escaped through the window which he had forced to give her freedom, and fled into the outer darkness alone and unattended. Uchon then compelled Naame's two maids to follow him, so that he could conceal them in a place secure from pursuit until everything had quieted down. Instead, however, he placed them in the house from which the treasures had been removed, then barricaded the doors from the outside and set the house on fire. The poor girls screamed for help and sought desperately to escape, but no one came to their rescue, so they perished.

Then Uchon said to his wife Hella, "There is no one left from Yoram's house. Embrace our son Nabal, and call him Azrikam."

As they were talking, the neighbours began to assemble at the scene of the fire. Upon seeing the people coming, Uchon and Hella began loud lamentations over their misfortune, and Yedidiah and Tirzah came and clasped their hands in despair, and they hastened their steps to Naame's home, but found it empty. They pressed Hella with the question, "Where is Naame? Where is Naame?"

"Alas, alas," said Uchon, "a terrible catastrophe has befallen us! I was late in coming from the fields tonight and as I came nearer to the house, an door of smoke assailed my nostrils. My eager walk broke into a run, only to be arrested in horror as I beheld my mistress's house in flames! I tried, but unavailingly, to save my mistress and her children, but, alas, I was too late, too late! As I approached the house I saw Haggit hand Hella her son, Azrikam, through an open window. Then, bent evidently upon rescuing her other two children, she was

lost to our view in the smoke and swirling upwards flame. The crash
of falling timbers reached our ears and the echo of destruction smote
our hearts with terror. Fear haunted, I ran to Naame's house to warn
and inform her, but I found her house abandoned and untenanted.
Then I hastened to the servants' house to save my son, but, alas, too
late, too late! My son had perished and only the night winds heard
the agonized cry of a father's heart bereaved!"

Then Hella cried out bitterly, and said, "The jealousy of Yoram's wives has brought about this desolation and destroyed so many
innocent lives, my own, my only son's amongst them!"

And Uchon said, "Yesterday, Haggit and Naame quarrelled
bitterly. Haggit said to Naame, 'In vain are you depending on the
love of our husband, Yoram. He is no longer here, and my children
are his heirs. You are building your hopes on air. When my children
grow up, they will eject you from your possessions; to them you will
be a stranger here.'"

Yedidiah and Tirzah were astonished to hear this and clasped
their hands in despair. Then Haggit' relatives appeared and precipi-
tating themselves upon the group shouted: "Where is that wicked
Naame? The incendiary! If we could only seize her we would quench
the fire with her blood!"

And Yedidiah said, "Have patience. Time will bring forth the
truth." Then turning to Uchon and Hella said, "Carry the child Azrikam to my house, and you, Hella, stay with him and be his nurse.
Let at least one heir be left of my friend Yoram, that his name be
not extinguished."

Who can imagine, even by superhuman effort, the pitiful plight
of the innocent Naame? Through the fear of being falsely accused of
incendiarism, she fled from her luxurious home, in the dead of the
night, apparelled only in the house garb she was wearing when she
heard the conversation between the conspirator-minions of Matan's
vengeance, without a thought or purpose whither to direct her footsteps. In oppressed fear of constant pursuit, she plunged into the
darkest labyrinth of life. Unconsciously she took the road to Bethlehem, then suddenly bethought herself of her relative, Avicha, overseer

of her husband's flocks. Sure of welcome there, she made her way to his home. Upon her arrival there, Avicha, having heard her story and thinking his place not sufficiently secret, sent her to his brother Sisry, in Carmel. Sisry secreted Naame in a little cottage near the woods and there Naame, twelve days after her foot-sore pilgrimage, gave birth to twins, a boy and a girl, to whom she gave the names of Amnon and Peninah.

Sisry went to Jerusalem for two purposes, first to receive his orders concerning Yoram's estate and secondly to ascertain all that he could about the disaster which had befallen Naame, and in what light the public regarded it. Upon his arrival in Jerusalem, he opportunely heard the testimony of Hepher and Bukkiah before the judges: "We came from the boundary of Phillistia. On our way hither, on the road to Achron, we met Naame. She was beautifully attired, and seated beside her was a handsome young man. Behind them ambled a drove of laden camels, and in their midst rode Naame's two maid-servants. One camel, richly caparisoned and guarded by armed men, bore Yoram's treasures. We accosted Naame whither she was going, to which she made answer, 'I am carrying these treasures to the Commander of the Phillistines, for the ransom of my husband, Yoram. The young man beside me is the Commander's special envoy.' We said to Naame, 'May God prosper you in your mission and may you return with Yoram in safety to your home.' Not until we had reached Jerusalem did we hear of the great misfortune that had befallen Yoram's house. Now that we are here, we only desire to testify before the elders all that we have seen and known and heard."

After this testimony, the judges with one accord agreed the case was clear against Naame. And Matan as one of the judges, exclaimed, "I move that the testimony of these worthy men, Hepher and Bukkiah, be recorded in the Archives of this Court, to justify our unanimous verdict of Naame's awful guilt."

When Yedidiah heard the result of these procceedings, he said, "Now it is clear to me that the jealousy of Yoram's wives has wrought all the disaster that led to the sacrifice of human lives. Oh, that such misfortune and calamity should so overwhelm my closest and dearest friend! To think that his best beloved wife proved false, and he is himself a helpless captive! To think that Naame, the pure and gentle, should set fire to Yoram's house, consuming Haggit and her children, to forget her own approaching motherhood and flee to the arms of a strange lover in a strange land!"

Then Tirzah said, "Therefore, it is best for man to have but one wife and enjoy that peace and love that my husband does, and so we shall enjoin and advise our daughter Tamar when her time comes."

Yedidiah said, "Naame's actions prove her heart is not pure and her offspring will be no better; therefore, let us take care of Azrikam, the only heir of the house of Yoram."

At the end of the year, Tirzah bore a son and named him Teman, and the three children, Tamar, Teman and Azrikam, grew up together in Yedidiah's house.

Tamar and Teman grew like two beautiful plants, Azrikam like one with menacing thorns. He was by nature wicked, and in face and figure most ill favoured. From his earliest childhood the difference between him and the other two children was so marked that it attracted the notice of all who observed them. In study or at play, Yedidiah, because of the love for his friend Yoram, forbore the reprimand that often trembled on his lips for Azrikam, and endeavoured to shield and condone his faults.

When Sisry saw that Naame's misfortunes reached their climax upon the testimony of the suborned witnesses, he hid her and her children in a more secluded sanctuary of refuge, and his wife supplied them with food and clothing and other incidental necessities. Upon reflection, Sisry, fearing Naame's embarrassment and circumstances would not permit her to properly care for the two children, took the boy, Amnon, as soon as he was weaned, and entrusted him to the care of his brother, Avicha. Avicha gave him in charge of an old shepherd and told him that he bought the boy from a stranger who found him by the wayside.

Amnon grew up to be a good and handsome lad in the shepherd's home, and his guardian, Avicha, who knew the secret of his birth, looked upon him with a love that increased with years, and when the old shepherd died, Amnon assumed his charge. All the other shepherds regarded him as a foundling, but the sweetness of his nature, the graces of his person and such rudiments of knowledge which it was in Avicha's power to impart to him, won from them a willing affection and recognition of superiority, unquestioning and abiding.

After a lapse of several years, Naame moved from her hiding place and occupied a cottage which Sisry built for her, concealed behind a rampart of rocks and screened by trees and brushwood. Here she lived with an old woman, her daughter secure from the intrusion of strangers, while she worked in the fields of her husband's estate with the other poor of the place. She passed as a Philistine widow, who had been married to a man of Judah.

Chapter four

I t came to pass in the fourth year of the reign of Hezekiah, King of Judah, and in the seventh year of the reign of Hosea, King of Israel, that God, in his anger against the Ephraimites, who had reached the last stage of corruption, sent against them Shalmaneser, King of Assyria, with his mighty army. They overspread the land of the Ephraimites like an overflowing river. After a siege of three years the King of Assyria conquered them. All the captives were sent to Halah and Habor, cities near the river Gozan, and also to the Cities of the Medes. He removed the high places designated for the altars of worship, broke their images and banished their priests and prophets.

Judah, her sister country, seeing that Israel, because of her wickedness, was punished by the hand of God, took it as a lesson to themselves and turned their hearts to God, followed the teachings of their prophets and loved God's chosen king, Hezekiah, in whose reign they lived in peace, while Israel was in much disgrace. At this time one of the fugitives of Ephraim, coming to the southern boundary of Zion, threw his idol into the ditch with these words, "Lie there, in disgrace, thou little wooden image, a god who is of no use in the land of Judah. Ten years have I served thee. I was thy mouthpiece and thou wert my god. With a procession of priests, together we marched as far as Shechem. We robbed, we did evil to our hearts' content. We drank the wine which was brought to please thee. We ate the meat brought as an offering for thee. Even our clothes came from thee. Oh, how good were those days! But, alas for the present! Thy altars are removed, the worshipers were taken captive. Where shalt thou go? Shall I carry thee to Zion? Why, the people there worship only the living God, the God of Hosts, who dwells amongst them! Thou wilt then be but a hindrance to me. Lie there, then, thou little wooden image, naked in thy disgrace. I will take thy gold and silver ornaments; they are of no use to thee, but to me they will be a recompense for my service to thee."

So spoke the fugitive Zimri. He was one of the unprincipled, villainous priests, who intercepted the people going to Jerusalem to worship God on the Holy Mountain, and persuaded them to turn and adore their idols.

Zimri, knowing the Lord Hananeel of Samaria, crossed the river Chebar and went thither and asked Hananeel to give him the name of his son-in-law in Jerusalem. Hananeel not only gave him his name, but also a sealed letter and a seal which he was to give to Yedidiah.

Zimri came to Jerusalem through the gate Ephraim at nightfall. A beautiful sight met his gaze. It was a glorious night. The sky was clear and the stars shone in their splendour. Everything there was life. The palaces were aglow with light. On the piazzas men and women in evening attire were promenading, and laughter and music could be heard from all directions. People were going hither and thither. Carriages and chariots, with the young lords and their wives, could be seen driving in all directions. Some few pedestrians were also seen going to the home of some friend. It is no wonder that Zimri forgot for a while his purpose in Jerusalem. The sight overwhelmed him, after living for three years in the besieged city, where everything had become one vast wasteland.

"How gloomy and desolate is Samaria," he said, "and how beautiful and bright is Zion! Samaria has gone to her decline, while Zion is blooming in the splendour and glory of the king who rules there. Ephraim has fallen and the land of Judah is rising in her beauty. A new earth and a new heaven I see here—a peaceful land where the inhabitants are enjoying peace under the blue dome of heaven, for the king has established law and justice—law and justice to protect the wealth of the rich, and to guard the poor and help them in the time of distress. But what is all this to me, whose future maintenance is uncertain, since King Hezekiah has destroyed all the idols in the land?"

A new idea suggested itself to his mind. "Who knows," he said, "maybe there are still some who in secret continue their worship of idols. What is idolatry? A mere empty form and nothing more. And what is their service? The robbing of the innocent. Let me, therefore, search this large city and I will surely find wicked men; for what city is without them? There are many rich people here, so there are many who are jealous of them, and if I combine jealousy with wickedness, and wickedness with handicraft, why then I am in my sphere. What need then of an idol? My brains, my tongue and my hands will serve me. Since justice is established here and righteousness dwells in this place, justice and righteousness shall be my constant motto, but wickedness shall dwell in my heart. This same righteousness shall be a wall to hide the schemes of my mind. I will bow my head like the bulrushes and my lips shall repeatedly speak of righteousness and the fear of God, for I have seen many thrive on such a course. For who is so blind as the righteous, the God fearing and the innocent? How easily they are deceived! They are so unsuspecting of evil that they never think of looking into one's actions, if the actions are but pleasing to them. Therefore, I will disguise my wickedness with the mantle of truth, and I will conduct myself in such a manner that everyone will respect and honour me." And Zimri did so.

The next morning Zimri climbed the mountain to the Temple of God and went to Ezarihuy, the High Priest. Zimri found him in the afternoon, and addressed him thus: "Let your Holiness lend an ear to thy servant. I am a merchant from the Tribe of Ephraim.

From my earliest childhood my father reared me in the fear of the idols and in the belief of their prophets and their priests. The name of God was strange to me. Our people scoffed at the teachings and morals of the Prophets of God. My father fed me on unripe fruit, but shall my mouth therefore be always shriveled? Now I can see that the prophecy of God, through his prophets, has come true. The tribe of Ephraim has come to ruin in the day of judgement, and they were driven from their lands. Samaria has been tossed in agony for three years, like a sick man in his sufferings until death claimed him. And all the priests and prophets, who have poisoned their lives with false doctrines, are bemoaning their lot and are ashamed of their wickedness. Now, with the mercy of God, I saved myself from the hand of the oppressor, for God knew my heart, which was yearning for his Holy teachings. Hungry for words of God and thirsty for His mercy, I came here, and I pray thee, oh High Priest, anointed one of God, teach me how to approach and gain forgiveness for my past misdeeds! If with offerings, alas, I am poor, only my heart can I offer to Him. Teach me to approach Him, not with silver and gold, but with righteousness and goodness."

And the priest answered, "God forbid that the sons of Aaron should ask any reward from those who are seeking knowledge from them. All our aims and desires are to instruct those who come to us for guidance. You shall know that a contrite heart is more acceptable in the sight of God than a burnt offering. Frequent the house of God every day and then thou shall find the path leading to life. But tell me, have you any relatives or friends in Zion?"

Zimri then answered, "I have a letter to Yedidiah, Finance Minister, from his father-in-law, Hananeel, at the time he was taken captive, together with other prisoners."

"Stay here then until evening," said Ezarihuy, the High Priest. "Every evening and morning, when the priests offer their daily sacrifices, Yedidiah comes here to worship God in His holy house. He is a pious man, and I will speak well of you to him. I will also endeavor to obtain shelter for you in his house or in some other home among the nobility of Zion."

Yedidiah came as usual, and when he had finished his evening prayer, the High Priest spoke to him in flattering terms of Zimri, and Yedidiah took him home to his house. Zimri then gave Yedidiah the letter from Hananeel. The seal he kept, thinking that he might need it in the future for some scheme. Yedidiah read the letter to his wife and children, as follows:

"Hear, my daughter Tirzah, and listen well my son Yedidiah, to the words of your father, who is going into captivity. Surely you have heard the cries of Ephraim, for the lamentations of Samaria have reached the gates of Zion. Woe unto the day when Samaria was silenced, when her king and her people were taken captives. I expected the fall of Ephraim long ago, so I unchanged all my wealth into gold, silver and precious stones. These I hid in a secret place, thinking that when the turbulent days should cease I would carry my wealth to Zion, persuade even my sons to become inhabitants of Zion, and come under the banner of the King of Judah. These were my thoughts, but God willed it otherwise. My sons fell in battle during the three years of siege, and so also fell the city.

"I had to leave the graves of my sons and my treasures, and march at the head of the captives. We marched until, at twilight of the seventh day, we reached the river Chebar. After I ate my scanty bread, mingled with tears, I fell asleep on the banks of the river, and I saw in my dreams a tall youth of comely face, beautifully attired, a sword girded to his side, and wearing an open helmet. He had raven locks crowning his brow, and rosy cheeks; his forehead was as white as the driven snow; his jaw was firmly set and he had pearly teeth; he was astride a beautiful black steed. When I looked upon his handsome face, I cried bitterly and called, 'Oh, God, my God, I too had sons as handsome as he, and now none are left to close my eyes in death nor to inherit my wealth.' As the youth heard my cries, he alighted from his horse and took my right hand, saying in his gentle voice, 'Why, I am he who is in love with thy grandchild, Tamar, and I am seeking thee in the land of thy captivity so that I may release thee and take thee to Zion to thy beloved children.' And I asked him his name and that of his father, and he said, 'This I cannot tell thee now, because some deep mystery enshrouds it, but it will come to light in the near future.' He showed me the ring which I gave to Tamar, and he said, 'Tamar gave it to me as a sign of her love for me.'

"Then I awoke, and, alas, it was only a dream, but a dream which was very dear and precious to me in my loneliness. I raised my eyes towards Heaven—the stars were shining and darkness enveloped the earth; and I called unto God with these words: 'So may the words of that dream shine in the depths of my heart.'

"Then I fell asleep again and dreamed that I was sitting in your palace. I saw Tamar attired in a purple gown, bedecked with jewels, beautiful in her loveliness, standing at the right hand of this youth, and you were looking at them with joy depicted upon your countenances; and just as the youth was about to speak to me, a hand shook my frame and awoke me, and I heard the gruff voice of the captor saying, 'Wake up, wake up! Come with the other captives; the morning star is already shining in the heaven.'

"I got up and marched with my fellow prisoners, and my heart palpitated at the recurring of my dreams. I inquired of those who could interpret dreams the meaning of mine, and they told me it was no idle dream. And the hope that Tamar's lover will come to release me and inherit my treasures, keeps the spark of life aglow within me.

"Therefore, my children, I wish you to watch future events so that you may see if my dream in any way is realized, and may peace be with you all."

Yedidiah and Tirzah wept when they read this letter, and Zimri, who was present, said, "Pray do not weep, for your dear father is now much better off than he was during the time that Samaria was besieged. In Assyria, where the captives are being taken, he will find many of his countrymen who had settled there before the war, and he will feel at home among them. These dreams, which he dreamt on the banks of the river Chebar, will be a great consolation to him, because he feels the conviction that they will surely come true."

While Zimri was thus comforting them, Tirzah looked searchingly at Azrikam. Yedidiah, understanding the meaning, bade the lad leave the room, and said to his wife, "Please, dear love, do not believe in such dreams, which comfort your father in his trouble, and do not compare Azrikam with the lad of his dream. You may turn the heart of Tamar from Azrikam, because he has red hair and is short and is not handsome, while the youth of your father's dream is tall and handsome and has raven locks. You know that I have made a covenant with my friend Yoram, and how can a dream break such a pledge made while awake?"

"Who knows?" said Tirzah. "Maybe Naame bore a son who may correspond with the lad in my father's dream."

"Why, Naame ran away with her lover, and how can a son of hers wipe out such disgrace?" answered Yedidiah. "Even should Yoram return today, he would not acknowledge him as his son, because of the disgrace of his mother. But why should we talk such nonsense? How can Naame return and produce her son after what she has done? Why, the law is after her, and the sword of justice hangs over her head. No, my dear, let us not mention her name; it is a blot upon Yoram's house."

Yedidiah was known for his innocence and his good heart, and because of his love for his fellowmen, he did not endeavor to search into the heart of man. He looked upon man only according to his actions, and especially when his deeds were outwardly righteous. It is no wonder, therefore, that Zimri found grace in Yedidiah's eyes, after the good recommendation of the High Priest. And Zimri was made head butler in Yedidiah's house. Zimri thanked Yedidiah and said, "I will serve you with a true heart and be trustworthy."

But Zimri was unaccustomed to work—he always followed the dictates of his wicked heart—and when he saw what was going on in the house of Yedidiah and could look into the future, he knew that he could put his rascality to use. He kept the seal of Hananeel and he said to himself, "This seal will be of great value to me. When the time comes I will know how to use it."

When Azrikam was ten years of age and growing up together with Teman and Tamar in Yedidiah's house, he was continually quarreling with them, making their lives bitter. He was even spiteful to

---

Tirzah and Yedidiah, and Tamar and Teman despised him. Therefore Tirzah said, "Like the tree, so is the fruit; as Haggit was quarrelsome, so is her son."

Yedidiah, seeing that Azrikam was causing continual discord in the family, sent him back to his father's estates to avoid the quarrels between them, and also in the hope that Tamar might despise him less when out of sight. He bade Uchon take care of him and watch him as the apple of his eye, and told him to bring the child to the house every Sabbath and holiday. Uchon did so.

Chapter five

Azrikam grew in his father's house like a thorn, becoming uglier as he grew. Tamar, however, grew more beautiful day by day. The contrast between these two children was not only noticeable in their looks but also in their actions. While Tamar was all that was good and noble, sweet and gentle, Azrikam was cruel, quarrelsome and disagreeable; he was unkind to his servants and would not stretch out a helping hand to the poor and needy. Tamar was kind to her servants and ever ready to comfort the sick and help the poor. Azrikam continually bragged of his birth and looked down upon those who were not of noble birth and not as wealthy as he; but Tamar was meek and gentle with her mates and associated even with the poorest of them. Azrikam was like a wooden image that had to be bedecked with gold and jewels to make it look presentable; Tamar on the other hand was like a sapphire set in gold, which did not increase the value of the jewel but only enhanced its beauty. At the age of sixteen, Azrikam was still of small stature and was peculiarly built. His head was small and set deeply between his shoulders. He had red hair and his face was covered with freckles. Tamar was like a rose in her beauty, and when she was sixteen she was a woman, both in looks and actions. She was not only a joy to her parents but was loved by everyone with whom she came in contact. She and Azrikam were as different from each other as day is from night.

There would have been no thought of uniting these two had not Yedidiah wished to fulfill his promise to Yoram. He refused, therefore, to listen to all the suitors for Tamar's hand.

Tirzah kept her father's letter, and Tamar, finding it one day, read its contents. She mused over the dream of her grandfather, and the more she pondered over it, the dearer the vision of the youth became to her. He was continually in her thoughts by day, and at night she saw him in her dreams. She had studied the description of the youth in the letter so carefully that she could see him in her mind's eye. Tamar came to love this lad of her dreams, and the more she saw Azrikam the more she came to despise him, and she shuddered when he approached. Her whole mind was intent upon her dream-lad and no one else could please her.

Azrikam noticed Tamar's aversion and ascribed it to the reading of Hananeel's letter. Azrikam was in despair, and calling Zimri to his house said to him, "Look here, you have turned Tamar's heart away from me through the letter you brought from Hananeel. She despises me and thinks only of the youth that her grandfather saw in his dream. You unwittingly wronged me; therefore, you must use your wit and your wisdom to remedy it. I will reward you generously."

"I know," said Zimri, "that Tamar is dearer to you than all the treasures, and I also know that her heart is far away from you and that with no wealth can you buy it. But anything can be done with scheming; without money, however, you cannot scheme. Therefore, if you will open your purse, I am ready to be your accomplice and supply you with my advice. Wait for me three days, and in that time I will devise some plan of action."

After three days Azrikam inquired of Zimri what plan he had made, and Zimri answered: "The first thing you must do is to put your confidence in me. Make Tamar disbelieve the reality of this dream, which is the cause of her aversion to you. Then I will try to bring her affections back to you. Now, give me three hundred shekels for the one who will accomplish our purposes; I assure you I will succeed."

"You know," said Azrikam, "money is dear to me, but Tamar is dearer. Tenfold the amount you shall receive from me when you fulfill your promise."

Zimri found a man from the boundary of the Land of Judah, and bribed him with the money received from Azrikam, giving him Hananeel's seal, which he had kept from Yedidiah. Zimri taught this man what he was to say to Yedidiah. The man went to Yedidiah and repeated Zimri's words, as follows: "I have just returned from Assyria. There I saw your father-in-law, Hananeel, lying sick on his dying bed. He called me to him and said, 'Behold, you are a man from Judah. If God will bring you back to your land, give this seal to my son-in-law, Yedidiah, and tell him that my treasures are hidden, but give me your oath that you will disclose the secret to no one.' Ere he finished the sentence a convulsion seized him; he groaned and passed away. And here is the seal."

Yedidiah recognized Hananeel's seal and therefore gave credence to the old man's story. He wept over the sad end of his father-in-law, and, taking the seal to his wife, told her the sad news. "Alas to our hopes; they have failed," said Yedidiah.

Tirzah would not believe her husband. She thought he told her of her father's death only to put an end to her faith in the youth of her father's dream. But Yedidiah solemnly assured her of its truth. Thereupon she wept bitterly. Even Tamar took for granted that her grandfather was dead. She did not, however, cease to despise Azrikam. When her father chided her for her actions, she made answer, "Let Azrikam keep away and I will honour him, but if he calls here I will surely insult him; I cannot treat him otherwise. I hate him!"

Tirzah intervened between father and daughter, and said, "Leave the child alone until she is twenty. She will have plenty of time to suffer at the hands of Azrikam then."

Azrikam saw that he was in the power of Zimri, and, fearing

that he might betray his plot to Tamar, gave to Zimri one thousand silver shekels. From that day Zimri was Azrikam's accomplice.

Chapter six

It was one of the first spring days, when the birds seemed to be calling to everyone, "Come out! come out! Enjoy this glorious day! See, the flowers are peeping forth and the trees are clothed all anew to greet you!"

It was on just such a day as this that Tamar asked permission of her father to leave the tumult of the city and go into the country with the other maidens of Zion. Tamar's father, who always granted her slightest wish, sent her, with her maid Macha, to Bethlehem, to the house of Avicha, the overseer of Yoram's flocks. He made her return after three days. Yedidiah also sent his son Teman to Carmel, to be the guest of Sisry until he should be able to bring a sheaf of the first harvest and the first fruits to Jerusalem. Teman took with him three servants.

The sun was slowly sinking through the masses of purple clouds which were floating over the eastern skies, when, emerging from the forests, Tamar and her maid saw before them a lovely plain, cultivated like a garden. Rows of orange and citron trees were backed by the dark green foliage of vines. Further on the horizon to the north side of Jerusalem, the outline of the mountain on which Bethlehem was built, the cradle of the Kings of Judah appeared to the travelers. Nearing the outskirts of Bethlehem, the scenery was even more picturesque; wells and streams as clear as crystal could be seen surrounded by olive, date and fig trees, whose branches were bent under the weight of their ripening fruit. On the mountain feasting was going on, and in the valleys, covered with wild flowers and roses, the lambs were playing at the feet of the sheep. On one side herds of cattle were grazing. The land was flowing with milk and honey. Here could be seen the three large cisterns and the water tower built by King Solomon, by means of which water was brought into Jerusalem. These cisterns looked like a sheet of silver, and were surrounded by willow trees amid whose branches pigeons and turtle doves were cooing.

In these places Amnon was feeding the sheep belonging to his father, Yoram. He was looked upon as a shepherd boy and was loved by all the shepherds of the place on account of his good looks and his fine voice. He often played on the harp and sang to them, much to their delight.

The spring gathered to Bethlehem all the young nobles, their beautiful wives and sisters; and Tamar, in all her splendour, arrived at Avicha's house. She was profusely welcomed by her host.

After resting a little while, Tamar, with her maid, went to explore the fields and see the dwellings of the shepherds. When she passed them in her walk, the shepherds were astonished and said to one another, "Look! The most beautiful of all the daughters of Zion!" Amnon, who chanced to hear the remarks, said, "Oh, foolish lads, how dare you stare at this high-born lady! You would do well to look after your sheep and not aspire to one so far above you." Notwithstanding this speech, Amnon stood gazing after the fair Tamar long after the other shepherds had gone back to their work.

The sun poured out its light and warmth over the dwellings of the shepherds. The streams were murmuring, the leaves rustled in the soft breeze and the birds twittered on the branches; the sheep bleated in the fields, and the combined harmony of all these sounds, echoing from the mountains, awoke in the shepherds a mood for singing; and the fields rang with the music of the flutes and the song of the shepherds.

Tamar, upon her return from her walk, was attracted by all this music, and especially by the voice and song of Amnon, who was singing these words:

> *Rich and poor alike rejoice in nature's pleasures,*
> *Wealth can buy only the prize of earthly treasures—*
> *Jewels, splendour idleness and mirth,*
> *Vanity, false vanity of earth.*
> *Prince and peasant share the glory that the sunbeams*
> *   bring,*
> *Both enjoy the sweetness lavished by the hand of Spring;*
> *Peace and beauty, hills and fields enfold,*
> *While contentment broods over wood and wold.*
> *All the city's restless tumult must the rich man bear,*
> *But when springtime summons, leaves he all his treasures*
> *   there,*
> *Seeks the shepherd's cot and happy hours,*
> *Seeks his pleasures mid the flocks and flowers.*
> *Costly diadems of gold, rich set with jewels rare,*
> *Princely lords bestow with pride upon their maidens fair;*
> *Fragrant roses are the shepherd's gems,*
> *Garlands richer far than diadems.*

"Hear, Macha," said Tamar to her maid, who sat near the stream, "listen, if you are not deaf, and look if you are not blind!" And Macha, not understanding Tamar's meaning, answered, "Why, the spring spreads its beauty and sweetness wherever we go, but we city people, shut up in our houses, never enjoy it. Come, my lady; let us climb the mountain and watch with the rest of the lords and ladies, the dancers, the shepherds and their sweethearts with their tambourines making merry."

"Leave me alone," said Tamar, "I am rooted to the spot. All the sweetness of the visions of night which I have seen in my dreams I now see before me. Behold, I see the youth of whom my grandfather dreamed! In his looks and in his stature he is the same. Look, Macha, at the shepherd boy who has just finished singing. See his locks! They are as black as the raven, and his forehead how white! It is even whiter than snow. How rosy are his cheeks and how sweet is his voice, and he carries a bow and arrow! If he had a helmet on his head, he would look like a knight in the panoply of war."

Macha looked at Amnon and she, also, fell in love with him. She said to Tamar, "Do not let dreams influence you. You see, you became distraught over a mere coincidence. You know your grandfather is dead, and all his visions are therefore vain. The fact that this shepherd boy carries a bow and arrow I can easily explain, as all shepherds carry them, for in the spring of the year, when Jordan overflows, the wild beasts leave their caves and play havoc among the herds; therefore, the shepherds must protect themselves against them. Now, let us go from here, dear lady, and join the crowd on the heights."

Tamar paid no attention to her maid, and she went up to Amnon and said to him, "If you are as generous as you are handsome, pray give me that garland of roses in your hand."

Amnon's face turned pale when Tamar spoke to him and he said, "If you will stoop to take anything from the hand of your servant, you are welcome to this garland."

And Tamar answered, "I heard you singing these words, 'Roses from the valley for the shepherd's crown, to put on the head of his beloved.' Tell me, please, who is thy beloved? I wish to see her, so that I may repay her for the flowers which I have deprived her of."

Amnon dropped his eyes to the ground and said, "As I live, my lady, even I have not seen her, though I have met thousands of damsels."

Tamar replied, "Oh, lovely youth, you will seek your beloved among thousands and thy choice shall be more precious than ten thousands."

Macha took Tamar's hand and said, "Stop that, my lady; let us go away from here. Someone is coming and your actions will be misunderstood."

While Macha was thus speaking to Tamar, Uze, the servant of Avicha, appeared, and Tamar and her maid went away. Uze asked Amnon, "What did Yedidiah's daughter say to you?"

"Is she Yedidiah's daughter?" asked Amnon. "I did not know that. How sweet she is! I am displeased with you—you frightened her away."

"Are you not aspiring a little too high, Amnon?" said Uze. "Know she is very good and modest. She does not think it anything to stretch out her bejeweled hand to help the poor and cheer the sad with her sweet voice, whereas the other girls in her position deem it a disgrace to be seen talking with one in your station. I saw her today walking in the garden, and she looked like a rose washed in the dew of heaven."

Amnon said, "I see her as the morning star. Sweetness and kindness, beauty and goodness, simplicity and grace are embodied in her. Her beauty and goodness are above my power of description. This I will tell you, Uze, that did she dwell among the stars she would outshine them all; and were she planted among the most beautiful roses, they would seem insignificant in comparison with her beauty."

"Granted all this," replied Uze, "yet you must remember, Amnon, that the lady is the daughter of Yedidiah and that you are a shepherd boy; therefore, look after your sheep and forget her."

Tamar, after leaving Amnon, said to her maid, "I wish I might live among these shepherds all my life. The garlands of flowers with which they crown their maidens' brows are dearer to me than all the jewels with which the noblemen adorn the maids of Zion. The music of their flutes is sweeter to me than all the music in the ballrooms of Jerusalem."

Macha laughed and said, "This shepherd has so bewitched you that in consequence you are thinking that all shepherds are like him, and dream of them even in your waking moments. I warn you, my dear lady, that such impulses in a young heart are dangerous. Even were your grandfather, Hananeel, alive, who would take a shepherd and raise him to such a height to become worthy of you?"

"That will do, you foolish girl," said Tamar. "What difference does his being a shepherd make? He has a good heart; shepherds' garments do not disgrace him. How sweet are his songs, how wise his words and how handsome he is! His eyes speak of kindness and love; his lips are like roses. Would that I could bring him to my mother's house, so that she might see him! I am sure she would agree with me and would recognize the resemblance between him and the youth whom my grandfather saw; he is the image of that youth." And so talking they reached Avicha's house.

Tamar retired to her room and sat and mused over the events of the day. She thought only of the shepherd and could not sleep. "Oh, if it were only morning!" she said. "I could then go into the fields alone and speak to him." And so, without thought of sleep, Tamar spent the night waiting for morning to appear.

That same night some wild beasts, coming out from their hiding places, played havoc among the herds. In the morning, when the shepherds came to care for the sheep, many were missing, and they immediately divined the cause. They armed themselves with spears and bows and arrows, and hid in the valleys and amidst the bushes to await their prey.

Tamar, unaware of the danger, arose early and went into the fields in the hope of seeing Amnon again. On her way, she heard the shepherds excitedly calling to one another to beware of a lion which had escaped them and was going in the direction of the fields. Tamar did not realize the significance of these warnings and went calmly on her way. She gathered flowers as she walked and wove them into a garland. When she reached the stream where she had seen Amnon the previous day, she was sorely disappointed not to find him there. But behold, looking once more, and directing her gaze on the other side of the stream, she saw Amnon watering his sheep, and her heart rejoiced. They were both abashed and neither dared look at the other; therefore, they feasted their eyes on the image of each other in the stream. Both were silent, but Tamar at last broke the silence with these words: "I am here, my dear, to pay you my debt," and she showed him the garland.

"You see, fair lady," said Amnon, "the stream is between us and I cannot reach the garland."

"If your arm is short," said Tamar, "mine is not." With these words she threw the wreath across the stream.

"Beware! Beware, dear lady!" called Amnon, in a frightened voice. "There is a lion approaching you!"

Tamar turned, and a frightful sight met her gaze! Coming out from among the bushes was a lion; his aspect was fearful; his hair stood up on his shoulders like bristles; his eyes were shooting fire; his jaws were yawning like an open grave; his tongue was as red as fire, dry and bloodthirsty. And the lion, directing his gaze towards the sheep on the other side of the stream, walked slowly but steadily towards them as if ready to make a leap across the water; in that instant he noticed Tamar. Quickly Amnon aimed at the beast. His arrow pierced the heart of the lion, and, with one awful groan, the beast fell dead only ten feet from the spot where Tamar lay unconscious.

Amnon, though brave enough to fight with a lion, was not proof against the sight of Tamar lying in a swoon. He left his sheep and, wading neck deep through the stream, stood perplexed before the unconscious girl. He could not see for the tears that were streaming down his cheeks. He called her by name and shook her until she showed signs of life. The first thing that met her gaze when she opened her eyes was the dead lion, and she heard the soothing words of the lad saying, "Calm yourself, gentle lady; have no more fear; the danger is over. God gave thy servant strength to overcome the monster. He lies there bathed in his blood. Look at him and rejoice."

Tamar was not entirely recovered from her fright. Her eyes, full of tears, were raised first to heaven and then to the face of her beloved, her rescuer. She wished to thank him but words failed her. Amnon continued to pacify her with gentle speech until she was herself again; then she spoke these words: "Oh, God, worker of wonders, who can see life and death in the same breath and still live! As young and as frail as I am, I have seen both. Why should not my heart quiver within me? Here lies the lion. Oh, how fearful he is! His teeth are like swords; his eyes look as if he could devour me and crush me." She took Amnon's right hand and said, "But thine arm, dear lad, saved me from becoming a prey to that beast. Like a brother in distress you were borne to me, and like a helping angel you hastened to my rescue. Your brave deed cannot be rewarded with mere thanks."

Amnon replied, "It is God's act, not mine. He gave me the strength to overcome the monster. Rise, and let us thank God for your deliverance."

"Pray, what is your name?" asked Tamar.

"My name is Amnon," he replied.

"Permit me," said Tamar, "to call you by your name, Amnon, my savior. Pray accept this ring of mine and let it be as a token of remembrance, not as a reward, but that you shall not forget me. The reward is with my father. He is a philanthropist and will raise you to a better position. It is not for a lad like you to dwell in a hut and mingle with the ignorant, to show to the beasts of the forest your strength, to waste your sweet songs on the trees! My father is a lord and very wealthy, and has power to give you honors worthy of you."

And Amnon answered, "Do not force me, dear lady, to accept a remembrance from you. I am only a shepherd, and if I remember you, I shall forget the world." The tears rolled down his cheeks as he spoke.

Tamar said, "Thy tears, which are like pearls on your cheeks, are the signs that you will not forget me, as I did not forget you until today."

"Why, where did you see me before?" asked Amnon in surprise.

"In my dreams," she answered with a kind smile. "And I really think it is the work of God to show you to me when I am awake."

"Pardon me, my lady," Amnon replied, "I do not understand your riddle."

Tamar only laughed and said, "When you come to Jerusalem for the next holiday, you will be welcome to my father's house. He will assist you to enter the military ranks or the theological school, whichever you may choose, for he is very influential in the former, and superintendent of the latter. Then you will understand my meaning. Now I charge you, by the roes and the hinds of the field, do not fail me when in Jerusalem. Farewell for the present, and may peace be with you. Think sometimes of Tamar, who awaits you with longing, as she will often think of you."

While they were speaking, Tamar's maid came towards them, and seeing the dead lion lying so near her mistress, was momentarily overcome. She chided Tamar for having ventured out alone. Tamar then explained how Amnon had saved her life and bade Macha say nothing about her solitary ramble, but merely to repeat what a great service the shepherd boy had done for her. Macha was very happy when told that Amnon had been invited to be the guest of Yedidiah, for she too loved the lad, and rejoiced that he would be so near her.

A few days after the two young ladies left, Amnon was sitting in the field, musing over a withered rose. Uze passing him, heard him speak thus to the flower: "How charming were you, gentle rose, when the morning star shone upon you, when your cup was full with the dew from Heaven! Even the cedars were jealous of you. How sweet you were to the passerby when the morning sun was rising and the dewdrops looked like so many diamonds on your petals, and so you grew in your beauty till noon! But, alas, you drooped your proud head and withered. Even from you, poor little rose, one can take a moral lesson. The heaven is like an open book to us, and the earth and all thereupon is spread before our eyes like a scroll; God's words are engraved upon it, and it says to man, 'Read in this great book all your lifetime, and then you will be wise and will understand what to do,' for, like the rose, man is like a bud in his youth and bursts forth into full bloom when love, like dew to the flower, touches him. Then, when love is denied him, he withers and dies, like the rose when the sun shines too strongly upon it."

"What has happened to you, Amnon?" asked Uze. "You have acted so strangely for the past few days. You look ill and are so restless. You hide yourself in the woods like a lonely bird, and at times you gaze at the stream like a roe. You wander from mountain to valley, from valley to mountain, as if seeking something you could not find. If you continue to act in this manner, we shall be afraid to entrust you with the sheep, for they will wander away from you and we shall be unable to find them. You talk as though you saw visions; really, I cannot understand you."

"Listen, then," said Amnon, "and I will tell you something that will surprise you: You know Tamar, whom I did not dare look at nor even think of? I saved her the other morning from a lion. She then approached me with her love and she bade me come to be the guest of her father, who, she assures me, will raise me to some honorable station. Now, can you wonder at my restlessness? How can I, a poor shepherd boy, aspire to one so far above me?"

"I am indeed sorry for you," replied Uze. "You would do well to put her out of your mind altogether, for it seems so impossible."

Uze told Avicha all that had passed between him and Amnon, and Avicha was deeply troubled over it. He then sent Amnon to Botzra to buy sheep.

When Tamar returned home and told her father all about Amnon, Yedidiah sent for him, but Amnon was then in Botzra, and his visit had to be postponed.

Chapter seven

When Teman arrived at Carmel he was gladly received by Sisry. The day following, Teman and his servants went into the gardens. The sun was shining brightly over the heights of Carmel and everyone was joyous. The gardeners were singing drinking songs and love songs. When he came to the ripening trees, he said to his three servants, "Any branch that is tied with a blade of grass, put aside, as it is the first fruit and belongs to the priests." Then he turned to the gardeners and said to them, "Do not forget yourselves, eat all you wish, but remember the poor and let them also have as much as they want. They come here to forget their sorrows; therefore, do not turn them away, for who knows what the future may bring to us? Perhaps our children may have to seek food in strange fields and gardens. Leave on every tree one branch with fruit, as that is the revenue we pay to God for his blessings to us."

The gardeners all worked very earnestly; they were singing and laughing joyously. Girls and boys were emptying their baskets into the boxes and men carted them to the vineyards until midday. Then the tired gardeners wandered over the garden with their sweethearts and made merry.

Teman, walking in the garden alone, noticed among the fig trees a girl picking the fruits that were left on the trees. She was not taking part in the merry-making of others. A smile now and then flitted across her face at the sound of the others' laughter, and it seemed to illumine her whole countenance like a ray of sunshine, but it soon passed and sadness seemed to overspread her face. Teman stood and watched her from a distance, and was charmed with her beauty. He could not take his eyes away from such loveliness, and was rooted to the spot. A sigh broke from his heart, and he said, "A treasure like this will be the lot of one of these poor gardeners, while I, with my rank and wealth, will have to marry some lord's daughter. Give all this, my Lord, to whom you will. Give rank to the ruler, riches to the needy, a lord's daughter to one who loves pomp and show, but give me that girl, whom I would not exchange for kingdoms. Just give me a piece of land with a garden and a little hut to live in, and this lovely maiden; then I will be the happiest man on earth." Before he had an opportunity to ask this maiden her name, a servant came to tell him that all the people were seated at the table and were waiting for him to bless the bread and wines. When he came back to the place where he had seen the beautiful girl, she was gone. He came and looked the second and third day, but in vain.

On the fourth day, Teman with two of his servants went hunting on the mountains of Carmel. They espied a deer, which they followed. After a long chase, the deer succeeded in reaching the bushes and two servants chased him. Teman, taking another direction, lost his way; he called to his servants but received no answer. He walked on, not knowing whither to turn, whether to the right or to the left. As he neared the rocks he saw something white in the distance, and hastening his steps towards it, he was surprised to see the same girl he had seen in Sisry's garden a few days before. She was walking around the house, which was built among the rocks, and when she saw Teman she stepped back, frightened.

"Do not be afraid," said Teman, "after fate has been so kind as to allow me to meet you again. I would ask you to give me back that which you took away from me."

"Pray do not, my lord, pray do not accuse me like that," she said, with tears in her eyes. "God forbid that I should take anything that did not belong to me. I did come into your gardens for four days, and I gathered only those fruits which were left for the poor. On these my poor mother and I live."

"Who is your mother, and what tribe do you belong to?" asked Teman.

"My mother is a Philistine and my father I never knew, but my mother knows you, my lord."

"Where does your mother live?"

"She lives in this little hut," answered the girl, "but she is gone and I expect her back in three days. Tell me, my lord, why did you frighten me so with your question? What have I taken that belongs to you? Pray do not keep me longer in suspense!"

"Very much have you taken from me, fair girl," answered Teman. "You took from me that which no wealth can buy. Give me back the sleep which I have lost and the peace of my heart; both of these have I lost since I saw you."

The girl, not grasping his meaning, was very much confused at his words, and asked, "And what did you see in me to have thus disturbed you?"

"The world and all that is in it," answered Teman. And taking his ring from his finger, he gave it to the young girl. "Tell me, pray, what is your name?"

"They call me Rose."

"That name suits you," answered Teman. "Mark you, lovely Rose, as this sapphire is fastened in this ring, so is your image fastened in my heart. And one of two things will come to pass—either I will raise you to live with me in my palace, or I will come to live with you in your hut."

And the girl looked at him perplexed, and not understanding his meaning, said, "How good you are, my lord, and dear is your kindness to me! There is hardly place for myself and my mother, and why should you leave your beautiful home to live in this wretched little hut? Come here after three days and my mother will understand you better than I can."

Teman could not resist her loveliness, so he kissed her and said, "You are right, my dear; I will speak to your mother. Please show me the path which I have lost." She then directed him to Sisry's house, and he went away with throbbing heart, longing for the third day.

And on the second day after this interview, Sisry prepared the sheaves of corn and wheat, and filled fancy baskets with the choicest fruits from the gardens, and also pigeons and turtle doves. These were loaded unto the backs of asses, and with them, early on the morning of the third day, Teman and his servants started on their way to Jerusalem. Heading this procession was a steer, with his proud horns bedecked with gold; on his head was a crown of olives, to show that he was the king of the beasts of the field, and also to indicate that with his strength he helped to bring these sheaves of harvest as an offering to God; and that after his work is ended he bids farewell to the fields, to the heights, to the valleys, to go to Jerusalem and there end his life, so that through his death God and man rejoice, by giving his fat and blood as a sacrifice to God, and his meat as a relish for his master.

Teman, when he was some distance from Carmel, said to his servants, "Move on slowly. I am obliged to go back; I forgot something. I will meet you this evening." And turning back, he rode as swiftly as a light cloud to Rose's dwelling, and when he arrived at the hut, alas, she whom he looked for was not there! He found there only an old woman, who gave him back the sapphire which was in the ring that he had given to Rose three days ago, and she said to him, "The Philistine woman, who lived here, bade me to tell you about her daughter Rose. The sapphire is separated from the ring, and no human power can unite them again."

Teman asked in despair, "Where did these two women go? Tell me, I beg of you, and I will give you whatever you ask."

"I know no more about it than you do, only that she told me she would never come back to this place again."

Teman went away very sad, pondering over the occurrences of the last few days. He rejoined his servants, and together they made their way to Jerusalem.

And Yedidiah, according to the law, brought the first fruits and the offerings to the Holy Temple.

Chapter eight

On the fourteenth day of the month of Tishrei, the day before the Feast of Tabernacles, Tamar, stationed at the eastern window of her home, was distributing, as was the usual custom, alms to the stranger, the poor, the widow and the orphans, so that they might provide for the holiday. She then sent them to her father's granaries, where Teman, her brother, was distributing corn, wheat, wine and oil. Tamar's mother came into the room and behind her a servant, carrying on his arm five suits of clothes, both civil and military, which were in readiness for the shepherd, Amnon, Tamar's rescuer, and said to her daughter, "You told me the stature of the youth was like this servant, and these garments were made accordingly. I leave them here until Amnon shall arrive."

"Will you not be glad, mother, to meet the shepherd boy who rendered me such a great service?"

"Indeed, my daughter, it will be a great pleasure to know him."

Turning to her servant, Tirzah said to him, "Take those thirty white robes, which are in the next room, and carry them to the quarters of the theological students. Give them to the students to whom they are assigned, and invite them to have dinner with us tomorrow."

When Tirzah left the room, Tamar put the clothes aside and returned to her charitable work. While she was thus engaged, Azrikam entered and said to her, "This charitable work is not meant for such delicate hands, dear lady, nor should you even lower yourself to speak to such wretched beggars."

"Tell me, Azrikam, what right have you to degrade these poor people? Did they do any wrong? Do they steal or rob? Perhaps their poverty came through their simplicity. One who does not pity them has no heart, or else his heart is like a stone, which even their tears cannot soften."

"Beggarly bread is sweet to them," answered Azrikam. "They are lazy; therefore, they are poor. A person who does not work has no right to live. I, therefore, command my butler to give them nothing, and to tell them that if they want anything they must work for it, and the result has been very good. It has taught them to work, and they have ceased coming to my house."

"Do you know," said Tamar, "why they have stopped coming? Because they know that your house is the den of a serpent. I wish that some day these poor people might unloose their tongues and tell you what they think of you, and humble your pride a little. They would speak to you thus: 'How did you accumulate your wealth, and what are you doing at present, more than sitting at a heavily laden table and enjoying yourself? You do not even dress yourself, but have many servants to do your bidding. Do you call that work?'"

"Please, Tamar, do not be a mouthpiece for these low-bred people, to insult a lord of Judah and the lord of thy youth."

"Tell me, why did you come today?" asked Tamar. "You are invited for tomorrow. Did you come to quarrel?"

"I could find no rest at home, so came here to find comfort and see what encouragement you would give me, fair one. But, alas, my hopes are in vain. I know why you act so: you are so beautiful that you are sure I will not reproach you for your insults to me. Therefore, you care not how you treat me." And taking her hand in his, he said, "I am at war with God, because he created you so beautiful. Were you less so, I would speak to you in terms less gentle."

Tamar, in disgust, withdrew her hand, and said, "That is enough for today. I am also of the same mind, and I, too, am at war with God. Had he made me ugly, you would not have favoured me, and then I should have been happy."

"Tell me, my love, what shall I do to please you?"

"Just despise me, that is all; then I will indeed be pleased," replied Tamar.

Azrikam's face turned pale and he said, "I wish I were strong enough to break the ties of my love, so that my misery might cease."

"You only imagine that you are tied to me," said Tamar. "If you will but examine your heart you will find that any ties which may exist, imaginary or real, are burned away with the wrath which dwells therein."

"It is only your beauty which prevents me from being angry with you; I wish I could quarrel with you. I would return sevenfold the insults that you have heaped upon me. I shall yet humble you. I will marry other wives before you, who will honour and respect me, and to whom my wish will be law. From them you will learn how to honour a lord like me."

"I already know your ways," she answered with a sigh. "Now you are so kind as to teach me even the ways of the wives which you are going to take unto yourself, so that I may know how to respect a lord like you. But those times are very far away. I would ask of your lordship a great favour: Leave me, I pray; your greatness is somewhat too much for me today and I want rest."

"You never were very favourable to me and always acted in a manner to displease me. Ever since you were rescued from the lion, five months ago, you have acted very strangely. The sudden fright must have caused some disorder of the brain, for you are wild and uncontrollable, like the lion you saw."

"Leave me alone, then," answered Tamar. "Everyone shuns a wild beast, and do you likewise."

So Azrikam, in great anger left her. Then Tamar in despair, said, "Oh, God, who puts an end to all darkness, end, I beseech Thee, my sufferings and deliver me from the love of Azrikam!"

Tamar, left alone, sat in a downhearted and mournful attitude, gazing through the window looking towards the east. The sun was declining, sending its golden rays on the Tower of David. Its bright light flashed like lightning and was reflected from the several shields and armors of this tower, giving the effect of sparks flying from a large tongue of fire—a very beautiful sight. The streets of Zion were thronged with people. Country folks were coming for the holidays; they were met by their friends. Everyone left his work and was hurrying home to sanctify with his wives and children the holiday of the Feast of the Tabernacles.

Tamar, looking upon this happy scene, was very sad, for he, for whom she looked, was not among the throng. The door creaked on its hinges and she did not hear it. Macha, her maid, entered and walked to her mistress, but Tamar did not notice her until she said, "Why art thou so sad, my lady, when everyone is so joyous and happy? Thy thoughts seem very far away."

"No," answered Tamar, "my thoughts are not very far away; they are between heaven and earth, between Amnon and Azrikam. From early morn till sunset I have stationed myself at this window in the hope of seeing Amnon coming to our house as he promised me in Bethlehem, and now I see these people coming in every direction, but Amnon's steps I do not hear. The sun has set and he is not yet in our house. God knows what has befallen him. Every minute some other thought occurs to me; therefore, I am sad and my heart is palpitating."

The day passed and night came, ushering in the sanctified holiday. The men left their dwellings, to live for a week in their tabernacles. They greeted each other with good wishes. Groups of merchants meeting on the streets had smiles and kind words for one another. Strangers, gathered in the wine-houses, interchanged holiday greetings. The City of Zion was rejoicing with gladness. Tamar alone was sad, for Amnon did not come. She went to sleep, but her heart was troubled.

The next morning the sun shone brightly through the windows of Tamar's chamber, and played lightly upon the purple curtains which hung around her bed, to protect the delicate Tamar from the sun's hot rays and put her, as it were, in the cool shade. Tamar was still slumbering, and her dreams, which had disturbed her rest all night, had become, as the morning approached, more pleasant. She was dreaming of Amnon, and with his name on the lips she awoke. And Macha, quietly entering the room, drew aside the curtains and let the beautiful sunlight fall upon Tamar's countenance. She gently shook her and said, "Awake, dear lady, awake; it is late. You know, today is a holiday. Attire yourself and we will go to the Holy Mountain and see the sights and rejoice with the rest. See, they are leading the steers and sheep for the peace offering and burnt sacrifices!"

And Tamar answered, "How beautiful is the sun when mingled with the face of Amnon, which shone on me in my dreams! Oh, if I could but see him so when awake!"

Macha laughed and said, "Such sights as you have seen in your dreams you will see sevenfold more beautiful in reality; dreams are only deceiving."

Tamar then got out of bed, dressed herself in her finery and went with her maid to the Holy Mountain. A most beautiful sight met her eyes: She saw people coming from all directions, leading their steers and sheep for burnt sacrifices and peace offerings to the living God, the Lord of Hosts. She and Macha passed the high bridge leading from Mount Zion to Mount Moriah, the bridge which King Solomon built to connect his palace with the Temple. From there Tamar saw the whole multitude coming to the Temple with song and thanksgiving, and she said, "My beloved Amnon is superior to all of them. I wish I might see him among that throng. But what is the use? If he were in Zion, he would have come to our house; he would not have broken his promise." And when she reached the Temple she fell upon her knees and prayed, "Oh, God, send Thy help from on high, shield Amnon with Thy great kindness and let no evil befall him wherever he may be. Be not angry with him, oh Lord. He has not kept his promise, but I am sure something unforeseen has occurred to prevent him, for I know that he is honorable, and Thou, oh God, knowest the innermost thoughts of his pure heart. Lead him with Thy goodness and grant all his wishes."

After walking around the Mountain a little longer, Tamar and her maid returned home. Tamar, seeing that Amnon had not yet arrived, could not rest, and going to her mother said, "I will refresh myself with some sweets, and then I shall go out and see the newcomers; the young folks and I will return at noon."

"Do so, my daughter, but do not be late. By the way, Tamar, what can be the matter? That youth from Bethlehem has not yet come."

"I cannot myself imagine," answered Tamar. "He is not a man who would tell a falsehood or break his promise." And Tamar, after refreshing herself, went with her maid into the streets of Zion. She looked in all directions in the hope of seeing Amnon, and so they passed the morning until noon. And Macha urged her to go back home, saying, "See, the sun is already over the king's palace." And Tamar, sighing, said, "Let us go. I did not find what I was looking for."

Amnon called at Yedidiah's house while Tamar was out walking, and when he was ushered in Yedidiah greeted him and asked, "Who are you, my lad?"

"I am the shepherd over the flocks of Avicha, your overseer. Your lordship's daughter bade me call at your house when in Jerusalem, and I am here to fulfill her command."

Yedidiah looked at him with kindness, and said, "Is your name Amnon?"

"It is, my lord."

"Was it you who saved my daughter from the ferocious lion?"

"God strengthened the arm of your servant," answered Amnon.

"May God bless you, my son," said Yedidiah. "You shall become a man of distinction in Zion. You have rendered us a great service and I will reward you accordingly." And Yedidiah introduced him to his wife and son, and said, "This is Amnon, the shepherd who rescued Tamar."

Tirzah said, "Be thou blessed by God, most noble youth. You saved my daughter's life, when death stared her in the face. Had your hand been less strong, your eye less sure, had you delayed but a moment, Tamar's name would now be but a beautiful memory. Therefore, two-fold will we rejoice today! A great reward awaits you."

Amnon very modestly answered, "I am already rewarded, and my deed was God's."

And Tirzah said to Amnon, "Attire yourself in the garments which I have prepared for you. You shall never be a shepherd again, having come under the shelter of our roof." And she bade her servant show the lad to the rooms assigned to him, and to assist him.

Amnon came back, attired in his new costume. He was completely changed and was even more handsome than before. Teman was so charmed and took such a fancy to him that he treated him like a brother.

"Entertain Amnon," said Yedidiah to Teman. "I must go to the theological school and will return as soon as possible."

"Let us go into the drawing room, Amnon," said Teman. "Tamar will soon return and she will be surprised to see you. She will not recognize you—you have changed so in your appearance."

While they were talking, Tamar and her mother came into the room, and when Tamar saw Amnon her face turned crimson and her heart fluttered. She tried to conceal her emotions, and said, "You are a man of your word and have kept your promise. You have rendered a service to those who will never forget it." Amnon bowed low and thanked her. And Tirzah said, "For good deeds there are good rewards, and instead of a shepherd's hut, you will henceforth live in a lord's palace."

Teman, who had been intently gazing at Amnon, turned to his mother, and in an undertone said, "See, mother, the young man looks just exactly like the youth in grandfather's dream on the banks of the river Chebar! Nothing is missing."

"Nonsense, Teman," replied Tirzah.

"What did Teman say to you, mother?" asked Tamar.

"Oh, nothing," answered Tirzah. Although she herself recognized the resemblance, she would not admit it.

The drawing room, a large spacious room, was most beautifully hung in rich silk tapestries. Massive furniture was tastefully arranged around the room and beautiful statures were placed in little nooks and corners. On one side the windows overlooked the gardens, through which the sweet perfume of the flowers floated. From these Teman saw a man standing, evidently looking for someone and talking to himself. And when he went to see who it was, he saw that the man was middle-aged and his face showed that he had been drinking the red juice of the grapes, and Teman said to him, "What is your name, and where do you come from?"

"I am from Hebron, my lord."

"Perhaps," answered Teman, "you are from the children of Anak, who lived in the City of Arba (that is Hebron), for, like Anak, you drank wine."

"Wine is good for a man like me, with a bitter heart," said he.

And Tirzah came to the window and said to the man, "Why do you not come into the house if you want something?"

"Do not look upon me, dear lady, as if I were intoxicated or that I am here without a purpose. I have seen my benefactor going into this house. I, your servant, came from Hebron to Zion to worship God, and on my way hither, robbers fell upon me and took away my cattle and my sheep and all the gifts which I had loaded on my camels as a sacrifice for God. I tried to defend myself to save at least the valuables I had about me, but when I saw that I could not withstand them, I gave them all and asked them to spare my life. Tell me, dear lady, how can a man see God, empty handed? I arrived yesterday, hungry and thirsty, to the gates of Zion. The city was full of rejoicing but my heart was sad. Oh, the pangs of hunger, who can withstand them! I asked some merchants to help me but they paid no attention to me, because they judge a man according to his dress. I told some of the lords of my misfortunes, and they asked me to prove it. How could I prove it? Could I cut my heart open to them? 'May God have as much pity on you,' I said to them, and walked away, with a bitter heart. Then that handsome young man there," pointing to Amnon, "without any questions, immediately satisfied my wants and gave me money and clothing. After he did that charitable deed he disappeared, to my sorrow. When I thought of that young man's goodness, I could not sleep. Was not he God's angel, I thought to myself. I arose early in the morning and walked all over the city trying to find him, but I was unsuccessful, and I went to the Temple and behold he was there! I approached him and embraced and blessed him, but he laughed and said, 'Leave me alone. I am not the man you are looking for.' You may be sure that I did not lose sight of him. I followed him until he came to this house, and you shall decide, my dear lady, between that young man and me. I have decided not to leave until he will receive my blessing."

Turning to Amnon, Tirzah said laughingly, "Come here, kind lad, and accept the blessing, as you deserve it."

Amnon, going to the window, addressed these words to the man, "You are mistaken, my man; you must have been drinking."

"Swear to me that you are not my benefactor and then I will leave."

So Tirzah, Tamar and Teman all said, "The man is right."

Then Amnon said to the man, "Come to me tomorrow. I live in the house of Juna, from Carmel."

"Your words are sacred to me and I swear by God who dwells in Zion that the more you hide your kindness the more I will make it known," said the man. "Are you ashamed of your deeds? May God bless all the lords of Judah with such sons as you, and then the throne of King David will be established forever."

When he ceased talking, Tirzah and Teman were surprised to hear of Amnon's kindness and were very much pleased over it. And Teman embraced him and said, "I approve of your deeds and I love you for them. I will be a brother to you."

While they were talking, Azrikam came into the room and the stranger, who was about to leave, returned to the window and said, "This is the lord who refused to help me last night and he seems to be rich. He has no heart. He should not be admitted to a house like this."

Azrikam gruffly said, "Who wants you beggars to come to Jerusalem? Have we not enough of our own drunkards? Go away from here, or I shall hand you over to the officers. They will punish you and teach you how to address a lord."

The stranger replied, "People who have no heart and who know not charity, lords who think only of themselves and are not humane, they should be punished."

Amnon interposed and said, "Go away, go away; do not speak in that way to a young lord."

"You are kind; you ought to scold him," answered the man. "He does not act like a lord." And when the stranger saw that Azrikam was coming out, he went away and became lost in the crowd.

Then Teman said to Amnon, "You know, that young man is Azrikam, to whom Tamar is betrothed. I hope he will reward you for what you have done for his beloved."

Azrikam, noticing Tamar and Teman acting so kindly and friendly towards Amnon, asked of Tirzah, "Who is that boy, and where is he from?"

"Why, that is Amnon, from Bethlehem," answered Tirzah. "That is he who rescued your beloved from the lion."

"Is that Amnon, the shepherd?" asked Azrikam in surprise.

"Yes, he was a shepherd until today," replied Tirzah.

"I am glad," said Azrikam, "that he is such a strong boy, so that he can take care of my sheep. I will pay him according to his worth, because of his service to Tamar. I will make him the head-shepherd over my flocks. But I notice in him something strange; he is a shepherd, yet he is dressed like a lord. Is he already tired of his occupation because he is aware of his strength?"

And Tamar replied, "A person can change his attire for the occasion, but he cannot alter his heart and spirit."

In anger Azrikam spoke, "That is right. You did not alter your spirits since yesterday. I ask you only why a shepherd wears princely garments, and you answer me entirely to another purpose."

"Even if Amnon does not belong to the nobility, yet God blessed him with noble sentiments, which are far above family and pride. He is blessed with kindness, strength and beauty, and as you love Tamar, you should love this young man for the service he rendered her." So spoke Tirzah to Azrikam.

Azrikam, anxious to change the subject, said to Amnon, "I heard that Avicha sent you to Botzra to buy sheep. What kind did you buy? Were they fat or poor?"

"They were good," said Amnon, "but here is not the place to talk of business, and besides it is a holiday."

"God will not charge it against us as a sin," answered Azrikam, "because we bring sheep as an offering to him. Now, I see that you are a strong boy. Be a man and do not be ashamed of your occupation. Continue to work, and even if you are of low birth, be satisfied with your strength."

Tamar, who could control herself no longer, angrily addressed Azrikam with these words, "Only the heartless people like you when they meet a man will inquire into his pedigree, his wealth, his occupation and his profession, and they value him accordingly."

"By all these, I looked into your heart and I found," said Azrikam, "that it was not right. Before you began to speak I knew that you wished to quarrel with me. Just as I told you yesterday, there is something wrong with you. I cannot imagine the reason for it."

Tirzah, seeing that the young people would soon be quarreling in earnest, said to them, "You men go into the Succa; there you will find fruits and wine. Entertain yourselves until my husband shall return."

And Azrikam answered, "I will not taste a morsel of anything until one of the priests will come and assure me that the fifty burnt offerings which I brought today have all been consumed on God's altar, for how can a man satisfy his own wants before he has satisfied God's with his sacrifices?"

"Why did you not bring peace offerings instead? I think God would be better pleased if the poor and the priests were helped than that such a magnificent offering should be consumed in smoke," said Teman.

Tamar, with mischief in her eyes, very sarcastically intervened, "Who would soil his hands to give to those low, ill-bred poor, or who would talk with them? A man who does not work must not eat. All he deserves is to be punished sevenfold for his laziness, and sent to work, so that he will not come and knock at our doors."

Everyone looked at her in surprise and even Azrikam dropped his eyes, for they all knew that Tamar was charity personified.

"Do not look at me like that," she answered. "Think not for one moment that such were my sentiments. That lesson I learned but yesterday from our friend here, His Lordship Azrikam."

Just then one of Azrikam's servants hastily entered and in great excitement said to Azrikam, "I beg your pardon, your lordship, but your butler, Uchon, bade me come in haste and bid you return at once to your house. There is great disturbance there!" When Azrikam and the servant left, another servant came for Azrikam, for Uchon had become impatient of the delay. Tirzah detained him and told him that his master had already departed. She gave him a glass of wine, and asked, "What is the trouble at your master's house?"

"Here one can readily see that it is a holiday, but, alas, not in my master's house. We do not celebrate. We received only a piece of dry bread; we get nothing else. We are waiting for the day when your kind daughter shall become mistress of our house, so that she may change it for the better." Turning to her brother, Tamar said in a whisper, "That day will never come."

Tirzah insisted that the boy tell her what the disturbance was that necessitated such haste and the sending of two servants for the master, and this is what he told her:

"Your ladyship, no doubt, knows that it was the custom of Yoram's house to set a table for four hundred poor orphans, widows and strangers every holiday, but since Azrikam became master he changed that custom and bade his butler to give them, the day before the holiday, some corn from his granaries. But the butler is even worse than his master, and did not even do that. When the poor came yesterday he told them to come in the evening when the master would be home, but the master did not come. When they returned this morning and received the same answer, two of the spokesmen said in their anger, 'Because you and your master have refused aid to the poor, there will come a day that both of you will be thrown out of this house as an olive tree drops its leaves, and will be wiped out of existence as an unrighteous nation.' When they ceased talking the entire multitude surrounded the house and cursed it with the most bitter invectives. The butler, seeing that he could do nothing, sent me after the master. I think it is entirely the fault of Uchon; he even tries to starve us."

"Do not repeat this to strangers," Tirzah warned him.

"Oh, no, God forbid," answered the boy.

Just then Azrikam returned, and seeing his servant he looked at him very angrily and sent him home, and said to the others, "God has blessed me with wealth, but I am most unfortunate with my servants. They do just the opposite to my bidding, and every one of them, from the highest to the lowest, is at this moment intoxicated. I entrusted the charitable work to the hands of the butler. How could I know that he had drunk so much wine yesterday that he forgot to give the poor according to my orders? They came this morning and cursed me; therefore, from today on there shall be no more wine or oil in my house. We shall be Nazarites."

Tamar laughed and said, "They have not yet broken their first temperance. They are Nazarites still."

Before Azrikam could answer, Yedidiah, with the invited guests, Avicha, Sisry and the students from the theological school, entered. Avicha and Sisry, seeing Amnon, greeted him very kindly and Yedidiah said to Avicha, "What can I do for that young man to repay him, in a measure, for all that he has done for me and mine?"

"I have made a study of that boy, and I know," answered Avicha, "that knowledge is dearer to him than wealth. Even as a shepherd he devoted all his spare time to study. He is very bright and well advanced in poetry and song."

Then Yedidiah turned to Amnon and said, "Tell me your wish and I will grant it."

"If I have found grace in your eyes, my lord," said Amnon, "give me a seat among these students."

Yedidiah, granting his wish, said, "Henceforth you shall be an inmate of our house and eat at our table." And addressing the students said, "I recommended this noble youth to your kindly care. Be friends with him, if you regard my friendship. Let him share with you all the lessons and teach him the ways of God and man. He is already advanced in poetry and other branches of knowledge."

The students unanimously replied, "Since the boy is seeking knowledge and in search of Godly teachings, may he be blest with God's goodness and be one of us."

Yedidiah, satisfied with their sentiment, said, "The table is set. Let us, therefore, go into the Succa and enjoy the plenty of God."

Chapter nine

Everybody was delighted upon entering the garden, for not every home in Zion possessed one like it. The well kept grass was like a green velvet carpet. Large trees shaded the guests from the heat of the sun, and the perfume of the flowerbeds was like a soft accompaniment on the lyre. In the midst of this natural splendour stood the Succa. Here, as was the custom, one week was spent in prayer and thanksgiving to God for all the blessings He had showered upon His people.

Yedidiah's Succa, as can well be imagined, was most luxuriously furnished. It had but one immense room, the walls of which were hung with tapestries; branches and fruits were used as decorations about the room and the effect was very pleasing. In the centre of the Succa stood a very large table, heavily laden with the choicest viands, and wine there was in plenty.

Yedidiah placed at his right Azrikam, Teman and Amnon; to his left, Avicha, Sisry and the students. After the blessing of the bread and wine, they all joined in the feast and made merry.

Tamar, standing in her room, was gazing at Amnon through a window which looked directly into the Succa, but she did not deign to notice Azrikam. At that moment she was a picture of loveliness. Her hair was of the richest chestnut hue and a golden light played through its darkness. Her large, deep hazel eyes, shaded with long dark lashes, were gazing lovingly at Amnon. Her complexion was so clear, so pure, that one would think roses were blooming on her fair cheeks. Her nose was of that fine Grecian mould and her mouth was so exquisitely formed that love himself might delight in it. In her cheeks two dimples came and went as her thoughts were intent upon her beloved Amnon. Her beautiful gown of purple and embroidery was a fitting background for all this loveliness, so perfectly did it envelop her lovely form.

While the feast was in progress, Yedidiah addressed his guests with these words: "Behold, how good and pleasant it is to live in peace and unity, and to dwell in protected homes. So may God shield us in His tent and alleviate our fears of Sennacherib, King of Assyria."

"If we could enjoy unity within," one of the students answered, "we should be safe and should not fear the invader from without. One bad feature is that the scribe, Shebna, has divided the people with his advices and now there is no longer any unity. He said there is no depending upon the help of God and His prophets. But let us hope that the words of our prophet, Isaiah, will come true, 'We shall be delivered from the hands of the Assyrians, and because Shebna disturbed the unity, God will wipe him out of existence and destroy his peaceful home.'"

And Sisry interrupted, saying, "But why shall we anticipate trouble? God bespoke peace to his people through his prophets. Let us, therefore, sing songs of peace."

Yedidiah then said, "Let Amnon sing to us one of the songs of Zion. Avicha told me that he has a very fine voice and that his poetry is good."

Amnon very modestly answered, "I have never sung before such a distinguished audience. My songs were sung to the trees and to the shepherds. But how can I refuse you, my lordship, being your guest? Of peace, therefore I will sing." And forthwith he sang the following:

> *Spread over us your peaceful tent,*
> *Thou God of Zion, shield our shade;*
> *As in the days of Egypt's great release,*
> *Now strengthen with thy help, oh Lord!*
> *Your right hand worketh wondrous deeds,*
> *From your high throne to your Jerusalem.*
>
> *You crushed the Assyrian hosts and Baal o'er-threw,*
> *And Zion joyed in home and fertile field,*
> *The mountains high your praises sung;*
> *Peace from God's throne in heaven high,*
> *Peace from Messiah's throne on earth;*
> *Thy peace shall gird us with an armor strong.*
>
> *Spread over us your peaceful tent,*
> *And with Thy wings, Almighty, shield us all,*
> *Watch over us as with a father's care,*
> *And peace shall blossom as an olive tree;*
> *Grim strife no more shall 'round us rage,*
> *But peace, sweet peace, with two-fold joy enrich.*

Everyone was delighted with the song. Some of the students said that Amnon should be placed among the fine singers, and others said that if he were but from the tribe of Levi he could lead the choir in the Temple of God. And Yedidiah said, "He is fit to be a lord in Judah!"

And Tamar, in her room, said, "Would that he were my lord, the lord of my youth!"

Azrikam saw that Tamar had eyes only for Amnon, and his jealousy consumed him but he concealed it and said, "Such songs and delivery are very commonplace in the city. New ones are created every morning in Zion. We are so accustomed to them that we pay no attention to them. We city people are all intelligent, we are all wise; even God shows himself to us. The nobility, the priests and the prophets are all excellent orators, but that is not the case with the farmers and shepherds. In the country, where everything is so simple and they hear nothing except the noises of the herds, the people are ignorant and do not even know God. They do not know how to speak and have no sense; therefore, such a song as we have just heard must seem something marvelous, something new."

"It is right for a city man to praise the city," said Sisry, "but I live in the woods on Carmel, and I will therefore tell you the good qualities of the farmer and shepherd. You must forgive me if I offend you, Azrikam has addressed some very cutting remarks to the farmers. He maintains that they are so ignorant that they do not even know God; therefore, I will answer him:

"Honour may dwell in the palaces, the knowledge of God in the dwellings of the righteous, God's glory in His Holy Temple, but the fear of God dwells in the villages. Though they are far from the house of God, God is in their hearts and the name of God is ever on their lips. They feel God's hand upon them in all seasons of the year, when they sow and when they reap, in want and in plenty. Sometimes, when they are in need of rain, they raise their eyes towards heaven and pray that God will send rain to refresh the dry fields; and again, when the fields are covered with the crops and they can see a year of plenty, you hear the prayer of thanksgiving in every home. In the time of harvest and the gathering in of the fruits, they rejoice over the gifts of God. They have plenty for themselves and the poor.

"If you would spend the night in the village you would see how early the shepherds and the farmers are awake. When the quiet of night is still over the earth, and the hills and mountains are just beginning to grow light after the heavy mire of the night, the men go to their work, and their handsome, buxom wives spin the wool and flax for clothes for the household. And later on, when the sun rises on the mountain tops and the birds, awakened by the great light, chirp and sing from their nests, the farmer also sings his song of praise to his God and Maker, and his prayer ascends like incense to heaven. Then they return to their homes, and their wives, with beaming countenances, meet them on the threshold, and their children, already awake, greet them with joy and gladness. They eat of the plenty of God, and are thankful. Then back to work again they go, and the women busy themselves with the household duties, and the children, after their work is done, play in the fields.

"In the cities it is vastly different; there, he who calls himself the son of Zion is still asleep in his ivory bed, and at noon, when he does awake, he calls for his servants, who hasten to carry out his slightest wish. They bathe him and anoint him with perfumed oils; they adorn him like a helpless idol. When he looks at himself and at his costume, his face changes; he is dissatisfied with himself; he thinks the material in his garments should be brought from Egypt and his linen should be woven from the flax growing near the Black Sea, and he promises himself that he will wear that costume for the last time. And what, think you, does this gallant youth when he leaves the house? He walks from the inner gate to the Benjamin gate, and sometimes to the water gate. There he meets his social equals, and with them he goes to the wine house and drinks to intoxication. Then everything that is wrong is right for him, and everything that is right is wrong. Is it any wonder then that he grows to be a man devoid of principle and honour? What does he speak about in such company? About jealousy, gossip, evil of his neighbours; he ridicules the righteous, and even love is not sacred to him. Family pride and wealth are like a stone wall between him and his wooing; his heart is far from the object of his wooing.

"I have seen fathers, for the sake of family pride and wealth, sell their beautiful and delicate daughters to some haughty noble, who boasts of his ancestors and immense wealth. These poor victims tell their misfortunes to the moon and stars; they wither away like frost-bitten roses when they fall a prey to such heartless men, whom they despise. The result is that the city people have no peace during the day, and sleep is far away from them at night. Such is not the lot of country people, though they know nothing of fineries and pleasures, neither do they know what jealousy, gossip or slander means, nor do they ridicule the righteous and desecrate love. Their strong will is their pride, and their wealth consists of their good deeds. They bloom, therefore, in their youth and grow stronger in matured age. They thank God for their inheritance with which they are blessed, and are satisfied with their lot. Inquire of the great doctors of Gilead where exist all diseases and sickness. In the villages? They will answer *no*; they are in the cities, because the health of the people is wasted away by their debauchery and wickedness. The least change in the atmosphere affects them. If these nobles would but take a lesson from this comparison, they would leave the cities and dwell among the fields."

And Yedidiah said to Sisry, "Leave your preaching for a fast day and then the people will listen to you, but today is a holiday; let us drink!" And he put the wine before his guests, saying, "Pour the wine into your goblets and so may God pour his blessings upon the city and the country people alike." The wine went around very freely, and Azrikam, to forget his embarrassment and grief, drank to excess. Yedidiah said to him, "I heard that your butler locked your gates against the poor."

"I scolded him," answered Azrikam. "I will send one of your servants at once and order Uchon to open the granaries and give to the poor today."

"That is very good, my son; be charitable and follow in the path of your father Yoram," said Yedidiah. Azrikam fulfilled his promise, even against his own wishes.

The students, after spending the day in Yedidiah's house, blessed him and his household, assured Amnon of their sincere friendship and then left. Amnon also wished to go, but Yedidiah detained him, saying, "I have assigned to you a suite of rooms in the house in the garden. There you will find everything you need." Yedidiah himself showed Amnon to his apartments, in the presence of Azrikam, Avicha, Sisry and Teman, and said to him, "Here is everything for your comfort, even a harp and a lyre for you to play on, for I hear that you can perform well on these instruments." Amnon thanked his host, and said, "Surely I am not worthy of all this kindness and goodness that you are showering upon me!" And left alone, he sat deep in thought in his new home.

Azrikam invited Tamar and Teman to go to his house to spend the evening there. Tamar refused, but Azrikam insisted that Teman go; so, taking Zimri, the butler, with him, Teman went with Azrikam.

The night was already far advanced and Amnon was still sitting at the window, musing over the sudden change that had taken place—from a shepherd boy to a theological student; from a little hut to apartments in the home of Finance Minister; from the companionship of shepherds and farmers to the society of noblemen and scholars; from a seat at the table with shepherds to a place at the table of the first of Zion. But who, no matter how engrossed, could resist gazing upon such a scene of merrymaking as was being enacted that night in Zion? Amnon was not proof against it, and as the music and laughter from the city reached him, he put aside his thoughts for a while and gave himself up for the moment to the sights before him. And such a sight! The city was alive with merriment of the feasters: Some were singing on Mount Zion; others were singing in the streets, accompanying themselves on their tambourines. On the piazzas, young men and women were dancing funny dances; jugglers were performing their very best feats for those who did not take an active part in the merrymaking. The city was lighted with thousands of lamps, which outshone the stars in their brightness. Even the moon shone in full splendour upon this festal night, as though she, too, would take part in the rejoicing. The large Tower of David and surrounding towers looked as if they were set in precious stones.

Amnon was gazing intently upon the scene, when Tamar, walking in the garden with her maid, saw him. On some small pretext she dismissed Macha and approaching Amnon's window said, "Great news I have for you, dear lad; great expectations are in store for you, for a lad of your countenance, who will come to greatness in our house, my grandfather, Hananeel, has seen in his dreams. And I would that the dream may be realized; you will conquer and a great future will be yours. Now, I pray, tell me, who are your parents?"

At these words Amnon's eyes filled with tears, and he answered,

"Most gracious lady, do not, I beg of you, instill vain hopes within me because of your grandfather's dreams. What do you see in me that makes you predict greatness for me? I am very miserable; I have no name. My birth is even a mystery to Avicha, who bought me from a stranger."

"Do not be downcast," said Tamar. "People can see very much in you—beauty, strength and a kind heart. And who, of all the young girls of Zion, can look upon you and not love you?"

Amnon sighed and said, "Who is there who would accept beauty in lieu of wealth, and strength rather than family pride?"

"Who knows; perhaps there is a girl in this city to whom your love is dearer than life, and to whom your family history will be of no account, and—" But ere Tamar finished her sentence, Macha returned, and told her mistress that her mother wished her to go out and see the sights. Tamar invited Amnon to accompany her, and together they went out to join Tirzah. They went into the streets to enjoy the merrymaking. When Tamar thought about Amnon's family mystery, her hopes were strengthened, for the lad in Hananeel's dream had said that his birth was a mystery.

When Azrikam reached home with his guest, he asked Uchon, the butler, whether he had carried out his commands concerning the poor. Uchon answered that he had done so, and that he had opened the granaries generously and distributed corn, wine and oil among the poor. Azrikam was very much provoked upon hearing this, but said nothing until Teman left. Azrikam's wrath was kindled against the servant whom he met in Yedidiah's house, and who, he suspected, had been telling many things to the disadvantage of his house. He punished him unmercifully, and to Uchon he said, "From today on, you shall regard it as law that when I say, 'Open the granaries and give,' you shall do the opposite. You shall do what you know is in my heart, and not that which is on my lips."

"Why do you make me a target for the curses of the poor? When in the presence of the poor, your lordship commands me to give; I must do so, or they will think that I, not you, am the one who refuses them," said Uchon.

"Oh, you wretched, low slave! Do you fear the curses of these poor more than the anger of your master?" said Azrikam. "You have heard my command. Woe be to you if you fail to carry it out. My father humored you when you were young, but I shall let you feel my heavy hand upon you in your old age."

Uchon, fearing his master's displeasure, fulfilled his commands explicitly, and was therefore cursed by everyone.

The whole household of Yedidiah had returned; already the lights in the city were dying out. Only here and there one could be seen. One by one the palaces were clothed in darkness. Now and then one could hear a late reveler singing a wine song, and the watchmen giving their signals, "Blessed is the God of Zion, dweller in Jerusalem. Hallelujah!" to one another.

Amnon returned to his room, but he could not sleep. At one moment his heart filled with joy because of the beauty of Zion and the encouraging words of Tamar; then again he grew sad, for he thought, "Yedidiah might notice Tamar is favourably inclined towards me, and he may think that I am an obstacle in his house and send me away in disgrace. She is as far from me as the heaven is from earth." When he thought of Azrikam, a shiver passed through his frame. "Oh, you poor innocent, pure-hearted Tamar," he said to himself, "mountains surround you and I am afraid of their enormity." And when the pious men were going to early morning worship, Amnon was still tossing on his bed.

Nor did Tamar sleep that night, and as soon as daylight permitted, she went into the garden with her maid. She approached the house in which Amnon dwelt, and saw a light still burning in his room. She heard him softly accompanying himself on his lyre, and sweetly singing these words:

> *Calm, peaceful is the shepherd's hut,*
> *Why did you leave it, foolish one?*
> *You soar too high, lost shepherd lad,*
> *I pity you your flight begun.*
> *Thy love, oh, Tamar, gentle maid,*

> *Encouraged me for love to sue;*
> *Above my lot you lifted me,*
> *Who has no name to offer you.*
>
> *Turn from this ill-fated lad,*
> *Whose heart is fire, whose hot tears blind,*
> *Low born is he, a noble you,*
> *So in your rank a lover find.*
> *Why did I come to chase the wind?*
> *Leave Zion proud, the home of lords,*
> *Sweet peace in Bethlehem you'll find.*

Macha loved Amnon from the time she first saw him in Bethlehem, but, seeing that Tamar also loved him, was afraid to make it known. As she heard Amnon's song, she said to Tamar, "You see, my lady, how miserable Amnon feels in your house. He is not accustomed to living in a palace and he longs for his shepherd's hut. He just came here and is already in love with you. What do you think of that, my lady? Would you return his love for you and disgrace your parents?" Macha said this with a purpose, thinking that when Amnon was turned out of Yedidiah's house he would marry her.

"My heart tells me," said Tamar, "that Amnon came here to become great. You see, everybody who meets him loves him; that is a sign that God favours him. And who knows what time may have in store for him?"

Chapter ten

Let us leave for a while the love-making of Amnon and Tamar and turn again to the disaster which had befallen Yoram's house.

The two false witnesses, Hepher and Bukkiah, had left Zion, rich with their ill-gotten gains; but God's curse was upon them and soon they were reduced to beggary. They lost all their lands, their money and their possessions. No matter what they undertook, they were unsuccessful. So the years flowed by, and as a last resource they returned to Zion, and with their tale of misfortune, went to Matan. "We were your tools," they said, "in your revenge against Haggit. We aided you in burning the houses and we were the ones who carried Yoram's treasures and concealed them in your house. We frightened poor Naame away with our words; and to put a climax to the whole, we swore falsely against the innocent Naame, and now, because of our false accusations, she is an outcast. All this we have done for you, and now that fortune is against us, we come in our turn for aid from you; if you fail us, we will confess our wrongs, and you will have to suffer the consequences."

"Do not be so hasty, my dear friends," said Matan. "I too have fared badly since that day. I cannot assist you myself, for all the treasures I then received are gone, and there is nothing left but remorse in my heart. However, I will see that you get aid from another source. Have patience, friends, until I have spoken to one who will not dare to refuse you. Everything will be satisfactory to you then, I am sure."

The next day Matan went to Azrikam and said to him, "You sit in your palace in quiet and security, little knowing what evil awaits you. Hepher and Bukkiah came to me last night and said, 'We are guilty of perjury. We cannot bear on our conscience any longer the wrongs we committed against Naame. We are going to confess to the elders, let what may come of it.' No doubt Uchon told you that Naame, at the time of her flight, was expecting to become a mother. If a son were born to her, and she were proven guiltless, then that son would fall heir to half of Yoram's wealth, and would take Tamar from you, for she is engaged to the son of Naame, not of Haggit. If you wish to remain undisturbed in the inheritance of your father, you will have to compromise with these two men. They are very poor and think that they have nothing to lose by a confession, whereas, if you bribe them sufficiently, they will keep your secret. I have already spoken to them to that effect. I am your friend."

"You have done me a great service, Judge, and I shall never forget it. I will supply Hepher and Bukkiah with all their wants."

When Uchon, Azrikam's butler, saw that Hepher and Bukkiah were living in idleness on his son's wealth and that he and his wife and other children were sold as slaves forever to their own son, his heart melted within him and he wept bitterly and said to his wife, "A curse be upon Matan, the villain! He influenced me in a moment of rashness to make our own son master over us. I am tired of it all and it may not be long before I confess everything. I don't care what the result may be."

"God forbid," said Hella. "If you utter one word, ourselves

and our children are lost. Do you want to acknowledge that you are the father of a lord of Judah?"

"Well," said Uchon, "the worst has not yet come. This lord of ours will show us how miserable he can make us. This much I know—that if it were not for you and our children, I would not endure his mastery another day." Shortly after this conversation, Uchon went to Matan and complained to him about the cruelties he suffered at the hands of his son.

"Your son's honour shines in the dark," said Matan. "Should you bring it to the light, you would only bring shame upon him, and make known your own guilt and that of your wife. Both of you would be put to death as soon as you divulged your secret; and if your heart aches because of the small insults you receive at the hands of your son, how much more must my heart ache and how bitter must be my lot? I only enjoyed my revenge against Haggit for a moment, and thereafter lost forever my peace of mind. When I think that I influenced you to destroy the entire household of Yoram, a man who had implicit trust in me, and made Naame a fugitive—Naame, who never harmed me!—remorse consumes my very soul. I walk in darkness during the day, and the nights, how terrible they are! And who has derived the most benefit from our wrongdoings? Surely not you or I. Your son, only, enjoys the harvest of our wickedness."

Uchon, clasping his hands, said, "Woe unto me! Were it not better to be punished by Haggit than to receive ill-treatment from my own son, the serpent? And when I think of the poor, innocent Naame, my heart aches. Who knows what has become of her?"

Then Matan brokenly answered, "Let us, therefore, seal our lips; I am sick at heart." And for the first time Matan spoke truly; he was sick at heart. He looked like a shadow, and nobody knew the cause. What good was his revenge? He did not gain Haggit, nor could he enjoy his stolen treasures, for he feared to bring them to the light.

Chapter eleven

A mnon was advancing rapidly in his studies and all the other students loved and respected him. Yedidiah and Tirzah did everything in their power for his betterment. Teman regarded him as a brother, and Tamar loved him. But Zimri, though he professed affection for Amnon, secretly spied upon all his actions, for Azrikam had bribed Zimri and said to him, "This shepherd boy is like a thorn in my side. Every day Tamar loves me less, and bestows all her affection upon Amnon. What shall I do, Zimri? Pray advise me." Since then Zimri watched Amnon's and Tamar's every step, and what he saw he told to Azrikam.

Three months had already passed since Amnon had become an inmate of Yedidiah's house. As was the custom in those days, the first day of the new moon was celebrated with a feast. It was upon such an occasion that Azrikam was invited to dine with Yedidiah. As it happened, Amnon was late and Yedidiah seated him at the right of Teman. "How scholarly," said Yedidiah to Amnon, "did Isaiah, the son of Amos, speak about the future of Zion; and I noticed, Amnon, that you were very attentive to his words. No doubt you understand his meaning."

And Azrikam answered, "Pray, who does not understand these brilliant orators and their morals?"

"It is not so, Azrikam," said Yedidiah. "Everyone can listen but everyone cannot understand. Do not you think so, Amnon?"

"Yes, my lord, the words of the son of Amos carry with them more strength and truth than the discourse of all the other prophets in Zion. When Isaiah speaks, his heart burns with the flame of God and his enthusiasm reaches such a state that his very heart seems to be removed from its place. He leaves the world and all that is in it; the noise and the tumult of the earth he hears not; his soul takes wings like an eagle, and soars through space to the skies and circles round the heavens until it reaches the throne of the God of Hosts. His eyes are open and he sees the vision of the Almighty—a pure vision. His ears are attentive to God's will for the future. From there his eyes look to the ends of the world, and with his penetrating sight he searches the deeds of the people and understands their doings. And when he sees that the iniquities of Judah are spread in their land, he comes down upon the people like a falcon upon his prey. He carries with him the wrath of God. He roars, he storms and, like a giant, he raises his mighty voice. From his mouth shoots a flame of fire, to burn the workers of iniquity and to destroy the evil doers. But his wrath lasts only a second, and like a calm wind after a storm, so a quiet spirit comes over him, and his words are all of consolation and hope. At times he reveals to us the God of Hosts and His cherubim, when He shines in His glory on the throne, surrounded by seraphim with their outspread wings, ready to fly whither they may be sent. And at other times he discloses the secrets of God to the people. He tells them what God has spoken in His holiness. Then, again, his soul carries him to other neighbouring nations and he prophesies about their destinies, whether for peace or trouble. He sees all this for us and so vividly does he portray the picture that we see it as if it were before us. Such is our prophet and such is his inspired delivery which God has bestowed upon him. And with a magnet he draws his listeners to him, and with his teachings he guides them in accordance with his will."

Everyone at the table listened to Amnon's words with wonder and pleasure depicted upon their countenances, and Yedidiah said, "Your interpretation of the prophet was most scholarly. If you continue to progress as you have begun, I shall indeed be proud of you and I shall rejoice." And Teman, overflowing with pride and pleasure, said, "Thousands of people listen to the words of the prophet but only few understand him. Those who do understand should be marked from among the thousands."

At another time, Yedidiah, in the presence of his family, said to Amnon, "It was most fortunate that you were present to rescue my daughter from the teeth of the wild beast. Why shall I not reward you accordingly? Accept, therefore, from me as much money as you will need to establish a home for yourself. Azrikam is willing to give you land as your reward for your service to Tamar. To him she is dearer than all the treasures in the world. Then you can secure your future."

"I thank you, my lord. I have once said that I will accept nothing from you, but, if you will protect me as you have done so far, I will consider my service more than repaid."

Tamar was very much pleased with his answer, but Yedidiah, though he said nothing, always remembered Amnon's reply.

So the winter passed, Tamar craving for her lover and Amnon longing secretly for his beloved. So the spring came, and on a bright day Amnon went to Yedidiah's house. There he found Tamar and Teman alone, Yedidiah not having yet returned from court and Tirzah being at the home of one of her friends. After the usual greetings, Tamar asked, "Why so sad, Amnon? Is anything worrying you?"

"Yes, even I," said Teman, "am frightened at the prophecy of Isaiah concerning Zion's future. He foretells a dismal outlook, because the fortifications, he thinks, are not strong enough and the army not large enough."

"Leave all this," answered Amnon, "to the God of Hosts, Patron of the City of David. But I tell you, Teman, we have a larger army than you think."

"Yes," said Teman, "there will be a large army if God sends down his angels to fight for us."

And Amnon replied, "When God sees that there are no men to fight for us, He will send us aid from heaven, but so far we are strong enough to fight. If the Assyrians should come to our boundaries, everybody—the great and the small, the low and the high, all who were born on this holy land—would fight, because they are patriots to their fatherland. The farmer works on his land, the priests and the Levites are at their holy posts, the mechanics are busy with their handicraft, the judges are sitting on their benches dealing out justice, the city officials maintain order; all this is the order of things in the time of peace, but not so in war. When the people see that the enemy comes to rob them of their birthplace, then the farmers will leave their fields, the priests their altars, the Levites their services, the mechanics their work, even the judges their benches, and, like one, they will all volunteer for soldiers to help their land and their king. Even I, hearing the prophesies of the son of Amos concerning the war, was stirred up as with a bugle call to war. I was thrilled, and my heart seemed to be clothed with a new strength! I said, 'There is my chance! My arm is strong and my arrows shall fly. My horse shall paw the ground with impatience to be off to the battlefield. I will join the horsemen and I will do wonders with my sword and my arrows.' How beautiful are the ranks of our cavalry on their trained horses, when, in the drill in the king's valley, they rush like the locusts! If I can only be one of these knights and pour my blood for my country! For what is my lot in life, when my hopes are fled?"

"Why should you give up all hope?" asked Tamar, trying to keep back the tears. "Why should you not hope, Amnon? Hope is dearer than life."

"I think you yourself are to blame, Amnon," said Teman. "Why did you not accept my father's gift? You would then have had a future before you. But I will tell you, Amnon, that you have won Tamar's heart. You have even conquered her. She feels kindly towards you. She honors you and, I think, she even loves you." And with a smile he looked at his sister. Tamar blushed at his words, and, turning to leave the room, said to Teman, "You are trying to guess my thoughts."

When Teman was left alone with Amnon, he said, "As I live, I assure you that Tamar loves you, and I also will call you brother. Where you go, I shall go. I know that my father will give you a commission in the cavalry. I too, will enlist, so as to be at your side and enjoy your honors. I am positive that you will accomplish great things and be ranked among the great in Judah. I will disclose to you a secret, my brother: I, also, have lost my hopes. Do you think that I am happy because I am the son of Yedidiah? All my father's wealth cannot give back to me the peace of heart which is robbed from me. My hope is hidden in Carmel. There I have seen the crown of the beauties, the ideal of my life, and that vision flew from me, leaving a waste and longing in my heart. But let that be sealed in my heart; I will not carry it on my lips. This you shall know—that my love for you is a recompense for that love which escaped me. Let our hearts be united."

"How happy you make me, Teman! I have won so much in your father's house, more than wealth. Love is sweet, even love between man and man. Love is born in heaven and is like the crown of glory on God's head. He sent it down to earth and made it the heritage of the people to comfort them, as a tender mother comforts her children in their grief. The Creator, who has created a remedy for all ills, has created love to heal the sorrows of the people. A man who loves, his cup is full of sweetness, which alleviates his bitterest disappointments. What is a man without love? He is like a ship without a mast and a captain. Without friends, a man will spend his life in misery and loneliness, but a man whom God has blessed with sincere friends gets comfort in time of distress, and their sympathies are a balsam to his wounds. Therefore, I say, love is dearer than wealth."

While Amnon was talking, Yedidiah and Tirzah returned. They sent for Azrikam. At the table Teman asked his father to talk with the commander, to give Amnon a commission in the cavalry, and Yedidiah promised to do so that very day. And so it came to pass that

Yedidiah made Amnon a present of an Egyptian horse, and Amnon began his new career and was successful.

Chapter twelve

The harvest time was again approaching and Azrikam sent his butler, Uchon, to hire reapers for the fields, which lay near Jerusalem. Uchon went through the valley gate until he reached an obscure street where the poor people lived. From among these he usually hired reapers and gardeners. As he walked, his gaze chanced to rest upon a very small hut, which was sunken to its windows in the earth. Into this hut Uchon went, and there he found a woman and a girl talking together as they worked. The woman had a kind face, but sadness was written upon it. The girl was very beautiful. Uchon greeted them with these words: "God be with you, virtuous women."

"God bless you," they answered.

Uchon asked them whether they wanted work as reapers or whether they would rather be gleaners. "I see that you are poor," he said, "and to the delight of the poor, the harvests are at hand. No doubt the old corn has disappeared with the winter. In a short time they will offer the sheave of the first fruits, and, according to the Mosaic law, the poor may eat the bread, parched corn and green ears from the new crop." Uchon looked at the two women very attentively while he talked to them.

The women answered, "We stay at home and do not go into other people's fields."

"How do you maintain yourselves?" asked Uchon.

"By handiwork. We embroider girdles, collars, table spreads and other things. These we sell and with the money we earn, we manage to get along. We do not live in idleness. Idleness is the root of sin, and sin leads to hell."

"I see that you are a widow and that young girl must be your daughter. With her beauty she need not be confined in this poor hut. If some young noble could see her, he would put her in a palace."

"Yes," answered the woman, "in the palace lurk treachery and wickedness, and in the hut purity and goodness dwell."

Uchon looked again at the woman and his heart ceased, as it were, to beat. He recognized Naame, his former mistress, Yoram's beloved wife. However, he did not let her see that he had the slightest idea that she was known to him. Uchon, broken-hearted and dazed, left the hut. When he returned home, he told his wife, Hella, about his unexpected discovery, and said, "My heart aches when I think of that gentle, delicate Naame, and my pity was awakened when I saw our master Yoram's beautiful daughter. She blooms even in her poverty like a rose in the desert. Woe unto us! We have done so much wrong to Yoram's house, without bettering our own conditions."

Hella was very much astonished to hear the sad news and said to her husband, "Remember if you let fall one word of this, our son's career is lost and our lives will be cut off. Seal, therefore, your lips, and bear your lot in silence."

And Uchon replied, "I will buy their embroideries and pay them in grain and fruit from Azrikam's granaries, tenfold the value of the embroidery. I shall not be wronging my son, because everything belongs to poor Naame and her daughter, and I shall only be giving them their own."

"Do so," answered Hella, "but do it wisely and carefully. Should Azrikam find it out, we are lost."

A year had gone by since Amnon had rescued Tamar, and Yedidiah gave a feast in honour of the occasion. He sent word to Azrikam the day before, to be one of his guests.

Azrikam sent for Zimri, and when he came, Azrikam said to him, "I will not keep it from you, Zimri, for you are my friend. This feast is very distasteful to me. Amnon's praises will be sung on every side, and his very name grates upon my nerves. I know that he will gain all the honors and praises tomorrow and that will degrade me in the presence of Tamar."

"Have you seen Amnon in his uniform, Azrikam? He is indeed handsome. With his armor, sword and helmet, he looks like a knight in the splendour of war. Not only Tamar but everybody who sees him adores him."

Azrikam, angered by this praise of Amnon, said, "I will not go to that feast. I will send word that I am sick."

Zimri answered, "You know that Amnon stands like an iron wall between you and your beloved Tamar. If you cease coming near her, do you think that you would better your position by turning your back upon the enemy? No! Ask even the wild beasts and they will teach you. The lion and the leopard will tell you that you must lie in ambush for your enemy. The lion crouches when he waits for his prey; the leopard hides himself when he is athirst for blood. They do not roar and herald their coming. They allow their enemy to pass and then they stealthily fall upon him. As they do, so should every cunning man do. God has given to the beasts sharp teeth, and to men false tongues. If you study it well, you will find that the teeth of the beasts have killed thousands, but the false tongues of men have killed tens of thousands. On the lion's mouth are left the blood stains of her prey; she treacherously consumes her victim and wiping her mouth, denies her evil. She is like a leopard awaiting its prey, only she is clothed in a sheep skin. Therefore, listen to me and I will teach you wisdom. These are the teachings of a man in this city. He who wants to live shall watch them and he shall surely succeed. And these are his instructions: 'To plan evils at night and to seek God's teachings from the priests by day. To tear with your teeth and with your lips speak words of welcome and peace.' And thus shall you do to Amnon. Thy mouth and thy tongue shall offer him peace and love, and in thine heart thou shalt ambush him. If hatred burns in thee, show it not. Let thy wrath be like lead hidden in you, that it may not bring the flame to thy cheeks and the smoke from thy nostrils. If you will follow these plans you will surely destroy Amnon and you will wash your hands of all guilt."

"Witchcraft is on your lips and your words are like the words of an oracle. But, Zimri, how can you break up the friendship between Tamar and Amnon? They are like brother and sister."

"Leave it to me. I will make them the target for my sure aim, and I will strike them even in the dark. That is the way treachery succeeds. I will be to Amnon like the dew to the plant, his love and kindness in the hearts of Teman and Tamar; and my praises will bloom in the day that I plant them, but they will never bear fruit. I will secretly poison the roots of that love and wrench them from Tamar's heart like the chaff from the grain; and I will cut the threefold thread with a skillful hand and entangle them with my schemes and wisdom, until the smoke from the fire will blind their eyes, so that they will not even see the flame that burns in them. Let us do our work in the dark and that will give us light. The fishermen choose a cloudy day for casting their nets, when the waters are muddy."

Azrikam put wine before Zimri, who drank, and then said, "Wine tastes very good, but we require hands to get it, to plant, to cultivate, to gather and to press the grapes. You understand me."

"Your words are as deep as the sea, my friend; I am not wise enough to understand them. Tell me, pray, what do your words signify?"

And Zimri explained, "Treachery is very sweet in our mouth but it takes skillful hands to accomplish it, and these hands cannot succeed unless they are filled. You see, I have bared my heart to you and I have concealed nothing from you. Now, then, you open your heart and your hands when necessary."

Azrikam answered, "Your words are indeed rich, and richly will I reward you. From today on, my heart and my hand shall be open to you; only fulfill your promise." And Azrikam ordered his butler to sell the old grain, in order that he might have ready money without touching his treasury to supply Zimri's wants. And he said to himself, "We shall see who is stronger, Amnon or I."

The next day, Azrikam, attired in his best costume, went to Yedidiah's house to attend the feast. He arrived before the guests began to assemble. As Tamar entered the room, Azrikam asked her how she was feeling, and she answered, "I am well, my lord."

"It is already time that you should call me lover, not lord."

Tamar laughed and replied, "If I remember rightly, when I was still too young to understand the meaning of love, I was in the habit of calling you Azrikam. You chided me and bade me remember that you were a lord, and you wished me to address you by that title. Now that I have reached the age to understand, I have conformed to your request; you are still dissatisfied. Pray, then, why are you angry?"

While Tamar was speaking, Teman entered, and walking to the front window, raised his hand and beckoned to someone. Tamar also went to the window to see to whom Teman was beckoning, and she saw Amnon in full equipment, mounted on his richly caparisoned charger. Under this saddle was the skin of the lion which almost proved so fatal to Tamar. One would think a knight was riding by, so imposing was Amnon on his steed! A noble charger indeed! Sometimes he trotted with an even step, and then reared upright and curveted and leaped. His ears were pricked up, his nostrils sent forth vapors as from a furnace; his eyes glistened like fire; he snorted and neighed aloud. Amnon, however, was master, and sat his steed boldly.

"Where are you going, Amnon?" asked Teman.

"I am going to the King's Valley, where we drill. My horse knows his time."

"Why does not his rider know his time? You know this feast is in your honour. Shall your seat be vacant?"

The charger, impatient, reared on his haunches and snorted.

"I know my animal," answered Amnon. "Therefore, I must go and exercise him. I shall then return."

"Your charger is very proud of the lion's skin with which he is covered," said Teman.

"Some horses," said Tamar, "are just as vain as some men. They are proud of their coverings, forgetting that they did not work for them, that they were given to them."

Amnon laughed, and giving rein to his horse, was off like the wind.

And Teman said to Tamar and Azrikam, "How fine Amnon looks and how pleasant he is! His military uniform suits him so well!"

"If so beauty were given the reign of a kingdom, then surely Amnon should be a king," said Tamar, "for he is as handsome as King David, King of Israel."

"Yes," said Azrikam, "like King David when he changed his behavior."

Tamar looked at Azrikam in disgust, and Teman asked, "What is it that you do not like in Amnon's behavior?"

"I do not like his change of purpose, he is so vacillating. First he is a student among the young prophets, and now he is in the military ranks. Through these changes, he forgets his beginnings and his ends. In the beginning he fed sheep, and now he will feed the wind and all his work will be in vain. If he had accepted the reward from your father, he would have done wisely. What good to him are his beauty, his strength, his voice and his knowledge? Can all these conceal his low origin and his poverty?"

And Teman answered, "Think well, Azrikam, and you will see how wrong you are. Were Amnon a lord's son, like you, I would say that ignorance is becoming to him. What would he need of wisdom? His father's wealth and his family name would shield him, but God kept all these from him and gave him instead beauty, strength and wisdom. Will you ignore all these Godly gifts?"

"His beauty, strength and wisdom," said Azrikam, "I can bear, but his smooth tongue I cannot forgive. Of what good can all these things be to a lowborn man? Will the multitude listen to him? Who are these learned people in Zion? Even these young prophets, who are continually talking to the people about morals or the future, are all from the poorer classes. They are living in misery, even in contempt. They are prophesying for nations' future. They tell us of what is taking place in heaven and here below; they have hardly enough to subsist on. What do they want with heaven? Heaven is for God, and a wise man will seek his livelihood on earth, which God has allotted for his dwelling. He will enjoy himself, and even the altars will not be forgotten. You ask these learned men and they will tell you that God does not want any offerings and He does not care even for the wine which they pour on His altars. But I will ask them how they know all these things. Are they in such confidence with God that He tells them His secrets? I despise their poetry and their proverbs. They are tiresome."

Teman replied, "If all the people think as you do, Solomon's proverbs and the psalms of King David would sound like jests. I will tell you, Azrikam, your arguments have no foundation. If you would plant them, you know what fruit they would bear."

Tamar interrupted and said, "I know what the fruit would be—gall and wormwood." With this remark, she walked to the window to see if Amnon was returning.

Azrikam did not attempt to answer, fearing to arouse Tamar's anger, and to Teman he said "I will tell you for the last time: As it is most unbecoming for a king to act the part of a jester, so it is for a poor man to preach. He only brings ridicule upon himself. I regard these poor men as pedlars. If they offer you real silver for sale, the purchaser will say, 'It is only lead.' The young lords despise them and the old laugh at them. It were better that they cease their preachings."

"Yes," said Teman, "you never listened to them attentively; therefore, you do not understand them. You can see that there is a brighter future for the learned poor than for the ignorant rich. Their riches die with them, but not so the wisdom of the learned. The learned man dies, but his wisdom endures for centuries. Their souls rest with God, and for all ages to come homage and honour will be given their memories. They are a monument to their descendants.

Now listen, Azrikam; if you cannot take a lesson from what I have said, at least do not say any more foolish things."

Tamar, growing tired of hearing all this wicked talk caused by Azrikam's jealousy, said, "I will put a stop to this talk. It is known that since God founded the languages of the people that he separated them into different sects, with different thoughts and deeds. The wise will talk wisdom, philanthropists will speak charity, clowns will utter nonsense and Jerusalem is full of them. Therefore, let everyone take his own way and let him seek friends according to his taste, and he will reap what he sows."

Azrikam had already forgotten the good lesson which Zimri gave him and he regretted having spoken against Amnon in the presence of Tamar. So thinking he might win Tamar over, said, "I was only trying you, Tamar. I spoke against Amnon to see what you would say. You must know that I think as much of him as you do. Did I not want to give him a large farm as a reward for his services to you, so that he might have his own home? I am also anxious to see him progress. Pray, Tamar, tell me how I can atone for any wrong I may unwittingly have done?"

"It does not matter to me how you feel towards Amnon, nor what you may do. Your faults may remain with you all your life, or they may leave you—it is all the same to me."

Just then the rain began to fall, lightly at first, then gradually gaining until in a very short time it came down in torrents. Azrikam took his rebuke in silence and leaving Amnon out of the conversation, began to speak about the weather.

Tamar was still standing at the window and as she watched she saw Amnon returning as swiftly as an eagle. The rain prevented the drill, so Amnon immediately returned. A short time after, both Amnon and Zimri entered the room. Zimri saw at a glance that Azrikam and Tamar had been quarreling. Turning to Teman he asked, "Pray, what was the topic of your conversation this afternoon?"

"We were trying to find out what constituted a righteous man."

Zimri, bending his head like a bulrush, and lowering his eyes, sighed and said, "What is the son of man, O God! Our iniquities are innumerable. With every step we sin; our hearts will the evil of our eyes follow. The meeting of a young girl and a young man is a mortal sin. If a man listens to the sweet voice of a woman singing or reciting, it is wicked. And not this alone, but with the doing of our hands, with the steps of our feet, with the words of our lips and with our taste, we sin."

And Teman interrupted, saying, "Who knows? Maybe man sins with his nose too."

"Do you deem that a trifle?" asked Zimri. "It just happened to me today. I came this morning into your fruit garden, the garden house whose fruit has not been eaten because they had not passed the third year, and the sweet odor of the tender grape was wafted to my nostrils and I enjoyed it. Would you call that a trifle? It is not right for a man to carry even such a small thing as that on his conscience. If I were not so poor, I would at least bring, as a forgiving sacrifice, a pair of doves."

Teman laughed and said, "If a man should live up to your ideas, there would be no sheep left in the fold, no pigeons and doves in the coop—not even all the wild beasts in the forest would be sufficient for sacrifices to atone for the sin we are committing every minute of our lives, and it would seem that the very ground we walk on is also wicked. If a man should have to account for all our sins, we would have to perish for them. No, Zimri, people cannot live with such a standard. It is more fitted for angels. Let Amnon give his idea." And turning to Amnon he said to him, "Now, do not put a wall around God nor soar too high like the stork. Confine yourself to the earth and remember that we are mortal."

And Amnon modestly answered, "It is not for me to lay out the road for others to follow, or to pass judgement. What wisdom can I give you? At best I can but repeat the words which I have heard from older people, and these few words of Micah, the Morashite, will answer your question. He says, "He hath showed thee, O man, what is good; and what doth the Lord require of thee but to do justly and to love mercy, and to walk humbly with thy God?"

"Amnon is the only one," said Teman, "who can answer a question and answer it in a way that everyone can understand."

Tirzah, who had been entertaining a friend in the other room, came in and said to the young people, "Why do you stay here? My husband, with the other people, is waiting for you." They all joined Yedidiah and together they went to the Temple to offer the peace sacrifice in honour of the occasion. On their return they feasted and made merry. Everyone spoke a few words in praise of Amnon, and he very modestly thanked them. Even Azrikam, though it required a great effort, met his obligations. On their departure, the guests thanked Yedidiah for his hospitality, and Azrikam, even though he had put on a bold front, could not subdue his jealousy, and went home very sad. And Teman, still thinking of Zimri's words, could not refrain from a little fun, so turning to him, laughingly said, "And pray, Zimri, tell me, what did we sin with today—with our taste or with our smell?"

"You see, you have just sinned with your laughing. If you think it is becoming in young men to laugh, do not think so of me. I am burdened with too many sins to laugh. My eyes fill with tears when I think of the follies of my youth."

Yedidiah overheard these words, and sending Zimri from the room on some pretext, chided Teman and said, "Why do you laugh at such a pious, innocent man? I wish you would learn his ways. You should see how devotional he is and how, with tears in his eyes, he prays. Even the priests praise him for his piety and respect him."

Yedidiah then went back to court, and Teman said to Amnon, "In three days we shall leave our winter palace and go to our summer home on Mt. Olive. Wait for me at twilight tonight and we will go up there."

"Let us all go," said Tamar. "The rain has ceased and the sky is clearing."

When Azrikam arrived at his home, one of his servants told him in secret that Uchon, the butler, had loaded an ass with the best fruit and grain, and had driven away with them, and that he had not yet returned. As can be imagined, Azrikam was very angry and in impatience awaited Uchon's return. When Uchon entered the house, Azrikam asked him, "Where is that band of thieves to whom you carry your master's wealth?" Uchon was so taken aback at these words that he could not answer. Azrikam's anger increased, and seizing Uchon by the hair, he threw him to the floor and kicked him unmercifully. Uchon could not endure the strain any longer, and in a voice choked with anger, said, "Beware, you lowborn 'Nabal,' or you will die with me!" Uchon would have done violence to his son, but Azrikam called his other servants and said to them, "Bind that rascal and throw him into the cellar. Let him have only bread and water, and keep him there until he repents."

Hella came into the room and begged and pleaded with Azrikam that he show mercy to her husband for her sake, who was his nurse. Azrikam pushed her from him in disgust. "It is my own hand," said Uchon, "which strikes me. Do not talk to that low life. I shall have my revenge some day." The servants carried out their master's commands. Azrikam then put the servant who had told him of the theft in Uchon's place as butler. He questioned Hella where Uchon had carried the grain. She knew that Uchon had taken it to Naame and she knew that her husband had not done wrong, for he had only returned a very small part to the poor woman to whom it all belonged, so she told Azrikam that she could tell him nothing.

Chapter thirteen

I t was an ideal night for such a walk as our young people had planned. The rain of the morning had settled the dust and the grass was greener and fresher. The sky was aglow with stars and the moon shone in all its splendour. At twilight, as had been arranged, Amnon and Teman left the house for their walk to Mt. Olive. They could not have chosen a more beautiful spot, and one which harmonized so perfectly with the night, for their destination. Mt. Olive! The name brings to our mind a most beautiful picture. It is synonymous with peace and rest. There, under the shade of its olive branches, one finds at this season of the year the keenest pleasure in nature. One is glad to know that he lives under the blue of the heaven. Nature was so lavish with her gifts to this Mount. The grass was of the greenest, the trees of the largest and affording the best shade, and the sky seemed bluer here than anywhere else. Everything was in harmony.

It was to this most favoured of all nature's nooks that Tamar, Amnon and Teman directed their steps. When they reached Mt. Olive, they sat down under one of the large trees. For a moment they sat in silence, drinking in the beauty of the place. It was Tamar who broke the silence by saying, "In three days we shall be living here. How I love this place!"

"How curious," said Amnon, "are the desires of the different people! In the villages they long for the din of the large cities, as a change from their continual quiet. They think that they would reach the haven of their desires if they could but leave the country and live amidst the bustle and noise of the city. On the other hand, the city folks weary of the excitement amidst which they live and are anxious to come to some quiet spot to be away from the tumult around them. How dear is this Mount in which both the tumult and quiet are combined! To the east lies the Salt Sea Plain, for centuries a sight of utter desolation, and a death-like quiet dwells there. From the west of Mt. Olive can be seen the city of Jerusalem in all its beauty."

"Did you ever see that Salt Sea Plain?" asked Tamar.

"Yes, I saw it," said Amnon, "on my return from Botzra. Our fathers tell us that before Sodom and Gomorrah were destroyed by the hand of God, because of their iniquities, it was like the Garden of Eden, and now it is the most fearful spot on God's universe. In its depths there is brimstone, Napthis, salt, and the atmosphere is full of the odor of burning tar. It is a pathetic waste; nothing grows upon its surface, not even grass. You cannot hear the song of birds, because the winged creatures will not nestle there. Even the wild beasts shun it, because God's curse rests over it ever since Sodom and Gomorrah were wiped off its surface. Over the whole Plain the echo of that mournful dirge can be heard. Satan hovers over it on the wings of darkness. And the King of the Satyrs dwells in the ruins of Sodom and Gomorrah, overlooking the Salt Sea waste. There is not a breath of life on this Plain. To the border of that Salt Sea Plain the Jordan overflows its banks, and the fish, which are left after the ebb of the tide, die on its surface. It looks as if the Inferno had opened its monstrous jaws and swallowed every living thing on or about this place."

"Turn from that gloomy sight," interrupted Tamar, "and look to the west and behold the City of God. How pleasing is the tumult of the people gathered there! See the beautiful eastern gate and the water gate covered in the evening with the water carriers who come for a supply for the home. See yonder the rush at the gate of the horse-market, where the lords and the wealthy merchants ride in beautiful chariots and carriages. And turn your eyes to the driveway leading to the Temple; you can hear the echoes of the carriage wheels upon the road even here, and how pleasant is the sound!"

"Look over there," said Teman, "at the gate of the fish-market, the large crowd of buyers and sellers. They bring into this place the riches and wealth of the great waters. And on the other side, see, there is the market-place where the cattle are sold. You can hear the bleating of the sheep which are brought from Kahdor and the rams brought from Neves."

"Behold," said Amnon, "this great city full of perfections! Its palaces are colossal and its towers, like giants, are so high that they seem to reach to the sky. The multitude hurry through the streets, directing their steps whither their desires lead them. The will and desire are the axles upon which the deeds of man turn. In a word, the eye sees, the ear hears, but a wise heart will understand that this agitation among men and their desires and hopes are altogether vain, unless combined with the higher idea of God. Just as the Temple of God on Mt. Moriah is the highest of all the palaces, so is the will of Him who dwells there above the will of mortals. He directs the ways and the deeds of the people, and without Him all thoughts are idle."

And Tamar said to Amnon, "Pray sing us one of your songs to Zion, for from here we can see the entire city, and the song would be very appropriate."

Amnon, without hesitation, sang the following:

> *Praise God, oh Zion, with new songs!*
> *The morning beams the mountains light;*
> *Your enemies in darkness grope,*
> *Your open gates the throng invite.*
> *They let the faithful nations in,*
> *To celebrate your feast within.*

The skies are dropping heavenly dew,
And words from heaven fall on thee,
God's word unto His prophet given.
Thy great Creator nations see,
And Him the nations glorified
Who brought your children, scattered wide.

Rejoice ye, in the sun and moon,
Rejoice, ye nations saved from strife!
Let Zion's daughters know their God,
Who slew who threatened their dear life,
Who made both young and old rejoice,
And lovers add their praising voice!

"Behold!" cried Teman enthusiastically, "Behold, I have heard and seen many things, but never such a sweet song as this!"

"Like the sweetness of the voice of God," said Tamar, with a joyful heart.

Amnon continued, "Who can speak enough about the beauty of Zion, and describe her praises in song! Consider her courts where justice is established; there are erected benches for those who sit in judgement. Elders, judges, scribes, reporters, all sit in their glory, each busy with his own work. Every outrage and misdeed committed in the city is brought before the elders and judges, and is punished accordingly. Blessed be the God of Justice, who gave us a king who is good to the righteous and furious against the wicked; who seeks justice and inspires righteousness. Therefore, little wickedness is done in this city. Not without reason did Isaiah, son of Amos, call it the 'Valley of Visions,' and a searching eye can see wonderful visions which the painter cannot sketch on his canvas nor the penman describe on parchment. Who is there who understands the doings and the workings which are being done inside and outside, and in the Holy Temple, and will not praise the creator of these charitable hearts? Some are teaching wisdom to the simple, others are maintaining the needy, and still others judge them. The scholar, the farmer, the city officials assist each other and help in their endeavors. Look at the mountain on which the Temple of God stands, where the people are swarming from all directions with their peace offerings and their daily sacrifices! Notice when they open the gate of the assembly court how the people hurry to hear the words of the prophets. There again in the streets the noble, the merchant and the mechanic, everyone, with his ready step, goes to fulfill his duty with confidence. A righteous nation! All law-abiding citizens! We can see with a clear sight that God's eyes are watching over this city and He spreads peace upon it like a flowing river. And, therefore, jealous people look with a keen dislike upon it, and contemplate its destruction. Woe unto thee, Assyria! With thy sword hast thou destroyed nations which have forgotten God, annihilated Somana and put an end to all the nations which believed in idolatry, because God has made thee His tool. But here thy sword cannot prevail against the sword which is pointed against you from heaven. The living God is our stronghold. Here thy arrows will break when they touch our armors. God dwells among us. Our King and our nations are depending upon His help, and our city will be our stronghold."

Tamar was so enrapt with Amnon's words that she seemed like one in a trance. Only when he ceased talking did she realize where she was, and, with a start, she brought her thoughts back to earth. "I forget everything but your words when you speak, Amnon," she said. "Your words are so sweet that I could listen to them forever. But tell me, Amnon, are all the people in Zion so perfect that there are no wicked among them?"

And Amnon answered, "You see, gentle lady, these olive trees, which are planted on this mountain, are all in blossom, but will all the blossoms bear fruit? Most of them will fall and maybe only a tenth of them will bear fruit. And so it is with the people. Everybody seems to have truth on his lips; they all speak of good deeds, but are we sure that all will fulfill them? There may be only one among ten who is upright, yet which of the ten we do not know. Therefore, we must think that each is the one of the ten."

"If that be true," answered Tamar, "what advantage have the

righteous over the wicked, and why shall not the good be preferred rather than the bad?"

"Even if we are in the dark concerning the wicked," said Teman, "the wise will make it clear to us by degrees. As the moon from a small crescent grows until it has become a full moon, and as it pays no heed to the howls of dislike directed against it by the wild beasts and loses none of its brightness, so also do the good deeds of the righteous gradually unveil themselves and suffer nothing from the proximity of the wicked."

"Forgive me, my brother, and I will correct you," said Tamar. "The moon gives light but no warmth. I should compare the wise with the sun when it rises in its splendour, for it is the joy of all the living because of its warmth and its light. The wicked I should liken unto a snail, which, born blind, cannot distinguish light from darkness. And so the wicked, hardened by their sins, cannot discern right from wrong."

Teman laughed and said, "I know whom you have in mind in your comparison to the snail. It is the snail who, under cover of darkness, has wicked intentions against you and wishes to torment you. It is—"

"Oh, do not profane the holiness of this place by mentioning his name," cried Tamar, hastily putting her hand over Teman's mouth. "He walks in darkness and his name will remain in darkness, and as the great mountains will not tumble into the seas, so I will not stumble to fall a prey to him. Those evil times, when fathers sacrificed their sons to Moloch and their daughters to an idol adorned with gold and silver, have passed. Now I will mention that despised idol's name; it is Azrikam. He is abominable to me! I even despise the gold and silver with which he is covered, for they are the cause of his arrogance and pride. And what is this family pride of which he boasts? I am surprised that my father allows his friendship for Azrikam's father to influence him to be so indulgent when that son proves to be so unworthy. No, my brother, I will not be his, I swear by my innocence!"

"I have studied you, my sister, and I guessed who was the snail which you despised. Now tell me, who is the sun in whom you rejoice? Do not conceal it from me, I charge you by your innocence."

And Tamar answered, "To the searching eye, the sun is visible even under a cloud."

"Do not speak to me in riddles, Tamar." And turning to Amnon, he said, "You are wiser than I. You understand proverbs and poetry; therefore, dispel the cloud and stand forth as her sun."

Both Tamar and Amnon blushed at Teman's words and lowered their eyes.

"Your confusion," said Teman, "shows me that I do understand riddles. I watched both of you attentively and I know that your hopes have the same end. If love is sin for you, forget it; if not, why so confused? Now, I wish you to make clear to me your intentions."

Amnon said to Teman, "It is just a year ago today that I saved Tamar's life, and my reward—" But Amnon could not finish. He was choked with his emotions and the tears coursed down his cheeks. Tamar also turned away from her brother and wiped away her tears. And to Amnon she said, "Your kindness shall not wilt like grass in the fields, but shall bloom like a rose in my heart."

When Teman heard the word "rose," he exclaimed, "A rose!" He remembered his Rose of Carmel. "Oh," he said, "The Rose is blooming in her splendour, but my heart is wilting!"

All three were silent, engrossed each with his own thoughts, when suddenly their attention was attracted by a most pitiful sight. An ossifrage, with outspread wings and open beak, with iron-like claws protruding from behind him like spikes, was chasing a beautiful dove. Its wings were white as silver and it was so exhausted that it nearly fell a prey to its pursuer. But our young folks, seeing the peril of the dove, screamed, and the ossifrage, taking fright at the noise, turned to see whence the sound came, and in the meantime the dove, regaining a little of its strength, flew on. The ossifrage renewed the chase, and the dove, exercising all its strength, tried to reach some hiding place. Teman, seeing the dove could not last much longer, gathered some stones and in hot pursuit, followed the ossifrage, pelting at it as he ran. Thus Tamar and Amnon were left alone together. Amnon, in his pity for the dove, unknowingly took Tamar's hand, and said, "Oh, poor innocent dove, you are like Tamar!"

Tamar pressed his hand and said, "This hand, which saved me from a fierce lion, will also rescue me from the ossifrage which pursues me. I raise my hand towards the Holy Dwelling of God and swear that I was yours since that day at Bethlehem, and you will again win my heart by saving me from the hand of my tormentor. Then I will be yours forever."

"Forever I will be yours," Amnon repeated after her. "See, my beloved, I too swear by the Holy Mountain that I will either go through life with you, or die in loneliness. You alone I love. You are my first love and I shall never know another."

Tamar took Hananeel's ring from her finger and gave it to Amnon, and said, "The name of the living Tamar and of the dead Hananeel are engraved on this ring. Let this ring be an omen to us that we will either live or die together."

Just as Amnon was about to speak, Teman, very much exhausted, returned, carrying the dove in his hand. When he approached them he said, "I have seen that God is favourable to the oppressed and punishes the oppressor. The poor dove could never have saved itself, and even my strong arm could not have helped it, when just as the ossifrage was about to destroy it, and eagle swooped down upon the pursuer, and, in the twinkling of an eye, the ossifrage was caught in the claws of the eagle; and the dove, all its strength gone, fell to the ground, and I picked it up."

"So shall be the end of all the oppressors," said Tamar, looking lovingly at Amnon.

The fate of the ossifrage was considered a good omen by all of them. And Teman, with satisfaction depicted upon his countenance, said to Amnon, "That is a sign that God will not give the life of your dove to her destroyer."

"What makes you so searching after secrets today, Teman?" asked Tamar. "However, I hope your words will come true. My heart is united with Amnon's. But how can we hope when Azrikam is chasing me like an ossifrage?"

"Therefore," said Teman, "let Amnon be the eagle and shield you with his wings, and release you from Azrikam's hand and destroy him."

Tamar laughed and said, "Give me that dove, since you compare me with it."

Teman gave it to her and said, "Raise it and let it be your good omen."

"I will watch it as the apple of my eye," said Tamar.

Teman and Tamar brought Amnon to their summer home and showed him his rooms. There Teman noticed Hananeel's ring on Amnon's finger, but he said nothing.

Zimri came for them, and said, "Why do you stay here so late? Your parents are impatiently waiting for you."

Zimri noticed that Amnon had Hananeel's ring, and, like Teman, he ignored it and spoke of other things on their way home. Teman apologized to Zimri for his jests at the feast. "As I live," said Zimri, "I had forgotten your insults. You know, it is a sin to carry hatred in one's heart."

Chapter fourteen

The next morning Zimri met Azrikam on the street. They passed the sheep market and the fish gate, and came to the old gate situated south of the eastern gate. Large crowds were out this morning and Zimri said to Azrikam, "Look at these people. They are buyers and sellers, sharpers and simpletons. How foolish people are! They buy articles, they buy victuals and they buy cattle, but they do not know that they can find everything which they desire in man. Purify a man's heart with the test of silver and you have obtained a tool for thy work, whether for good or for destruction. You can even recreate him, making him a horned-ox or a wild bear as it pleases you."

"I see," answered Azrikam, "that you are full of news. Come to my house and tell me all about it."

"Home is not the place to talk," said Zimri. "They say walls have ears. Neither can we talk on the street, where at every step seven eyes are directed upon you, and where the ears of seven are attentive to catch every word ere it is spoken."

"I have a place," said Azrikam. "Let us go to Carmi's wine-house. He is wise and cunning, and can keep a secret."

"I know him, but with all that," said Zimri, "I will not let him know my secrets. Let us go to the valley at the outskirts of the city; it is just the place for secrecy. You know that King Hezekiah routed all the witches from there, and since then it has been deserted. Therefore, I say, let us go thither to discuss our plans."

"Let it be as you say, but if you should need me at night, you can go to Carmi's and he will send for me. He is my confidant. However, that which you shall tell me today, I will not tell even to him; it shall be known only between us."

To this lonely place they went and seated themselves in the seclusion of many bushes.

"Yesterday," said Zimri, "Tamar, Amnon and Teman were on the Mount of Olives, and they lingered there until late in the evening. I was sent to call them, and, to my great surprise, I saw Hananeel's ring on the finger of Amnon."

Azrikam started back in surprise and exclaimed, "Your words astonish me! Hananeel's ring on the hand of Amnon, the shepherd! Woe is to me! Hananeel's dream is fulfilling itself. What did you do to me, Zimri? I asked you to make Tamar detest him, but you have chosen the wrong course. You continually praised him in her presence, and did your work so slowly that you allowed Amnon to be rooted in Tamar's heart from the first. Now he has developed into a large tree. Can you bend his head now, think you, like a bulrush?"

"You make me laugh," said Zimri. "How could I make Tamar detest the shepherd? Could I blind her? Could I tell her that Amnon is not handsome? Everyone who sees him must acknowledge that he is without fault. Therefore, I must keep up my tactics. I tell you, a man who has not a righteous mask on his face is like a fish without fins and scales. People call him unclean and shun him; therefore, we must praise that which we despise."

"But why did you not tell Yedidiah about the ring?" asked Azrikam.

"Shall I be both tool and adviser?"

"Now," said Azrikam, "you must advise me and find some scheme. That low-born shepherd is like a bone in my throat, which I can neither swallow nor remove. The stork knows when to fly north and south, so surely a wise man, such as you are, should be able to devise some plan to help me. If you wish to manage and not be the tool yourself, have someone else tell Yedidiah."

"That is what I told you," said Zimri. "Test a man's heart with silver and you have a tool with which to work. On one hand, with a large reward, I will bribe Peroh, Amnon's servant, to spy on all of his master's actions; on the other hand I will buy Macha's services and make her a tool to do my bidding. Now, give me some money and let me scheme for you."

"I told you before," answered Azrikam, "that money is nothing to me, if you can only buy back Tamar for me. And to you, Zimri so far as you are concerned, if you ask half of my wealth, I will not refuse you."

"Now, be quiet and have no fear," replied Zimri. "I will find a time for everything. In a few days my scheme will be developed, and then we can both have our revenge on Amnon."

They then returned to the city, and Azrikam gave Zimri sufficient money with which to bribe Peroh and Macha.

Two days later, Yedidiah and his household moved to their summer palace. Amnon went with them and gave up his rooms in Jerusalem to Sisry, who had come from Carmel to stay in the city for a few weeks to arrange matters of importance.

On the third day after Yedidiah's stay in his summer home, Judge Matan's servant came rushing in, and, in great excitement, asked Yedidiah to come to his master at once.

"What is the matter with your master, that you come to me at night in such haste?" asked Yedidiah.

"He was taken deathly ill, very suddenly," answered the servant.

Yedidiah, upon hearing this, immediately mounted his horse and rode quickly to Matan's house. When he entered the sick room, he seated himself at the bedside and asked, "What is the matter with you, Matan?"

Matan looked up at him but could not speak, and his wife said, "Some peculiar illusion has taken possession of him, and he is insane. He is frightened at every little thing."

"Some time ago I noticed that your husband looked very melancholy," said Yedidiah. "I asked him what was the matter and he answered that he did not feel very well but that he would soon be all right again."

"So he did answer everybody," said Matan's wife, "but he kept getting worse every day. He would go about downcast the whole day, and at night such fearful visions possessed him—I cannot begin to describe them. Especially at midnight, he would shiver and jump from the bed, clasp his hands and stamp his feet, shriek and cry out, and say such fearful things, that when I think of them my blood curdles. And so, for a whole month, I have lived in misery and pain. But tonight I was so frightened by his deliriums, when the evil spirit had so terribly possessed him, that I sent my servant for you."

As she spoke she glanced at her husband, and at the sight of his frightened looks, she moved from her place in fear. Matan shrieked in terror, "Woe is me! Haggit and her children! Woe is me! The lioness and her cubs! Woe is me! Who will extinguish the flame in my heart? Go away. Go away, you wicked woman! Do not consume my life with your wrath! Why did not Naame's house burn? Oh, you wicked woman! My sins destroyed you! Woe is to me! My trespasses are too many for me to endure. Woe is to me! A perpetual fire!"

This delirium exhausted him and he could not speak. His fever increased and his burning lips closed. He took a key from under his pillow and gave it to Yedidiah.

Matan's wife then said, "That is the key to a cave to which no one has access but Matan himself. Oh, my poor husband, my poor husband! He is going to leave me! He is going to die!" And with these words, the woman wept bitterly.

Yedidiah comforted her and said, "Is there no doctor in Gilead? Have patience, there is hope. God will send His help from on high. Take no notice of his words. He speaks from delirium. I will go home now and shall be back in the morning."

Yedidiah left Matan's house, preoccupied with his thoughts concerning Matan's ravings. When he rode home and was but a few blocks away he noticed flames in the skies and smoke rising in large columns. Yedidiah turned back in the direction of the fire, and, as he neared the place, he heard a voice calling, "Help, help! Judge Matan's house is on fire!" When Yedidiah came near the house he saw that the fire was beyond control. The odor of sulphur was very strong, and Yedidiah concluded that someone had set fire to the house. He asked the people gathered there whether they had saved the inmates, and they said, "When we came here, the fire had surrounded the house on all sides, and nobody dared risk his life to save them."

Matan's house and all its inmates were destroyed. At daybreak everything was charred.

Yedidiah took with him city officials and they opened the cave door with the key Matan had given to him. You can imagine how greatly surprised Yedidiah was to find all the valuable vessels, precious gems and all the treasures of his friend Yoram. And Yedidiah said, "Now the affair is clear, and Matan spoke the truth in his delirium." And he bade the officers take the treasures to the elders, to be left there until an investigation could be made concerning the calamity which had taken place in Matan's house. Then Yedidiah hurried home.

Tirzah was awake the entire night, not knowing why her husband was so urgently called to Matan's house at night. Her fright increased when she learned that there was a fire in the city. She arose at daybreak and walked among the olive trees, awaiting her husband's return. Being impatient at Yedidiah's delay, she sent one of her servants to the city, to bring her tidings of her husband and of the fire. In the meantime, a man came up the mountain and Tirzah asked him what had happened in the city, and he answered, "A fire has destroyed Matan's house before any of them could escape."

Tirzah clasped her hands in terror and almost fainted at these words, but she recovered instantly upon seeing her husband approaching, and ran to meet him, and embracing him, said, "You frightened me so! If you had not gone to Matan's house I would not have had a sleepless night."

"And if I had not gone," said Yedidiah, "I should not have seen and heard some most outrageous things. I am only at peace when I am with you, my love."

Tirzah laughed and said, "How nicely you say that, my lord, and I, like a woman, believe everything you say. But tell me, dear, is it true that the fire destroyed Matan's house?"

"Yes, it is true. The house and its inmates were burned before assistance arrived. Matan died the death of the wicked." And Yedidiah related all the occurrences of the night from the beginning to the end. He said, "Alas, there is no honesty, and righteousness is cut off from the earth. Matan's friendship to Yoram was false and wicked. Poor Yoram regarded him as his best friend."

And Tirzah sadly replied, "Woe is to my friend Naame! Though innocent she had to flee. She was not false to her husband as we had thought."

"I think so now myself," said Yedidiah, "but Hepher and Bukkiah, who were always found to be honest men, testified against her. My mind is confused. I will go to the Temple and give thanks to God that peace and quiet are with us. When I return I will talk the matter over with you."

Yedidiah arrived at the House of the Lord when the priests were offering the morning sacrifice. There he found Sisry. When Yedidiah finished his worship, he invited Sisry to his home. On the way thither, Yedidiah told him of the sad disaster which had befallen Matan's house.

The recital of these events brought back to Sisry's mind poor Naame's sad flight to his home and the facts of the affair as she had told them to him. Sisry had always felt that Matan alone was the guilty party. At that time, however, the testimony of the two false witnesses was too strong against Naame, who had no one to speak in her behalf. But now Sisry hoped for a brighter future for her. He thought that, with Yedidiah's testimony and Naame's character, everything would be cleared up and that she would again be thought of as the good, upright woman that she was. There was only one cloud on this bright and hopeful picture: Sisry feared that the judge would not accept the words of the dying man as evidence, because it was in delirium that he spoke. Therefore, he thought it best to wait yet a while before he told Yedidiah what he knew about the affair. So Yedidiah and his guest arrived at the summer house. Seating themselves at the table, they continued their conversation, in which Tirzah joined, saying, "There are no more honest people. Who can distinguish, in these days, an honest man from a dishonest one?"

And Teman, who was present, said, "Is it the same Matan who always prayed so much, with his hands raised to heaven, and who wept so much? Is it he who brought so many sacrifices to God and who was regarded by everyone as a most pious man?"

Yedidiah chided him and said, "I have told you, my son, several times, that when older people are talking, you should hold your peace. You are not old enough to give us your wisdom." And turning to Tirzah, he answered, "Let us not accuse the whole world for the wrong of one man. Let us believe that there are honest people, and, if some do wrong, their sins will find them out."

"Honesty!" exclaimed Sisry, with a sigh. "That is the word which is on everybody's lips, but you can scarcely find one in a thousand among the city people who has it in his heart. Honesty! Scores of thousands mention it continually; thousands of people wear it for an ornament, as a seal ring on the finger, so that everyone can see it. There are scores that wear it as a girdle around their waists. Many feign piety among the pious, and, in the assembly of the righteous, pretend righteousness. The people use it for two purposes: some for honour they think it may bring them, others for the money they can obtain through it. Both classes use it as a garment with which to conceal their wickedness when they are seen, but they remove it when in their own homes. If you will bear with me a little longer, Yedidiah, I will tell you. I never regarded Matan as I did you; therefore, I am not surprised at the crimes he has committed. He always sent the widows away empty handed. In vain did they plead with him. Orphans prayed to him for justice until their very throats were dry. He always answered their petitions in such a sweet and gentle way, saying, 'Why do you come to me? I can do nothing for you. I am only a tool in the hands of the law. It is God who is punishing you; it is He who is lashing you.' Even when Matan quarreled with his equals he would say that it was God's quarrel and not one of his own making. When he had to use his tongue as a sword, it was with God's name on his lips, saying that it was God's revengeful sword. All the goodness which he did never amounted to a straw. When he returned to the people what his father robbed them of, it was done only to entrap the innocent victims."

"That's true," said Yedidiah, "but tell me, how can we test the ways of man? Can we look into a man's heart as into a window? Now, I looked upon Matan as a man, and his actions seemed right to me. If I should change now and regard people as you picture them, I should think that these people whom I see in the morning, like angels, will look to me like satans and messengers of evil when evening has set in. Then I will reduce the number of my friends and increase my enemies day by day, and in this great City of Zion I will be left alone, like a man who is lost in a desert."

"Forgive me, my friend and my lord," answered Sisry. "Allow me, and I will teach you to distinguish a pure hearted man from a wicked one. We are not yet left without good and upright people. Look at our king in his glory—beauty and greatness, goodness and sweetness shine on his countenance. He is like a well of life, and is kindness to the upright and a source of fear to the wicked. Look at the son of Amos and the others of God's prophets! Their righteousness shines from their faces. The lovers of God look like the sun; they shine with a great light and spread their wrath upon the world, and their words are penetrating. But not so the unrighteous; they wear a cloak to conceal their faults. Even if their words burn like red-hot coals, they give no light and no warmth; their purpose is to burn and destroy everything around them."

"Your lesson is very good," said Yedidiah, "but how can that help us? We can see today that the calamity which has befallen Yoram's house was brought about by the wickedness of the unrighteous

Matan. But who were those who revenged themselves on Matan for his rascality? And who were those who burned Yoram's house? Naame's guilt was established before the elders, through Hepher and Bukkiah, but Matan, with his dying words, testified that Naame was innocent. Whom shall we believe now? You can see that these testimonies contradict each other. Who knows what has become of poor Naame and her child?"

"Our Lord is a righteous God," answered Sisry, "and if He has begun to disclose some of the things that were in darkness, we may be sure that He will make everything clear in the future. We will find the guilty one who put Naame in such disgrace. Many such acts are committed in large cities. I praise God, therefore, that my abode is near Carmel, in the woods. I dislike the noisy city, in which wickedness is so evident. And you, my lord and friend, take more notice hereafter of what is taking place around you. Do not trust everybody. Your trust in God is right but your belief in man may bring trouble upon you. May God shield you from them and bless you with peace."

On the same evening that Matan's house was destroyed, Azrikam, Hepher, and Bukkiah were assembled in Carmi's wine house. Hepher and Bukkiah said to Azrikam, "In a short time, a fire will burn Matan's tongue and he will never open his mouth to harm you. His wife and children will also be destroyed, so that no one may be left to testify against you. Now hasten and take Uchon out from his imprisonment. Speak kindly to him and reinstate him as your butler, for, if you keep him confined in the cellar, it will give cause for suspicion, and your end will be bitter."

Azrikam hurried home as he had been advised, and released Uchon. He appeased him with a tract of land and a garden for himself and children, and promised to do more for him, and he made him his butler again.

So the elders began a new investigation. They sent for Hepher and Bukkiah, also for Uchon and Hella, to testify anew regarding the calamity which had happened so many years ago in Yoram's house. Their evidence remained the same as heretofore, for they were afraid of their lives. All the judges agreed that Naame had conspired with

Matan to revenge themselves on Haggit, their mutual enemy. And all the treasures found in Matan's house were ordered returned to Azrikam. Matan was a curse in everybody's mouth, and poor Naame had to bear all the insults and disgrace heaped upon her, in silence. No one knew her, because everyone thought that she was a Philistine woman.

Chapter fifteen

Before Sisry left for Carmel, he said to Amnon, "I am very glad to see you prosper in Yedidiah's house, where you have gained so many honors."

"What good are all my honors to me," answered Amnon, "when I am a man without a name?"

"Make for yourself a name with your wisdom and knowledge," said Sisry. "That is the only honour a man can gain for himself. Be prepared to meet my brother Avicha, in three days from now, and he will disclose to you great news, which you little dreamed of." With these words, Sisry bade him farewell and departed for Carmel.

Amnon was left alone in his new abode, with only his servant, Peroh, to wait upon him. He thought he was well secured in his home, not suspecting that his servant, bribed by Zimri, was watching every movement, and was even watching an opportunity to steal Hananeel's ring from him. In this he was unsuccessful, inasmuch as Amnon never took the ring off his finger.

Macha, Tamar's maid, had not yet received instructions from Zimri concerning the plot.

One night, while Amnon was peacefully sleeping in his bed, he was awakened by a knock at the door. He awoke with a start and wondered who it could be that disturbed him so late at night. He recognized Avicha's voice, saying, "Open the door, Amnon." When Amnon opened the door, Avicha entered. Amnon, lighting a candle, said, "What brings you here, master, at this time of night?"

"Dress yourself and come with me," said Avicha.

Amnon hurriedly dressed and left with Avicha. In silence they passed the streets and markets, until they arrived at the gate of the valley.

"I heard you complain so often because of your low birth," said Avicha.

"That is true, my master. It is the only thing that embitters my life. I do not know my origin, and I do not know where I shall end."

"Swear to me by God," said Avicha, "that you will never disclose a word of that which you hear from me, and I will tell things which will greatly surprise you."

"By God I swear to you," said Amnon, "that I will never disclose to a living being one word of what you may tell me. May your words be a comfort to my yearning soul."

Then Avicha led the way till they came to a poor hut. To Amnon's great surprise he saw a most kindly looking woman sitting at the scanty table, and by the light of the candle in a copper candlestick, he could see that the face of the woman was worn with worries and tears. To her right sat a beautiful young girl, who arose upon his entrance. Amnon was so bewildered and astonished that he was unable to move or speak. He could not understand why he had been brought to this lonely hut, and wondered what would happen next. Avicha broke the silence by addressing these words to Amnon: "Go thither and kiss the hand of your mother—she is your parent. And embrace that young damsel—she is your twin sister."

Amnon's heart nearly stopped its beating from the surprise of

Avicha's words. Both mother and daughter, crying, embraced and kissed Amnon, and the mother said, "Oh, Benoni [son of my mourning], whom I have not seen since you were weaned!"

The girl, looking at Amnon with tearful eyes, said, "Oh, my flesh and blood! Are you my brother Amnon, of whom my mother has told me so much? Are you the one whom I could only imagine, never having seen you and knowing you only by name?"

Avicha, thinking the reunion of Amnon and his mother and sister too sacred for a stranger to witness, quietly left the room.

And Naame said to Amnon, "May God be gracious to you, my blossoming bud! But why are you so silent, my son?"

Amnon embraced his mother and sister, tears streaming down his cheeks, but he could not speak. His mother repeated, "Why do you not speak? Let me hear your sweet voice; you know how sweet it is to a mother's ears."

And Amnon wept and said, "Your love, my dear mother, your sweet kisses and your tenderness, of which I was deprived for so many years, all gathered in my heart just now, and I could not withstand it. Therefore, I was silent. Oh, how sweet you are, my dear mother! How beautiful you are, my sister! I found you like roses in the desert. But woe is to me! I see you are so poor and hiding yourselves in such a wretched hut. Tell me, dear mother, why have you acted like a stranger to me all these years? Tell me your name and my sister's name. To what tribe do I belong? And what was my father's name? I want you to know, my dear mother, that in vain I try to make a name for myself to be respected. I am looked upon as low-born, and all my hopes are vain. Tell me, dear mother, your troubles and anxieties. Am I so weak that I cannot help you? If at present I cannot raise you from your poverty, I shall do it, with the help of Yedidiah, the philanthropist, who offered me a fortune for the life of his daughter, whom I saved from death. I refused it, but now I will accept it, so that you may live in comfort."

"There is one request I will ask of you, my dear son: Do not press me to tell you that which I have kept from you so long. Do not be impatient to find out who your father was and to what tribe you belong. I will tell you only one fact; that is, that your father belonged to the nobility of this land, and he is now dead. After his death, his creditors came and took everything away. If I had not saved my life and yours, my dear children, they would have sold us into slavery. Even yet I fear them, for they are cruel. If that is not sufficient for you to know, my son, you shall know that many, many hardships await us if they find us out. Therefore, I am hiding in darkness and poverty, until God, in His time, shall bring light upon your birth. I can see, my dear son, that God in His mercy, has begun to favour your father's house, for he raised you from a shepherd boy to a high station, to live among the nobles and to be an inmate of Yedidiah's house."

Amnon sighed at his mother's words, and, with tears in his eyes, said, "To my great sorrow did Yedidiah raise me to that lofty station. My desires are too far above me. Oh, if I had not left the shepherd's hut I would be at peace!"

"What does that mean?" asked his mother. "What do you mean by the word 'desires', and that they are too high for you?"

Amnon could not keep back the tears, and weeping, said, "You see this ring on my finger? Tamar, Yedidiah's daughter, gave it to me as a pledge of her love."

Naame looked at the ring and wonderingly gazed first at Amnon and then at her daughter. Amnon's ring brought to her mind the ring which Teman had given to her daughter while in Carmel. And she asked Amnon what was the significance of the names engraved on the ring. And Amnon told his mother all about the dream and everything that had taken place up to that very day. Then his mother said, "Pacify your heart and depend on God." Thus she comforted her son until the morning star shone and its light penetrated into the room through the tiny window. Naame embraced her son and daughter, and said, "So may your light shine like that morning star. May I see it and rejoice."

Amnon, kissing his mother and sister, said, "I will see you often now."

"If I want to see you," said his mother, "I will send Uze, the servant of our protector, Avicha, and I will appoint a place of meeting. Be very careful when you come to see me, and guard your words concerning our secrets."

Amnon left his mother and sister with a fluttering heart.

Peroh, Amnon's servant, who was spying upon every step of Amnon, was glad of the occurrences of the night. To him they seemed very strange, because he had watched Amnon from the moment he left his room with Avicha, and had followed them at a distance until they reached the hut. He did not linger there, fearing that Amnon might return soon, and, missing him from his place, might suspect him.

The next morning, Peroh related to Zimri all that had occurred the previous night, and Zimri scolded him and said, "You were very foolish, Peroh. Why did you not look through the window and learn what Amnon did there? Now be more careful in the future and watch closely all his movements. Do not consider the occurrence of last night a trifle."

Chapter sixteen

Uchon, after he had been reinstated as butler of Azrikam's house, was treated with more consideration by his master than heretofore, but with all that, he was not happy. The thought of Matan's end weighed heavily upon his conscience and he continually thought of his share of that heinous plot enacted so many years ago. And one day, feeling more downcast than usual, he said to his wife, Hella, "You saw Matan's end and in what agony he died. Just so I often think will be our end, for were not we accomplices in the crime? As God punished him, so will He punish us, unless, even at this late date, we do something to atone for our sin. Therefore, I have decided upon a plan by which Yoram's wife and daughter may be put in their rightful places."

Hella, hasty in her conclusions, said, "Are you going to deprive our son of his possessions now that he has begun to be a little kind to you?"

"Listen attentively until you have heard my entire plan: I will bring Naame and her daughter to their possessions, and at the same time not harm but better our son's position. This is my plan: I will go to Naame and tell her how Matan had burned the house and how, fearing me, he made me say that my son was Azrikam, so that he might be the heir. She shall know that Matan did all this out of revenge against Haggit. Then I shall ask her to give her daughter, Peninah, to Azrikam in marriage. Peninah is a beautiful girl and I am sure Azrikam will fall in love with her when he sees her. Thus, you see, both mother and daughter will be given their own, and our son will suffer nothing by it, and my conscience will be so much clearer that at last I shall be at peace. Nobody will know who the girl is and everybody will think that Azrikam married a Philistine woman, and no questions will be asked."

"But what will Yedidiah say? You know that he will not allow Azrikam to marry anyone but Tamar, he being engaged to her."

"You have not heard the end of the plan yet, Hella. Listen, and when I have finished, you shall tell me if my plan is not good. Zimri told me, in secret, that Tamar and Amnon are in love with one another, and Tamar gave Amnon Hananeel's ring. I will tell Amnon that the story of Hananeel's death was concocted to deceive him. Then, to carry out the dream to the letter, he will go to Assyria in search of Hananeel. I am sure that he will succeed, for half of the dream has already been realized. He looks like the youth of Hananeel's dream and he already has the ring, so the end will be that Amnon will marry Tamar. Then it will leave Azrikam free to marry Naame's daughter. With all this accomplished, we shall have done so much good that we can begin to hope that God will forgive us for the wrong we did Naame."

"You see, my husband," answered Hella, "you put yourself in a great labyrinth, and I am afraid that you will never find your way out of its winding paths."

"Do not fear," replied Uchon. "Only let me carry out my plans."

"How can an inexperienced lad like Amnon attempt such a great undertaking?" asked Hella. "How can he take so great a risk as to go in search of Hananeel to Assyria, where they are constantly at war?"

And Uchon answered, "There is a traveling merchant here, from Zedon, whom I know. He told me that there is a place between Zedon and Tyrus and the other islands; that there is a treaty among the central isles for the exchange of merchandise, and that there is no danger to merchant ships and caravans on their way to and fro. I will introduce Amnon to this merchant as a native of Zedon. I am sure that he will allow nothing to prevent him from going, because of his love for Tamar."

"Your plans are too deep for me to comprehend," answered Hella. "Do as you deem best, but be careful that you do not fall into a snare."

"I will not let Azrikam know anything about it until Amnon shall have gained his point. Then, when our son sees that Tamar is lost to him and grieves over his loss, I will show him Naame's daughter. Then he will forget Tamar and will fall in love with Peninah. At the same time I will tell Azrikam that Peninah is Yoram's daughter and that he is my son. I cannot keep the secret forever; he must know it some time. That time will be as good as any, and I do not wish to keep the burden of my son on my conscience any longer than necessary. He must know that we are his parents."

While Uchon was repenting and trying to repair his wrongs, Zimri was scheming how he could best deal out his deadly blows upon Amnon. He sent Amnon's servant, Peroh, to the gate of the valley to find out who lived in the hut where Amnon had gone the night before. When Peroh reached the hut, he found another woman there, and he said to her, "Do you know Shoav, the Moabite, who lives here?"

"No, I do not," answered the woman.

But Peroh did not give up so easily, so he inquired all through the neighbourhood, and they told him that not a Moabite but a Philistine woman and her daughter had lived there. After learning this, Peroh returned to the city and found Zimri in Carmi's wine-house, and told him everything that he had found out.

"Here are thirty shekels," said Zimri, "for the work you have done today. Twice that amount you shall receive if you succeed whither

I shall send you. Now, go to Teman and tell him, as a secret, that Amnon left his house last night and that it was so unusual an occurrence that it aroused your suspicions and you followed him, and saw him enter a lonely hut, occupied by two women, and that he remained therein until morning. And tell him you thought he should know that Amnon did not conduct himself properly. Make him promise, however, that he will not tell who told him."

And Peroh answered, "You can depend upon me. I know how to talk to Teman. I will go at once and do your bidding."

"Do not be in such a hurry," said Zimri. "Wait a few days and perhaps, in the meantime, you may learn more, and I, too, may find out things that will be of use to us. Then we can put them all together and use those facts which will give us the best results."

"Very well; I will do as you command me," said Peroh.

The next day, Uze came to Amnon and told him that he should come at twilight to a certain valley at the outskirts of the city and wait there among the bushes. And Amnon said, "I will do so."

Peroh, the spy, overheard this, and immediately went to Zimri and told him. Zimri said, "Now be quick! Go to Teman and tell him all that you know."

Peroh went to carry out his orders, and Zimri, satisfied with what he had accomplished, said to himself, "Now I will break up the brotherhood existing between Teman and Amnon. When Teman finds out that Amnon is not so innocent as he pretends to be, he will find fault with him."

Amnon impatiently awaited the appointed time of the meeting. When he arrived there, he found his mother and sister dressed in black and heavily veiled. Amnon was in excellent humour, because of the good news he had heard from Uchon the previous day—that Hananeel was alive and that the traveling merchant would leave in three days for Assyria. He was glad to see his mother and sister before he left. But his happiness left him when he noticed the troubled face of his mother. She also had heard the news from Uchon, which caused the worried look in her eyes. But Peninah's face was calm, because she was not aware of anything that could disturb her, and she said to her brother, "Shall we act as brother and sister only in secret? Oh, cruel fate!" The mother cried when she heard these words.

Then Amnon said, "Please, mother dear, do not cry! The sight of your tears breaks my heart. Tell me, dear mother, what is my sister's name?"

"Will it please you to know that her name is Rose?"

Then Amnon, turning to his sister, said, "That name is as becoming to you as a precious jewel is in a beautiful crown."

"I will tell you, my son," said Naame, "a great change has come over me lately. There will come a day when you, my son, shall hear them; then you will wonder and be surprised. You shall know that you will not see us for a long while. We leave the city today and go to some other place, where we shall stay indefinitely. Avicha will know our abode."

"I, too, am going to leave the city," said Amnon, "for I have heard news which I never expected. Oh, to my joy, I heard that Hananeel, Tirzah's father, is alive! This ring, which Tamar gave me, is a treasure to me. I hope that Hananeel's dream will come true. I can clearly see now that all the things that have happened so far carry out my dream. I resemble the youth of Hananeel's dream. I saved Tamar's life. She loves me and gave me the ring which is required for my purpose. My birth also is a secret, which corresponds exactly with the dream. If I can find Hananeel and bring him back, then my future is made."

"Put your hopes in God, my son, and depend upon Him. He will bring you to your destination. You will find Hananeel and God will bring you back in safety. Then I shall see you and rejoice. And who knows, perhaps by that time God will have pity on me and bring my innocence to light."

Amnon then kissed his mother and sister and they embraced him. Amnon went towards the city and they went in the opposite direction.

Teman, directed by Peroh, had gone to the appointed meeting place. On his way hither, he met Peninah and her mother, returning. Peninah recognized Teman and started back in confusion. Teman also recognized her and trembled with surprise, and he exclaimed, "Oh fate, did you show me again my beloved Rose?" Peninah, astounded, could not answer, and Teman said, "Are you not the Rose whom I met on Mt. Carmel, and who kindled the fire of love in my heart, and who then escaped from me like a vision of the night?"

Peninah, still overcome by her emotions, could not answer, and looked from her mother to Teman in utter bewilderment.

Teman continued, "Oh, gentle Rose, give me back what you took from me! Give me back the peace to my soul and the rest to my heart! With one look from your glorious eyes you have bewitched, me, and my peace is gone forever. Come to me, my beloved, and I will take you to my father. I will tell him that you are my treasure and that I love you, and will die if he refuses his consent to our union."

Naame interrupted this outburst with these words, "Pray, young lord, do not call for Rose nor lift thine eyes to her with love. She is a stranger to you. She is engaged to another."

"Are you her mother," asked Teman. "Did you not send me word, through an old woman, that the sapphire is removed from the ring? Now you tell me that she is engaged to another man. Who can that man be, who, having found a treasure such as Rose, does not attire her like a princess? He must be a poor man. Tell me who he is, and I will give her weight in gold and silver if he will release her from her promise. I am my father's only heir. I am sure the man will gladly exchange and he will be satisfied with the price. Then your daughter and I will live in happiness all our lives. My life depends upon her."

"Is it not enough," asked Naame, "that God has blest you with wealth? Do you want a beautiful wife also? Should the poor have nothing? You ask too much, my lord."

Teman, seeing that he could gain nothing by talking to Naame, turned to Rose and said, "Oh, dear Rose, have pity on me!"

Naame turned to Teman, saying, "We do not understand what you are talking about. My daughter's name is not Rose. Go back to Carmel and look for the Rose who took away your heart, or go home and sleep over it; I see you are dreaming."

"If I do dream," answered Teman, "I dream of love for your daughter. I have been dreaming of her for the past year, ever since the first time I saw her."

"You must forgive me," replied Naame, "if I tell you that you are dreaming about roses. It will make no difference how many beautiful girls you may chance to see; they will all look like roses to you, because you love roses! Who can prevent you? You can find many of them in Zion. Turn to them and leave my daughter alone."

Then Teman turned to Rose and said, "Can you be cruel, too? Can you act as a stranger to me? Could God endow you with so much beauty and kindness and loveliness, and fill your heart with treachery? God forbid that I should think Him so unjust! Not for evil, but for love, God has created you; therefore, look at me, and tell me you have not seen me before. Did you not take a ring from me in Carmel? I will not leave this place until you can tell me why the sapphire is removed from the ring. When you tell me that, I will ask you, as a favour, to point out the man to whom you are engaged. I will see the fortunate one, and then I can measure my own misery."

Peninah could not restrain her tears any longer, and choking with sobs, said, "Ask my mother. I can do nothing. Let her do as she pleases with me."

And Naame answered, "Put your confidence in me, just as you have put your love in my daughter, and believe that in three days I will send you a decided answer concerning her. Now, I charge you, my lord by the hinds, and the rose of the field, not to mention our names to any living being."

"I swear," said Teman, "by my life and the life of your daughter, which is dearer to me than life, that I will keep it secret."

Then Peninah addressed Teman with these words, "Now go in peace, my lord, and wait for my answer. By God do I swear that I will send you word in three days."

When Teman left them, he said to himself, "Amnon, who must have seen Rose, naturally fell in love with her. What a man could see her and not fall in love with her? There is, therefore, only one course for me to pursue: I will give Amnon hopes of marrying Tamar and talk to my parents about Azrikam. If I can accomplish that, then Amnon can take but one wife, my sister. However, I will wait for three days; I will govern my actions by the news I shall receive from her. I have good reason for good hopes. I could see that Rose looked very pityingly and favourably upon me."

Amnon, after his return, sat in his room and pondered how best he could remove the obstacles in his way. He thought that if a high ransom was demanded for Hananeel's release, he could not accomplish it. So he made up his mind to tell Tamar on the morrow of his intended trip to Assyria, with the hope that she might advise him. When Amnon saw Tamar the next day, he told her that he wanted to see her about a very urgent matter and that he would wait for her at the well-known rendezvous on Mt. Olive, at twilight.

At the appointed time, Amnon stood among the trees behind the summer house. The sun was setting and the moon could be seen in the sky. Amnon, while waiting for Tamar, carved in one of the trees, his name and Tamar's name. When Tamar came, she said, "Your name God has long since engraved in my heart."

"Let our names," answered Amnon, "be engraved on this tree, and, like this olive tree, so may our love bloom in our youth, and spread and grow in strength until we have both grown old. May this tree always be our shelter and resting place. Let it be the omen of our love. Now listen to me, my love, and I will tell you some unexpected news. Do not chide me for not telling you sooner, for I have but just found out the truth. This shall open for us the gates of hope. Therefore, listen most attentively, my dear: Your grandfather, Hananeel, is alive. Tomorrow evening I am prepared to leave for Assyria, with a traveling merchant, for Zedon, to bring back your grandfather from his captivity."

At these words, Tamar's heart was turning from fear to joy, and, taking Amnon's hand in hers, said, "Can a person hear such tidings without receiving a shock?"

"Now, my love," said Amnon, "I will not see you again until I have accomplished my purpose. You will have to use a little strategy and tell your father that I have changed my mind, and will accept the thousand shekels he promised me for your rescue. With that money I shall be able to ransom your grandfather from captivity. I know your father will not refuse it to me."

Tamar cried while Amnon spoke, and he too wept at the thought of their parting, and he said, "Wait for me until my return." He raised his eyes to heaven, and seeing the setting sun and the rising moon, said, "Even you, with your charitable coming and going, be witnesses to our covenant, and keep our secrets until the right time! Then you will shine upon us when the lovers shall walk by your light, and bless God, your Creator and the Creator of love."

And Tamar raised her hand towards heaven, and said, "I also take you, everlasting moon, as a witness, and I swear again that I will always be yours, Amnon." And taking his hand, she continued, "Guard this ring more than all the treasures."

"I will guard it as the apple of my eye, for my life and your love depend upon it."

"Tomorrow I will ask my father about the money," said Tamar. "I cannot trust myself to speak today, because my heart is overwhelmed with the tidings you brought and with the thought of the intense longing I shall have to endure during your absence. Every day shall seem a year to me."

While Tamar was speaking and holding Amnon's hand, Yedidiah, unnoticed by the lovers, was approaching. Suddenly he confronted them and said, "Behold, a curious sight I see! The hand of a man clasping that of a girl to whom he is an utter stranger!"

Amnon and Tamar, as can be imagined, were very much astounded to be so interrupted. In their surprise they dropped each other's hand, and could not speak for confusion. Yedidiah, as though rooted to the place, stood and looked at them. When he saw Hananeel's ring on Amnon's hand, he turned his eyes away and ignored it. Yedidiah, seeing that Amnon and Tamar were still confused, said, "You ought to be ashamed of yourselves. What shall I say to my daughter? She is like a young dove, irresponsible for her actions; but to you, Amnon, I will speak. Is it thus that you repay me for my trust in you? Do you think you are acting honorably, according to your own standard of honour? You know that I was willing to give you a reward for Tamar's life, and you refused it. But I see now that you have wanted a greater reward—life for life. Do not try to deceive my daughter with false words, for you will not succeed. She is engaged to another, not to you. Go back to your rooms and do not see Tamar again."

Yedidiah took Tamar by the hand, and when he had reached the house, he brought her before Tirzah and said, "It is your fault, Tirzah, and you must repair the wrong." And he told his wife all that he had seen.

Amnon returned to his rooms, full of shame and heartbroken. He thought that all his plans were upset, and he was in agony of mind all night.

Zimri saw that something unusual had happened. Tamar went about with tearful eyes and a downcast countenance. Teman also looked worried. And Macha related to Zimri all that had taken place in the house. Peroh told Zimri how wretchedly Amnon had spent the night. Then Zimri hastened to Azrikam and told him that the fish had been caught in the net he had set for them.

Chapter seventeen

It was the third day and, according to Peninah's promise, the day that was to bring Teman news from her. Therefore, hoping to see her again, Teman went to the former meeting place to await either her appearance or a messenger from her. When he arrived there, a boy approached him and asked, "Who are you, my lord?"

"What business have you with me that you ask me who I am?" asked Teman.

"I am looking for a young lord," answered the youth, "who made an appointment for a meeting here; therefore, I ask, 'Who are you, my lord?'"

"I am lord Yedidiah's son, my boy."

At these words, the youth took a sealed letter from his pocket and handing it to Teman, said, "A strange young lady gave me this letter this morning, and, paying me, bade me give it to Yedidiah's son, who would be waiting here for it. So I brought it, my lord."

Teman forthwith opened the letter and read as follows:

"My lord Teman: —

"Your lips, not your eyes, deceived you. You recognized me as the girl you met in Carmel, but you called me Rose. That is not the name given at my birth, although I was known by it. Therefore, forgive me, my lord. Twice have I deceived you—once in Carmel, when I told you my name was Rose, and again at our second meeting, when I still kept my name from you. This time, though, I will tell you all my thoughts and feelings towards you; my name and my station in life I must keep secret.

"When I called myself 'Rose,' in Carmel, I was like a rose, calm and peaceful. I knew no other love than that for my mother. Then I was contented with my lot. But now, since I love you, I have no more peace and am dissatisfied. I was like an innocent lamb before I met you—I did not even know my own heart—but since your eyes bewitched me and your tender words penetrated to the innermost sanctuary of my heart and conquered me, I know my heart, and I know how unhappy I am. When I gazed upon you, I said to myself, 'Do not look at the sun—it is too high and its rays are too bright; they will only hurt your eyes and will leave darkness in your heart.'

"Give back, beloved of my heart, give back to the rose the dew of youth which you took from her! Give back her quiet heart, her innocence and peace. Why did you begrudge her blooming in the desert? Turn away from her, beloved. Thorns surround the rose, and if you attempt to take it, you will only hurt your hands and never reach it. Should you, however, succeed, it will lose its bloom when in your hands, or some invisible power will snatch it from you. Therefore, I say, turn away from her. Pray, my lord, keep me dear in your heart. My heart yearns for you, but it is afraid to see you. Let me be to you like a night's dream, which vanishes at daybreak and is forgotten forever. And you shall be like the vision of an angel of God, who came down in a flame from heaven to light the fire for the sacrifice of an innocent lamb, and then disappeared. Oh, I am that sacrifice, burned on the altar of love! Pour your tears upon it, beloved. Such is the lot of the Rose whom you know. She has seen that which her heart longs for and she is destined to hide herself from it. Let that be your kindness to me, and the reward of the fruit of our first love, to keep our secret as you have pledged and forget me. Pity an unhappy soul and forget her as one dead, and give your love to a more fortunate one than she."

When Teman finished reading the letter he clasped his hands, and, with a deep sigh, exclaimed, "Oh, misfortune and calamity! Oh, beautiful Rose! Your puzzle is as strange as your love. You love me too. What, then, can be the obstacle which keeps us apart? Oh, sweet Rose, you have wounded and broken my heart! Who can cure it? If you are unhappy, how unhappy am I? I have seen you only twice, but I can never forget you."

The bearer of the letter, noticing that the contents brought sadness instead of joy, said, "I am very sorry for my disappointment. I was in hopes of receiving a reward for the glad tidings I brought you, but I see that the letter did not please you."

"Show me the place where the lady who sent the letter lives, and then you will see how liberal I am," said Teman.

"Believe me, my lord," answered the youth, "I did not notice where she lived, nor did I even see her face. When she mentioned your name, I was overjoyed, thinking of the reward I would receive from the son of the great Philanthropist, and I noticed nothing but her direction to me."

"You made no mistake in that thought," answered Teman. "Here is a shekel for you."

The boy thanked him and left. And Teman returned home with an aching heart, and he thought to himself, "Tomorrow I will go to Amnon and indirectly question him about the two women. I will also interrogate Sisry. Perhaps from their combined answers I may be able to form some conclusion."

Amnon was sitting in his room, dejected and lost in thought. He could devise no plan of action. All the plans which he had thought out were in one way or another inadequate for his purpose. "Woe to me is that third day, from which I hoped so much," he thought. "The day which I thought would be so bright has been clouded with a dark cloud of shame and humiliation. Instead of honour, I received disgrace; instead of love, a broken heart. And now my rival, Azrikam, will have the upper hand of me. Oh, woe is me! How can I live and see my beloved given to another! How shall I shield myself from such shame? There is only one thing left for me to do; that is, to go away and wander about without hope."

These thoughts so affected Amnon that he could not refrain from tears, and his frame shook with sobs. The night came and the tumult of the city had ceased, but Amnon's heart did not feel that calm in which the city was wrapped. The thought that he might lose Tamar forever aroused in his heart a storm of agitation and alarm.

At that moment, Yedidiah walked into Amnon's room, and Amnon, very much surprised, rose to his feet. And Yedidiah said, "Send your servant away. I wish to speak to you."

Peroh left and went to Zimri. He was afraid to listen through the door as usual, lest Yedidiah see him.

When Yedidiah looked at Amnon's haggard face, stained with tears, he said, "You are crying, Amnon. You are repenting the injustice you did me and the deceit you worked upon me when I thought I was safe in you. But I did not come here to reprimand you nor to teach you morals, which your teachers failed to teach you. One thing

I will ask you, Amnon. Be honest with me for a moment—tell me the truth—did Tamar swear to you eternal love?"

"Yes, my lord; she pledged that a year ago, in Bethlehem, when I saved her life. But the token of her love, which she gave me, you took from me yesterday."

"You showed yourself truthful upon my first question," said Yedidiah, "and I am very much pleased. Now, tell me, Amnon, what will you do if Tamar's father disallows her oath?"

"I will bemoan my bitter lot all my life," answered Amnon. "I will live in loneliness and I will never know another woman. So I have sworn, and I will not break my oath."

"Why, Tamar has a father," said Yedidiah, "and therein you were wrong that you did not think of him."

"Neither did the lion think of you, my lord, when he was about to devour your daughter."

"You have only saved Tamar's life. How can you ask such a high price for your service?" said Yedidiah. "You want her life and her honour. Her honour belongs to me and that Tamar cannot give without my consent. Oh, why did I not know your ways before! Now, if you do not want me to be your enemy, accept from me these thousands shekels as your reward. Hananeel's ring, which Tamar gave you as a token of her love, I return to you; let it be a reminder of your wrong to me. As there is no more value to the ring since Hananeel is dead, so shall Tamar's love be dead to you. Take these, and leave before daybreak, and do not be a stumbling block in my house for my daughter. See, I warn you."

Yedidiah did not wait for Amnon's answer, but leaving the money and the ring on the table, left the room.

Amnon was very much gratified at the turn events had taken. He had feared the worst from Yedidiah's anger, but the result made his project possible. He took the money and the ring. The lion's skin he placed under the saddle of his horse, and he rode to the abode of the traveling merchant, in readiness to leave for Assyria.

When Peroh returned to Amnon's rooms, he found his master

gone. He waited until morning for Amnon's return, and when he saw that Amnon did not come, he went to acquaint Zimri of the fact.

"I know all about it from Yedidiah," said Zimri. "Amnon went on a voyage from which he will never return."

"Where is my pay?" asked Peroh.

"We will need you in our service, and when we have accomplished our end, you will receive your reward," answered Zimri.

Three days had passed since Amnon left Zion. Azrikam was very low spirited. He heard that Yedidiah had given Amnon money and returned Hananeel's ring, thinking that, Hananeel dead, the ring had no more value. He sent for Zimri, therefore, to hold council with him as to what should be done before Amnon should return with Hananeel. Zimri advised Azrikam to press his suit for Tamar's hand, and hurry the marriage. He promised, for his part, to continually belittle Amnon in Tamar's eyes. To accomplish this, he would see Macha, who, being in love with Amnon, would stoop to anything in order that her rival should not have him. When Tamar should send Amnon from her, then Macha would have hopes of winning him.

Azrikam went to Yedidiah's house. He met him as he was coming down Mt. Olive, and addressed him with these words: "How long will your daughter exalt herself over me? She despises me. Is she going to break the covenant you made with my father?"

"Do not fear," answered Yedidiah. "You know that I was your father's friend. You are Yoram's son; Tamar is my daughter. Who can break this threefold thread? Go to Tamar; she is home. Talk to her the best you can. I am sure that you will find her willing to listen to your advances."

"I hope that Tamar will learn to love me as she despised me heretofore," said Azrikam.

"I told you that I am her father, and therefore she will obey my wish in the matter." Yedidiah left Azrikam and went to the city.

When Azrikam reached Yedidiah's house, he found Tamar very much downcast and lost in deep thought. As she perceived Azrikam, she turned her face towards the window. Azrikam turned to Macha and said, "Leave me alone with Tamar. I wish to speak to her in private."

"Stay, Macha," said Tamar. "I do not want any secrets."

"So it goes nowadays," said Azrikam. "Those secrets which we do not wish to be disclosed are brought to light in spite of our carefulness. Therefore, let those things, which need not be hidden, become secret."

"Why, what is the matter, Azrikam?" asked Tamar. "What can have happened? You are so wise today! You choose such brilliant remarks!"

"I have become wise since you were foolish enough to follow a crooked path," said Azrikam.

"No, Azrikam, I was not foolish. I am going the straight way, and my senses will carry me so far, that just as a deer cannot be caught by a rider on the swiftest horse, so I will not be caught by the wicked."

"Even a swift deer," answered Azrikam, "is not swift enough to catch a disobedient daughter when she follows a lover in spite of her parents' wishes."

Turning to Macha, Tamar said, "That is just what I said before, Macha, that Azrikam chose wise remarks. You had better tell him, Macha, that such wise words he should not be ashamed to address to a large assembly as moral teachings. And Azrikam tells them as a secret to a girl who does not even care to listen to him!"

· "You are mistaken," said Azrikam. "There is only one whose secrets you do not care to hear. If you would listen to my secrets, I could buy you thousands of such speakers whose secrets you enjoy listening to, and not one of them would be worse than the one you have chosen."

"Now have you spoken the truth," said Tamar. "You have thousands because you are rich, but if you can afford to buy, buy wisdom. Buy yourself an upright heart; then you will understand that a fool without a heart speaks to no purpose, and that a man without a soul should not speak. How long will you boast of your wealth? Do you know that riches and honour crawl in the darkness, and they never find what they seek? If truth would light your ways, there would be a new creation in the world. We would see then beggars dressed like lords, and fashionable men in rags. The low would be raised and the highborn would bow before them. Wealth and honour! There is an old saying concerning that, 'That wealth becomes a fool like snow in summer, and honour to the ignorant like rain in the harvest.' You know, Azrikam, that gold and silver are taken from the earth. A man who has nothing but gold and silver is considered like the dirt of the earth, and Tamar will not stoop so low as to mingle with it."

Azrikam could not control himself, and with anger consuming his very being, said, "I am not strong enough to argue; there is too much wisdom in you lately. You always have some lesson to teach me, and all that I can hear is, that you belittle the great and raise the lowly. It is a wise plan for your parents, who know when to raise the lowly. But you shall know, fickle hearted lady, that a stronger hand than mine shall govern you; then you will not be so wise."

Tamar arose with disgust, and leaving the room, said, addressing herself to Macha, "Send that lord away and tell him that if he comes to see me again, I shall insult him so that he will not recognize his own shadow." With this parting thrust, she left the room.

Azrikam, grinding his teeth in his rage, sullenly left the house. He went to the city, searched out Yedidiah and said to him, "Tamar spoke to me in another manner, my lord. Oh, her tongue! It is like a sharp sword! I am getting tired of listening to her sarcastic remarks. That is the harvest that you have reaped for the kindness to that shepherd boy. Now, try to cure Tamar's insanity, if you can."

"You are too hasty, Azrikam. Do not press your suit so. I will speak to her in your behalf and she will make up with you. Give me a little time and I will try to direct everything in the right course. After Tamar shall have finished her eighteenth year, I will fulfill your wish."

That same day at the dinner table, Tirzah was seated on the right of her husband, and Tamar and Teman on the left. Teman was preoccupied with his thoughts concerning his love affairs, and Tamar was sad. Yedidiah looked at them but said nothing during the meal. At the conclusion of it, however, he said, very crossly, "Ye take too much upon you to eat a mourner's meal, to sit at the table with downcast faces and embitter my soul. You shall not see my face before you brighten your countenances."

"Please, my dear husband," Tirzah interposed, "if I am dear to you, do not become angry with the children."

"Your life is very dear to me," answered Yedidiah. "In exchange for your heart, I gave you my wealth and my name, but it is not so these days. The men wish to win the heart of a girl, without wealth and without name. They want to find a mate without looking for them!"

"Consider," said Tirzah, "the first days of the creation. God made man alone. What did he give for his wife, Eve—only one rib. And did you notice what the prophet Isaiah has prophesied these days? He says, 'And in that day seven women shall take hold of one man, saying, we will eat our own bread and wear our own apparel; only let us be called by thy name.' And these days are approaching. A new era is at hand, when girls will have to ask the men in marriage."

"Woe is those days!" sighted Yedidiah. "Woe that this has happened in our house and that this new era you speak of has found its first victim in our daughter, to disobey her parents and give away to her own choice. Ask your daughter, and she will teach you the ways of these days."

Tamar wept continually while her father spoke, and Yedidiah continued, saying to Tirzah, "Do not think for a moment that these are tears of repentance. She cries for her lover who went away. Therefore, she insulted, today, her lord. Pay no heed to her tears. They are like the morning dew, which the sun dries up. Do not, my daughter, do not mourn and yearn for your lover. He went away out of your reach, and he will never return to you. Do not cry for him but, rather, over your own heart and deeds, which are not right, and over the shame of your youth. You see that Azrikam is still very lenient with you, inasmuch as he is willing to overlook all your past wrongs to him. I give you seven days in which to repent of your wrongs. In that time you shall think over the wrong you committed by loving a stranger without your father's consent. You shall not see me until you can tell me that you are sorry for your foolishness." With these words, Yedidiah sent her away. Tamar left the room, crying bitterly, and Teman also left the room. Then Tirzah said to Yedidiah, "Think, my husband, upon whom you inflict so much pain. We have only one daughter. Why, then, make her life so wretched?"

"That is what I said," answered Yedidiah. "It is all your fault, Tirzah. I see that you approve of her actions even now to despise the son of my friend Yoram, with whom I made a covenant, and to choose a strange boy from the low classes. I must be just to him—he is very wise and has a good heart, and is handsome, but what shall I call him? He has no name. I would like to give him some name. Think that matter over yourself and give me your advice. There should be something done; the time of our daughter's marriage is approaching."

And Tirzah said, "You are searching after Amnon's parentage. Why do you not search Tamar's heart, as my father did mine when he gave me to you? He asked me what I thought of you—I never thought of looking into your origin. I saw you, loved you and decided to be yours; and afterwards I found out who you were. Do you not know, my dear, that sometimes a rose will grow in the desert, and on Mt. Camel and Schuron a thistle and thorns may grow?"

"Now, listen, my love," said Yedidiah, "I know what makes you say that. Your father's dream is still on your mind and you look upon Amnon, with that handsome countenance, as the youth your father saw in his dream. If your father were alive, I would give Amnon all my wealth and send him to ransom him; but you have seen what the dream came to. Therefore, try your best to influence Tamar to care for Azrikam."

"I will do so," answered Tirzah.

When Tamar came to her room, Macha said, "You see, my dear lady, that my words came true. I told you beforehand that Amnon had no hopes for you and that he would have to leave this house; that you would not be allowed to return his love, to disgrace yourself and your parents. I am very sorry for you, my dear lady, that you still love him and endure insults from your father. Why do you despise Azrikam so? His name is great, because of his father's rank; his wealth is immense. Everything he has will be yours; what can poor Amnon give you? He can give you his heart, for he has nothing else. Oh, my poor mistress, my heart aches to see you grieve! Your father has sent you from him in disgrace."

"I wish my father would send me away forever! I would gladly leave all my father's palaces and go in search of Amnon. My whole life depends upon him. It will be sweet to me to live in a shepherd's hut; it will seem like a king's palace, if only he is there. Let him lead me to the desert and I will follow him with all my heart. Under his footsteps flowers grow, the deserts rejoice at his words, and a desolate land will be full of song from the echo of his voice. And, as I do not care for wealth and do not desire honors, I have therefore said to myself, 'If I were a princess, if I possessed all the gold of Ophir, if I were the most beautiful woman in all the world, then, even, I would not be worthy of the goodness of Amnon's heart.' You said that he could give me only his heart. Why, his heart is dearer to me than all the pleasures in the world!"

And Macha answered, "That is true. When I saw him first I thought he was handsome, but when I grew accustomed to him, I found he was not any handsomer than other young men in Zion. If you would grow accustomed to Azrikam you would soon forget Amnon, and the best advice I can give you is to forget him, for he will never return."

While they were talking, Tirzah entered the room and asked, "What answer will you give your father? You know, he has made up his mind, and who can persuade him to change it?"

"I am in my father's hands. He can do what he pleases with me," said Tamar. "Let him bind my hands with a rope and sell me like a slave to that low life. I will be dumb and bear my grief in silence. But you shall know, my dear mother, that only my body he can sell and that golden bridle and silver cannot hold me. My soul flies after Amnon. I am his, and with him I shall die!"

Tirzah sighed and said, "Oh, my only daughter, how great is my sorrow!" Then she went to deliver Tamar's answer to Yedidiah.

The seven days of Tamar's banishment passed, and Yedidiah could get no word from her. He said to her, "Be prepared for Azrikam, your lover. In ten months you will be eighteen years of age. On that day you shall be his, whether you wish it or not."

Tamar bore all this in silence and her heart was heavy.

A few days after, Teman came into Tamar's room, and, after sending Macha away, said, "Listen, my sister, and I swear by God that I have no falsehood on my lips."

"Why, I know, my brother, that you are truthful. Speak, I am listening," said Tamar.

"You know, Tamar, that I loved Amnon like a brother and that I hate Azrikam. You remember that evening when you swore you loved Amnon, and our father so suddenly frightened you, and the next day Amnon left and you do not know whither? You did not hear the reason for his going. Therefore, listen and learn that there are wicked people in the world: A man came to me from the heights of Benjamin and said to me these words: 'I came to Jerusalem to see God on the Easter holiday, and I saw among the girls one who was very beautiful, the daughter of a poor man, who is dead, and her mother is a Philistine woman. I fell in love with this girl, so I went to her mother's home, which is in the neighbourhood, at the gate of the valley, and asked her for her daughter in marriage. The girl consented and I gave her presents in abundance. I told her to wait a month, until I should divide my father's inheritance among my brothers, and that then I would return to her. The girl agreed to wait, and before I went home I had a boy in the neighbourhood watch the ways of that girl, to see if they were proper. When I came back to Jerusalem at the end of a month, I did not find her again. The boy told me that a handsome young man came there one night and stayed there until morning, and when he left the house, the boy watched him and saw him go into your father's house.' So the man told me, and I, wishing to find out if there were any foundation to the story, questioned Peroh, Amnon's servant, and he told me that Amnon did leave his rooms one night, returning the next morning. If I did not know other mysteries about Amnon, I would dispute both the man and Peroh, but, alas, it is true—just as though I had seen it with my own eyes! Now, my loving sister, you shall know that if our father should change his mind and give you to Amnon, you shall look out for yourself that he shall have no other wife beside you. And if he is married to that girl, he must divorce her before he marries you."

Tamar was so astounded by her brother's tale, that her heart palpitated within her, but she hid the fact from him and said, "Do not be so foolish as to believe everything you hear. Let all the people be false, but Amnon will never be false to me. Leave it to me, my brother. I wish my father would not separate us. I would laugh at all these tales."

Yedidiah, seeing that Tamar despised Azrikam with the bitterest hatred, never broached the subject again, and left her to her own thoughts. He said to Tirzah, "Let us wait and see to whom God has willed our daughter."

Chapter eighteen

Three months had passed since Amnon left Yedidiah's house, and there were no tidings of his whereabouts. Tamar, since Amnon's departure, arose every morning, after a sleepless night, and walked alone in the garden. One morning, as she was walking in the garden as usual, a Zidonian approached her. He held a letter in his hand, and, when near Tamar, said, "Are you Tamar, the philanthropist's daughter?"

"Yes, I am," answered Tamar.

"Pay me," he said, "and I will give you this letter, sent to you by a young man in Assyria, whose name is Amnon."

"Come a little later in the day," answered Tamar, "and I will liberally reward you."

"Very well," he said, "I know you will not deprive me of my reward—you are a lord's daughter." With these words he handed Tamar the letter and made his departure.

Tamar, trembling, broke the seal, and read as follows:

In the land of Nimrod, in Nineveh, the city of a mighty nation, am I. Come, my dear noble Tamar, and listen to the words of Amnon from afar.

I loved you in Bethlehem, I longed for you in Zion, and now, in the other end of the world, you are my treasure. I am far away from the sources of my life, but your presence is with me always. It leads me and comforts me in my sleeping and in my waking.

Are you not the one who took me from the shepherd's hut to live in Zion? And then did you not honour me by making me an inmate of your own home, giving me the privilege to enjoy the sweetness of your countenance and to learn your gentle ways? But that was not all; you did more than that. With your kindness, with your charity and love, you implanted hope in my heart; you promised to see life and joy with me forever, and I compared you with the morning star. I always thought your station as far above me as the earth is from the heavens, because I am poor and helpless; therefore, I thought of giving up my hopes, and I especially feared your father's anger, and, alas, my fears were realized.

Your father surprised us together, but fortunately he returned Hananeel's ring to me and he also gave me a thousand shekels. You know for what purpose I am going to use the money. Oh, I wish that I might find your grandfather, Hananeel! I will ransom him and bring him to you. Then I will say to you, 'Here is the interpretation of the dream.' I will wed you and your parents will then admit that Amnon has accomplished great things.

I am in Nineveh, a big city in the land of Assyria, a

land of corn and wine, and from her skies the dew falls in abundance. Now I want you to know about the great city of which so much is spoken:

In the time of the first creation, when God created the mountains and the people, cities were built, and the City of Nineveh was erected on her foundations from the very beginning of the centuries, after the mountains were created. The hands of Ashur built the city, and, to establish forever the name of his son, Nin, he called the city Nineveh. The city is built on both sides of the River Hiddekel; it is three days' journey through this city. A high wall surrounds it. A channel brings the water from the river to the city, and fills the brooks and valleys. Such is the strong city, built so many years back. But do you think it can be compared with the beautiful Zion, even though it is young? Nineveh's brooks are not like those in Zion. A pure light is spread over everything in Zion, while a gloomy light is over the waters of Nineveh. You do not see joyful faces here; the people are dull and their eyes are dim with tears of the oppressed. Every day captives are brought here in battleships and in the fisherboats.

Not like the Mountains of Zion, Mt. Moriah and the Mount of Olives, crowned with a bold splendour. Not to them can you compare the smoky mountains of Assyria, which shoot out flames or fire and burn all the surroundings. Zion is the dwelling of our Creator, and Nineveh is the abode of lions. I call Nineveh, therefore, a sweet and fearful city. It is like a leopard adorned with a fine skin—pleasant to look at and fierce with the roar issuing from its mouth.

From this city, King Sennacherib comes forth like a lion from the heights on the Jordan and darkens the surface of the earth. He crushes the homes of Kedar and Raamah, and destroys the inhabitants of Sepharidin. His arm is ready to strike the Holy Mountain and plant his standards there and establish his throne. He wants to see all the kingdoms of the east and west crawl at his feet. He is fierce, and so are his hosts. Even the bravest knights are afraid of his chariots and horsemen, whose armor glistens like gold, and whose horses are as swift as the water of the River Hiddekel. The earth shakes beneath the weight of his armies and the strongest nations are afraid of them. They deaden the rush of their wheels with their joyful war songs. They roar like leopards, and at the onslaught of the battle, the war-cry rages and the victims fall like sheaves before the reaper. Their captives number into thousands.

The sun is setting and the moon is shining on the River Hiddekel. I look at them from the heights. Oh, thou dear moon, how sweet you were to me when I saw you over that Holy Mountain, when I stood on the Mount of Olives and your light shone like a sheet of silver from among the branches upon Tamar, who stood like a rose on my right! How beautiful did thy light shine on her hand, when she raised it to swear to me eternal love! But you are not truthful, oh moon! As a truthful witness, Tamar called upon you, and right there you were false to her, for by they light I saw tears on her cheeks. Three times have you rendered your light since that night, but you have not renewed new spirits within me, and as many nights as you have come and gone, I have spent in misery. With thy light came the dreams, all vain and empty dreams; they remain with me during the night but vanish at daybreak. The day vanishes like a shadow, and the evening passes like a wind, and it is midnight.

All the people are enveloped under the wings of slumber, which ends the toil and misery of the day. And beneath them all the low-spirited revive, but I, alas, neither sleep nor slumber! With the lion's skin I have made my bed. Thoughts without any connection come crowding through my head.

My heart is like a tossing sea, and my soul moves on its broken billows. My eyes are intent upon this sheet, and sleep is strange to my lids. But what has robbed my sleep? The stars in heaven are restful and quiet, and they look down from their far height upon the peaceful earth. Why am I not at peace? Oh, if I had wings like a bird, I would fly to you, if only for one second, to see your face and to know my own destiny! If you were at peace, my heart would be at ease also. I have studied it and found it sitting alone in my room, a joy suddenly came over my heart, and I did not know the reason. I went to see you and found you joyous also. At another time, my spirits were low, without knowing why. I went to you, and you, too, were sad. When I called your attention to that fact, you said with your sweet lips, 'Do you not know, Amnon, that since we made our covenant of love, my lot is thy heart and thy lot my heart? Our joys are intermingled, and the sorrows of one are the sorrows of the other.' I treasured your sweet words in my heart and found them true. So shall you love what my heart loves, and despise what my heart despises. It is so, my love; we both have one soul, and why shall I not tremble when my heart is sad?

How are you, my beloved Tamar? Did your father rebuke you? Did Azrikam annoy you, or are you worrying about your beloved Amnon? But pray, dear one, do not take all this too seriously. Let no grief and sadness reach you, and, if they should come over you, let them pass away like a cloud from your beaming face, for your shining countenance is a source of life and goodness to the oppressed. And I pray to the God of our ancestors that you may be free from all sorrows and that all your burdens may be put upon me, for I am strong and will bear them without a murmur.

Hush, my soul! I hear sickening voices, a strange murmur is audible, a murmur which disturbs the quiet of the night! What can it be? Oh, it is the cries of the captives which fill the streets of Nineveh! My heart cries with them. God had confounded the languages of Nineveh. Some of the captives roar like bears. They yell with broken hearts, 'Oh, how we are conquered!' And their captors, like wild asses, wildly exclaim, 'Behold, we have devoured them!' Again we hear those that curse the day and pull their hair in grief, and call out, 'Oh, calamity and misfortune!' And their oppressors, with pride, repeat, 'Victory, victory!, I see only strange sights and languages that I cannot understand. Some heave deep sighs from their burdened hearts and bemoan their lot in the Egyptian language, and some bewail in the speech of Kedar, Arvad and Raamah.

When I think of Jerusalem, I tremble, and when I think of you, Tamar, my very heart melts. Then I ask myself again, 'What does the roar of nations amount to, and what are their kingdoms? They are only like small insects, like ants, which can be crushed by the foot of man. So these kingdoms must retreat before the God of Jacob, and be silenced forever. It is still night and my soul is still awake. Shall the night last forever? Will it never be daylight? Leave me, ye phantoms of the night! I long for the light! I opened the window of my room and I saw that the morning had already spread its faint light over the mountains. The birds had begun to sing, and with them the morning stars also sang. And my heart rejoiced with them. I wish it would remain so forever. Oh, how sweet it is!

As I sat and mused, the eastern sky became red with the bright morning light. In a short time the rising sun broke forth like a spark of fire on the tops of the heights. Oh, how beautiful is his light, shining over the mountains! And how pleasant is the sun when it shines upon the surface of the Hiddekel, the river which comes from Eden—a pure light, like the light of God which shines upon pure hearts. The sun comes forth like a knight, overcomes the darkness and overwhelms the earth with its glorious light. All the winged creatures sing and praise the might of God, and all creation rejoices that the light overpowered the darkness. The sun rises until, at midday, it stands, worn out, in the middle of the heavens. The birds cease their singing and gradually the sun goes down, the shadows lengthen and the day is gone.

And so is the life of man on earth, and so move the wheels of time. How sweet is the morning dew of his childhood! How pleasant is the light of his youth! All the darkness shuns him and all the hopes dance before him and sing in his ear like the songs of the birds. But, alas, hope remains with him only to his middle age and comforts him like a mother. The man becomes a shadow; only a slight memory remains of his youth, and even that memory leaves him in later years. All his pleasures depart and in his heart is left only a dense darkness, which remains with him day and night.

When I speak of hope my heart shrinks within me. Do you remember, Tamar, my beloved, that first spring day, when I lived in your father's house, when your sweet lips told me, in the presence of Teman, 'Hope, Amnon. Hope is better than life!' What hopes can comfort me? Hope is dear and very comforting to a broken heart, like the rainbow in a clouded sky, but just when a man puts his trust in it, it is shattered. Hopes are like bubbles on the water, which become quite large, but, when you reach for them, they disappear. These hopes are like strong towers, which stand firmly when the elements are at peace, but which totter when the slightest storm arises. Recollect, dear Tamar, that evening of our hopes and distress? We were suddenly separated, and our hopes, alas, where are they? That terrible night ended and another day passed, and then my hopes returned, but, as yet, her ways are a mystery to me. I followed in her path until I reached this place, and now I am undecided where to go.

Already the great light has shown five times over the mountains of this glorious City of Nineveh since I came here, but the sun of hope did not shine upon me to crown my wishes. My eyes are continually searching the streets of Nineveh in the hope of finding Hananeel, and my soul soars towards Jerusalem, where are the sources of my hopes. But as quickly as it soars, it is forced back, because my fears are also there. My soul is like the rushing waters, that can come only to the banks and then flow back. So my soul flies back and forth. Sometimes my soul hovers over the Mount of Olives, and nestles on the olive tree where our names are carved and where our hearts are bound together. 'Behold,' I say to my soul, 'Wait, there are hopes. In vain do the mountains rise between us; they cannot separate us. Even the River Hiddekel and the rivers Prosse and Jordan, and all the great lakes which flow between us, cannot drown our love.' I can still hear your sweet voice which thrills in my ears, and your pure lips sending me peace from afar, saying, 'I am yours.' When I think of those words, my hopes carry me on the wings of love, but soon after, my reason says to me, 'Oh, you foolish creature, do not soar to the heavens! There the eagle and the ossifrage fly. Stay in your humble abode—there you will have peace.' Who will not listen to reason? And if I shall listen to reason, where will my hopes be? And so my thoughts continually turn in my mind, like the flaming sword which turned every day, to keep the way of the tree of life. And my soul is like the river which comes out of Eden and never returns. And my heart, oh, my heart, broken and shattered, quivers from the perpetual change from hope to fear when I think of you, my sweet one.

Live in peace, my sweetheart. Wait for me a little longer, and do not give your love to another. Raise thy voice once more, gentle daughter of Zion, and say, 'Hope, Amnon. Hope is better than life.' Say that, my dove, on the Mountain of Zion, and I shall hear thy voice from afar.

The traveling merchant, with whom I came, went to the Island of Mudah. Behold, there are still hopes for me to find there what I am seeking! Would that my travels might end instantly and an unseen hand from above carry me from the smoking mountains of Assyria, the rumbling mounts, to the quiet and peaceful mountains of Zion. Would that I might fall asleep and awake to rejoice in thy presence!

When Tamar finished reading the letter, she joyfully pressed it to her lips and said, "Who can speak of love like Amnon, or who can express his thoughts as he does? Like a divine flame is his love, and his words are like sparks of fire! I do not possess these gifts. Even if my thoughts are very strong within me, I cannot give expression to them. Only my soul, which is within speech, possesses them. Ten thousand words cannot explain one thought of Amnon's love and how I feel towards him. It is not necessary for me to express my feelings, for Amnon gave voice to all my thoughts in his letter."

Thus Tamar soliloquized, when suddenly Teman's words flashed through her mind. She gasped and stood there, pale and trembling, but almost instantly a feeling of perpetual faith replaced her momentary apprehension, and she said, "He will never fail me with his love." Then she read the letter again and again, and carefully studied every word, and found a very few words which she could not satisfactorily explain to herself, such as "So shall you love that which I love." "Can Teman's tale concerning Amnon have any significance? Why, if your heart were as wide as the sea, it should be full only with my love, that there should be no place for any other love. Can another woman have touched thy heart, Amnon? Oh, my heart burns within me when I think of it! But woe is to me and woe is to that stranger! Though my love for you, Amnon, is stronger than death, my jealousy is deeper than the grave. I will crush that stranger and scatter her before the wind of my wrath; and with the storm of my vengeance I will destroy her. Amnon's heart belongs to me, and to me alone. No stranger shall come between us. But why should I let such thoughts worry me? It can never happen."

Tamar was still deep in thought when Macha approached her and said, "Why so absorbed in thought, fair mistress?"

"Advise me, Macha," said Tamar. "How can one test the heart of a lover, as to whether it be true or false?"

"If he raises his eyes to another woman and speaks of love to her, he has broken his pledge to his first love," answered Macha.

"Your advice is very good, Macha, but I have a secret to tell you: I have a letter from Amnon."

Teman's story still rankled in Tamar's mind, and she asked Macha to find out from Peroh all about Amnon's actions during the last few days he was there.

Macha, seeing that Tamar was uncertain about Amnon's truthfulness, tried to awaken a jealousy in Tamar's heart towards Amnon, rejoicing at the opportunity of destroying the love between them, so that in case Amnon returned, she might have Amnon for herself. And she took council with Zimri as to her future course of action, and he advised her to do all the mischief she could towards creating a hatred in Tamar's heart. Then Zimri sent word to Azrikam to meet him at the usual place.

Chapter nineteen

The news of Sennacherib's numerous victories and his approach to Judea created great excitement in Zion. Day by day the tidings were more eagerly looked for.

It was a bright morning and the inhabitants of Zion and the vicinity left their homes and their work, and hurried to the assembly rooms to await the reports of the war council, which was assembled in the presence of the king, as to what should be done to strengthen the city and the fortresses during the siege. Those who could not get within roamed to and fro like locusts, and the habitual idlers, who did not have the slightest idea of the significance of war, mingled with the crowd. The news mongers, who arranged their lies at night, were also there to sell their tidings for drinks. In one corner a crowd gathered in a circle around a man who spoke favourably, with hopes for the nation, saying, "Our king has sent his ambassadors to ask help from Pharaoh. He is our ally and will not refuse us aid."

"In vain we hope for aid from Pharaoh," answered one of

the listeners. "How can the Egyptians help us? They are weak and lazy."

In another part of the square a traveller, returning from across the River Prosse, relates to the crowd which surrounds him the following: "All the roads are deserted. No travelers are to be seen. The lion and the leopard, with their cubs, have come from their hiding places. The terror of nations, with his hosts, is on the march, and with him are the Assyrians and the Illums, carrying their standards. Rawaseka is also with him. His hosts are as mighty and strong as the cedar of Lebanon. Their roots begin at the River Hiddekel and extend to the River Prosse, and they are besieging the fortresses of Carchemish, which are situated where the two rivers, Chebar and Prosse, join, and even these two great fortresses are like toys to them. How can the fortresses of Judea stand against them? In a short time they will cross the river Prosse and the Jordan." All the listeners shook their heads and sighed, "Oh, what fearful tidings! Who will help us in Zion?"

And Hepher and Bukkiah, who were among this crowd, laughed and mockingly said, "Come, let us have some wine and forget our sorrows."

"Come," said Bukkiah, "let those who have money buy wine for those who have none. In a short time people will throw their gold and silver into the streets and no one will even pick it up. Therefore, let us wash our throats with the blood of the grape before the enemy shall wash our feet in the blood of their victims."

"Hush, hush!" someone exclaimed. "The King and Isaiah, the prophet, are approaching." And thereupon the crowd dispersed. And Bukkiah said to Hepher, "Come, let us go to Carmi's and have some wine."

Carmi was a shrewd hypocrite. Outwardly he was very pious but he was the accomplice of all the wicked men in Zion. Even to them he assumed a righteous mien, giving them some excuse for his wrong doings, saying that in all his dealings he never wronged anyone, that he hears and sees everything but says nothing. He exchanged his wine for stolen property and anything which would increase his wealth. His house was a refuge for all those whose actions could not stand the light. So he grew rich and influential. He was seen every morning and evening in the Temple, prostrated in prayer, and was regarded as an honest man. Zimri and Azrikam came to Carmi's house early that same morning as they had planned the previous day. Carmi brought them wine and seated them in a private room. When Carmi left, Azrikam said, "I am sure that you bring good news."

"Do you know that all my strivings are for your welfare?" said Zimri. "Do not relinquish Tamar yet; there is still hope. You shall know, my lord, that Amnon sent a letter to Tamar from Nineveh—a very ardent love letter. She read it to Macha, who told me all about it. I taught her how to conspire with Peroh to change Amnon's sweet words to gall and wormwood. She succeeded, and kindled the fire of jealousy in the heart of her mistress. You know that Peroh is one of your accomplices, and with his falsehoods he made Tamar believe that Amnon loves another girl. Now she is consumed with a mighty feeling of revenge."

"I am exceedingly glad, Zimri, that we are both on the same track. Listen! What I tell you will correspond exactly with your words. That tale in regard to Amnon knowing another girl is not idle talk. Amnon is in love with another, and it is true. I heard it from Uchon. He noticed that I have been rather downcast of late and he came into my room yesterday, and said to me, 'How long are you going to bemoan Tamar, who despises you? Is she the only one in Zion?' And I asked him whether he thought I could see Tamar given to another and not feel downhearted, and he said to me, 'Tamar is not the only one whom Amnon loves. He has found another girl, who is even more beautiful than Tamar, whom he would not exchange for seven like Tamar, but she is poor. Therefore, Amnon went in search of Hananeel in order to get rich, so you outwit him and become betrothed to that beautiful girl. I am sure that you will cease thinking of Tamar when once you have seen her.' I asked Uchon where the girl was and he told me that within ten days she would return with her mother from the boundary of Judea, where she is at present, and I could see her then."

"I wonder how Uchon knows all this," said Zimri. "But what

is the difference? I know that there is no other girl than the one who lived with her mother at the gate of the valley. Teman is also in love with this same girl, and he was refused by her mother, and since then he walks about like a shadow. Now you can rejoice! The devil himself could not have planned anything better. I will prepare a hell for Amnon, Tamar and Teman. Let Amnon come back and I will crush him to the ground. Oh, I am satisfied with myself! I have the whole plan in my mind. Now, let us wait until the girl returns and Amnon comes back from Assyria."

As they were talking, Hepher and Bukkiah noisily entered Carmi's place, and Hepher said to Carmi, "We have heard so much bad news from afar that we came here to drown our sorrows in your wine." Carmi, knowing that Zimri, a very pious man, was in the other room, bade Hepher and Bukkiah make less noise, so that Zimri should not think that he kept a disorderly place, and he said to them, "This is no time to rejoice."

Hepher looked scornfully at Carmi and said sarcastically, "What is the matter today, Carmi? Have you a preacher here to preach about the drinking laws?"

"I will tell you the law," said Bukkiah to Carmi. "Listen and understand. You and I are empty people and your casks are full of wine. We will empty your casks into us; then we will be full and the casks empty. Is that not so?"

"Never mind," said Carmi. "Sit down and drink."

"Someone must be in that room," remarked Hepher, "and I must see who it is. I am going to look into every room and see who is there, come what may."

Carmi put his hand on Hepher's shoulder and lowering his voice, said, "Azrikam and Zimri are in that room."

Bukkiah laughed aloud and said, "Why, they are good people. We know them. They will buy us wine."

Azrikam heard and recognised their voices, and opening the door, invited them into the private room. Upon entering Hepher and Bukkiah noticed Zimri, deep in thought, intent upon the wine before him. He did not raise his eyes as they entered, and Hepher said, "Your thoughts are deep in the wine, as if you would like to find in the wet juice of the grape your schemes that you lose when you are dry, or as if you would like to fish out news which has not yet been created."

"You told the truth," replied Zimri, emptying his glass. "Old and new secrets are hidden in that red beverage, and they are very profitable if kept secret."

Then Bukkiah interrupted, "There is a peculiar element in wine. We drink it in secret and the results are manifest to the public. As soon as the wine penetrates us, it revolutionizes our whole system, and all our secrets, which should be buried, rise as if on wings to our lips. Surely it is God's curse."

"What great secrets have you?" asked Azrikam. "Are you afraid that your secrets will take wing and fly from you like birds? We give you wine to drown your secrets, but when you drink to excess they come to your lips and burst from you like a bottle when the wine in it ferments, and your secrets are exposed."

"It is not so with me," answered Bukkiah. "It is true that my soul dwells among these casks and my heart is united with the juice of the grape since my youth, but with all this I am a trustworthy man. But why speak of such idle things? Lazy hands and foolish words will never bring success. You had better call for wine and the best that Carmi's house affords. If trouble and sadness turn our hair gray, a goblet of wine will renew our youth."

And Azrikam did as Bukkiah suggested, ordering Carmi to bring in some wine, and Hepher called to Carmi, who took the order, "Be careful and see that you bring honest measures."

"Long live the King Hezekiah," said Bukkiah. "Since he is on the throne our drinks are not adulterated and our measures are honest and full, and we are not cheated. Yesterday the city officers searched the house of Izhor, the Carmelite, and they found adulterated wine and false measures. They broke all his casks, put him in custody and confiscated the wine. So you see, Carmi, that you will have to look out for yourself or you will suffer. They will treat you as they did the Carmelite."

"Very well," answered Carmi. "Fill yourselves with wine but do not fill yourselves with nonsense. Joking does no good nowadays."

"Now, be quick, you honest man," said Hepher. "Do your work quickly before Sennacherib besieges our land."

Carmi brought the wine and they drank to intoxication, and Bukkiah, feeling in excellent humour after the wine, sang the following drinking song:

> *How nice are our inflamed faces,*
> *Like the red fluid from the blood of the grape;*
> *Good wine tastes sweet to its drinkers,*
> *It burns in us like a river of flame.*
> *But with its deluge it drowns sorrows,*
> *It is called Noah's water—he was the father of it.*
>
> *We take too much upon us, eating a mourner's meal,*
> *Walking downcast in this great city,*
> *And fearing misfortune from the south;*
> *We are safe in this chosen day,*
> *Why worry for the morrow when today is good?*
> *Drink today, the earth may cover us tomorrow.*

"I always said that," Bukkiah broke in, "—eat and drink, for tomorrow we may die. A man who wants to live shall not trouble himself about the past, and should not even think of the future, but should live only for the present day and keep it fresh with drinking."

"I see that the wine has imparted its spirits to you," said Hepher. "You drank sweets and your lips are uttering sweet words."

"I am speaking the truth," answered Bukkiah. "I wish that I were appointed to comfort the people in these troublous days. Who would not listen to me?"

"That is true. The times are troublous," said Carmi. "But what good will it bring to become discouraged? The city is our stronghold; it will protect us in the day of siege. Its walls are strong, and its towers reach the very clouds. When Sennacherib's hosts come and see our strength, our fortresses and our mines, they will be ashamed of their own strength. Why, our ambassadors are in Egypt, and we sent messengers there to bring horses and chariots, and, besides, we have our own ammunition. We will equip ourselves. We are good soldiers and God will help us!"

And Zimri, who was quietly listening to the conversation, drained his goblet and said to Carmi, "Your wine is not diluted but your words are somewhat mixed. Jerusalem's stronghold can only protect the swallows. The nation is not strong. We have nothing to depend upon in time of trouble. You are all brave men when you sit here with your wine before you, but when you see the flash of the swords and the glitter of the javelin and spear, you will be struck dumb and be unfit to meet the enemy. You can boast of your bravery to people who do not know, but you cannot tell me such things, for I know. I have seen the misery when I was in Samaria, during the siege of Shalmaneser. No, my friends, you cannot make war against the Assyrians with mere words."

"Woe!" cried Bukkiah, with a sigh. "Sennacherib has conquered so many nations and plundered their wealth! He attempts to swallow our peaceful dwellings. Has he not enough wine in Assyria that he comes here to drink up our wine and consume our grapes? Oh, Assyria is like Death, whose desire for souls is insatiable!"

"Be quiet," said Zimri with a laugh. "Do not fret. Let us make a covenant with death that he may not cut us off from the juice of the grape."

"I swear by God," said Bukkiah, "that no man shall leave this room until he tells us all that he knows about the pending calamities, and I know that you, Zimri, hear all the news in your master's house and in other places which you frequent. So tell us, so that we, too, may know."

"If you will swear to me that you will not disclose the facts until the right time comes, I will tell you," said Zimri.

"May our wine and our juice turn to gall if we divulge the secrets," Bukkiah swore with great solemnity.

"I can depend upon you," said Zimri. "Therefore, listen to me, my friends. Though I am a Samaritan and have no property nor friends in Zion, my heart bleeds within me at the sight of Zion's disaster. In vain does the son of Amos comfort the people with his eloquence and false visions. He soothes them as a mother soothes her little one to sleep, with gentle lullabies. Let us not listen to him; we may fall asleep never to awaken. He who is anxious for life should listen to Shebna; at least his life will be safe. Shebna takes another view of the matter. He advocates peace with the king of Assyria and that will insure freedom to all. But it is no time to talk. I told you one thing, and you will hear two things after the effects of the wine are gone."

"May Shebna's plan succeed," said Azrikam.

"Therefore," said Zimri, "let us not neglect to support Shebna, because he is at war with the king, but we must keep it secret until later developments."

They all swore secrecy, and Zimri left, returning to his work. Then Azrikam said to Hepher and Bukkiah, "I am young yet, but you were men in the reign of Ahaz, when our forefathers, by means of secrecy and witchcraft, obtained their knowledge about the destiny of nations. But we stand here like fawns in the ruins of Jerusalem, and grope like the blind in darkness and know not which way to turn. All that we have to look to are the prophecies of the son of Amos. I wish that I knew some sorcerer. I would pay him well to tell me what will become of Zion and about my own destiny."

"Listen to what happened to me about four months ago," said Hepher. "I was walking in the outskirts one evening, and I saw among the bushes a heavily veiled woman and a girl—the most beautiful girl I have ever seen in my life. I asked them where they were going, and the woman answered, 'I came to Jerusalem from Beersheba, and my daughter asked me to show her the city.' But while I was speaking, I saw a man approach and, fearing to be suspected, I walked away. The women ran among the bushes, like a hind and roe of the field. I cannot forgive myself for leaving them; they must be witches."

"Look for them in the city and if you find them, let me know," said Azrikam. And with that they separated, each going to his own home.

Chapter twenty

Two months had passed and Tamar had not received another letter from Amnon. Since Amnon left, Tamar went into the garden early every morning and poured out her heart to God, and prayed that Amnon should be sent back to her in safety, with a pure heart and pure in his love for her. One day, as Tamar was absorbed in her devotions, her maid, Macha, approached her and said, "Do not be surprised, my lady, if I tell you that Amnon and Hananeel have arrived and are now in this house.'

"Amnon! Hananeel!" exclaimed Tamar with mingled fear and joy, and, with heart beating violently, she rushed past Macha and into the house. As she excitedly opened the door, a most touching picture met her gaze. In the embrace of a venerable old man, with snowy white hair and a slightly bent though powerful frame, Tamar saw her mother and heard these thrilling words, "Oh, father, father! Source of my life!" Turning from this scene she saw another and no less enchanting picture: There, with his arms outstretched, stood Yedidiah, waiting for Amnon to come to his arms and receive his blessing. "Oh!" exclaimed Yedidiah, "I have seen that which I have never expected! Truly, it is a miracle!"

Tamar was so overwhelmed with joy and surprise that she stood on the threshold, motionless and speechless. Teman and Zimri were also present, and they, too, were too bewildered to break the silence. At last Tamar exclaimed, "Oh, joy of my soul!"

Then Yedidiah went to Tamar and, taking her by the hand, led her to Hananeel and said, "Behold, my father, your daughter Tamar." Hananeel embraced Tamar and Yedidiah, and said, "In return, you behold your son Amnon, my ransomer and my heir. Oh, happiness, my dream came true to the letter! Amnon has accomplished great things with your daughter, and still greater with me. Therefore, his honors shall be in accordance with his deeds."

"Yes," said Tirzah, "Amnon has done great things for us, and great were the insults he received at our hands. Now we are helpless. We are hardly able to ask his forgiveness." Tears gathered in her eyes as she spoke.

Yedidiah embraced Amnon, saying, "Forgive me, my son. I did not understand your ways, and therefore used unkind words to you. Now, renew your love for Tamar and woo her. The dream is realized. Now, you know that a covenant exists between Yoram and me, and I cannot break it. Therefore, ask Hananeel, for Tamar is his daughter, and he will willingly grant his consent."

Tamar was still as if in a dream and Amnon approached her with these words, "See, my beloved, there is your father, Hananeel. I have kept my promise, and have ransomed him and brought him to your presence."

Tamar awoke from her amazement and said, "Oh, my light and life! You have returned the parents back to their children."

Hananeel took Amnon's hand and said, "We have brought with us all the treasures which I had hidden in Samaria, and today I give them all to Amnon, as a reward for my release. Now I am poor, and Amnon is one of the wealthiest lords of Jerusalem; and in addition I give him Tamar, in return for the services he rendered her." He joined their hands, addressing these words to Tamar, "Here is the handsome youth who risked his life to release me, for the sake of your love. His birth is a mystery, but through you and through the big heart which he possesses, he will gain more than family honour. Now, my son Amnon, Tamar loves you, and twice have you risked your life for her; therefore, let her heart be dear to you, and you shall not take other wives beside her. Drink together from the cup of pleasure to your hearts' desire, and let not a stranger come between you."

"Tamar is the only one to her parents and so she shall be to me—always alone and beloved forever and ever," answered Amnon.

And Tamar, sanctioning his words, repeated after him, "Forever and ever will I be yours. Dearly have you purchased me." A stream of tears rolled down her cheeks as she spoke.

And Tirzah said to Amnon, "Now everything is at an end. Tamar is yours. Take her into the garden and speak to her. She is still as if in a dream."

Amnon went to Teman and embraced him, and he cordially greeted Zimri, who was standing near. Then taking Tamar's arm, he walked with her from the room. When they reached the garden, Amnon said, "Now, my beloved, the dream has passed and we see its interpretation. Let the brightness return to your fair cheeks, for in them I see life."

"Would to God that your heart may always be as faithful as it is today," answered Tamar.

"Do you still doubt my sincerity?" asked Amnon. "Do you not yet know that I am ready to stake my life for you? I will throw myself among the wild beasts and encounter any danger for your sake. On you alone my life depends. Your advice I will follow all my life. By the living God, do I swear it!" He kissed her tenderly, and Tamar returned the caress. She took the letter which he had written and showed it to him, and said, "I did not part with this letter, because I trusted you, and I will always believe your words to be true." And Tamar ceased thinking of Teman's words about Amnon, and had implicit trust and belief in everything he did or said. And so they spent their time in happiness until they were called to the midday meal. When the wine was served, Amnon refused, saying, "I have vowed to God to be a Nazarite for thirty days from that day on which my feet touched the soil of Zion."

"After the thirty days of your vow shall have passed," said Hananeel, "we will rejoice on your wedding day."

Macha felt sick at heart when she saw that the low-born Amnon had risen to such a height—rich, and Tamar's husband, and she had no hope of ever being even his concubine. Burning with jealousy, she went the next day to Yedidiah and told him that Amnon was false in his love for Tamar and that Teman knew that he fell in love with another girl, after he had pledged his love for Tamar. Yedidiah questioned Teman about the matter and Teman told him what he had heard from Peroh and that he knew where the meeting place was. Yedidiah was very much discomforted and surprised, and bade Teman say nothing to anyone until he himself had looked into the matter more closely. Yedidiah also commanded Teman to return Peroh to Amnon, as a servant, and tell him to watch all Amnon's actions and report to Macha, who in turn should indirectly tell Tamar. "If," said Yedidiah, "suspicion should strengthen and Tamar break with him, then I will give her to Azrikam as I have promised, and Amnon will have no right to complain, for it will be his own fault. Until then, act friendly to Amnon, and do not let him see that you suspect him."

The next day Yedidiah said to Amnon, "I have made arrangements for building a house for you on the Mount of Olives, in the same place where you and Tamar pledged your love together. Now, you stay in your summer house until the wedding, so that you can superintend the work and hasten the completion of it." Amnon consented and that same day he moved into the summer house.

Peroh took up his position again as Amnon's servant. Amnon kept him busy, sending presents and sweets every day to his beloved Tamar. Tamar also sent Amnon many little tokens of her love for him. During the time that Amnon lived in the summer house, he sent word to Sisry, telling him of his return from Assyria. Impatiently he waited for the end of the thirty days. In all this time, Peroh noticed nothing to attract his attention, and so twenty-seven days passed. On that night, Uze came to tell Amnon that Avicha was very sick and his brother, Sisry, of Carmel, was there, and he expected to see Amnon's wedding. When Uze left the room, Amnon followed him, as he noticed that Uze wanted to tell him something that he did not want Peroh to hear. When out of hearing of Peroh, Uze said, "Come tomorrow night to the same little hut, and there you will see what your heart mostly wishes, but be careful that no one sees you." Amnon rewarded Uze liberally and waited for the morrow with impatience, for he knew that he would then see his mother and sister again.

Then next morning Zimri went to meet Azrikam at the bank of the river. On his way thither he passed the monument of Absalom, which was near the hill on the north side of Jerusalem, and he saw one of the prophets standing there, talking as follows: "Oh, wicked children, come here! You conspirators, come and see! Look at Absalom and take a moral lesson. There is warning to all who raise their hands against their parents! They shall have an end as he had. Who is the father of this nation? The king! And who is the wicked son? Shebna, the counterpart of Absalom! Oh, you disobedient son, forgetful of God and God's anointed! Woe is to you! You are conspiring and you will receive your punishment, and, like Absalom, you will die lonely and forgotten, between heaven and earth. Absalom, with his own hand, prepared for himself that monument during his life, and you also are making yourself a name which will end in your grave. God will shift you to another land. Absalom died hanging on a branch of a tree, and you in God's curse shall dwell as Isaiah prophesied."

These words penetrated through Zimri like an arrow from a bow. He stopped and addressed the prophet with these words, "Why do you waste your words on the birds and trees? Are there no people in Zion? Have they no ears for your words?"

"They are like grass," answered the prophet, "like dry grass, which will burn like fire with the words of God. Their ears are hard of hearing; therefore, it is better to talk to the desert where there are no people, than to talk in the city to people who are not human."

"You are insane, you high spirited man," said Zimri.

"It may be because I tell the truth," answered the prophet, and walked away.

And Zimri stood, thinking over the words of the prophet, when Azrikam approached and said, "What do you say today Zimri? The feeder of sheep has become a lord, and the lord has become a feeder of false hopes."

"You are always feeding false hopes. It is no wonder, therefore, that you are so easily discouraged," answered Zimri.

"Why, how can I help it?" said Azrikam. "I want you to know now that I live only in the hope of revenge; that gives me life. It is not enough that Tamar has thrown me over as an unworthy wretch and has raised the low-born Amnon and given him her love, but Amnon himself chases me like an unmerciful angel upon all my ways! Listen to what happened to me, and you will be surprised yourself: At noon yesterday, Uchon took me to that beautiful girl whom Amnon fell in love with before he was betrothed to Tamar. As we entered the hut at the gate of the valley, we found her sitting with her mother, working at some embroidery. What shall I tell you about that girl, Zimri? I can tell you this—that if Tamar is as beautiful as the moon, this girl shines like the sun! As soon as I saw her, I fell in love with her and I wooed her in the presence of her mother, and told her that I would raise her from poverty to make her mistress of my palace. The girl glanced only once at me and then she continued her sewing, and never spoke a word to me. I said to her, 'Do you know who I am? I am the son of Lord Yoram, and I wish to make you happy. Why should you refuse me?' But the girl still kept silent. Then her mother said, 'You will forgive her. She is not accustomed to speaking to men and specially to a lord like you, even if you lower yourself to speak of love to her, but—' I did not let her finish, and I said, 'I know the reason why your daughter has no word for me. She believes in the love of the shepherd, Amnon, the pretender. Know, then, that he swore to Yedidiah that he would not have any other wives besides his daughter, Tamar.' As I mentioned Amnon's name, both mother and daughter cried out bitterly and trembled, and the mother said to me, 'May God punish me and my daughter if I give my daughter to Amnon for a wife! Now, give her a month's time to consider your proposal. If I can obtain a satisfactory answer, I shall then let you know.' 'You can take her word,' answered Uchon. 'She is a truthful woman.'

"So I left the hut with a better heart. At night I went again and alone, and I saw a light in the house. I did not have the courage to enter, so I stood under the window and peeked in. How great was my astonishment to see Amnon embracing and kissing the girl, and she hanging on his neck, with tears in her eyes, and her mother embracing each of them in succession! My heart stopped beating, my eyes became dim and my ears wearied of the sound of their kisses, and I thought to myself, 'Is that most beautiful, innocent girl, who was afraid to talk in the presence of a man?' I told them, though, that Amnon is a charlatan, but that did not alter the girl's feelings towards him. Evidently she would rather become his concubine than his wife. My feet shook under me and my heart told me to burn the house with its inmates, but I ground my teeth and resisted the temptation. When I came home I told Uchon about it, and he said to me, 'Do not be so hasty. If I do not bring that girl to your house, you may turn me out of your sight forever.'

"But how can that help me? I have seen it with my own eyes! That pretender, Amnon, stands like Satan in all my paths. Oh, Zimri, if my heart were as cold as ice, it would burst with sparks of fire! If milk and honey would flow in my veins, they would turn to gall and wormwood. I have suffered enough disgrace and pain from Amnon. Now he even wants my life! We cannot both live on! One of us must perish; the other can enjoy life."

Zimri started as if from a sleep when Azrikam finished speaking, and said, "Tamar has taken a serpent into her house to play with, but he bit her so badly that there is no cure. Now, my lord, the time is ripe for my schemes and I will speed my work. Every second that is delayed counts for a day. In a very short time, you will see the great flame which will consume Amnon, Teman, Tamar, and the strange girl. And if you want one of these two girls, I will rescue her as a cinder from the fire."

"Do not sell the leopard's skin before it is caught," said Azrikam.

"That is so," answered Zimri. "But leave it to me this time. There is not a moment to lose." And he left Azrikam, to do his wicked work.

Chapter twenty-one

I n the afternoon of the same day, Tamar was sitting in her room, joyful and contented. She was humming a love song, from sheer joy at the near approach of her wedding day, as she put the finishing stitches in a cap which she intended to present to Amnon on her wedding day.

Macha busied herself about the room, arranging her mistress's jewelry and finery. In her evil heart there lurked only mischief, and, in order to attract Tamar's attention, she sighed heavily. Nor did she fail in her little strategy, for Tamar, so happy herself that she could not imagine how anyone else could be sad, turned and asked in surprise, "What is the matter, Macha? Why do you sigh?"

Macha sadly shook her head and said, "How can I take part in your joy when it passes like a shadow? It just came and has already flown, and a deep mourning takes its place."

"Cease your foolishness," answered Tamar.

"Yes, I know I am only a poor, foolish servant, but my heart knows, through signs that have never failed, that certain things will happen. It is already three nights in succession that I heard a crow cawing on our roof, and it is an undisputed fact that this bird portends evil tidings. And, alas, my forebodings have come true! Oh, my young lady, I am compelled to acquaint you with the evil which is in store for you, for I cannot keep it any longer! I have done as you bade me: I questioned Peroh concerning Amnon's actions, and he told me that he secretes himself with witches."

A gloomy darkness overspread Tamar's face when she heard these words, and she cried out, "Merciful God, turn thy gracious help upon me, and let Macha's words be false!"

"I, too, was astonished upon hearing of that outrageous act," answered Macha.

Tamar trembled and asked, "Does Peroh know who these witches are and where they live?"

"These witches are two in number—a mother and a daughter. The girl is very beautiful and is a witch. She ensnares innocent young hearts with her beauty. With their witchcraft they have already ruined many families. They are ready for all the outrages that can be committed. Peroh knows their abode, and yesterday he saw Amnon spending a very jolly time there with them. Peroh's first impulse was to save Amnon from these wicked women but he was afraid of his own life, thinking, 'Who can stand up against witches and be in peace?' They are fearful! They have their covenant with the wild beasts of the desert, and the serpents crawl at their feet and harm them not. Even a burning flame cannot consume them and the sharpest sword cannot destroy them. They darken the moon and the stars with their witchcraft at night, when they are at their work. And especially at midnight, when a thick darkness is spread over the quiet earth, these daughters of hell come out of their hiding places and direct their steps to places forgotten by human feet, to places where one cannot look without fear. They go as far as the River Kidron, where all the refuse is thrown, and to the valley of Tophet, where they used to sacrifice their children to Moloch. They remain through the night among the graves, and in secret caves. They bring up the dead from the graves. Woe is even to the eyes which behold this! Let them that curse the day, curse it!"

Tamar grew sick at heart when she heard these words, and embracing Macha said, "Oh, Macha, Macha! Only tell me that you are talking in your sleep, and I will regard you as my sister! Tell me that you are only trying to test my faith in Amnon and that you are speaking falsely, and I will give you all the wealth which my grandfather, Hananeel, gave me! Oh, give me back Amnon, for without him I am poorer than you! But if your words are true, what is Amnon to me?"

Macha sighed and answered, "Woe is me, my lady! I have fulfilled your command and learned this. What unfaithfulness it would be for me to keep it from you! Amnon stealthily left his room yesterday and did not return until this morning; that certainly has some significance. Speak to him, my lady. Maybe he will repent and give up his evil ways."

"Leave me, Macha," said Tamar, clasping her hands. "Let me be alone, and I will bemoan my lot in loneliness until I shall see for myself the misfortune which is to befall me. My calamity is as great as the mighty ocean. This night shall be a night of watchfulness, to watch Amnon's steps, and let what may become of me. Tell Peroh to let me know as soon as Amnon leaves his room tonight, but say nothing to my parents."

Macha left her mistress as she was bidden. Then Tamar told her misfortunes to her brother, and Teman, full of wrath and excitement, said, "I am ready to go with you and see the outrage that is going on in the house at the gate of the valley!"

Darkness had enveloped the earth, and Peroh came to the window of Tamar's room where Macha, as arranged, was waiting for him. Macha, upon receiving the news, went to her mistress and said, "Come, my lady; do not delay. Amnon has just left his room and is hastening away." At the same time, Tamar's mother entered the room, and upon seeing tears in Tamar's eyes, asked, "What is the matter, my child? Why do you weep?"

Tamar quickly made excuses for her tears by saying, "Amnon was just here and is very sad because of Avicha's illness. That is why there are tears in my eyes, mother dear. I was about ready to go with Teman to Avicha, so that I might comfort Amnon in his grief."

Tirzah, who anticipated all Tamar's wishes, did not wait for her to ask permission to go with Teman to Avicha, but said, "Certainly, my daughter, you shall go. I will have the carriage ready for you, and you and Teman need not walk."

Teman bade Peroh, who did the driving, go to the gate of the valley. When they were about two hundred feet from the hut, Teman said, "Stop here. I will go with Tamar to the hut." Upon reaching the hut, they looked through the shutters. In the room, they saw a beautiful young girl, attired in exquisite silks and embroidery, standing at the right hand of Amnon, like a bride blooming in her glorious beauty. Amnon was bedecking her hands with jewels and putting costly gems in her ears. He gazed upon her with loving pride and stooped to kiss this most beautiful maiden. The girl kissed Amnon in return, and she seemed to be very happy. The mother, seeing this happy picture, went up to them and kissed one and then the other, with joy and contentment written on her countenance.

"Oh, open thy jaws, oh earth, and swallow them!" Tamar hoarsely whispered.

"May the lightning destroy them!" exclaimed Teman in a low voice.

"Come, let us hurry away from here," said Teman, and he took Tamar's hand and dragged her from the window. And Tamar, with trembling feet and leaning on Teman's arm, returned to the carriage. Peroh asked Teman what he had seen, and Teman answered, "I wish that God had not given me sight to see this wickedness of Amnon's."

When they were seated in the carriage, Tamar said, with tears in her eyes, "Can that be my beloved Amnon?"

"Oh," said Teman, "yes, that is thy lover, Amnon, who is in love with another, who blooms at his side like the rose of Carmel, but you are destined to wither away."

"Woe is me, my brother! God has turned against me this night and he has shattered me. A fire burns within my breast!"

"Oh, this terrible night," groaned Teman. "Let darkness seize upon it and let it not see the dawning of the day. This night, like a reptile, has swallowed all Amnon's good qualities and has destroyed the brotherly love which existed between us."

"Oh, miserable calamity," wailed Tamar. "This night will turn my days into nights, and even the light of midday will be dark to me. I have seen the bright morning star fall from the heights of heaven to the depths of hell! Oh, if I could only release him from that hell! If I could only make that hell a paradise for him! But, alas, who can get good from evil?"

In the midst of these moanings and wailings, the carriage stopped at their house. After sending Peroh away with the horses, Teman instructed Tamar what to tell their mother about their supposed visit. When they came into the house, Tirzah said, "What is it, my children? Why are you so changed?"

And Tamar answered, "Oh, mother, a misfortune has befallen me! A witch has frightened me so! She said to me in Teman's presence, 'Beware, my young girl! A calamity will befall you if you marry the young man whom you love.' And with these words she disappeared. Do you not think, mother, that she must have been a witch?"

"Oh, stop talking such nonsense!" said her mother. "Go lie down and sleep, and that evil vision will pass. And do not grieve Amnon with your tale tomorrow. Azrikam must have hired the woman to scare you." Tirzah tried to persuade Tamar to get the vision from her mind, but Tamar, knowing the bitter truth, could not be comforted, and she spent a tearful and sleepless night.

Chapter twenty-two

I t was the day before Tamar's wedding. The morning was very bright and Macha awoke Tamar, who had just fallen asleep after a very restless night, with these words, "Awake, my lady! The sun is already high in the heavens!"

"But my sun has already set," answered Tamar, with tears in her eyes. "Tomorrow the sun should brighten my wedding day, but, alas, it will be a day of darkness for me."

"No doubt you will be surprised to hear that Amnon is here waiting for you. He is talking with your grandfather in his room," said Macha.

Tamar groaned and said, "Oh, destroyer of my life! But tell me, Macha, did you ever see such a handsome and perfect young man? If all the maidens in Judah should see him, each and everyone of them would fall in love with him. When I am with him, I cannot take my eyes from his face. My heart is interwoven with his. How can I turn him away from me? How can I bear to part from him? Oh, Lord, my God, God of my strength, harden my heart like a rock, so that

I can talk to him harshly and send him away from me!" But after a moment's hesitation, she exclaimed, "No, no! He acts cunningly false to me and I will do likewise. Go tell him, Macha, that I will be ready to see him in a few minutes." Then Tamar arose and, making a very elaborate toilet and assuming a bright and happy countenance, went downstairs to meet her lover.

When Amnon entered the room, he said, "Are you well, my love? Did you spend a restful night?"

"Oh, it was a long night for me," answered Tamar.

"Only one more night," said Amnon, with a happy smile on his countenance, "and then you will call me husband and I will call you wife. Then I may kiss you in the presence of everyone without blushing." With these words he kissed her tenderly on the lips.

Tamar's face turned deathly pale and she said, "Your lips, Amnon, burn like fire. Is it only for that purpose that you came here so early this morning?"

"If it is a trifle for you," answered Amnon, "not so is it to me. It is of great concern to me, because I love you a thousand times more than you love me. The real purpose of my early call, however, is this: I swore to you that I would do nothing without your knowledge and consent; therefore, I came to ask you whether I might go to Bethlehem today, to see my foster-father, Avicha, who is very ill."

"Will you always keep your oath as you have kept it until today?" asked Tamar.

"I swear by God," answered Amnon, "that I shall always fulfill your wishes."

"Therefore," said Tamar, "I will ask one favour of you, because I loved you until today—leave my father's house! Leave the land of Judah, so that in three days you will be far away from here!"

"Oh, Tamar," exclaimed Amnon, with a quivering voice, "are these your words, my beloved, my dove?"

"I am not your dove nor your beloved any more," answered Tamar. "I am your foe. I do not love you any longer. I was false to you. I repent that I did not listen to my father's words. I have changed my mind and I am going to renew my covenant with my first lover. I am going to be the wife of Yoram's son. You see, Amnon, I am a false and wicked girl. Despise me! I am not worthy of your love!"

"Tamar! Tamar!" said Amnon, in amazement. "Do not trifle in such a serious manner. My life depends upon it." Then he became speechless with wonder and doubting. Regaining his composure, he began to laugh and said, "I am ashamed of myself, Tamar, to think that I believed your joke for a moment. Your lips and your eyes do not agree. Your lips utter very bitter words, but your loving eyes still look at me in the same way—full of love. I know that you will comfort me in another moment. Oh, speak to me, loving Tamar, as you used to! Why did you choose to speak to me in this way to torture me?"

He took Tamar's hand in his, but she hastily withdrew it and said, "That is enough, Amnon; not another word. Remember what I told you and remember your oath. Now, leave me and do not mention one word to my parents. Remember, I command you!" And with these words, she turned and left the room.

"Oh, arrows of the Almighty!" cried Amnon, with a wildly beating heart. "Oh, desolation and destruction! Who will comfort me in my loneliness?"

Amnon left the room, frightened, broken in spirit and downcast. He hurried from the house, so that no one should notice his troubled countenance. His heart was like a stone, his eyes were dim and his feet shook under him. He had to exert all his strength in order to reach his house. He went into his room and fell among the pillows, he wept bitterly. Then he arose and paced the room like one who is insane. Then he stopped suddenly and said, "It cannot be true! It is only one fearful dream! Either I must have been dreaming or Tamar must have been dreaming when she spoke to me. Or it may be that she is trying to ascertain how strong my love is for her. What shall I say! Tamar commanded me to leave and wander in a strange and distant land. I swore to fulfill her wishes. Oh, if I could only unburden my heart to Hananeel, but, alas, I will have to bear my lot in silence!"

In the afternoon of the same day, Tamar sent for Zimri. He came into the garden, and when Tamar approached him, he said,

"What is it, my fair lady? You look so pale and so downcast at a time when you should be joyful and happy."

"I have always found you trustworthy," said Tamar. "Therefore, I sent for you to tell you my troubles, and I hope you will keep them a secret from my parents."

"Your secrets are sacred to me and shall never pass my lips, most gracious lady."

"Therefore," said Tamar, "be astounded to hear of my misfortune. That good lad, Amnon, whom I love like the apple of my eye and who is betrothed to me, has become wicked and was led astray by witches."

"Do not say that, my lady," said Zimri, wonderingly. "Do not jest with me. Surely a young man like Amnon will not do such things."

"In vain you try to comfort me," said Tamar. "No one told me about it. Alas, I saw it with my own eyes. Cursed be the night which has swallowed all my joyous days, and cursed shall be the witches who entangled such a dear lad in their net! Oh, Zimri, the arrows of the Almighty have struck me! Eden has been turned into a desolate waste. And with all this, my heart is undecided between hate and mercy on Amnon or to flee from him and hate him. Woe is to me! A war rages in my heart between love and hatred, jealousy and mercy, for Amnon's love has become so deeply rooted in my heart that I cannot uproot it without breaking my heart in twain. In my wrath I sent him from my sight this morning. Now my anger has subsided and my better feelings awoke within me, and I reasoned thus: Whom have I despised to cast away? Amnon, my only treasure in the world. What am I without him, and what is the world to me without his presence? Oh, Zimri, have mercy on me! You know what is taking place in my heart. Bring Amnon back to me!"

Zimri clasped his hands and said, "My heart cries for both of you. Oh, how suddenly your love was cut off and separated you!" He put his handkerchief to his eyes to wipe his tears. He was like a whale, which, when it is about to swallow a man, begins with his feet, and, finding the head difficult to swallow, groans and forces tears to his eyes. Just so were Zimri's tears and his bemoaning of Amnon.

"I will ask a great favour of you, Zimri. Spend one sleepless night for me and talk to Amnon. Do not be harsh with him. Speak to him like a father. Perhaps he will turn from his wicked ways and he will not break the covenant of our love."

"If the fear of God is not too far from his heart, that will bring him back to you," said Zimri. "And if he will listen to my moral advice, he will return and be the lord of our youth."

"May God favour him," said Tamar, "and so will I favour him. Then he will once more gain my heart with more strength and with more love."

Chapter twenty-three

That was a miserable day for Amnon, who could not reconcile himself to his abrupt dismissal. He spent the day in brooding over the events and did not touch a morsel of food, and it was in this condition that Uze found him when he came at twilight. Uze was very much surprised to see Amnon looking so depressed on the day before the wedding, and in wonderment he said, "Why, what has happened to you, Amnon? You look as though you were entirely broken down. You seem worried and exhausted, as if some great calamity has befallen you."

"Tamar has cast me down as suddenly as she raised me," answered Amnon, with a groan. Then he related to Uze all that had taken place that day.

"I told you before not to try to catch the stork. It soars too high," said Uze. "You were like a swallow that builds its nest over the window of a dwelling, unmindful of the fact that any change in the elements or the hand of man could easily destroy it in its unsheltered place. I told you to find a girl of your own station, and marry her and be happy, but you did not listen to me. Tamar only deceived you, and you, like a simpleton, believed her. You want to live in Zion among the nobles, whose ways you never knew. These nobles have no God in their hearts and they have no pity on their fellow-men. If Tamar had only one spark of God's fear in her heart, she would not have turned to be so cruel to you."

"Why, before I knew her, you praised her beauty and her righteousness before me," said Amnon.

"But you see how changeable these people are," said Uze. "The righteousness is only a mask by which they obtain praise, and they change it as their fancy leads them. She has shown love for you all the time and now, all of a sudden, she inflicts agonizing pain upon you. You had better cease chasing her, for you will fall into the pit before you. Forget you ever loved her, and pluck her from your memory and your heart."

"Stop, stop!" exclaimed Amnon. "I might forget my right arm, but Tamar I could never forget!"

The entrance of Zimri interrupted the conversation, but suddenly Uze exclaimed, "Why, I have almost forgotten the purpose of my visit! My master, Avicha, is very ill and wants to see you."

Upon the departure of Uze, Zimri said, "Peace be with you."

"I am far from being at peace," Amnon sadly answered.

"I know of your trouble and have therefore come to comfort you. Oh, what times are approaching! There is terrible news in the city. All day I have been studying the situation, and this evening I went into the city to see what was going on and a fearful scene met my sight. Anxiety and fear were written on every face. A subdued excitement pervaded the city. Most of the wealthy people are preparing to leave the city before it is besieged. Some of them are going to seek shelter on the distant islands of Greece, and others are going to the shores of Zidon and Tyrus to take ship to Tarshish. When I returned home I found no peace there, either. Such a terrible change has taken place! I heard that Tamar had rejected you and has decided to marry her first lover, Azrikam. I tried to persuade her in your favour, recounting to her all the noble acts you had done to her and to her father's house. I even chided her and told her that she was wrong. She scolded me and said, 'Who made you an adviser and a teacher of morals in my father's house? You are already too long in our house.' I was astonished to hear her talk that way, for she was always so amiable and kind to everyone. That is why I came here, to ask you whether you committed any wrong against her."

"By God I swear I am innocent! Tamar turned me out today and commanded me to wander in strange lands. I must do her bidding. I will leave behind me the land of life and go to a deserted land," answered Amnon, with bitter tears.

Zimri shook his head and continued, "Do not weep, Amnon. Your grief makes my heart ache and your tears cause mine to fall. If both of us give way to our feelings, what counsel can I give you? Stop crying, therefore, and let us talk the matter over and see what course we should pursue."

Amnon wiped away his tears, and said, "Let me hear your advice, Zimri, for I cannot gather my thoughts together."

And Zimri began, "Most of the misfortunes and troubles befall young people by falling too hastily in love, and especially when the parties are of different positions in life. I hinted to you several times, thinking that you would understand me, but you did not comprehend. I saw the end of the beginning, because I had known Tamar since she was a little girl. As much as she is kind and gentle, so much is she stiff-necked. She always made the life of her parents bitter, long before you ever met her. She always loved what her parents despised, and what they praised she scorned. She hated Azrikam because her parents loved him, and now that they love you, she hates you. She is very fickle minded. But that is not the end of what she is going to do to you; she will find new reasons for accusing you. Do you know why she acts thus? Because her parents favoured you. I wish that her parents would despise you; then Tamar would instantly go to your side. I am telling the truth when I say that she has no heart. In my own heart I always thought, 'How unlucky that poor Amnon is, to have fallen in love with Tamar. Her wooing is like a spider's web. He will never reach his destination. His hopes will fly from him like a bird, and Tamar will disappear from him like a vision of the night. Her love began with a dream and with a dream it will end.'"

"Oh," sighed Amnon from the very depths of his heart, "how sweet that dream was to me! I would that that dream might last forever, to wake from it, and then sleep the eternal sleep."

Zimri laughed and said, "Did I ever tell you that some simpleton once asked me where he should seek a wife for himself, whether in a city or in a village. I answered him according to his simplicity, 'If you want to seek a wife, put on iron shoes and provide yourself with provisions for many years. Then travel until you reach the other end of the world. Then you will be able to say to yourself, "I have seen them all and have not found one to please me; therefore, I remained single." ' Now, Amnon, it is immaterial to me whether you ever take my advice again, but this one time I want you to heed what I say. Is this a time to think of marrying, when both the wealthy and the poor are fleeing from the city with their wives and children, who are only a burden to them and whom they are in constant fear of losing should they encounter the enemy? But that is not the case with you or me, who are unmarried. Come, Amnon, we are both turned out of Yedidiah's house. We are both swift of foot, like the hind and the roe. Come, let us run away before we stumble on the mountains of Zion! Save yourself! Who knows what other evils Tamar has in store for you? She began with a pretense. The next time she will accuse you of some crime for which you will not be able to vindicate yourself. She will do everything in her power to prove to the world that she is in the right. How shall you be able to defend yourself?"

"Woe is to me!" cried Amnon. "Woe is to me that Tamar has brought me to think thus of her! From the other end of the world I hastened to her, and I will flee again from her. Now, Zimri, like a brother in distress you were borne to me. We are both in distress, but your misfortune is not so great as mine. You are alone in the world, but, alas, I have a mother and sister. How bitter and painful it is for me to leave behind those poor strayed lambs! My oath to Tamar necessitates my leaving the boundaries of Judea. You will ask me whither

I shall go. I will go to the sword or captivity, or to any misfortune that may first befall me. What hope is left to me? But you, Zimri, why should you leave the city when it is in distress? Why should you notice that some wealthy flee from the city? How can people forget that Zion is their tender mother that nursed them in their childhood with her tenderness, and which was their playground in their youth? She raised them and reared them to greatness. How can they have the heart to forsake her and leave her desolate in time of her trouble? Oh, dear Tamar, you know just as well as I do that my heart is entwined with love of Zion, and that I am faithful to her God, her Temple, her king, her priests, and her prophets. You know all this, Tamar, and yet you are going to break all these holy ties with one word!

"I will tell you the truth, Zimri," Amnon continued; "if I had not sworn to Tamar to obey all her commands, I should never have thought of leaving Zion in these troublous times. I would choose rather to suffer cold and hunger in Zion during the siege than to live in a palace in a strange land. Stay here, Zimri, and wait for the help of God, who dwells in Zion, for one of the two alternatives shall come to pass: If God is favourable to Zion, He will send help and relief such as has never been heard of before: and if the people of Zion have displeased God to such an extent that He has turned from them, what help have they even if they do flee from God's wrath? All escapes are cut off. At every step and in every path the sword will await them or the leopards will consume them; famine and hunger will end their lives. Oh, how I wish that Tamar had not forced me to leave the city! I would pour out my blood for Zion and I would die in peace, and my life would end in the arms of my dear mother!"

These words were like thorns in Zimri's heart. He saw that Amnon was still faithful to his God and to his faith. A fear awoke within him when he learned that Tamar's belief in the witches, by whom Amnon was ensnared, was a false story and that these supposed witches were Amnon's mother and sister. Should that secret be discovered and Amnon's innocence come to light, what would become of Zimri's schemes? Therefore Zimri said to Amnon, "I will not go back on my word. I am ready to go with you wherever you may go. I am going to Yedidiah, to tell him that I intend leaving his house. I know he will release me and will willingly pay me for my work. It may be that I shall be sufficiently fortunate to persuade Tamar to return to you. Oh, how great would be my joy if I could bring that about!"

"A man has thousands of friends in the time of his prosperity," said Amnon, "but only one is left in the time of his distress. Oh, how dear that one is! Like Tamar, all my friends left me, you alone coming to comfort me in my grief. How can I repay you? When a friend does not comfort you in the time of trouble, he is like a lyre, which hangs on the wall and gives forth no sound, but is there to be gazed upon."

"But I am not one of them," said Zimri. "Depend upon me and be sure that I will bring you some good tidings."

Then Zimri left Amnon and went to Carmi's wine house. When there, he sent for Azrikam, and upon his arrival told him everything

that had taken place in Yedidiah's house during the past two days.

Chapter twenty-four

When Azrikam arrived at Carmi's wine house, he found Zimri there. Azrikam locked the door behind him, and for a while both men sat in silence, gazing at one another. Zimri saw before him the face of a man with disappointment written on every line, with eyes that shifted uneasily like one who is about to disclose bad tidings and dislikes his task. For this very reason, Zimri's eyes gleamed with intense joy, for he thought, "My news will be so contrary to what he expects and will be so welcome to him that now, after all this time, my reward will be forthcoming." Finally Zimri broke the silence with these words, "Now you can be proud of me. Thanks to my schemes, I have succeeded in setting your enemies one against the other. Tamar has cast Amnon from her father's house and commanded him to leave the land of Judea. Then your path will be clear and you will have both Tamar and that beautiful girl to choose from. But why are you so sad? I see that my good tidings did not chase the gloom from your face."

Azrikam clasped his hands, and said, "In vain, Zimri, have

you used all your wisdom to untie the knots and to make my way clear out of the labyrinth, but, alas, before you loosened two or three knots, the thread broke and cannot be tied again. You just raised me from the grave of my jealousy when Satan came from his hiding place and destroyed all my hopes and aspiration. I will tell you only a few words and you will be amazed. You know, ever since I knew Uchon he was always unfavourable towards Hepher and Bukkiah, because I supported them, and they also hated Uchon and kept a watchful eye on him. Just lately they learned that Uchon frequents the hut of the two women who live at the gate of the valley, so they spied upon all his movements. This morning I went with Uchon to visit the two women, and the mother said to me, 'Why did you hurry here today? You know that I set the time for a month, and the time is not yet here.' And I answered, 'Because you are in such haste to break your oath. You received Amnon here last night, with such a joyful countenance that I could not help judging that you were more in favour of him than of me. But I do not blame you so much as I do your daughter.' And I turned to the girl, saying, 'Do you know, my dear, that a fire of jealousy burns in Tamar's heart, and her wrath will follow you to destruction and you have no one to save you? Let me, therefore, be a stronghold in the time of your distress. I do not wish to know who you are nor how you live here. My love for you covers everything. Come, be my wife, and I will place you in my palace and give you every comfort. Your mother may enjoy the same with you. But woe unto you if you reject me! Your beauty will fade from the calamities which will befall you. You will perish at my hands and your mother will also end her life in misery.' Then the mother said to me, 'You are a lord's son, and my daughter is low and poor. If you take her as a wife, you will put your greatness to the dust.' While she was speaking, Hepher and Bukkiah came into the room. As Hepher looked at the two women, he said to me, 'Why, these are the same two women of whom I spoke in Carmi's house.' Uchon, much displeased at their presence, said to them, 'Why did you come here and talk secrets?' Hepher, thinking that the women were witches, said, 'You came here to learn secrets of the future from these two women and we have come to disclose secrets of the past, to make the darkness of the night as clear as day, to disclose what a treacherous servant will do to his master when he is displeased with him. But why do we ask witches for these things? You, Uchon, can tell us all about it.'

"The girl, hearing all this talking and not understanding the meaning of it, trembled, and taking her mother's hand as if for protection, said, 'Tell me, mother, what is the matter here? These people, whom we have never seen before, have gathered in our hut and are talking so wildly, with hatred and evil shining from their eyes. I cannot understand it.'

"Then Uchon said to Hepher, 'Leave this place and leave these two poor respectable women in peace. Do not say another word or I will silence you forever!'

"Hepher only laughed, saying, 'Wait a little! Before you silence me, you will grovel like a serpent in the dust. You are practicing witchery here. Come, Bukkiah. Let us go to the elders and disclose Uchon's iniquities and tell them that he holds secret meetings with witches. And it is better that you, my lord Azrikam, leave this place. Why should you suffer innocently? Why do you listen to Uchon? He wishes to ensnare you with these two women, whom he calls respectable.'

"And Uchon answered, 'Let the three of us go to our destruction. Our time has come. I will go to the elders myself and I shall disclose all I know and put a stop to all these false intrigues.'

"Then Uchon whispered something into Hepher's ear, which made him tremble. Hepher looked at the two women and his heart stopped beating. After recovering himself, he said to Uchon, 'Let us not injure each other. I am sorry for what I have said. Forgive me.' He spoke these words tremblingly, and turning from Uchon, whispered something to Bukkiah, which made him also tremble.

"You can imagine my feelings when I saw these two men, so hardened in their wickedness, tremble at Uchon's words. I knew then that it must be something out of the ordinary to bring such an expression to their faces. Uchon, no doubt, holds the secret of some mystery concerning these two women.

"Then Hepher and Bukkiah left the hut and Uchon and I followed them. I was very anxious to know what it all meant. Uchon told me that I should not be hasty and harsh towards these two women, and that my welfare depended upon their peace, and that we should be in harmony. Therefore, Uchon said to Hepher and Bukkiah, 'Come to my master's house this evening and we will hold counsel about our secrets.' And they agreed to come. After we returned home I insisted upon Uchon telling me all about the proceedings of the morning. Uchon then locked the door and, falling upon my neck, he embraced me and kissed me, saying, 'Now the time has come for me to relieve my conscience of the heavy burden which has weighed upon my heart almost since your birth. Today is the time to unveil to you a great secret! Now you shall know that, through robbery and murder, I made you the heir of all which you possess. These two women, whom you have seen today, are Naame and her daughter!'

"My whole frame shook when I heard these words, and I asked him, 'How did you dare to persuade me to marry my own sister, the daughter of my father, Yoram?'

"Then Uchon continued, 'I told you that a heavy weight lay on my heart. Do not decide to release me and put the burden upon yourself until this evening, when Hepher and Bukkiah will come, and we shall advise ourselves how to avoid the evil which awaits us.'

"Now, Zimri, you have heard, and now you may understand the calamity which awaits me and what is taking place in my heart. And you boast that you have cleared the way for me!"

Zimri was indeed astounded at what he had heard, and he said, "Uchon, Hepher, and Bukkiah are terrible people. They are the possessors of fearful and terrible secrets, but this is not the time to follow them. I have not finished with Amnon yet. He is still in the city. If these two friends of ours will disclose their secrets before the elders, then the wheels will turn on us. How can you be sure that these rascals will hold their tongues? Now, Azrikam, you have seen all the work I have done for you and you know that I was always faithful. Now give me my reward, so that I may not be an addition to those who seek your life. Your enemies will then rejoice. You know that I can open Tamar's eyes and she will see unexpected things, which will bring you to your destruction. You know that Amnon is a brother to that girl and the woman is his mother; this Amnon told me yesterday. If Tamar hears that, then Amnon's innocence is established."

Azrikam was very much confused, and in great anger said to Zimri, "A half of my wealth you have already and you can depend upon me that I will not fail you at the last. I know that I am in your hands. Help me, therefore, and advise me what to do."

Zimri paced up and down the room, devising some new scheme. Suddenly he stopped and took Azrikam by the hand, saying, "Hepher and Bukkiah will come to your house this evening. This is what you shall do to end your troubles: Make them drink to intoxication and then put fire to the house, and their secrets will go up in smoke. Now go and do as I advise you, but do it wisely and carefully, and I will go to put my last arrow into Amnon. My reward you shall pay me in cash. I do not want any field or garden. This time I am working both for you and for me."

When Zimri left Azrikam, he prepared some poison, so that he might be ready to bring his scheme to completion. Knowing that Amnon was waiting for his answer, he went to his house. When there, Zimri said, "Yedidiah is not at home. He is at the Senate, where all the high officials are discussing what should be done for the city in case it should be besieged, and the rest of the household are asleep. But while walking hither, a good plan presented itself to me. Listen, Amnon, and hope this may be the means of bringing back Tamar to you:

"Send a loving cup of wine to her and some fruit, as usual, and write a letter full of endearments, and sue for mercy. When Peroh comes in the morning, send the wine and the letter with him to Tamar. She will be walking in the garden. At the same time I will be in the garden and will approach her and plead for you. I will take courage, if necessary, to tell her to her face the wrong she has done you; I am not afraid of her. I do not ask any favour of her. I have worked for her father with clean hands and a pure heart. My righteousness testifies that I am a trustworthy man. Do, therefore, what

I advise, and thereby you will test Tamar. If she ever loved you, you will gain back her affection with renewed strength; if not, then you can be sure that she never cared for you."

"Your advice is very good," said Amnon, "and I hope that Tamar will again feel towards me as she did. Now, Zimri, do not leave me. Stay here through the night. I am half crazed with sorrow and your presence puts new life into me."

"Do not be afraid," said Zimri. "I am with you for good or for woe, because I can feel your sufferings."

Amnon then sat down to write a letter, and the tears poured down his face. These are the words of the letter:

Turn to me once more, most beautiful of all women. Let me know, dear Tamar, in what way I have sinned against you. Why are you angry with me? Wherefore have you sent me from your side and commanded me to leave my country, which is the only inheritance that God gave me? Remember, my dear one, that I was only a shepherd and that I never dared to think of you. You were the first to make advances to me. I never dared hope that you would love me. You implanted the hope in my heart and said to me with your sweet voice, 'Hope, Amnon, hope is better than life!' Then I girded myself with strength to raise myself above my station. You and yours sanctioned my ambitions. You lifted me to the station which I now hold; now you cast me down into the depths of the earth. You made me as strong and as firm as gold; now you make my heart melt like wax. Think, my gentle Tamar, that you have made me what I am. How can you wish to destroy me in a day? The world despises a sculptor who breaks his statue after it has been finished. Woe is to me! Your words have broken my heart and I feel them more than death. And even while I am writing this letter, the fear of your anger and the hope of your mercy causes my mind to waver. What will my end be? Oh, kind and noble Tamar, light up your countenance for me and look at me as you did that glorious day in Bethlehem, or let me know my fate, so that I may know how miserable I am! I have pondered over it the whole day, and, with God's advice, am guiding myself. I am sending you a goblet as a loving cup, behold I will raise my head and rejoice, but if you return it as if it were a traitor's gift, I will know that God has spoken, 'Go, be a pilgrim in strange lands!' And you shall know that I will never break your commands. I have once sworn to you and I will not break my oath. I will meet all misfortunes until my heart, which is true to you, will near its end, and my last words shall be, 'Perish, my soul, without a murmur! Tamar has willed it so!' Now, my dear Tamar, I am putting before you my peace and my distress, my honour and my shame, my life and my death. Speak, let me know whether I shall ascend to heaven or go down to hell! See, my beloved, my lot is in your hands. Awake your mercy for Amnon.

When Amnon finished writing the letter, he said to Zimri, "Read it." And Zimri read the letter over and said to Amnon, "If Tamar has a heart as hard as a rock, it should be shattered by the force of your words. And if it is made from iron, it should melt as wax and return to you. But if Tamar should not be moved by your words and should not listen to my pleadings, she is a leopardess, and the best thing for you to do will be to run away from her. Tomorrow will decide. Now, prepare the wine for tomorrow morning." Amnon did so and left the wine on the table. They then retired for the night. While Amnon was fast asleep, Zimri arose and put the poison into the wine. He kept this act secret even from Peroh.

Who does not await the light of day? Who does not rejoice to meet the glorious morning? The sun is the joy of all the living! It sheds its kindly light upon the good and wicked. And so Amnon waited for the morning light that would put an end to the darkness which was hidden within him. Zimri also awaited the morning to complete his wickedness. And as the morning star arose, Amnon and Zimri awoke. When Peroh came, Amnon gave him the wine and the letter to take to Tamar. Zimri said to Peroh, "May God favour your message and fill Tamar's heart with goodness and mercy, so that she may return to your master." And to Amnon, he said, "I will also go to Tamar and I will bring you her answer. You remain here, but do not show yourself, because we do not know how it will turn out. If Tamar should insist upon her first plan to injure you, she will put upon you such evils that you will not know how to escape from them. Go, therefore, and hide yourself yonder under the trees."

Amnon sighed and said, "If Tamar has hidden her face from me, there is no place for me to hide. The heavens will uncover my mystery."

When Zimri left Amnon, his heart raged like a tossing sea. His heart was full of treachery, murder, robbery, and rascality, like Satan who comes from the depths of hell with his destructive assistance to murder, to destroy, to confuse, to overthrow the world on the Day of Judgement, and he said to himself, "Behold, my harvest is ripe! In a little while my work will be finished and I will receive my reward in full!"

As Amnon was walking in the garden, Uze came to him and said, "Your mother and sister are in great distress because you did not come last night, and I did not tell them anything about your troubles."

"I have tried to see if I could win Tamar back again," answered Amnon. "I will know my fate in a short while, whether it is conviction or mercy. Stay with me! My heart trembles!"

"If you had listened to me in the beginning," said Uze, "all this misery would not have befallen you. The beginning of love is trouble; it is followed by treachery, and ends in tears. Her sparks do not give any light; they burn and consume the bone to the very marrow. Blessed be he who shuns it. But if you have fallen into this evil, make your heart as hard as a rock, and let not fear overcome you. There is no use crying. Even the summer heat does not dry the tears of the afflicted. There is always hope; if it does not come from heaven, it will spring forth from the earth."

Chapter twenty-five

The sun shone over God's city. The cattle dealers were leading their steers, sheep and fat calves to market, to exchange them for money. Other parties, bringing their wines, fruit, juice, and oil, passed Yedidiah's house on their way to market. Yedidiah and Tirzah were sitting at the window, looking at them as they passed, and Yedidiah said, "In spite of the prophecies that God hath called these days for weeping and mourning, the people are slaughtering more sheep, oxen, cows, and calves, and are buying more wine, fruit and oils than they have heretofore. It seems as though they want to fill their stomachs for a whole jubilee. The last part of the prophecy seems more true than the first—'And behold joy and gladness.'"

Tirzah sighed and said, "The mourning has begun in our house. You have ordered to slaughter and to prepare for Tamar's and Amnon's wedding. Everything is ready, but Tamar's spirit is not. She did not sleep all night. She cried and wept bitterly. She has taken the fancy to believe in the words of an accursed witch, whom she had seen on a dark night and who implanted in Tamar's heart the belief that Amnon was not true to her."

"I will tell you the truth, Tirzah," answered Yedidiah. "Since Amnon came to our house, we have had no peace, and Tamar has been changing from one extreme to the other. It is best to leave her to follow the dictates of her own heart and see what God has willed for her."

"She is out in the garden, lamenting," said Tirzah. "I tried to comfort her but her grief is very heavy upon her and she would not be consoled, so I left her."

"Let us wait until tomorrow and then I shall insist that she tell me what she wants. She is eighteen years of age," said Yedidiah.

When Zimri came into the garden, he saw Tamar reading Amnon's letter. Her face showed that her anger had disappeared and that she was full of mercy and goodness. He also saw Macha standing near Tamar with the goblet of wine in her hand. Zimri did not wait until he was near Tamar, but he clasped his hands, and from the distance called out, "Throw away that abomination and have mercy on your own life!"

Tamar raised her eyes and saw Zimri approaching with a fearful darkness on his face, uttering these words, "Are you well, my mistress, are you still alive? Oh, I am half crazed from that sight! Do I see aright? Is that the goblet of wine? Oh, my God, the goblet is still full and my mistress is still alive! Blessed be the God who did not withhold his mercy from my master's house!"

Tamar stood there, startled, not knowing what to think. She kept her eyes riveted on Zimri, who was swaying to and fro, murmuring unintelligible sounds. She could endure the sight no longer and in an agonizing voice exclaimed, "Speak, Zimri, speak! Keep nothing from me!"

"There are no words to express this outrage," said Zimri, regaining his composure. "Amnon's tongue is smooth, his words are soothing, but his heart is wicked. He is planning wicked things to accomplish his purpose. That is all. Throw away that letter and the wine, and forget Amnon!"

"Zimri," exclaimed Tamar, "do you think that Amnon grew

in my heart like a blade of grass which you can pull out with your words? No, Zimri, Amnon has filled every corner of my heart! Do you want to uproot in one second all the pure plants which he planted within me all these days, or do you want to cut Amnon off from my heart as with a scythe?"

"Woe," said Zimri, pulling his hair, "Satan himself must have drawn me into this terrible calamity! I wish that I had died last night; then I should not have seen what I did."

"Look here, Zimri," said Tamar, "you are not acting wisely. Your heart is full of hell and purgatory. You came here to scare me by degrees, and you are casting darkness around me. You can inflict upon me all the tortures of hell but I will not die without knowing why I perish! Do you think that you can show me the arrow and hide the bow? I want to know who my slayer is and what weapon he prepared for me."

"Therefore," replied Zimri, "therefore, listen to me and make your heart as hard as a rock, so that it may not be shattered by my words, which will fall like a sledge-hammer on your heart. You asked me to persuade Amnon and bring him back to you. I thought that speaking to the point would not accomplish my purpose, so I used a little cunning and acted as though I did not know what had happened, and complained to him of your actions, my mistress, saying, 'I do not know what fault Tamar found with me today, but she scolded me and insulted me. She commanded me never to darken her threshold again.' Then I asked him to plead to you for me, so that you might place me in favour again. At my words, he bade his servant bring in some wine, and bade me drink. He also drank, saying, 'Drink, Zimri! Wine is good for bitter hearts.' Then he continued, 'You ask me to plead with Tamar for you. I must tell you that she is angry with me, too. She bade me also leave. Now, I will tell you my past history. Avicha bought me as a child from a stranger, and I was raised to be a shepherd. It happened that my strong arm helped to lift me from a shepherd boy to a lord, and Tamar fell in love with me. I returned her love, because she is a noble's daughter and is very rich. But Yedidiah learned of our love affair and bade me leave the city. Then I risked my life. I went to Assyria. I ransomed Hananeel and he willed me all his wealth. Then I thought, "I am rich now and will establish myself among the lords." Tamar became jealous of me because I was so immensely wealthy. It must be that she has fallen in love with another. I wish it were so. I am wise now, too. I am no longer a shepherd, and I am no more a lost sheep. And you are wondering that she bid you leave her father's house? She even bid me to leave the land of Judea. But that does not disturb me. You think that Jerusalem is the metropolis of the whole world and that her inhabitants are before all other nations. I used to think so myself, but I do not think so now, since I have seen the great city of Nineveh. I have seen the wisest men of the East, astrologers and wizards. I have seen them all and I have become wise. Do not be afraid, Zimri. Cast your lot with mine, and, instead of being a servant to your master, you will be a master over your servants.'

"I could see that there were evil thoughts in Amnon's mind and that he was planning some secret scheme to destroy you, so I threw the bait into the depths of his heart and I said, 'What do you think, Amnon, about the King of Assyria? Will he conquer Judea as he did Samaria?'

"'You have said just what I think,' said Amnon, 'but guard your words and say nothing about it to those who love Zion. Be sure, Zimri, that Sennacherib will put an end to Zion and lower it to the ground. He will slaughter the people like cattle and even the young will be put to death.' And I said to Amnon, 'What will you do with your dove if she should plead to you for protection?' And he said, 'You mean my dove which is bedecked with silver? No, I will not give to the beasts the life of my dove.'"

Tamar aroused herself and a light shone on her countenance as she said, "Oh, how happy I am! Amnon loves me still! I wish that these last words may be the last that you will tell me."

"And I wish," said Zimri, "that I had been deaf and not heard those words. Do you want me to tell you sweet lies? Let me go!"

"Oh, you unlucky man," said Tamar. "You were not born to bring good tidings."

"I never heard Amnon speak as he did last night," said Zimri. "His words were always so sweet that God's angels could listen to them. But his words last night were so terrible that the devils would stop their ears in order that they might not hear them. He made me drink wine and beer, and he also drank more than he could stand. His frame shook, his eyes were red and he could hardly move his tongue, and he spoke such terrible words! They were words insulting to the king, to the lords and to the army. He spoke evil of the prophet Isaiah, son of Amos, and of all the scholars, his colleagues. Then he started to talk about you, saying, 'You ask me, Zimri, what I will do for my dove, eh? You shall know that she shall not be among those who will fall by the enemy's sword and she will not count among those who will perish from hunger in the time of the siege. I myself will dig her grave. She was false to me, and so I will be to her.'

"Then I said to him, 'You always spoke so lovingly of Tamar. What caused this sudden change?' And he said, 'Oh, we say many things with our tongues but the heart thinks differently. You will see, Zimri, that I did not go to Assyria for nothing. I gained wisdom there.'"

Tamar clasped her hands over her heart, and said, "Oh, God, give me strength to bear all this!"

Then Zimri continued, "My strength left me, also, when I heard Amnon's words, but I was intoxicated with his words and with the wine I drank, and a deathly slumber fell upon me. I fell asleep, but he did not let me sleep very long, and woke me at midnight, saying, 'Come with me, and I will show you my power.' I was still as though in a dream as I accompanied him. I staggered along, not having completely slept away the effects of the wine. A dense darkness had covered the earth and the heavens. We staggered on until we came to that old deserted valley, called Tophet. 'Behold, behold!' I heard a girl's voice calling, 'Behold, mother, my youth, Amnon, my lover comes!' And the mother answered, 'The altar is built. Light the fire and show your lover, Amnon, your power over all the fierce creatures of the world.' While she was still talking, an odor of burning sulphur and tar reached my nostrils, and a green and yellowish light ascended from the altar. By that light, I saw a very graceful woman and a beautiful girl, with their luxuriant hair hanging loosely down their backs. Standing over the burning altar, they fanned the flame with the black mantles with which they were enveloped, and mumbled these words: 'Burn! burn! Thou hellish fire, and kindle a hellish jealousy in Tamar's heart! Let thy flames burn her to a cinder!' Then the girl approached Amnon and said, 'Break your covenant with Tamar.' Amnon kissed her hand, saying, 'I despise Tamar and her riches, and with you, love, I shall live forever.'

"'Now, I want to have witnesses to our covenant,' said the girl. Forthwith she uttered an incarnation and immediately a terrible storm arose over the valley, and an unclean wind brought with it from all the four corners of the earth wild beasts. The lions and the leopards roared fiercely, the bears growled loudly, the wolves howled dismally, and the wild boars snorted wildly. After these, a whole multitude of winged creatures circled above their heads; these were eagles, hawks, and ossifrages, and the different shrieks of each could be distinctly heard above the roar of the storm. I could also distinguish all sorts of crawling insects, snakes, and serpents. While I was wondering at all this, the dead began to come from the earth, moving nearer and nearer to the altar. Then I saw Satan standing on the altar and evil spirits dancing around the fire. A deathly fear took possession of me, and I called, 'God, oh, my God, where am I?' As I uttered these words, one of the spirits came and shook me, saying, 'Silence! Do not mention the name of God here. The fearful king, Satan, reigns here. Bow down and worship him.'

"Then the girl approached the fierce lion and took his beard in her hands, and led him to the altar. She killed him and put him upon the fire, and, sprinkling his blood on the altar and upon Amnon, said, 'This is the blood of the covenant between you and me, and at the same time it breaks the covenant between you and Tamar, made at the feet of the lion which you killed when you saved her life.' The mother slew two wild boars, and a part of these she burned on the altar and the rest she put into a large caldron. She filled a huge vessel with wine, some of which she poured on the altar, and with the rest she filled some goblets.

"The girl called forth in a loud voice, 'Thou, Satan, and all these fearful beasts, shall be witnesses to our covenant!' Then she uttered another incantation, and all their fearful vision disappeared. Shortly after, they sat down at a table and ate the meat from the fearful sacrifice, and drank the wine. What they did not drink they put into a bottle and put some poison into it. They called me to feast with them, but I could not taste anything, because I was sick. The maiden then said to me, 'If you mention a word of what you have seen, your life will be forfeited.' Amnon made merry with these two women. The sight of all that I had seen and heard made me almost insane. My strength left me and a heaviness possessed me, and I fell asleep. When I awoke I was in Amnon's room.

"I arose early, and I saw Amnon give Peroh this goblet of wine and a letter to carry to you, and he said to me, 'I showed you, Zimri, how fearful I can be. Now I will show you my scheme, but do not say a word to anyone.' As Amnon left the room for a moment, I stole out and I said to myself, 'I will hasten to my mistress and tell her everything, let come what may of it.' Oh, how fortunate the goblet is still full and my mistress is still alive!"

At the conclusion of Zimri's story, Tamar awoke as from an awful dream. She seemed dazed, and in a hoarse voice said, "Oh, my head, my head, it is in a whirl! The earth moves around me and a mist is falling over my eyes. Come, Macha, hold me. I feel very faint."

"It is impossible," said Macha, "that Zimri could have seen all that in one night. He must have dreamed it. Let us test the wine and then we can see whether he spoke the truth." So Macha took the dove, which Teman had given Tamar on the Mount of Olives, and poured a few drops of wine into the beak. The little dove flapped its wings and then fell dead at the feet of its mistress. A shiver passed through Tamar's frame, and her face turned ashen pale. And Macha said, "Who would think that there was death in that goblet!"

"And what shall I say?" said Tamar. "I will say to the mountains,

'Cover me up!' And to the rocks, 'Fall upon me!' My destroyer has accomplished his end today!"

Zimri, pulling his hair and dissembling agony, said, "Would that I had died last night instead of that poor innocent dove. I would have been spared that terrible sight. Gather all your strength, Tamar, my mistress, and crush the head of the serpent that wants to bite your feet."

Tamar was so overcome with grief that she could not utter another word, and Zimri, frightened, lest his words had caused her speechlessness, said in vindication of himself, "You insisted, my mistress, that I should tell you all that I knew."

When Tamar regained her voice, she said, "How is it that the sight of all that sorcery did not affect you when the mere repetition of it caused me to lose all my strength and spirit?"

"I am a man, and Amnon is a perfect stranger to me; therefore, my mistress, make him also a stranger to you and forget him and his deeds. I warn and I charge you, in the name of God, not to mention a word of what I have told you, for I am afraid of Amnon."

And Tamar angrily said, "Oh, you coward, you have said enough! Leave me!"

Tamar left the garden and went to her rooms. Her father came to her and said, "What has befallen you, my daughter? You are like a shadow. Why do you hide your troubles from your father? Can I not help you?"

Tamar fell in her father's embrace, and, weeping bitterly, answered, "Forgive, father, the faults of your wretched daughter. I did not listen to your advice. As an innocent girl I met Amnon and fell in love with him, but now, alas, I see with my own eyes how great is his wickedness. He has steeped his soul in wickedness and henceforth I cast him off. Pray, father, do not let grandfather know what has happened. I have brought all this trouble into your house and I will free the house of it!"

Yedidiah shook his head and answered, "Woe is to me, and woe is to you, my daughter, that you did not confide in your father! Write a letter to Amnon and in it reproach him bitterly, and bid him never to enter our house again. I also knew about his wickedness, but waited in silence to see how far he would carry it."

Tamar wept, "Alas, it is true! Amnon went wrong. The heavens are crying because of his sins. The angels above weep bitterly over his lost soul. Even the hell below shudders at his wickedness. Leave me, father; I am sick at heart. I feel guilty when I look at you, because I did not harken to your words."

As Yedidiah left Tamar, Hananeel came into the room. When he saw her grief, he said, "What is it, my daughter?"

Weeping bitterly, Tamar answered, "Do not try to comfort me. You have seen many things during your long life. You have seen good times and also reverses. You have seen me happy, but a misfortune has befallen me. A disease came upon me and I lost my love for Amnon in the day for which I hoped so long."

Hananeel was perplexed when he heard these words, and said, "Pray to God, my child, and He will help you." And he left her, going to Tirzah and Yedidiah to consult about sending to Gilead for a doctor and remedies for Tamar's ills. And Tamar's sadness turned to a bitter anger. At noon she went to her room to pour out her bitterness to Amnon in a letter. Her mother insisted that she tell the reason for this sudden change, and Tamar said, "Please do not force me now. First, I will make the wicked Amnon leave the country. Then I will tell you all the outrages he committed, which I have seen with my own eyes."

"Woe is to me, my daughter, that you are taking so much upon yourself—to love and to despise as your fancy wills. Remember what Amnon did for you and for my father."

"If Amnon could live a thousand years," said Tamar, "and live them in righteousness and goodness, his last wicked act would wipe out all of them. You know, dear mother, how passionately I loved him. I rejoiced when I heard his name mentioned; and now a deadly fear comes over me when I hear it. Leave me to my grief."

As Tirzah left her, Uze approached Tamar and said, "Your lover, Amnon, is impatiently waiting for an answer to his letter, dear lady."

"Is he still in Zion?" asked Tamar. "Let him hasten and leave the city before every gate in the city is locked against him. A revengeful sword hangs over his head. Tell him that his smooth, false tongue will lead him to his destruction."

And Tirzah, who had not gone very far, overheard this dialogue, and coming forward, said, "Tell Amnon that he has only himself to blame and that God will lead him in the path that he has chosen for himself, and will reward him according to his deeds."

"Come back at twilight," said Tamar to Uze, "and I will give you a letter to take to the destroyer of both our lives."

Uze went away with a bitter heart, and after delivering the message, he went to Amnon's mother and told her what had befallen Amnon. Naame clasped her hands and said, "That was the only calamity that had not yet befallen me. Now desolation and destruction, like twins, come to me. Tell Amnon to get himself ready to leave and that my daughter and I will meet him in Bethlehem. Sisry will be there also."

But, alas, this last hope of seeing Amnon once more was not permitted to the distracted mother. Yedidiah had put a watch upon her and her daughter, and they were taken prisoners to answer the charge of witchery before the elders.

Chapter twenty-six

My heart panted, fearfulness affrighted me!
The night of my pleasure hath he turned into fear unto me.

Isaiah XXI, 4

T he sun was declining and sent her last rays upon the tree tops of the Mount of Olives. Amnon, having become impatient at the delay of Peroh with Tamar's answer, walked towards the city and sat down, very much disheartened, by a little brook which ran into the River Kidron. He mused thus to himself: "How sweet and peaceful does this clear stream babble! It shines like crystal and is as blue as the azure sky, but its pure clear water does not empty into a river as clear. It falls into Kidron, into which the refuse of the city is cast. Oh, alas, like this quiet brook, so quiet and peaceful, were my thoughts and my life! And like this brook, my life turns into a mournful and desolate life. My peaceful days did not last—days of misery took their place. Love came to me like a suckling. It grew and grew to the size of a giant, but I did not know that this giant had sharpened his sword to destroy me. He destroyed within me all the truthful plans which I had cherished and brought up with an innocent heart and clean hands. Oh, my spirit rebels within me, and my soul is bursting its bonds, and my heart is like a tossing sea on a stormy day!" Musing thus, he left the brookside and wandered back to the Mount of Olives, and he heard Uze calling from the trees, "Hurry, Amnon, hurry!"

"Oh, I was waiting so impatiently for you," said Amnon. "What is the news? And what have you in your hand?"

"Oh," answered Uze, "I have in my hand a sledge hammer, which I fear will kill you." And he gave Amnon the letter which Tamar had written, and the goblet of wine which she had returned, and said, "So spoke Tamar: 'This letter shall be the document of our divorce, to cut off all the bonds between us forever. Let him drink the wine, and he will forget his sweetness and his love.' When I went away with the letter and the wine, Macha came running after me, and said, 'Let not Amnon drink that wine. Tomorrow morning I shall come to him and tell him all the fearful things I know about Tamar. She has become unmerciful to him and she seeks his life.'"

Amnon opened the letter, which read as follows:

As a grape-gatherer selects the grapes for the baskets, and as the gleaner gathers the sheaves, so will I select and gather our sweet words, spoken when God united our hearts on the memorable and painful day. 'My friend', 'my lover', 'my companion', 'love of my heart'—these are the names I called you. You called me 'dove', 'my beloved', 'my heart's idol', 'my only one', 'the only one in the whole world for me'. So sweet and smooth were your words! But your hands! Oh, they have dug the grave for me! Your lips are like roses, but the thoughts of your heart are like thorns. Is that what you have decided to do to 'your dove', to 'your only one'?

Oh, you miserable fiancé! Let us cease cooing like doves and talking of love and friendship, and the sweet future. Let us rather choose to growl at each other like the bears and to howl like the leopards. Listen to my howling and to the roar of my soul! Listen, if you are not deaf like a serpent, like an unmerciful serpent.

Oh, but what shall I say? What shall I say! Your ears are stuffed up like your heart. You have sucked the milk of reptiles and the venom of serpents. Where is that Amnon who came like a helping angel to save my life from the fierce lion? Oh, my heart breaks within me when I have to ask! Where is that Amnon of Bethlehem, the saver of my life, and that same Amnon, who schemed to take that life once given away?

If I should mention your deeds, I am afraid that God would be so angered that he would lay waste the whole land of Judea. You shook the throne of God with your wickedness. Oh, be but a moment the Amnon of before, and think to whom you have done this thing! To your innocent partner, to your 'dove,' to your 'only one,' whom you said you would not exchange for all the wealth and treasures of the Kings and rulers of the world!

I have seen you as a blooming youth and have planted you in my heart, and in the day of my planting you blossomed. But woe is to you—you ripened into wormwood and gall! And woe is to me, that I must tear you from my heart, even if by the act I break my heart into pieces! You have wounded me with your smooth tongue and have broken me with your wicked deeds. You did not let the wild beasts destroy me, so that you yourself might destroy me.

Run away, therefore, seeker of my life. Run to the place where the mountains are smoking and the seas are roaring. Go where the lions hide themselves. Hide in the holes of the reptiles, but even there your wickedness will be found out. You are worse than they. The lion loves his mate and the reptiles have mercy on their young, but you have destroyed the life of your benefactor and lover. Run away, unmerciful serpent! Do not again try to ensnare me with your smooth tongue. Run for your life! Why should I see your blood flow before me like water?

A revengeful fire burns in the hearts of my relatives, and if they reach you, they will take your life without mercy in their revenge. Perhaps you will ask me, 'Where shall I flee from them?' Why, you know the way which leads to hell and the path that good people shun! There is where you should go! That is the path you began with and that you shall follow until your heart shall break with remorse, and your last days end in repentance.

When Amnon finished reading this letter, he tore his hair and rent his clothes, and groaned from the depths of his heart in his agony, and exclaimed, "Oh, day of trouble and perplexity, God confounded our speech! A letter full with pleading and mercy I sent her. In her answer, she sent me this, full of scathing words and merciless commands. She accused me of deadly crimes, even of murder, seeking her life. This cannot be Tamar's doings. There must be some mysterious enemy of mine who is at the bottom of this, and Tamar is childish enough to believe it. I will go and throw myself before her. On my knees I will beg and cry, and maybe she will listen to my pleadings and turn her heart to me again as before!"

"Do not go, Amnon," said Uze. "Do not hasten to your death. Her maid, Macha, told me to tell you that she will come tomorrow and tell you everything. She said that Tamar had become a terror, and seeks your life. There is poison in the wine that Tamar sent, so that you might drink of it and die. Why did that wicked girl not drink it herself?"

"Silence, Uze," commanded Amnon. "You break my heart when you speak harshly of Tamar!"

"Go then, if death is so dear to you! Go and meet her, but remember do not perish without vindicating yourself, and remember also that you have someone to live for. Run away, therefore, for your life!"

"Not for my life, but from my life, I will run," said Amnon.

"You must fulfill your mother's commands. She wishes you to

go to Bethlehem," said Uze. "They will meet you there and you will also find Sisry in the house of my master, Avicha."

Amnon awoke as from a dream, and, not having heard Uze's words, said, "Go quickly to Tamar, to my turtle dove, and tell her that her lover, Amnon, waits impatiently for her under the olive tree, upon which our names are carved—that I have so many things to tell her, compared with which what I have told her during all the time of our love is as nothing to what I have to tell her now."

"Do not deceive yourself any longer," said Uze. "Run away. The sun has set."

"That is right," said Amnon. "I will run to the gates of hell. My sun has set at midday. See, all the winged creatures have gone to their nests, but when will rest come back to my heart? Let me feast a little longer on this glorious sight of the stately trees and the Mount of Olives, where I spent so many happy hours with my beloved Tamar. Oh, who could foresee that there would ever come a time when I, in such distress, should have to muster all my strength and courage to run away from my only treasure in this whole world! Woe to that long desired evening in which I anticipated so much joy, and which should have become an evening of mourning! Tomorrow should have been my wedding day. Over yonder is my palace, but who will be there with Tamar? Oh, ye mountains and thou great city, to which I was so faithful, tell Tamar that I am innocent, that I am not that bloodthirsty Amnon she thinks me, but that I am accused of crimes that I never committed! Peace be with you, City of God, and peace be with you, my beloved Tamar! I have no gall. I cannot be angry with you, most beautiful of women. May God never be angry with you!"

As Amnon was speaking, Teman, on horseback, came riding towards him. He alighted when near Amnon, and said, "Mount this horse and fly for your life, before the bloody sword of revenge shall overtake you." Then Teman turned and walked away, not heeding Amnon's voice calling to him.

Amnon then said to Uze, "Go quickly and bring my mother and my sister, for I cannot linger there." And he rode towards Bethlehem.

When Teman reached home, he went to Tamar's room and found her still weeping, and he said, "Now, my sister, forget your old lover and prepare yourself for Azrikam. God has willed you for him and father has betrothed you to him. The elders will be here tonight and Azrikam will be betrothed to you in their presence."

Hananeel just then entered the room and said, "No, my daughter, not to Azrikam have I given my wealth, and that will never be. You shall never be Azrikam's wife."

"Oh, dear father," said Tamar, "save me from Azrikam's hands! Let me not see him in the day of my distress! Let Azrikam not think that I must love him in spite of myself. I hate him! I abhor him! I cannot bear the sight of his face! I have known one man, and if he could turn false to me, there is not another man on the face of the earth."

"Maybe Amnon's sins are not so great as your father thinks," said Hananeel. "It is impossible that an upright man like Amnon should so suddenly become so wicked as he is accused of being. Shortly the two women shall be brought here and then the judges will question them."

And while they were speaking, Tirzah came into the room and said, "The two wicked women are already here. It is no wonder that Amnon fell in love with the girl. She is as beautiful as Venus. I have never seen anyone like her in my life." And Tamar trembled. "Where is Macha?" she asked in surprise. But Macha was no longer there, for she had left the city in search of Amnon.

Chapter twenty-seven

Naame and Peninah were standing downcast in a corner of the room in Yedidiah's house. Naame's face was very heavily veiled, but Peninah wore no veil at all. Officers closely watched them. Yedidiah called Teman and Tamar into the room, and sent one of his servants for Zimri.

When Tamar entered and looked upon the two women, she stepped back with a shudder, and said, "Oh, father, these are the unmerciful mother and the wicked daughter who have ensnared such a noble heart and who put poison into the wine which Amnon sent me! They were not satisfied to ruin the heart of my choice but they wished to end my life also."

Naame was so surprised that she could not say a word, and only clasped her hands in silence. And Teman recognized his Rose of Carmel, and his eyes filled with tears, but his lips were silent, because of his emotions.

Yedidiah broke the silence, by saying, "Tell me, you wicked women, how long have you known Amnon?"

Peninah answered, "If false witnesses have falsely testified against us, take my life, for I am a girl and alone, without hopes, and I do not care to live in a land which is so corrupt, but leave my mother in peace."

By that time Zimri had entered the room, and looked frightened when he saw the two women.

"Do not be afraid of them," said Yedidiah. "They may have power in the valley of Tophet but here their spell is broken."

"Listen to me, you women," said Zimri. "With truthfulness God created the world and encircled the heavens, so the people should gird themselves with truth, and with mercy and truth God forgives iniquities. We must sow to reap mercy."

And Naame answered, "Bring the man who accuses me, face to face with me, and let him repeat his accusations. How have I sinned before God?"

"Silence, you accursed witch," said Tamar. "How dare you mention the name of God! Call Satan and bring forth, with your incantations, the fearful creatures of the darkness, and employ your witchcraft! Then perhaps you will find him who accuses you!"

"Where is Amnon?" asked Hananeel. "Surely you will not deny that you know him." And turning to the young girl, Hananeel continued, "Did Amnon fall in love with you? You cannot hope for mercy if you tell lies."

Peninah cried bitterly, and said, "God shall judge our innocence."

"Lock them in a room upstairs until the elders come," said Yedidiah to the officers. "They will make them tell the truth." Then he said to Teman, "Go and tell Azrikam to come here."

"Oh, have mercy, dear father!" cried Tamar. "Do not give me into the hands of that wicked man!"

"You see, my daughter, these are the fruits of following the dictates of your own heart."

"Let Peroh come here," said Hananeel, "and let us do nothing until Amnon himself comes to face his accusers, and give him an opportunity to vindicate himself."

While Hananeel was talking, Avicha, leaning on the arm of his brother Sisry, entered the room. Yedidiah responded to the greeting with a sad face. "I was very sick," said Avicha, "but with God's will I have recovered, and I am here to rejoice with you on the wedding day of Amnon and Tamar, which occurs tomorrow."

"You are an old man," said Yedidiah, "and you will see wondrous and curious things. Devils will dance around his wedding-canopy and the wild beasts will rejoice at his wedding feast."

And Sisry, very much surprised, asked, "What do you mean, Yedidiah?"

"Amnon was raised by you," answered Yedidiah, "and you do not know that he took himself a girl who reigns in the desolate places in the darkness of the night, and who enrages hell with her words."

"God must have turned the heavens and the earth, and the angels of heaven descended into hell, and all the despised of God ascended to heaven," said Sisry.

"Amnon was not satisfied," said Yedidiah, "that he stole himself into my house and disturbed its peace, but he even brought discord into the family."

"Your queer words force me to answer you," said Sisry. "I always told you that your blind trust in people was foolish and would lead to no good. Now you say that Amnon has disturbed the peace of your house. Therefore, listen to me, my lord. There are three things which disturb the peace—two of them are walking with their heads up and they the righteous shun. But the third hides himself in the dark and he ensnares the innocent. If any enemy comes to our land to disturb our peaceful dwellings, we depend upon the strength of God to conquer him. Law-breakers, when they spread their villainy to rob people and do injustice, the judge will deal out justice to them and they are punished accordingly. War and rascality do not last forever. The sword of war is put back into its sheath, the strong arm of the rascal is broken and peace is restored. But rascality, which is covered by the mantle of piety, if it is not punished by God, is never punished by law. That kind of rascal mingles among the righteous and destroys them ere they are aware of it. They are like reptiles, which are covered with a beautiful green spotted skin and crawl among flowers and bite the passersby, leaving their poisonous venom in their feet; and when the passerby looks to see whence the bite came, they can find nothing, the reptile having crawled quickly and stealthily back again among the flowers. Therefore, Yedidiah, my lord and my friend, do not pass your judgement upon Amnon before his enemies testify against and prove his guilt. These enemies are raising havoc in your home but you do not know it."

"Your words are true," interrupted Hananeel, "but where is Amnon?"

"He must be in Bethlehem," said Sisry. "Perhaps he has heard of Avicha's illness and gone thither."

"Let two messengers on horseback speed to Bethlehem and bring Amnon back," said Yedidiah.

Just then Tirzah came into the room and said, "Macha has gone, no one knows whither. This must have some significance."

Yedidiah then turned to Zimri and said, "Will you swear to Amnon's guilt to his face?"

Zimri trembled at these words, but he concealed his confusion, and with great composure said, "You will pardon me if I ask you why you do not insist that the elders examine these two women and learn what they do and who they are. I have heard much about them and I can testify about their old and their new wickedness."

A dense darkness has enveloped God's city. Everything is silent, only occasionally is heard the voice of the sentinel calling, "Behold, he that keepeth Israel shall neither slumber nor sleep!" And the watchmen in the streets, singing:

> *Thrice happy are they who peacefully rest,*
> *With conscience untouched and with righteousness blest;*
> *Their hearts are at rest, their souls are at peace,*

> *But sleep to the wicked brings never surcease.*
> *From doers of evil is banished sweet sleep,*
> *And the sinners night vigils of misery keep.*

And one watchman said to the other, "Look! Look yonder to the south! See how red the sky is? A huge tongue of fire seems to rise and fall again! What can it mean?"

"You are right," said the other, "but it is changing to a heavy smoke, which is enveloping the whole south side of the city. Let us hurry thither; maybe they need help."

And five of the watchmen hastened to the place whence the flames came. As they turned the corner they heard someone talking to himself, saying, "I put the sword into her heart, and they whom if reared would disclose my secrets will be consumed by fire in a little while. But why should I tremble so? Oh, my mind is wandering! Fears such as I cannot name come over me. These large palaces are dancing before my eyes like so many evil spirits, and the towers are like huge monsters which want to devour me. I am mad! I wander like a wild wolf in the darkness of the night. The heavens weigh down upon me and the earth trembles beneath me. A fearful voice is roaring in my ears, 'Keep out of the road, you unclean mind!' Oh, woe is to me! I am unclean! My mother's blood is dripping from my fingers! The waters from the great ocean cannot wash away the stains. And all the waters in the world cannot put out the fire which I myself kindled to burn my own father. Oh, where shall I go? Where shall I go? I am going to die in shame and disgrace!"

"You have told the truth," said one of the watchmen. "Seize him," he said to his comrades. "You have confessed your guilt. Now tell me who you are, for you cannot long keep it secret. The night does not last forever, and with the morning's sun all the secrets of the night are uncovered." While the watchman was talking, he and his comrades met some officers, who, returning from the fire, said, "A great calamity has happened in the city. A terrible fire is raging and it looks like the work of some incendiary."

"I think we have the right man in our hands," said one of the watchmen. "After we heard the fearful confession from his own lips, he became as quiet as a lamb, and would not give his name."

"Let us take him to Yedidiah's house," said the officer. "The judges are all assembled there. The victims from the fire will also be brought there. Come, let us hasten thither."

The judges had all taken their respective seats around the table in Yedidiah's house, and Zimri was telling them what he had seen in the valley of Tophet. The two poor women were standing astounded, weeping, for they could not find any words with which to deny his accusations. Tamar, who was in the next room, was weeping for grief and anger. In the midst of this scene, the officers brought Azrikam into the house. When Azrikam saw Zimri, he pulled out his sword from under his coat and rushing to him, stabbed him through the heart, and said, "Instead of silver, I give you steel!"

"Oh, murder!" cried the judges.

Azrikam, crazed as one who is possessed with an evil spirit, rushed with drawn sword towards Naame and Peninah, but Teman rushed upon him from behind, and catching him by the neck, hurled him away. The officers then took the sword from him and bound him as they were commanded by the judges.

Tamar, hearing the uproar, came into the room, and was bewildered at what she saw. Zimri groaned in his death agonies, "Woe is to me! Amnon is innocent! I and Azrikam are guilty!" All assembled looked at each other in amazement, and Avicha and Sisry looked at each other in triumph. Suddenly a great uproar was heard outside and the officers said, "They are bringing the victims of the fire." The door opened and Uchon's children came in with their hands clasping their heads, moaning and weeping, "Oh, our brother, Nabal, has committed a double murder! He locked up our father and Hepher and Bukkiah in a room, and set the house afire! And when our mother came near him, he stabbed her with his sword!"

"And who is Nabal?" asked all present. "Who is Nabal?"

And Uchon's children said, "Why, this wicked Nabal, our brother from one father and mother, who called himself Azrikam, the son of Yoram."

Then the judges ordered that the victims be brought in, and Uchon's children said, "Our father and Hepher and Bukkiah are still alive. We saved them from the flames, but they are like cinders." The officers brought Uchon, Hella, Hepher and Bukkiah into the room. Hella was already dead and Uchon, Hepher and Bukkiah were so burned that they were hardly recognizable. They were groaning bitterly with agony. "Woe," cried Uchon, "God is just! He punished me according to my sins. Eighteen long years ago, Matan, the justice, tempted me to set fire to the home of Haggit, whom he hated. I burned her and her three children with her. And my son Nabal, I called 'Azrikam', the boy who was burned. And I put the blame on my good mistress, the innocent Naame, the wife of my master."

"Woe," cried Hepher and Bukkiah, "these are our wounds! We are to blame for all this! We emptied all Yoram's treasures into Matan's house and we falsely testified against Naame before the judges and degraded her innocent name, and then we put fire to Matan's house when the evil spirit possessed him."

"Woe is to me," Uchon repeated. "The gentle Naame, with her daughter, is living in a little hut at the gate of the valley. Go, bring her back, and reinstate her in her husband's possessions."

"Woe is to me," groaned Zimri in his delirium. "I have falsely testified against Amnon and these two women, whom I have never seen until today."

Everybody in the room was astonished at these confessions. Yedidiah and Tirzah clasped their hands and shook their heads in remorse.

And Tamar said to Teman, "Is it any wonder that Amnon fell in love with Yoram's daughter, such a beauty? What am I in comparison to her? Amnon is innocent!"

And Tirzah approached Naame and before anyone realized her purpose, she raised the veil from Naame's face. They recognized and embraced each other, and wept in silence.

And Hananeel cried, "Where is the rescuer of my life and the heir of my wealth?"

Yedidiah approached Naame and said, "Forgive me, honoured

wife of my friend Yoram. With fire and sword has God dealt justice to those who wronged you. I insulted you, not knowing who you were."

And Teman fell at his father's feet, and said, "Have mercy on me, father."

Yedidiah raised him, saying, "What is it, my son?"

"There is the girl I have loved for almost two years," said Teman. "I love her more than my life. She loves me also, but she was afraid to make herself known to me because they were wronged by false testimony, and she feared lest she bring trouble upon me. My life depends upon her. I am naught without her."

"This is no time to speak of love," broke in Naame. "We must remove the hatred which exists between us. Tell me, gentle Tamar, what evil did you see in my daughter and myself that you have insulted us and called us accursed witches?"

"My love for Amnon," said Tamar, "was the cause. I saw him making love to your daughter, and jealousy kindled such a fire within me that it almost crazed me. Oh, if I could remain with your daughter and be also a wife to Amnon, together with her!"

"Oh, you hasty child," said Sisry. "Do you think that General Yoram's daughter should be the wife of a shepherd? Now, listen to me, gentle maiden, and listen all assembled here, and I will complete the tale: Amnon, the shepherd, and Peninah are twins, which Naame bore after the calamity which befell her. Amnon was raised by my brother Avicha, and Peninah and her mother lived in Carmel, as gleaners on Yoram's fields. Everyone in Carmel called Peninah the 'Rose of Carmel,' because of her rare beauty."

"Mother! Sister!" cried Tamar, and she embraced Naame and Peninah. The strain was too much for Tamar and she fell to the floor in a faint. Yedidiah and Tirzah carried her to her room and put her to bed. Then Naame said to Teman, "Send messengers on horseback to bring Amnon back from Bethlehem." And Teman did as Naame bade him. And the judges, seeing that Yedidiah's house was in confusion, returned to their homes.

Zimri was tossing in death agonies. His throat was dry, his

cheeks were becoming pallid and his eyes were bulging from their sockets, and becoming fixed and glassy. He had his gaze directed upon Azrikam, who lay near, bound in chains.

Azrikam said to Zimri, "Who put the poison in the wine and who tempted me to do all these wicked things! You, Zimri—you took upon yourself a quarrel in which you were not concerned, only for the money that you might receive thereby."

"Oh, Zimri," exclaimed Teman, "you hypocrite! You are dumb in your agonies. You hear Nabal's insults and yet you cannot deny them. Oh, you model of piety! You used to offer sacrifices and repent to God for that which you spoke with your lips and saw with your eyes, and that which you heard with your ears and even that which you smelled with your nostrils; and for what sin have you sacrificed today these human beings and made them burnt offerings? You are still gazing at me, oh, you poisonous reptile! Shortly your eyes will fall into their sockets and your serpent tongue will become dry in your throat, and you will cease hissing, like the snake that you are! You have defiled the sacred incense with your deeds, and with your wrathful tongue you have turned the rose to wormwood and heaven to hell! Now God sends you there with a broken heart, and God has sweetened all that you have made bitter."

"Now, my son," said Naame, "you can understand my riddle in Tophet. You can see the thorns which surround the rose and have caused all her troubles. But the thorns have been burned and death has consumed them. That miserable Nabal wanted to ensnare my daughter in his net, and promised to reinstate her in his possessions, which did not belong to him. When my daughter refused him, he attempted to kill her."

"Oh," cried Nabal, "come, Teman, thrust thy sword through me! I am full of shame and remorse. Release me from this wretched life!"

"No, you reptile," said Teman, "I will not soil my sword with your wicked blood. You will be thrown out into the fields, and the fox and the crows will feed on you."

Tirzah came from Tamar's room, and said to Teman, "Let them

clear the house of these victims, so that we may not see them again." Then Nabal was given over to his brothers, who could do with him as they pleased.

Tirzah led Naame and Peninah into Tamar's room. Tamar, who had recovered from her swoon, embraced them and said, with tears in her eyes, "Satan came up from the depths of hell to play havoc with us. Oh, had we heard all this a few days ago, then my lover would not have gone away. Now, forgive me, my dears; I have inflicted pain upon you unknowingly." Both Naame and Peninah wept at Tamar's grief and repentance. And Tamar continued, "God wiped away your tears today, and your honour and innocence are restored. But who can feel my agony? I loved Amnon when he had no name. How great must be my grief when I know that I have cast away the son of Yoram, a lord in Judea and the lord of my youth? Oh, woe is me! I sent him from me without thought, and who knows if he will ever return?"

Yedidiah very humbly said to Sisry, "You were always right. I am ashamed of myself. I learned just tonight how foolish I have been—a shudder will always pass over me when I think of it. I did not heed your advice when you told me how to study people's characters, but tonight Zimri taught me wisdom, for destructive fires and floods of water and wild beasts cannot destroy and do as much damage as a dishonest man cloaked in a righteous mantle. How fearful are thy punishments, oh God, and how wonderful are thy judgments!"

"And I thank God that Amnon is innocent and that my dream came true, and that, with God's help, Amnon will return and mitigate our grief," said Hananeel. Then turning to Naame and Peninah, he continued, "Now, gentle ladies, be prepared to take possession of your inheritance tomorrow, which has been in strange hands for so many years."

"Now," said Teman to Peninah, "let me take the sweet out of the bitter, and let the sapphire be restored to the ring."

"Let Amnon come. Then we will unite all of you," answered Naame.

All present, not understanding these words, looked at each

other and then at Teman, as if for explanation. Teman forthwith related everything that had occurred from the time that he had met Peninah in Carmel up to the present day.

"God knows," said Yedidiah, "how strong my friendship was for Yoram, and now I see that the friendship has extended even to our children. Now, gentle Naame, establish yourself in your possessions and hope to Him, who always protects the lovers of Zion, that the clouds will entirely disappear from over your head."

Then Tamar spoke, "Your righteousness came forth like the rising sun! So may the sun shine upon me and bring back my Amnon. I know that Amnon will forgive me, because my love was stronger than death; therefore, my jealousy was as deep as the grave."

That terrible night had passed. It ended with the destruction of all the wicked, who died in agony. Even Nabal was killed by his brothers, in revenge for the death of their parents. The same day, Yedidiah and his family accompanied Naame and her daughter to their new home. Avicha and Sisry were persuaded to remain with Naame as her guests, until the turbulent days should pass.

The news had spread that Sennacherib, the King of Assyria, had passed the River Prosse and that the people from the neighbouring villages had hastened to Zion because it was fortified. The messengers, who had been sent in search of Amnon, returned at eventide, and told Yedidiah the following: "We arrived in Bethlehem and inquired for Amnon, and a shepherd told us, 'Amnon came to my house last night and was impatiently waiting for his mother and sister. Seeing that they did not come, he hastily wrote something. When he finished, I saw tears in his eyes. He gave me the letter, which was addressed to Tamar, Yedidiah's daughter, and bade me deliver it. He left before morning, and I do not know where he went. Here is the letter, my lord.'" Then he continued, "The shepherds seized Peroh, Amnon's servant, on the outskirts of Bethlehem. He had fallen upon Macha, Tamar's maid, and stabbed her. We have brought Peroh and the maid, who is dying, with us."

When Yedidiah read the letter, he wept and told the messengers not to say a word to anyone, so that Tamar should not learn of the letter. "Tell Tamar that Amnon has joined a party, which immigrated to Tarshish with the wealthy of Judea." Just then Tamar entered the room, and Yedidiah hastily hid the letter. Tamar, however, noticed the tears on Yedidiah's cheeks, and said, "Why, father, what is it? You have been weeping!"

"Ask the messengers," answered Yedidiah. And they told what Yedidiah had instructed them to say.

Tamar, in despair, clasped her hands and exclaimed, "Oh, father, my life is cut off!"

"Do not be downcast and do not murmur, my daughter. Do not mourn for those who left Zion. Weep for those who remain here, whose lives are in danger. Would you feel satisfied to live here with your husband when the city is besieged? Compose yourself, my daughter, and hope to God, who guides the steps of the righteous, and he will surely bring Amnon back to you in the day of peace."

Yedidiah, Avicha, Sisry, and Hananeel all tried to comfort Tamar, but in vain. Her grief was inconsolable. But only the sight of the city's misery alleviated her grief and made her think of helping the needy.

When Macha was questioned, she said, "I am going to die, why shall I not confess? I loved Amnon from the day I first saw him, and I conspired with Azrikam to blacken Amnon's character, and I tempted Peroh, who was in love with me, to join us in the same plot. When Amnon's enemies had succeeded in making Amnon run away, I followed him. But I did not know that Peroh was watching me and following me. However, he was, and, gaining on me, he stabbed me. Had it not been for the shepherds, I should have now been dead."

When Yedidiah questioned Peroh, his confession corresponded with Macha's so they knew that they had both at last spoken the truth. Both Peroh and Macha were imprisoned until judgement should be passed upon them.

Chapter twenty-eight

I n the fourteenth year of King Hezekiah, Sennacherib threatened Judea with war, and King Hezekiah, not wishing to plunge his kingdom into a great war, sent to the wicked Sennacherib, King of Assyria, as agreed, all the wealth of the treasures, and even the golden doors of the Holy Temple, as a peace-offering, amounting to three hundred talents of silver and thirty talents of gold. All this Sennacherib accepted and the terms it implied, but his wickedness overmastered him, and he sent a large army, led not by himself but by his commander, Rabshakeh, to the walls of Jerusalem. At this time of our story, Jerusalem was besieged by Rabshakeh and his vast army. The city was in great distress, for, knowing that Hezekiah had sued for peace and that Sennacherib had agreed upon the terms, the city had not provided itself with sufficient provisions. The famine was already being felt in the city. Groaning and lamentations greeted one as one walked from street to street. From every direction one could hear the echo of the sledges, hammers, and axes breaking down the beautiful stone mansions and palaces for material with which to strengthen the fortifications. Everywhere one could see faces, gaunt with starvation, and some black with the dust of hard toil. Women went about with broken hearts, wailing and weeping. Zion was in the clutches of the enemy, and her children were in misery.

King Hezekiah sent three representatives, Eliakim, the son of Hilkiah, who was over the household; and Shebna, the scribe, and Yoan, the son of Asaph, the recorder, to plead with Rabshakeh for their rights and justice. But Rabshakeh not only refused to listen to them but also spoke insultingly of their good and noble king. He spoke to the people on the walls of Jerusalem and told them they should not put their trust in God, not to listen to their king's commands, for he could not deliver them out of the hands of the mighty Sennacherib.

Hezekiah gathered twelve thousand men, true to their king and their country, also their officers. When they were all equipped on the market-place, King Hezekiah came forth and spoke to them, as follows:

"Listen, my children! The great army of the Assyrians has come and is besieging the city, but do not fret nor let their great numbers weaken your courage. Their strength is only human, but with God's help our armies will conquer them. Gird yourselves with heroism, and carry with you the fear and love of God. Pray to Him and hope for His help. He will give you such wonderful assistance as you have never hoped for. For the City of Zion is not only for her inhabitants but also for all the inhabitants of the land from far and near, and from all the four corners and the distant lands. They all depend upon Zion; in her lap lies the destinies of the nations, and from her goes forth the laws for all peoples. When we conquer, the whole world will rejoice and they will flock from all the corners of the world to the God of Zion. Then you people of Judea will see that your Redeemer is strong. God of Hosts is His name!"

But Shebna put the city into confusion and incited the people one against the other. He had thirteen thousand followers, all of whom were cowards, without honour or without manhood. He placed one of these as leader over this multitude, who spoke these words:

"Who desire life, listen to my advice: Make peace with the King of Assyria before he shall break the city of Jerusalem into pieces. In vain is King Hezekiah seeking means and in vain do those who love Zion tire themselves strengthening their walls. That broken fence is full of cracks and holes. They are committing sins breaking the beautiful mansions and palaces, summer houses and winter residences. That will not strengthen your walls. Can you fix those cracks and holes with old material? The gates of Zion are still locked, but the gates of hell are open for us. If we will not secure some means of safety for ourselves today, we shall be among the dead tomorrow. Rabshakeh will not even accept ransom from us. He warned us once, in the name of the king, to surrender to him. What are our hopes in King Hezekiah? In his treasury? Why, he has not enough to maintain these few soldiers in the time of siege. He emptied the treasuries of all the gold and silver, even the gold from the doors of the Temple, and laid them at the feet of King Sennacherib. Do you expect to depend upon our strength? Go up on the walls and look down upon the army of the King of Assyria; they are as numerous as the stars in heaven. All the other nations tremble at the sight of them; all the other nations combined cannot conquer them. Then how can we, a mere handful, expect to do so? They have already taken possession of all the fortified cities in Judea. Our wealthy people immigrated, they flew like birds from their nests. Those who remained, both old and young, are tossing in their beds from hunger, and they who were raised in comfort are fainting in the streets. And many, many tender children were devoured by their starving mothers. There is no wisdom, no strength and no advice against the King of Assyria. Who can stand up against him and conquer him?"

In these turbulent days, Naame and Peninah lived in their beautiful palace. They had fed the poor of the city as long as their provisions lasted, but now there was nothing left them and they became dependent upon Yedidiah for sustenance. Teman and Tamar often visited them. One day Teman visited Naame's home and found Peninah alone, with tears streaming down her lovely cheeks.

"God be with you, noble maiden," said Teman. "Your cheeks

are like the sun and the moon emerging from the heavy clouds, and the tears on your cheeks are like the dewdrops on the sweet scented flowers."

"But I am miserable, my lord," said Peninah.

"Call me not 'my lord'," said Teman. "I am your servant and you are my mistress, since the day that I first conquered your heart, and I belong to you. Now, through those wicked enemies of yours, a source of life came to you. Your noble birth is now known and your future shines like the rays of the sun when they come from their hiding place."

"Oh, what good is all that to me?" answered Peninah. "I am a noble's daughter, the daughter of Yoram, but where is my father? What has become of him? If he is alive, his spirit is broken, and that is worse than death. And what is the lot of my mother, alone and bereaved? And what is my brother's future? Bitterness and lonely wanderings! And what do you think of my fate—only mourning, tears, and bitter disappointment! How can my countenance shine, when it was clouded on the day of my birth? How can I drink rejoicings from the well of bitterness and tears? Oh, heavily, indeed, did God's hand fall upon my father's house! Where are my hopes? The enemy has surrounded the city and all the daughters of Zion seek protection in the strong arms of their husbands, fathers, and brothers. But where is my father to protect me? Where is my brother, who should save me from the insults of the enemies? Shall I not weep at my lot?"

Teman, who had not taken his eyes from her face while she was speaking, said, "Are you the proclaimed witch? It is true, your lips are bewitching. You are longing for your brother Amnon, who was my brother also. If you but knew how strong our friendship had been from the first, you could realize how painful his departure was to me. Let me be a brother to you in the time of your distress and I will be more than a brother to you in the time of victory. Tell me that you are my sister and I will gird myself with the heroism of a giant. If you only look at me with your loving eyes and encourage me with your sweet words, you will implant strength within me, and I will be the strongest among the strong. If all the Assyrian hosts approach me, I shall smite them. I will devour them like a destructive lion. And as a lioness fights her enemies when they take her cubs, so will I defend you. I will be a strong fortress and a wall between you and misfortune. The arrows of the Assyrians, flying over my head, will be like drops of rain. Their swords and their bows I will consider as dry straws of a wilted leaf. Tell me, my beloved, that you are my sister and you will strengthen my heart."

"Oh, how can I give you strength when I am helpless myself?" answered Peninah, with a sigh. "What do you want with a girl who is so heavily burdened as I? My tears will melt your heart, and your hands will become weak with my sighs."

"What do I want with you?" repeated Teman. "I want what no other hopes or desires can equal. Behold, the thorns which surround the rose have been burned! Why shall I not reach for the rose? Give back to me, gentle maiden, what you took from me. Give me back my peace and my rest, and God will give you the joy of His helpfulness."

Naame, coming into the room at this moment, said, "You are sad, my children, because of the joys which were taken from you. You should weep for the city, which is in such distress, and for Amnon, who was cast away and has not returned. Therefore, I have once said, 'If God will be favourable to Yoram's house, He will not extinguish his name, and He will bring back Amnon to fulfill the covenant with Yedidiah.' But if God has broken their covenant, and my son Amnon, should not return, your hopes will not be fulfilled and the sapphire will remain removed from the ring. Bear, therefore, God's judgement. Stay away and do not make Peninah's life any more bitter than it is. You are a man; forget your sadness and turn your heart away for a while from my daughter. It may be that God will look down upon your suffering and comfort you, together with the fugitives of Judah."

"All my life depends on Peninah," said Teman. "In her eyes I see the world and all that is in it. If I should have to hide myself from her presence, then my ways will also be hidden from God and the light will be darkness to me. Oh, I am like a man without strength and my heart is like a woman's, ready to weep and moan! I am like my loving sister Tamar, and like Peninah, the treasure of my heart. We three have loved Amnon and all three of us will bemoan, with bitter tears, the loss of our beloved one, because with him went all our joys." And Teman wept bitterly as he spoke. Peninah also cried, but Naame hid her grief within her. From that day, Teman ceased coming to Naame's house. He joined Tamar in her grief for the loss of her lover, Amnon, the source of their mourning.

Chapter twenty-nine

Let us follow Amnon in his wanderings. Disappointed because his mother and sister did not come to meet him that night in Bethlehem, he rode away before the break of day towards Ezikah, and arrived there in the morning. There he joined a party of fugitives on their way to Egypt. As they neared Echron, they met a Philistine attachment, which took them prisoners and sold them to Greeks, who were landing in Echron on the way back to the Island of Kapthar, which was among the islands belonging to Greece. Thither they brought their captives and made them gardeners and vinedressers.

The overseer was a man from Judah, taken captive in the days of Ahaz. He was made overseer over his own people, because he had command of the Greek language besides his mother tongue. The captives worked on a beautiful mountain, which lay on the shore of the sea. The mountain was cultivated with beautiful gardens and vineyards, and the purity of the water around the mountain added to its beauty.

As Amnon looked upon the glorious picture of nature, the recollection of the beautiful City of Zion, which was so dear to him, and the loving hearts which he had left behind, came to his mind. A groan came from the very bottom of his heart when he thought of it. Amnon was like a coconut tree, which had been taken from the fertile land and transplanted in a barren land, whose leaves had wilted and lost their beauty.

Spring came again and the captives came to the gardens to cultivate and dress the vines. Amnon was working in one corner of the garden and his eyes were red with weeping. The overseer, approaching him, said, "Behold, the spring has renewed life to the earth! Why do you not renew your spirits? You are young; why are you so broken down? An old man finds it hard to renew his vigor, even in the springtime, but a young man should take up a new life, full of vigor, with the spring. Wake up, dear lad, and take courage! It seems that all the workers here like you, and I love you myself for two reasons—for your good looks and for your birthplace. They told me that you were born in Zion and for that city I yearn, as my whole life is connected with it."

"Even though I am young," said Amnon, "I have suffered and experienced more hardships and misfortunes than an old man. Now I am separated from the woman whom I love more than my life, and from a tender mother and from a beautiful sister. They snatched me like a bird from its nest and brought me here. A loose bird, nobody cares to comfort me, and I have no one to wipe away my tears. I can only tell my troubles to the wind and my distress to the waves of the sea, which will be carried away like the groanings of my heart. What comfort and vigor can the sweet spring give me? The fresh air does not comfort a man who is tired of life, and the beautiful sunshine cannot comfort a bitter heart. What joy do the flowers of the valley bring to me, when my flower flew away from me like dust? Oh, if I had wings like a pigeon, I would fly to the mountains of Zion and take the beloved of my heart and carry her where the seas end, to a place where there are no tattlers nor mischief-makers! There she would listen to my words and she would see my tears, and believe in them.

And if the walls of Jerusalem have been broken to the ground, and the beloved of my heart is dying among the ruins, then I will go to the ruins of Zion, to the desolate palaces and to the deserted Holy Temple. I will weep over the ruined city, over her victims and over my lost loved one. I shall cry until my heart shall have spent its life and put an end to my misery."

"I feel your misery deep in my heart," said the overseer. "But if you knew the agony of my heart, you would be silent. I belonged to the nobility of the land. I enjoyed my sweet peaceful life in a marble palace. I shone in the light of God. I enjoyed love in its sweetness, and I was happy. My misfortune came suddenly and my future is cut off. It is nineteen long years since my misery began. I became old, bent and grey in strange lands. God cast me to this place, but He was not satisfied with my own misery; His hand was heavy upon my household in Zion. A fire had consumed my home and wife, with two children, and my heart was broken with their misfortune. But a waste is left in my heart at the recollection that my beloved wife was untrue to me. Ten years ago, some fugitive from Judah told me all about it, and since that time I have had no rest in my heart. Why shall I conceal my name from you? You are from Zion, and you surely must have heard the name of General Yoram. Behold him now standing before you in his misery!"

Amnon looked at him and trembled, and started back. His face turned pale, his strength left him, and his heart was breaking with pity for the man who was brought so low, from the height of the mountains to the depths of the sea. He shuddered at the thought that Azrikam, his rival, was the son of this noble man.

"Why did my words startle you so noticeably?" asked Yoram. "A man is born naked. God raises him and brings him down to the dust."

Amnon sighed and answered, "How true were the words of my beloved when she told me, 'What man can see life and death in one moment and survive.' So I see this moment, high and low; therefore, my heart beats within me and my spirit is rebelling. Are you General Yoram, whose name and memory are in everybody's mouth?"

"Do you know Yedidiah?" asked Yoram. "How is he? Do you know my son Azrikam, and my friends, Avicha and Sisry?"

Amnon answered all these questions in the affirmative and he told Yoram the end of Matan, the justice. And when their conversation turned again to Yedidiah, Amnon could not keep back the tears which were streaming down his cheeks. Yoram could not understand the meaning of Amnon's tears. While they were both standing there weeping, the owner of the garden came and said to Yoram, in the Greek language, "Is it for this I made you overseer, that you should soften the captives' hearts with memories of their birth and kin?" And in a rough voice, he continued, "I put these people under your supervision and from you I will look for their work." Thereupon Yoram left Amnon and went to his duties, and Amnon went to his work.

The next morning, Amnon, even though he tossed the whole night in an agony of grief and in a burning fever, awoke as usual and went to work in his garden. It was a cloudy morning and before the day had advanced, a storm arose from the sea. The clouds gathered and darkened skies. Amnon was sitting on top of the mountain, with a lonely heart, and his eyes were raised towards heaven, where a ray of sun was shining from amidst the clouds, and he said to himself, "Thou great light, ruler of the day, thou beautiful light! As a true witness I regarded thee when I made my covenant of love with Tamar. Both of us looked upon you at that time, and by thy light we walked on the Mount of Olives, to rejoice in the hopes our future held for us. Bring me back, oh, thou sun, hope and healing on thy wings! Bring me, with thy glorious light, the sweet words of Tamar! Bring them to me when they are still warm, as soon as she utters them with her sweet lips! Make me hear her voice as she always said, 'Hope, Amnon, hope is better than life.' Let thy glorious light shine over God's city, that my innocence may come to light to my beloved Tamar. Woe is to me! Since Tamar cast me away, God's countenance also ceased to shine on me. What good is the sun to me? By his light I see only misery. Hide thyself, oh, thou sun! Hide thyself beneath the clouds, as my hopes are hidden in the darkness! Cease to shine upon the earth, as Tamar has ceased to shine upon me. Let the day be darkened without thy light. Let not the moon and stars shine. Let everything be extinguished as my life is extinguished. Let the light-giving bodies fall from their heavenly sphere like the leaves in the forest. Let brimstone fall from heaven upon the earth. Let there be no peace on earth, let there be no rejoicing and no gladness. Let love turn to hatred, prayer to blasphemy, charity to selfishness; and let the world of rejoicing be turned to a world of sorrow. Let the revengeful God cause the fire to burn even its waters, and let the waters to overflow the land. And let the heavens give war to the earth, let the earth rise with fury over all her inhabitants. And let there be a waste in heaven and a desert on the earth below. God Himself has rebelled against me! The pillars of the earth are shaking. What is the foundation of the earth? Zion! And who are the pillars? Jerusalem! Tremble, thou earth! Thy towers have fallen in the day of the rush of war! Shake, oh ye heavens! Your pillars are removed from beneath the dwelling of God! The light of the world is enshrouded in darkness and so is God's city, and her inhabitants walk the streets like shadows. They can only be seen by the flash of their swords and their muskets. Oh, how fearful is that terrible slaughter! The Assyrians and Uhlans have broken the walls and passed through the gates of Zion! They trampled the people under their feet, and they have slaughtered the innocent children! And the glory of Judah has been brought to the dust, and her lamentations ascend to the heavens. The moon has turned to the colour of blood, and the waters surrounding Jerusalem are red with the blood of their people. Oh, what a fearful sight! A sight of perpetual waste! Oh, the city of my cradle, the enemy has destroyed you! He destroyed the righteous with the wicked. The revengeful God has given the lash into the Assyrian's hands, and they have lashed God's people unmercifully. Like an epidemic which does not distinguish the wicked from the righteous, so all the inhabitants of Zion are swept away before the enemy!"

All this time Yoram had been standing behind Amnon, but he did not have the heart to disturb him. Amnon continued, "Woe is to me! Where are you, mother, sister? Where did I leave you? Go not to the valley of Tophet; that is the valley of the dead. The stabbed, the murdered are thrown like the dung upon the earth. Come, let us go to the Mountain of God, and let us pour out our hearts on the broken altar of God. Hasten, before you fall by the enemy's sword. Stop your roaring, ye waters! I hear a wail coming from Zion—a voice from those dying in agony on the Mount of Olives! It looks as though the Mount of Olives itself were destroyed. Woe is to me! Alas, my very life, my love, dwells there! Let me hear your voice, Tamar, my only Tamar!" (And he was silent for a moment, as though listening to a voice.)

"Woe is to me! There is no answer. You are ending your life among the other victims. As I call you, you lie immersed in your own blood, and your brother Teman lies beside you; his last drops of blood are flowing. A shame upon thee, oh sun! How can you dare shine upon such outrages! Come, mother, sister, let us fall among these victims and let us mingle our blood with these sweet tender ones. Life has separated us, and death will unite us!"

Amnon could not speak any more, and, exhausted, he fainted, and fell upon the grass where he had been sitting. With trembling hands, Yoram raised him and said, "My heart cries for you, poor lad. Your mind is wandering and you talk about visions and fearful dreams. Come, I will put you to rest. You have a high fever. Your mind tosses like the sea, and your brow burns like fire. Oh, you handsome, noble flower! Cursed may they be who cut you off from the earth wherein you were planted." And Yoram took him in his arms and carried him to the tent, which was in the garden, and laid him on the bed. When Amnon revived and saw Yoram standing by his bedside, he said, "Oh, have mercy upon me, my lord. I am very miserable."

"Be quiet, my dear lad," said Yoram. "I will take care of you just as though you were my own son, and will nurse you in your sickness."

Chapter thirty

Tamar, also, could not reconcile herself to her grief; she wept continually. It was on the fourteenth day of the first month of spring, when Sisry came to Yedidiah's house as usual, to be one counted on the Passover lamb. He found Tamar lamenting and bemoaning her lot, and he said to her, "The misfortune which has befallen the city is fearful. The lamentations have spread over the whole land of Judah. It was better that you bemoan the inhabitants of Zion in their distress rather than Amnon, who is in a place of safety, even though it is a strange land."

Tamar wept bitterly and answered, "I will cry forever for him, who has gone from me, never to return."

Yedidiah, who was present, said, "Why do you bemoan the dead? They who dwell in the dust will never come back to us—we will go to them. Weep over the living, whose lives are in danger, but not for the dead.

"Yes, Amnon is dead," said Yedidiah. "He fell at the hands of the Assyrians. A fugitive came back yesterday from the heights of Saul and told us the following: 'I saw the wealthy people of Jerusalem, who went to seek their safety in strange lands, disarmed and bound in chains, and among them was a young man of good countenance, with raven locks and a forehead as white as snow, who fell at the sword, fighting for liberty.' I am positive that according to description, the youth was Amnon. Not he alone fell, but many others were destroyed by the sword of the Assyrians. Why do you weep for one, daughter? Forget him who sleeps in his grave. He will never return to you."

"Perhaps the fugitive saw another youth answering that description," said Sisry, "but at any rate, cease your weeping, for if Amnon is dead, crying will not bring him back to life. And on the other hand, if the fugitive was mistaken, then he still lives, and there is hope that he will return after peace is restored. Therefore, dry your eyes, put your trust in the Lord and forget Amnon during these troublous days."

"No," said Tamar, "I will never forget Amnon—not in time of war and disturbance nor in the time of redemption and song. I will not forget him while awake or sleep. Woe is to me! I am broken down by the awful visions I see when I sleep. And the dreams are not idle omens. Listen and I will tell you: I retired with a broken heart last night and so I fell asleep. In my dreams I saw the king, with his sword girded at his side, at the head of his army, which was still true to their God and their king, standing on the outskirts of the east side, ready for an attack. Then they formed a circle around him to listen to his words, and King Hezekiah's eyes were full of tears and he raised them to heaven and said, 'Oh, God, look down from Thy heavens and see the King of Judah leaving his throne and his city to fight, with a handful of soldiers, against the King of Assyrians, whose army is more numerous than the stars of heaven! To Thee, I leave this great city, her women, her sucklings, her aged, her widows and her orphans. Shield them, oh God, under Thy wings. Be Thou the shepherd over these poor lost sheep. Remember Thy covenant with us. Do not extinguish the heirship to the crown of David. Shield us in Thy peaceful tents.' The soldiers and officers wept as the King spoke, and with touching voices they bade farewell to God's city, to God's dwellings and to their wives and children, who came to see them depart. From among this great army, Amnon came forth with lustrous eyes, with his sword girded to his side, with a shield and spear in his hands, mounted on his noble charger, with the lion's skin under his saddle. He looked like a knight in his glory in the time of war, and he called to me, saying, 'Farewell, farewell, Tamar, my only beloved! Even death cannot separate us!' As he spoke these words, he disappeared and I was riveted to the place, as if fastened with nails. I could not move I was so astounded. I wanted to speak, but my tongue clove to the roof of my mouth. I attempted to scream, but no sound issued from my lips. And not until the army turned and began to march did my tongue become loosened. Then I raised my voice and called, 'Oh, lover of my heart, lord of my youth, where art thou going? Why do you break the command of God? You are betrothed to me and are going to battle ere you have taken me! You are allowed by law to remain a year in your house, to establish it before going to battle.' And I was following the army farther and farther, lamenting and calling, 'Amnon, Amnon!' I raised my voice, I cried, I shrieked, but nobody heard me. I walked until I came to the last gate. I wanted to pass through the gate but the sentinels stopped me. I turned and joined the other women from Zion, who were gathered there, weeping and crying, with their hands clasping their heads. Then we all went up on the walls of the city and from there we went to the tower, where we could see the battlefield. As I saw the Assyrian army, I was astounded, and my flesh began to creep from the noise and roar of the army. I was standing and gazing at the standard of the army of Judah, which was moving with difficulty. Like a hailstorm the spears and javelins descended upon the warriors. Arrows were flying on the wings of death. The war fell very heavily upon our people and their dead were strewn all over the battlefield. Suddenly a voice from amidst the conquerors and a blast of trumpets was heard from the Assyrian army, proclaiming, 'The King of Judah has been taken alive!' And the army of Judah, hearing these words, turned their backs and retreated in disorder. Like a frightened herd of sheep they ran, falling one upon the other, with the Assyrians in hot pursuit, like hungry wolves. Then I heard the roar of the Assyrian commanders, howling like leopards, 'Wake up! Wake up, children of Assyria and Uhlan! Go up to the mountains of Zion and destroy the city to the ground! Kill, destroy, with fire and sword!' And in that great tumult and fearful disaster, I saw Amnon being trod upon at the very gates of Zion, and I heard his voice in his death agonies. I wanted to jump down from the tower and thus end my life together with him. Then I awoke, and it was only a dream. The fearful vision creeps through my frame yet. My spirit is like a waste from that awful night. Why, I am not the only one in the world! There are many misfortunes which we must endure from the hands of God. But there are some supernatural occurrences which God has chosen for me. From the first day I knew Amnon, our joy and our grief were peculiar and extraordinary. No, father, mother and all my friends, do not attempt to comfort me. I will never forget Amnon, neither in time of war and disturbance nor in the time of redemption and song. Neither when awake nor when asleep, will I forget him!"

"If the dream," answered Sisry, "sounds strange to you, to me it does not. Dreams come from things we think of and see during the day. And as we are in constant dread of the outbreak of war and fear its issue, so Tamar, taking all these things to heart, sees them in her dreams. And now, since she has heard the sad tidings concerning Amnon, it will add to her grief and make her dreams only more realistic. But there is no significance in that dream."

"I see it from the same light," said Teman. "We hear nothing but sighing and prayers from the Temple of God, and the Levites are blowing the trumpets ever since the enemy besieged the city, and our hearts and thoughts are so full of fright and uncertainty that we dream dreams even more fearful than the reality."

"What will be our end?" asked Hananeel.

"There are hopes," answered Sisry. "Listen and I will repeat to you what the prophet, son of Amos, said in his holiness: 'With fire will God judge, and with the breath of his nostrils He will set the whole army of the Assyrians on fire. A storm and a flame of fire will destroy everything around them. The flash of a sword will not be seen, nor will there be heard a clash of the spears. At God's hands the

Assyrians will tremble and they will be astounded by His voice. The sinners and the wicked will perish by His words, and the righteous will find safety and shelter until God's anger shall pass away. Zion's suffering will begin in the night, but ere another morning shall have dawned, with God's help, their sufferings shall cease. And through His help, we shall know which is His favourite nation. Then they who shall be left in Jerusalem shall be called holy.'"

The Assyrian armies had lain down to rest, feeling secure, as a lion might feel in the midst of a herd of sheep. For who could disturb their rest? Like a ball of fire, the sun sank in the heavens. The night, with its fearful darkness came, and the moon as red as blood shone over the Mount of Olives. It was the night of the celebration of the Passover—that memorable time when the nation commemorated the wonderful assistance which God gave in the land of Egypt. But, alas, that joyful evening had turned into a night of anxiety. The handful of people left in Zion, deprived of the holiday rejoicings, came to their homes, weeping silently and praying that God might turn His anger from them. The priests, like lost sheep, moved in the Temple, between the entrance and the altar, weeping and lamenting. The king had taken off his crown and covered himself with sackcloth, and the son of Amos was pouring out his prayers before God, praying, "Look down, oh God, upon Zion, the city of our assemblies! How joyful and holiday-like it used to be! And now her streets are full of lamentations, her mountains are deserted. Look down, oh God, upon Zion, the city of our assemblies! Fear is over all. Instead of the rush of holiday feasters, we hear the roar of the enemy. Instead of the voices of the singers and merry-makers, which were wont to ascend to the Holy Temple, we hear the trumpets of the besiegers. Instead of wine which we drank with Thy blessing, we now drink tears. Wake up, Thou Almighty God! Favour those who depend upon Thy help, and bring to account our enemies! Oh, the strength of Jacob, come down from thy throne and show thy strength, as thou didst of old in Egypt, and Thy helping hand at the Red Sea!"

How fearful is God when He sits in judgement and how

glorious and strong is He when girded with revenge—the Creator of great deeds! With His words, He changes the order of things. The heavens and earth will leave their places, the planets will change their stations, the elements will act against each other, the ice mountains will melt with one word from His mouth. When the God of judgement rode with mercy in His chariot to redeem His children, the waters stood up like a wall before Him. He roared at them and they buried the Egyptians beneath the seas.

Now, at that time, He came in a storm in His chariot and He roared through a flame of fire. With His seraphs beside Him, He passed over the Assyrian armies. A tremendous storm enveloped them, and the seraphs with their wings, fanned the flames of the raging fire. As they passed the sleeping army, they left behind them a quiet, fearful silence and a deadly slumber. God's anger lasted only a second, and in that time the Assyrians were consumed by an invisible fire. And as the morning star arose with good tidings, uncovering God's secret hidden in the darkness of the night, the rulers of the day and night, the sun and moon, were still vying with each other to be the bearer of the good tidings.

The sentinels on the wall were waiting to hear the usual movements of the enemy in their tents, but not a sound reached them. Surprised, they listened more attentively, and still everything remained as quiet as the night. Then they raised their voices in song on heights of Zion, singing, "Awake with the light, God's city! Thine enemy is asleep! Sing and rejoice! Thine enemies are dumb. God's right hand has done wonders, as in the days of old. He broke down the strength of our enemies, He turned the night upon them and turned them to dust. Oh, ye daughters of Zion, put on your mantles of strength, for thine enemies are clothed in shame! Thine oppressors are no more. Celebrate, Judah, thy festival!"

The night with its fears had passed. The sun shone forth and enveloped the City of David in a glorious brightness, and brought on its wings a healing to the hearts of the inhabitants. The sick left their beds of suffering, and those who were suffering from hunger, left their poverty stricken huts; the cripples laid aside their sticks, the lame forgot their lameness and danced about for joy, and the weak girded themselves with strength. Everybody living went out to the tents of the Assyrians. All the valleys, which yesterday were filled with chariots and horsemen, today were filled with dead. Everybody then gathered as much spoils as he could carry away. God's city, which was in deep mourning, became a city of great rejoicing. God had recreated Jerusalem. From all the corners were heard rejoicings and gladness. The celebration of the holiday was mingled with prayers and thanksgiving on the Holy Mountain. Rejoicing was everywhere! The misery was soon forgotten and there were no more sad faces.

Tamar also went to God's Mountain with Naame and Peninah, and, falling on her knees, prayed, "Oh, God, creator of wonders, let our dead return to life and rejoice with us!"

"Send us also consolation," said Naame and Peninah. "Console us, oh God, as Thou hast consoled Zion and its mournings."

Tirzah joined them and said, "Zion has recovered from its sickness. God is good to them who put their trust in Him. Let us hope that He will return Amnon to us."

King Hezekiah had ordered all the captives who had returned from Egypt and those from Ethiopia, whom the King of Assyria had brought with him, to assemble before the gates of Jerusalem, and spoke to them as follows: "Now, God has taken the yoke of the Assyrians from your neck. He has loosened the chains of your captivity. For the revenge of Zion, the God of Hosts has destroyed the Assyrians like flax before a fire. But this is not the time to speak of the works of God, when we can see them with our own eyes. The heavens and the earth are rejoicing and singing. Generations to come will hear and rejoice over this which we see before us. Look, ye captives, and wonder! Look at the dead Assyrians and Uhlans, like dung on Judah's soil! What has become of ye, destroyers of nations? Like a night robber ye came, and like a thief ye sneaked away at night. Ye could not withstand God's light and His righteous deeds. Ye have spread over the whole world. Ye have conquered nations and destroyed them, and also the idols of Carchemish, Chanla, Chmash, and Arpod. Ye cut down the throne of their kings to their dust, but ye did not cease there—ye were not satisfied. Ye raised thine hand against the daughter of Zion. Ye came with thy knights, commanders and allies from other kingdoms, and, like an eagle, ye soared from afar to the house of God. Ye did not rest, ye did not sleep, but now, from the voice of the God of Jacob, ye fell into a deep slumber; ye were tired. Now ye will rest upon Judah's soil in an everlasting rest. Now, ye captives of nations, ye have seen and ye will relate God's wonder to the distant islands that the God of Jacob hath wrought wonders!

"Your God is the only God," answered the captives. "Greatness and strength are His. Glory and honour are in His Temple! His name is great! He shields the righteous!"

The captives, when freed by Hezekiah, spread the news of the fall of the Assyrians in the miraculous manner, far and wide. In the furthermost islands they related God's great power and mercy, and from the corners of the earth could be heard rejoicings and thanksgiving to the God of Zion for His revenge on the King of Assyria. Day after day, gifts and congratulations poured in from other nations to King Hezekiah. The people of Zur also sent presents and returned the captives and fugitives of Judah as a gift to the King. Whoever applied for liberty in the name of Israel was immediately given his freedom for the sake of the God of Jacob.

The traveling merchant, whom we have before mentioned, whose business lay between Zur and Zidon, was one of the representatives who brought the greetings and gifts to King Hezekiah. Being in Jerusalem, he visited Yedidiah's house. He was cordially greeted and made welcome by all, for the helping hand he once offered Amnon. When he asked for Amnon, Tamar told him the sad story. He was surprised and sympathized with her over the misfortune that had befallen Amnon. Then the merchant said, "I have just made my voyage by sea, and I met many vessels and ships. They were all speeding towards Jerusalem, carrying the captured Israelites back to their homes. There are no storms in these days but a calm, peaceful wind blows, bringing the captives, with songs, back to Jerusalem. I am going back to my country now, but I am determined to make my business trip to the islands of Greece, and from there to go to Tarshish. I will not let my business engross me so entirely this time, but I will value the man of Judah higher than gold, and I will look for her captives as we search for treasures. And if God will favour me with the opportunity to meet Amnon, be assured that I will bring him to you as a present—not in any expectation of reward, but from sheer love of Amnon. He is very dear to me."

Tamar wiped the tears from her cheeks and said, "So may thy life be dear in God's eyes, and may He lead your steps to the place where Amnon is. May you bring him back from there, as you brought him back from Nineveh. Your heart will rejoice to see all of us around you, blessing your name for the good you have showered upon us. And our blessing will rest upon you and will remain with you to the end of your days."

"I will do all in my power," said the merchant. "Pray to your God that He should favour my journey and its purpose, because God is favouring these days, and showers His blessings and peace upon the inhabitants of Zion, so may He favour me."

Then they wished him Godspeed and gave him several presents, and he departed and left the same day.

Chapter thirty-one

Two months had passed since the fall of Sennacherib's army, and Tamar's hopes for Amnon were lessening day by day; but her grief and loneliness were increasing. Teman also, seeing that his hopes for Peninah were in vain, could not endure to be so near his love and yet so far from her as the other end of the world, so he left Zion and stayed with Sisry, in Carmel.

Tamar, all this time, lived in her summer home. She had a new maid, whose name was Peoh, a very bright girl. Yedidiah's purpose in giving Peoh to Tamar as a companion was that she might persuade Tamar to console herself and forget Amnon. One day Peoh endeavored to brighten her mistress by suggesting that she choose one of her many wooers in place of Amnon.

"Try not to console me, Peoh," said Tamar. "Throw not away your words of consolation on me, because they are in vain. 'The only one, thou art to me,' my lover said to me. Since then he is the only one to me. There is no one else on the face of the earth for me;

so in vain do you try to comfort me. Thy words are like oil on my burning love."

The summer passed, but Tamar's grief had not ceased. The month of strengthening (the beginning of autumn) had come, but Tamar's spirit had not strengthened. The poor lonely girl walked in the garden and stopped at every place where she was wont to sit and enjoy her loving chats with her lover, Amnon. All these memories increased the wounds in her already aching heart. Oftentimes she saw Amnon in her dreams, and the following day she was tortured with the visions of the previous night. At other times she would not sleep at all. Her thoughts wandered in the darkness of the night and brought her imaginings that Amnon's voice was calling her among the olive trees. Then with a joyful voice she would awaken Peoh, saying, "Oh, I hear my lover's voice in the garden!"

Then Peoh, listening, would answer, "I hear no voice." After that, Peoh ceased to answer her mistress when she came to her with such dreams.

On the fifth day of that month, Tamar, looking for some papers in her father's room, chanced upon one addressed to her. Thinking that it had been mislaid, she took the paper, and recognizing Amnon's writing, she went into the garden, where she would not be disturbed, to read it. Thus it ran:

Thou fields of Bethlehem, where my youth was spent,
Here fell the lion by my strength and art,
Here thoughts of friendship, love and murder dwell,
Here love blossomed like a flower in my heart;
My heart was sore disturbed, my spirit all aglow,
For love for all eternity o'erwhelmed me so.

Thou, Tamar, hast enthralled me with thy love,
With kindness hast enticed me near to thee,
Within thy palace offered me a home,
And with thy loving eyes enchanted me;

Thou, hopeful, prophesied for me a future great,
Alas! 'Twas false, for on our love grim sorrows wait.

My every thought turned but around thy lodge,
My heart was thine, mine eyes thy dear ones sought,
The treasures of the world I found in thee,
And thou my happy lot in life, I thought.
But hast, like the swiftly running waters I,
And all my hopes, like winged birds before me, fly.

Great wonders blessed the morning of my youth,
But enemies unknown have suffering brought;
They turned thy love, oh, Tamar, into hate,
My heart is broken and my ruin wrought.
My nights of joy, unkindness to sorrow turn,
Because, dear love, thou all my fond devotions spurn.

Instead of abiding peace, affliction came,
And swept my life with scorching, fiery breath.
Have I but sinned in seeking thee, my love?
Have I blasphemed that thus I meet my death?
My fond rejoicings all to deepest mourning turn,
For Tamar's thoughts with unforgiving hatreds burn.

Above me shakes the mighty vault of heaven,
The shining stars from me their bright lamps hide,
Alone in darkness, desolate, I roam,
And think of thee amid misfortunes wide.
What if from hunger here alone, forgot, I perish,
If thou no longer care our precious love to cherish?

Tears now on right and left encompass me,
All joys and brightness in my life are dead;
And where for safety shall thy lover fly,
When earth's foundations shake with terror dread?

At every trembling step some unseen trap is laid
By cruel beast and man, and I am sore afraid.

Forgetfulness alone will bring me rest,
There equal peasant stands with princess fair.
My grave, oh love, shall be my wedding couch,
And wicked hands will not disturb me there.
The Assyrian sword will not intrude upon my sleep,
The earth's strong armour will protect my slumber deep.

"That is enough, oh, God!" exclaimed Tamar, raising her eyes towards heaven. "I have mourned and cried enough in thy rejoicing city. Thou hast taken Amnon's life! Take mine also, and then will end all the mourning in thy city. How can I live, hearing Amnon's lamentations poured out in this letter! These were his last words, when his life departed from him. Oh, how fearful is that vision to me! It is breaking my heart! How beautiful wert thou, oh Zion, when Amnon graced thee with his beauty! What art thou now to me? Nothing but a valley of death; and I, like an owl, raising my screeching voice to sadden all the joy in this city and tire God and man. But there is one hope for me, and that is that I shall not last long after Amnon. His love was deep-rooted in my heart when he was alive, and now, when he is no more, his love blooms in my heart and with me it will die. But I wish I could end my poor life on the same ground which opened her mouth to swallow Amnon's blood."

Tamar's father, being in the garden, heard her. He approached her and said, "According to the law, a month is given to mourn for the death of a betrothed. You are mourning perpetually and are embittering your parents' lives."

"Why did you hide Amnon's letter from me?" asked Tamar. "Had I read that letter before, my life would have ended long ago, and you would not have to endure my grief so long."

Then her father tried to console her once more, and said, "Our Father, Jacob, considered his son Joseph, among the dead, and after many years he found him, and he was the source of life to his father and brothers. Hope, therefore, to God, my daughter. Nothing is impossible for Him."

"Woe is to me!" answered Tamar. "How can I have strength enough to hope? What is my end? Try not to console me, father—all the consolation is hidden from my sight. Let me cry and let me die in misery. Let death be my consolation."

Chapter thirty-two

"The voice of my beloved!
Behold! He cometh leaping upon the mountains,
skipping upon the hills."
The Song of Songs 11:8

I t was Yedidiah's custom every year, after the fruit and grapes were gathered, to invite to his summer home all his friends, and give a large feast on the thirteenth day of Tishrei. After this feast, it was his custom to lock up the summer house, which was left closed until the next spring. He remained then seven days in the Succa and returned to his winter palace in Jerusalem.

This year being the seventh year, the Sabbath of the land, there was no harvest, and all the inhabitants of Judah ate that which grew of its own accord. Even this year, Yedidiah did not change his custom, and made a fat feast for his friends on the usual day. And he said to his wife, "There will be great rejoicings in our city this year. There will be a very large crowd from far and near to rejoice in the Feast of the Tabernacles. But in our house, alas, there is no happiness! Let us, therefore, invite the young men and women, all the beauties and the young lords from Zion, and also the visiting young folks. Let us have music, dancing, and singing. Maybe it will enliven

Tamar and she may raise her eyes to some handsome nobleman and forget Amnon."

Tirzah shook her head and said, "That is just as you men all talk, but you shall know, my beloved, that women are not like men. Man looks at many women and loves them all. But the woman—if she chooses one and loves him, and if that one is lost to her, she will never forget him. But with all that, let us try your suggestion, and we may succeed."

On the thirteenth day of this month, at noon, a large crowd had already gathered in Yedidiah's house. Teman returned from Carmel and brought Sisry with him. The old man, Avicha, also arrived from Bethlehem, and many outsiders, young men and women, were present. Naame and Peninah also came. There was singing and dancing, laughing and music, but the merriment was not complete; it was mingled with sadness, even with tears. Teman and Peninah, looking at each other, hung their heads in sadness, and were silent. And Tamar, unable to take part in all the rejoicing, went to her room and cried bitterly. Her friends from Zion, and those visiting in Zion from the neighbouring cities, tried their best to comfort her, but all their efforts were in vain. Tamar could not be comforted. Teman and Peninah could not restrain their tears, and Naame and Tirzah wept too.

The guests remained until late in the evening and they related all the hardships and misfortunes they had endured at the hands of the Assyrian army, and then thanked God for His wonderful help and mercy. When they saw that the rejoicings in Yedidiah's house were not as whole-hearted this year as usual, they left for their homes.

Naame and Peninah were detained and invited to remain. Sisry and Avicha also stayed overnight, so that they might be ready early in the morning to cut the boughs of the thick trees and the willows of the brook, which were to be used for the coming festival, according to the Law. Tamar's maid, Peoh, drank a little too much wine that evening, and, feeling encouraged to talk to her mistress more freely than was her privilege, said, "Why do you mourn more than Peninah and Teman do? Their grief is jut as strong as yours. Even

Naame, the mother of Amnon and Peninah, composes herself. Why do not you do likewise?"

"You see," said Tamar, "Naame had two children—she rejoices with the other after the loss of one. But I had only one whom I loved, and that one is no more. Peninah can also rejoice when her lover shall return from his studies in Carmel; but where is my lost one, that I should hope for joy? The gates of Zion are open day and night for the captives and the lost ones of Judah who are returning from all the corners of the world, from over the lakes of Kush, from the north and the west; but the earth has closed her gates over Amnon, so that he cannot come out again from her bonds. Let all the other hearts rejoice and all the spirits be glad, but my heart is forgotten and my spirit is cast from my lover. He is no more!"

So Tamar spent her nights in bitter yearnings. When all the others in her father's house were sleeping, she alone was awake.

The sons of Zion, the pious ones, who are obedient to God's law, were awake early this morning, even before the morning star arose in the heavens. They scattered themselves among the palms and in the valleys and on the banks of the brooks, and in small groups were standing, busily engaged cutting boughs off the goodly trees—branches of palm trees, boughs of thick trees and willows of the brook, to be used as memorial of God's helpfulness and His strength, and for rejoicing and thanksgiving on the first day of the Feast of Tabernacles.

The evening stars were dim in comparison with the bright light of the morning star, which shone with reflection of greenish gold on the green hilltops. From the east, the sun was rising like a small flame and gradually increasing until it shone in its full glory as it came from its abode. The streams and the rivers lay quiet and looked like sheets of silver and like a mirror, reflecting a greenish red colour, the green being reflected from the surrounding mountains and the red from the glowing sun. Also the changeable colours of the sky, pale blue, and the stars, like silver dots in the heavens, increased the beauty of the scene on this glorious morning. The eagle awoke his young, and all the winged creatures began their warbling. All nature was awake and in harmony sang and praised God for His gifts, and from the mountains of Zion were heard the songs to the God of Hosts.

Yedidiah also arose early this morning and went to God's Temple, and Teman and Sisry went to cut boughs off the thick trees and the willows of the brook. The whole household was awake, but Tamar, who, tired with crying the whole night, was still in bed, restlessly sleeping. She slept, but her heart was awake. Her eyes were closed, but she heard every word and every move around her. The dreams created fearful and confused visions without any connection, without any meaning, and in her dozing she heard a sweet voice buzzing in her ears, a sweet voice coming from the olive trees which stand near the summer house, crying, "How beautiful and pleasant are these shady branches and twigs, covered with the dewdrops of heaven, which are shaken by the wings of the awakening birds and drop on the heads of the righteous, even on the head of the son of Amos, who passes here every morning to teach the people the ways of righteousness! How inviting are thy dwellings, oh, Zion! Thy heights are girded with joy! Peace in thy house! Song and rejoicing in thy palaces! The unrighteous enemy has disturbed thy peace but it did not last long. The anxiety has passed away, and quiet and peace have taken their place, and like a sleeping rose thou art awakening from thy slumber. Thy peace and comfort will increase still more; thou wilt continue to bloom; thy children will grow up peaceful and will awake with praises of God on their lips. Oh, how peaceful is everything! Here a father is relating to his children God's righteousness and His wonder which He showed to His people! And the children, rejoicing, listen attentively. There a mother, embracing her young one in peace and security, kisses him, and on her tongue is a blessing to God. Here again is a fiancé, rejoicing with his betrothed that the time of mourning and anxiety has passed away from Zion, and their hearts are happy with twofold pleasure. And there, early risers are swarming, with contented hearts, to the House of God, to sing His praises. The morning stars are also singing. 'Behold! I hear a voice from the Temple, the voice of God calling to the city, and the echo is heard in all the corners of the world! Hush, all flesh! Ye birds, be still and listen to the song coming from the Holy Temple!'"

And the voices and the blasts of the trumpets and the thrill of the singers were heard singing these words:

> *Jerusalem, our fortress strong,*
> *The city where our feasts shall be,*
> *Great Zion, choice of heaven's hosts,*
> *Our hopes are centered all in thee.*

> *Your walls and buttresses are strong,*
> *Defended by God's watchful care,*
> *The city where King David dwelt,*
> *And Ariel, Lion of God, was there.*

> *Thou mother city, beauty's crown,*
> *The king and all his hosts are there*
> *Your nation, faultless, stands alone,*
> *While peace is in your dwellings fair.*

> *Mount Olive in her glory towers,*
> *Her stately trees with fruit are fair,*
> *And Zion gleaming from the west,*
> *With life deep throbbing everywhere.*

> *On Mount Moriah's regal dome,*
> *The cherubim God's glory keep,*
> *Its rays illuminate Zion's homes,*
> *While Assyria gropes in darkness deep.*

> *The nations will to Zion bow,*
> *Our mother city, firmly made,*
> *God's city with her dwellers true,*
> *And God will keep her unafraid.*

Tamar awoke, and calling Peoh, said, "Wake up, Peoh! I have heard a sweet voice, the voice of my lover, talking ever so sweetly, but he has just ceased!"

And Peoh, who was still under the influence of the wine she drank the previous evening, would not get up. "Leave the tired one alone," she said. "There are no words and no voice. It is only a dream."

Tamar sighed and said, "Maybe I do dream again. I am so accustomed to that particular dream." She lay still for a while and she heard the same voice again, saying, "Behold, the voice from heaven like the songs of God. Her captives have returned like pigeons to their homes. Every betrothed claims his bride. But where is my bride? Where is the love of my heart? My beloved was given to another, and to me is given a broken heart and an eternal mourning. Oh, Zion, Zion, heaven is my witness! I have suffered with you, I have drained the cup of bitterness to the dregs with you! Why shall I not drink on your mountains from the cup of your deliverance? Like a stranger, like an outcast, I was driven from thy gates, and your misfortune and your tears have reached me even on the far islands. Take me back now to your home. My heart, which is full of bitterness, is yearning for you. I have carried my bitterness from the strange lands to pour it out on your holy ground. Oh, here is that pleasant olive tree, on which both my name and Tamar's are carved! The morning dew is still nestling on its branches, but the dew of my youth has been dried up. I am like a withered leaf, shattered and blown by the storm from one end of the land to the other. There is my palace and there are the trees under whose shade I was wont to spend many happy days. Now Azrikam is enjoying his honeymoon with Tamar, and I, oh, my heart, I will pour it out here under this olive tree, which shall be a tombstone for them who wish to remember me!"

He could not speak any more. He stood as if dumb, without moving a muscle. And Tamar, who was not sleeping, listened to all his words, and then loudly exclaimed, "No! No! I am not dreaming any more! My tears are streaming down my cheeks and my heart beats violently! Then I must be awake!" So she hastily arose and dressed herself. And when she touched the door-knob with her trembling hand, it would not yield, and she saw that the key was not in the door. She shook Peoh roughly and said, "Get up, Peoh, and give me the key! When I look for my lover, he may be gone! Hasten! My heart almost jumped from within me when I heard his voice!"

Peoh, rubbing her eyes, got up and said, "You must excuse me, my lady, but you will make the whole house insane with your dreams. What is it that you have frightened me so?"

"Oh, woman without heart," cried Tamar, "give me the key. This place is suffocating me!"

Peoh opened the door, and Tamar hurried out into the garden. She ran from one corner to the other, but her lover was nowhere to be seen. She walked on, calling, "Amnon! Amnon!" And she clasped her hands, and said, "Did I really dream again, even when I was awake?"

At that instant, the traveling merchant approached her and said, "Go thither, among the olive trees, and there you will find that which you seek. And you will see even that which you never expected to see. But do not tell anything to anybody. I was his redeemer and I want to be the one to bring the glad tidings."

Tamar ran like a deer to the place where she was directed, and the traveller went into Yedidiah's house.

"Amnon," called Tamar as she approached him. "Amnon, my light and my salvation, in the land of the living!" And she fell into his arms.

"Are you still my own little one, my love, my dove?" said Amnon.

They were both speechless with joy and they stood like statues in each other's embrace. Tamar was the first to break the silence, and said, "The heavens have proclaimed thy righteousness, and the earth has testified thy innocence. I am ashamed of myself. I was like a foolish pigeon to believe all the false accusations against thee. I have erred for a short while, and many a day I washed my faults with bitter tears. I wronged Amnon, the shepherd, and the Lord Yoram's son will forgive me."

Amnon, not grasping Tamar's meaning, said, "Leave me, Tamar! Leave Amnon, the shepherd, and go to Yoram's son, if he loves you still. Turn your eyes away from me. Why shall you see my life end before you?"

"No, lord of Judah, and lord of my youth, my heart is bound to thine. Raise thine eyes to thy beloved Tamar, who cannot live any longer without thee! In an unrighteous way, Azrikam enriched himself. He wished to swallow thy father Yoram's inheritance. He was only Nabal, the son of the miserable Uchon. But they all ended their lives in a shameful death. Also Zimri, Hepher, and Bukkiah are in their graves, and thou, my beloved Amnon, son of Yoram, will see happiness with me!"

While Amnon stood there, unable to speak from wonder, Yedidiah, Tirzah, Hananeel, Naame and Peninah, also Teman, Avicha, and Sisry came hurrying to the olive trees. Everyone embraced Amnon, with tears of joy in their eyes.

"My dear son," exclaimed Naame.

"Oh, my brother!" Peninah and Teman exclaimed together.

"Here is the joy of our hearts," said Yedidiah to Tirzah. "Here is our friend Yoram's son. God has returned you to us to heal all wounds, to remove all the bandages and to wipe away the tears from our faces."

"Oh, my releaser and my heir!" called Hananeel. "I can die in peace now; my dream has come true! Not one word failed!"

"Yes," said Amnon, with beating heart, "your dream did come true, but I am dreaming now. I cannot believe myself whether I see aright or whether I am still dreaming."

"Look around, Yoram's son," said Sisry, "and see all these surrounding you, who love you. Awake your love for your beloved Tamar! Think only of her, and no more of those false visions. All your enemies have perished in shame and disgrace, and you have risen from the dust, and with honour your name and birth have risen."

As Sisry was speaking, the traveling merchant and Yoram came out from among the olive trees. Yoram did not yet know that Amnon was his son, and neither Naame and her daughter, nor Yedidiah and his household, knew of Yoram's return. The traveling merchant kept the news unrevealed, because he wished to be the means of bringing the families together. And as they approached, Yoram went to Yedidiah, and embracing him, exclaimed, "Yedidiah, my friend and my true comrade!"

Yedidiah did not recognize him at first, and asked, "Who are you? You must know me, if you call me by name."

Then Yoram took his ring from his finger, and said, "Do you remember what you told me many years ago? You said that nothing could be compared with friendship, and that the remembrance of it is very dear to true friends. For twenty long years this ring did not leave the finger of your friend Yoram. I fell a captive in the hands of the Philistines. They sold me to the Greeks, who robbed me of all I had, but this ring I saved as my only treasure. When I looked at it, I forgot my captivity, my misfortune and my bitter lot, and I thought only of you and all I loved. Now, tell me, I pray, my friend, is there a kin left me, or am I all alone in the world?"

Naame, being preoccupied with Amnon, did not notice Yoram's approach, but when she heard his voice, she immediately recognised it, and exclaimed, "What do I see! Did God say to the earth, 'Give up thy dead?'" She could say no more, being overwhelmed with joy, and she ran into his outstretched arms.

"Only God could show us such joy," said Yedidiah, embracing Yoram again. "Wondrous things hath God revealed to us. How can we thank Him for all His goodness and mercy? There is your innocent wife, Naame, the love of your youth, and here are your beautiful children, Amnon and Peninah. They will repay you for your sufferings during these past unhappy years. Our friendship is everlasting and it even existed between our children, before they knew that their parents had been friends."

Then Yedidiah told Yoram all that had taken place from the time he had been taken captive until the present time. Yoram then embraced Naame again, and said, "Oh, my innocent wife! I have longed for you twenty years. Now all my sorrows have suddenly changed to joy, an everlasting joy, and I pray God may strengthen me, so that I shall not be overcome with this great happiness!"

"Oh, thou lord of my youth!" cried Naame, with tears. "For your sake, God hath given me strength to live after enduring so much pain and disgrace. But my bitter days have passed away like a cloud, and like midday will the new life shine for us!"

Naame then took Amnon and Peninah by the hand, and led them before Yoram, saying, "Embrace, my husband, my children, your offspring! They suffered with me in the days of our affliction!"

Yoram embraced Amnon, and kissing him, said, "Oh, you noble youth! Are you really my own son? You held a place in my heart on the Island of Kapthar. I nursed you in your sickness and your agonies. Since then my heart was close to yours. I loved you, not knowing what you were to me."

"Oh, father, crown of my head," cried Amnon, "I, too, loved you, not knowing who you were to me!"

Yoram then turned to Peninah, saying, "What is your name, my dear, sweet daughter?"

"Peninah is my name," answered the girl.

"Peninah," repeated Yoram. "Manifold are Thy mercies, oh, God! How happy I would have been if I had found but one kin, and how much happier I am that I have found you all again, and you, my friends and relatives! Avicha and Sisry, benefactors of my family, how shall I reward you? I give to you, Avicha, my possessions in Bethlehem, for your guardianship and care of my son Amnon. And to you, Sisry, I give my possessions in Carmel, for the benevolence and mercy you have shown to my beloved wife and to my darling daughter Peninah." Turning to the traveling merchant, he continued, "How can I repay you for all the services you have rendered to my son and to me? All my wealth is not enough to repay you for your deeds. You have brought back the hearts of the parents to the children, and united the hearts of the lovers."

"And I brought thee from the distant lands to be near thy loved ones," said the traveling merchant. "So I want to be near thy God, whose glory became known to all the inhabitants of the world.

The clash of swords and the roar of shots have ceased everywhere, and peace has returned to all the nations far and near. Therefore, I will attach myself to the people, for the God of Zion is greater than all the gods of other nations, and to Him belong the greatness, the strength and the glory. Let us go to God's house and let us approach Him with praise and offerings."

All present congratulated him, and called him "One of us," and they said, "May God of Jacob, who was favourable to His children, favour you forever and unite you to the House of Jacob."

Yedidiah, Yoram and the merchant went to the Temple, and there offered their thanksgiving offerings and praised God for His mercy and for His wondrous deeds. When they turned to the summer palace, they feasted together and made merry. And Yedidiah said, "See, my friend Yoram, that which I told you twenty years ago came true. I told you that when God brought you back safely to us, we would offer thanksgiving to God and would rejoice in this summer palace together with our families."

"Thank God," said Hananeel, when he saw Amnon and Tamar happy in their love. "Thank God, my dream is realized, and all the mysteries are unveiled!"

"I, also, am happy," said Teman, kissing Peninah. "I am happy that God gave back to me that which He had taken from me, and the sapphire and the ring are united forever."

And Tamar, taking Amnon's hand in hers, said, "Remember my words which I so often repeated, 'Hope, Amnon, hope is better than life?'" Amnon embraced her, and kissing her, said, "I have hoped, my love, I have hoped, and your love is dearer to me than life."

The Guilt of Samaria

Plot Summary and Extract

Translated by David Patterson

The Plot

In the reign of the evil King Ahaz of Judah there lives a certain Uzziel, an outlaw in a mountain cave in Lebanon, attended only by one faithful servant. A God-fearing nobleman of Jerusalem, he has incurred the wrath of King Ahaz because of his marriage to Miriam, the daughter of Shamir, a warrior of Ephraim. Ahaz himself loved Miriam in his youth, but she could not return his love because of her aversion to his evil practices. So long as Yoram was king of Judah, Uzziel and Miriam lived happily, and she bore him a son. But as soon as Ahaz ascended the throne, Uzziel was forced to flee. After wandering through Moab and Egypt, and encountering many misfortunes, he finally came to Lebanon and fortified himself in his mountain fortress, where he is now regarded as a lone bandit.

One day Manoah, the Hebronite, whose estates are close at hand, overhears Uzziel in prayer, and realizing that he is far from being a bandit, approaches him and recognizes him to be Uzziel. Manoah informs him of all that has transpired in Judah and Ephraim since his flight, and brings him to his own house under the name of

Eliada. There he meets Yehosheba, the widow of Elkanah, the king's minister whom Zichri, the Ephraimite warrior, slew in battle. She is now a close friend of Uzziel's wife, Miriam. He also meets Hannah, Manoah's wife (whom he married after the death of his first wife Noah), Zephaniah his son and Shulamit, Noah's daughter.

From Yehosheba, Uzziel learns that Shamir has sacrificed his son to Moloch to erase all trace of Uzziel, and that Miriam has adopted a foundling as her son and called him Eliphelet. But Uzziel knows that Eliphelet is his real son, the one who was sacrificed having been substituted for him. Yehosheba then describes the war which Judah waged against Ephraim and Aram, in which her husband, together with the king's son, Maaseiah, and Azrikam the king's steward were killed by Zichri. In this battle Maaseiah had placed Eliphelet on the most dangerous front, regarding him as an obstacle to his love for Kezia, Elkanah's daughter. But Eliphelet had fought and captured an amazon-like warrioress, Reumah, whom Keturah had borne to Zichri. Having sworn to love only the man who could overcome her in battle, Reumah had intervened on behalf of Eliphelet after the total defeat of Judah's army, and sent him to Jerusalem to return to her with his entire household. But Eliphelet, who loves Kezia, has not returned, and has been sent by Ahaz as an envoy to Assyria.

Yehosheba, however, plans to wed Eliphelet to Shulamit and sets out to Gilead to intercept him. But her servant Abishag reveals her plan to the villains Omri and Zimri, who inform Keturah, who, in turn, informs her daughter Reumah. On that same day, which is a festival at Beth-El, Reumah issues a challenge to the Ephraimite warriors to do battle with her in a tournament. The challenge is accepted by Daniel, Azrikam's son, disguised under the name of Ammihud. Daniel is searching for a maiden who showed him compassion when he was taken captive after the disastrous battle, but whom he has seen only once. Unknown to him, she is Shulamit, Noah's daughter. But he is also seeking an opportunity to take revenge on Zichri for his father's murder, hence his acceptance of Reumah's challenge.

Reumah is informed of her adversary's likeness to Daniel and decides to use him to wean Shulamit's affections from Eliphelet. She sends him with his servant Yoach in search of her, but they are separated at night in the hills of Lebanon. As dawn breaks Daniel hears Shulamit praying to God, and they are joyfully reunited. Daniel learns that she is the daughter of Elkanah, and they retire to her home, where they are joined by Yoach, who arrives with Uzziel.

Three days later Daniel sets off to return to Reumah, still bent upon revenge, and also in the hope of saving other Judaeans who are in her power. On the way he meets Eliphelet, who is returning from Assyria with rich treasure. Eliphelet has just saved the life of Hephzibah, a former wife of Zichri but a friend of Judah. She had been attacked by an Ethiopian at the instigation of Keturah and Reumah, as a prelude to an attack on Miriam. It transpires that Uzziel had many years previously saved Hephzibah's life from a similar attack by the father of this Ethiopian.

Near Jerusalem Eliphelet meets Manoah bringing Uzziel, disguised as Eliada, to serve as the steward of Miriam's estates, and gives him a letter for Miriam, disclosing that the king has destined Kezia for Daniel. Uzziel and Miriam are overjoyed at meeting after so many years of separation, but dare not reveal their secret. Meanwhile Magdiel, who had himself aspired to the stewardship of Miriam's estates, informs Eliphelet that Eliada and Miriam are meeting secretly at night. Unaware that Eliada is Miriam's husband, Eliphelet leaves Jerusalem in a rage, and is captured by the Edomites, who plan to sacrifice him to their gods. He is rescued by one of Miriam's agents, who is unaware, however, of his identity.

Meanwhile Uzziel receives a warning that his presence has been discovered and is forced to flee once again, leaving Miriam even more disconsolate than formerly. The irony of her plight is increased by the death of King Ahaz and the ascension of the righteous Hezekiah, who listens readily to Isaiah's teachings, for she realizes that her husband could well return to Jerusalem and live in peace. In Samaria, on the other hand, licentiousness and vice are rampant, every form of idolatry is practised, while the righteous suffer persecution.

The fame of Zichri and his daughter Reumah has reached its zenith. Daniel is imprisoned in Zichri's palace, and a rich ransom is placed on his life. Shulamit, too, is abducted from Manoah's house and carried there. But Reumah nurses hatred against her father, Zichri, who has engineered her mother's death, and so she furnishes Shulamit with the sword of her father Elkanah, which Zichri had taken after killing him. Daniel manages to secure this sword and wounds Zichri when he enters Shulamit's room.

Meanwhile Uzziel has come to Samaria to win converts back to the true religion, and there he meets Eliphelet, who is endeavouring to redeem Reumah's prisoners. Uzziel reveals to Eliphelet that he is his father and they are reconciled. With the help of Sharezer, the prince of Assyria, they rescue the captives. But Samaria, after the overthrow and exile of her king and nobles, is plunged into a state of dreadful confusion, and punished for her many sins.

The heroes return triumphantly to Jerusalem to celebrate the Feast of Passover. Uzziel is united to Miriam, Eliphelet to Kezia and Daniel to Shulamit. With Miriam's consent Uzziel takes the unhappy Yehosheba as a second wife. The king rewards Uzziel with rich estates at En-Gedi, to which he and his household retire to spend their remaining years far from the city's tumult.

Chapter one

In the days when Ahaz reigned in Judah, and Pekah son of Remaliah and Hoshea son of Elah were the kings in Israel, the prophets grew hoarse with rebuking the refractory people and wearied themselves with appeals to their erring and presumptuous hearts. In those evil times Ephraim knew only rebellion, and Judah deceit. Ephraim offered up his sons for slaughter, and Judah sacrificed his choicest offspring through the fire to Moloch. Thus did King Ahaz, and his people followed in his ways. The law disappeared out of Zion, while truth and honesty fled from Samaria's gates, to hide among the clefts of the hills, and in the crevices of the rocks. Righteousness dwelt only in the forest, and Faith in caves.

But to the end of time righteousness shall not perish, nor shall wickedness and folly cease. For where the shadows lurk, there light is found. Thus did the Lord create the world and thus did he establish it, summer joined to winter, night ever linked with morning. And even thus did the Lord create man, whose heart is always full of evil inclination, while his good sense protects him like an angel, that he follow not his rebellious desires. Its light is like the rainbow in a day of dark cloud, fashioned in ancient times as witness to the covenant of peace, to remind men that the Lord creates light and darkness, and from on high makes peace between them as they strive with one another. From the lowliest earth to the highest star the splendour of his work appears in everything created in his name and for his glory. For his actions are all weighed, and he will not destroy the good for evil's sake, but he takes forth the precious from the vile, the pure from the corrupt; and from a perverse and crooked generation he separates the pure of heart, those who are wise and know the Lord, who shine through the darkness like a rainbow through the darkest night. And the soul of man is like the light of God, searching the innermost recesses of the heart. And even when Israel and Judah broke all bounds, and profaned the glory of his might, and the pride of Jacob lay prostrate before the abominations of idolatry, even then the light of God shone forth upon the righteous, and the pure of heart glowed like precious stones upon God's earth. And when Ahaz closed the portals of the Lord, Lebanon threw wide her gates that all the faithful might enter therein. And there they served the Lord by torch-light, and in the secret places of the forest paid homage to the Holy One of Israel.

In the remotest mountains of Lebanon, which form the northern boundary of the tribe of Naphtali where the Hermonites dwell in bands, the peak of Amana towers aloft. At the foot of this mountain there unfolds a valley, the most beautiful and lovely in all the mountain ranges round about. And from the rocks rivulets gush forth and stream into this vale, where the limpid brooks unite and flow beneath the ground until they emerge from the bosom of the earth to form a mighty river—the river Jordan.

The dew of Hermon still lingers mistily over the valleys, enveloping the bushes, thickets, and pasture-lands, as the dawn stretches across the mountains, lighting in gold the glory of Lebanon and the great proud trees, whose roots dig deep into the soil while their tops grope towards heaven. These mighty cedars are ancient as the earth which carries them, and their leafy tops spread out and intertwine with one another. Their foliage forms a shady grotto even at noontide, and provides a nesting place for every sort of bird that sings the praise of Lebanon to the Lord. The ear can never weary of their sweet song and pleasant melody. And the mountain tops re-echo the roars of savage beasts; for there the lions and panthers have their lairs, and the soul thrills fearfully to the sound of their mingled cries. These mountains drip with the juice of the abounding vines that bend beneath the burden of their clusters. Even the earth breathes myrrh and frankincense, while the scent of spices creeps into the nostrils of the traveller. And hence the phrase "it bears the scent of Lebanon," for Lebanon is shrouded in delight, and how much more so when the dawn breaks over it, laying bare such beauty that the heart cries out in joy.

The summer was drawing to a close. It was the month before Ethanim, when the sun scorches the land and the fullness thereof, giving no respite from its heat. Wherefore travellers would arise at the first watch to journey through the morning mists. At that very time three travellers arose, who had lodged safely among the Hermonites. They were returning from Damascus, the land of their captivity, where Rezin, King of Aram, had brought the great captivity of Judah, throwing their princes in prison, but freeing the poor to return to their own land, that they might relate the sorrows of the princes held captive in iron fetters, and thereby hasten their redemption with rich ransom. And these three of the captivity of Damascus were of the poor of the land of Judah, and traversed the way of the Hermonites on camel-back, their faces set towards Jerusalem. They were accompanied by the servants of a rich man of that place who came to send them on their way; and all were well armed against the terrors of the night, for the wild beasts of Lebanon abounded at that season, and the lions could be heard snarling for their prey, while the mists of dew that billowed down upon them from Hermon blotted out the paths from before their eyes. These three impoverished men—one from Adullam, the second from Lachish and the third from Ziph—had no portion or inheritance in their own land, but found their sustenance in Jerusalem, serving in one of the houses of the great. And just as in times of peace they had beheld the grandeur of their master's house, so had they seen its pride overthrown in war and known its shame. Wherefore the Hermonite servants questioned them on what they had seen and what they knew of the dire destruction which had but lately befallen Judah.

"All three of us are of the poor of the land"—answered the man of Adullam, "and who are we to record a nation's story? My birth was lowly, but I beheld the highest in the land when I served in the house of Azrikam, who was the steward of King Ahaz, and in whose house I witnessed pride and grandeur. For Elkanah, that was next to the king, would come there with the lady Yehosheba his wife, and with their daughter, Kezia, the loveliest of Zion's maidens. And these two princes of Judah, who stood at the head of all the noble families, thought to join their houses in marriage. For Kezia, the daughter of Elkanah, that was next to the king, was destined for Daniel, the son of Azrikam my master, the steward of the king. But Maaseiah, the son of King Ahaz, stood between them like a rock. And what was the latter end of these high, exalted figures? Alas! Their doom was sealed, for Maaseiah the king's son, and Elkanah, that was next to the king, and Azrikam, the king's steward, were all slain by Zichri, the hero of Ephraim, in the war of the allied kings, Pekah son of Remaliah and Rezin King of Aram, against Judah. Zichri smote these three pillars of strength and shook the foundations of the land, for one hundred and twenty thousand valiant sons of Judah fell smitten before the might of Remaliah. Alas! The land of Judah is withered and lies mourning."

"Verily, it is so"—the man of Lachish replied. "Many homes lie desolate in Zion. Do you not know, have you not heard, how the noble Yoram met his end, a captive of the Philistines, while Naame, his beloved wife, ransacked his treasures, plundered his wealth and set fire to his estate for jealousy of Haggit, her adversary? And the flames consumed his children saving only one, Haggit's son, who alone survived like a brand plucked from the fire. Then Naame fled from her vile crime, and escaped to her lover. Five years have passed since that dread deed, but is it not enough to desecrate the land?"

"Misery has indeed befallen the great in Judah," the man of Ziph continued. "Do you not know the noble lady Miriam who dwells in Zion? I know her story well, for Achsah, my sister, is a handmaid in her house. This Miriam, who is both gracious and wealthy, inherited the fortune of her mother Deborah, to the great chagrin of Shamir her father, a bitter enemy of Judah and the house of David, for he is descended from Ephraim's kings. And he was sorely vexed to see his daughter Miriam following in the footsteps of Deborah, her mother, and loving her people, Judah. And his fury increased when Miriam fell in love with Uzziel, the son of a Judaean nobleman, a scion of the house of Uzziah. But Miriam loved him both for his beauty and his nobility, for he was of the royal blood. Then in his anger against his daughter Miriam and Uzziel her husband, Shamir swore a secret oath to blot out their memory for ever. Which oath he fulfilled, for he sacrificed their offspring to Moloch, and caused Uzziel to flee to the land of Moab in the early days of Ahaz's reign. And the lady Miriam has lived a miserable widow's life these fifteen years."

"No need to tell me that," replied the man of Lachish. "When Yedidiah, the ruler of the king's substance, sent me to the country of the Philistines to inquire after the treacherous Naame and to trace her footsteps, at that same time Miriam summoned me to her, and implored me search for news of her husband Uzziel, who had left Moab and gone to the Philistines, and from there to Egypt. Yet neither the money which she gave me nor my toil were ought avail. Would that I might have found him, for now I would be rich. Verily, there is no end to the wealth which Miriam received from Deborah her mother, and in bereavement and widowhood her whole desire is to perform good deeds. She is a refuge for abandoned orphans, and a shelter for the heroes of the war. And one orphan in particular, a handsome and valiant youth named Eliphelet, has she adopted. And by virtue of her compassion and love for him, she has made him a place among the young noblemen favoured by the king, and regards him as her son."

"That is all mere hearsay," answered the man of Adullam. "All Eliphelet's greatness came from Maaseiah, the king's son, whose weapon-bearer he was, just as I bore the weapons of Daniel, son of Azrikam, the king's steward. But listen now, and wonder, for Kezia, the daughter of Elkanah, that was next to the king, the most beautiful of Zion's maidens and a joy to behold—this Kezia would pay no heed to Daniel, my master, comely though he was, nor would she deign to notice even Maaseiah, the son of King Ahaz, but raised her eyes to Eliphelet, whom Miriam adopted, against the will of Elkanah her father. But he, together with his friend Azrikam, the king's steward, and Maaseiah, the king's son, were slain all three by Zichri, the hero of Ephraim. And Daniel, my young master, lies in prison in Damascus. Soon will he hear that Kezia, daughter of Elkanah, has fallen the fair lot of the low-born Eliphelet. For a kind of madness has beset the great ones of the land. Thus the lady Yehosheba, Kezia's mother, used to say, and thus I too observed when I passed through Gilead on the road to captivity with Daniel, my master, son of the king's steward. For there our captors let us rest, and there a maiden saw him, a lovely maiden beautiful as Kezia, daughter of Elkanah, in all her radiance. She saw him from afar and wept for the wanderer. Daniel, too, espied her and waved his hand to her in love, until our cruel captors let us enjoy the sight no longer. Yet the memory of this girl weighed heavily upon his spirit in the land of his captivity, for her image was ever before his eyes, though he had never seen her else and even her name was hidden from him, so that he would refer to her as 'his heart's desire'. Such is the folly that has overcome the great ones of the earth."

In this wise the sons of Judah, returning from Damascus, the land of their captivity, related their stories to the servants who had come to send them on their way, and still talking they reached the peak of Amana. And there the servants stopped and listened intently to the cry of a stag. And one of the servants said to his fellow: "Go, tell our master that the lion of Amana still lurks in his lair, and bid him arm his men and bring them to some fastness on the mountain, for he shall surely fall into our hands, and all the iniquity he has wrought in Lebanon shall descend upon his head. I pity the young deer that has fallen prey to him, and the poor doe that will yearn for her lost one. For these two young deer were the delight of Shulamit, our master's daughter, and they would eat out of her hand, and brought her comfort in her time of mourning for her mother. And now the one young deer will serve as food for this man of blood."

Then the men of Judah inquired of them concerning the matter, and one of the servants related that a murderous robber had found a lair on the peak of Amana since the beginning of spring, and was plundering Lebanon like a ravening lion. He had made his home high up upon the crag where even the wild beasts could not ascend, and on a nearby spur of rock a tawny leopard stood guard over his lair. For the man of blood was a sorcerer, and even the wild beasts quaked before him. And thus had he lived for several months: "He rises early in search of prey, and returns late at night to his hiding place, nor has anyone of us looked upon his face. And just as he is, so is the servant who accompanies him. But my master has resolved to put an end to the dread of this tyrant, and to storm his lair this very morning. Then shall his bloody deeds recoil upon him, he shall bear the penalty for his evil ways, and the wrath of Lebanon shall descend upon his head."

When he had finished speaking the three men of Judah thanked the servants for their night's lodging and the provision for the journey, and having blessed them rode off upon their way to their own land.

As dawn broke over the peak of Amana, behold, a man, clad in a coarse garment, appeared upon the rocky spur which even the wild beasts could not ascend, and stood listening to the voices of the servants talking far below. Then hastily he returned to a cave hewn from the living rock and composed of two vaults, the outer one for himself, and the inner one for his master. In this vault a hole had been driven through the wall which by day was covered with a plank of cedarwood to ward off the fierce heat of summer. But now the aperture was open facing the east, letting in the scent of Lebanon together with the morning light, which illumined everything inside. The floor was covered with the skins of wild beasts, and the walls were hung with every sort of weapon: bows, spears, lances and javelins, even a great sword encased in its sheath—a sure sign that this hunter was also a man of war. Outside this dwelling on a spur of rock a dreadful tawny leopard stood motionless. The outlaw had killed it and stuffed its skin, and set it on the crag to terrify whoever might be so brave as to assay the man who had overcome wild beasts in strength and courage. But even without the terror of wild beasts, this refuge was secure; for the sheer cliffs were its rampart, and those who lived there went up and down a ladder of rope. This ladder was securely fastened with an iron peg, and was lowered at need. And the servant, who attended to the outlaw, entered the vault and took down two powerful bows from the wall, to be ready for his master's coming.

Yet at that moment his master was not as a man prepared for battle, for every morning he prayed to the Lord. And even now, when his enemies were about to assault his lair, he stood in contemplation. He was a handsome man in the prime of life, and his thoughts were clearly depicted on his face as his spirit welled up and cried:

"O Almighty, whose ways are exalted above the mountains of God, and whose mercy is greater than the resounding seas, look down upon this lone soul that pleads with you, turn your face to one who is downtrodden and lost, who cries to you with stricken heart: why do I see evil strutting above erect and fearless, while righteousness hides stealthily in the crevices of the rocks; or wickedness enthroned in marble palaces, while honesty lurks in the thickets for fear of the sin of the land and the evil of its inhabitants? Wherefore, O Lord my God, did you grant me tranquillity and joy in my youth, to torture me in mature years with memories of my beloved, with long exile and with fears? For one brief space I witnessed life and happiness with my beloved Miriam. She sat in marble palaces at my right hand, and everything I beheld about me was clothed in delight, all Zion and her assemblies. But alas, my time of joy was all too short, and how long have been the years of affliction! For your anger, O Lord my God, has been raised against me all this time, and you have tossed me about through foreign lands—Moab, Philistia, and Egypt. And you have sated me with wanderings even as in the days of the kingdom of Ahaz. And now you have set me on this mountain peak like a black stone, to fill my soul with dread. Still have you not restored me to tranquillity and honour, for you have decreed the measure of my sufferings, O God of wrath. But in spite of all my misfortunes is the cup not yet full? Woe to me that am cut off from my people, from Miriam, my gracious wife and my soul's delight, and from Eliphelet, our beloved child, whom our hands lifted from our pleasant garden to plant amongst the thickets of the forest, that they might protect him from the evil man who sought to extirpate him root and branch. For those dear ones I have raised my hands in prayer all the days of my wanderings, and even today I lift my thoughts to them from the Jordan and the Hermon. Indeed, O Lord God, You have afflicted me sore, yet not consumed me utterly; and that is a sign that you have spared me for the sake of my beloved ones, and that I shall look upon them again when the time is ripe. But when will that time come? How long shall I be a stranger in the land? How long shall my way be wrapped in darkness? Behold, I am blown about like stubble on the mountains, afraid of Judah, fearful of Ephraim. Alas! I have been fearful, afraid and blown about these sixteen years. I came hither like a wayfarer that turns aside to tarry for a night, and chose the peak of Amana for my abode. And yet I have dwelt here full four months in vain. I was almost at peace, and thought I would remain here until your anger, O Lord God, had passed. But you have fixed the years of my affliction, and so affliction and sorrow will discover me wheresoever I be. O Lord, who looks into men's hearts, surely you have searched in mine, and know that I fear you. But why do I tremble at the sound of every falling leaf, for my heart is in my mouth continually? I hunt my prey with bow and arrow, return and lay me down to rest inside my abode, and behold, I am beset with fears of men who know me not, who plan to storm my lair and hunt me like a wild man. When, O Lord of my Salvation, will you bring my redemption, return me to Miriam, my wife, for whom I yearn, and to Eliphelet, my son, my delight and comfort in all my years of wandering? Shall God abandon me forever? Will you not set me free, for behold, the year of Jubilee has come!

"You, yourself, O Lord, decreed the year of Jubilee, the year of redemption in the land. But my redemption has not come. Liberty is in the land, but I am like a wandering bird. For you, O Lord, say to my soul: 'Fly to the mountains, fly from the hatred of Shamir, your father-in-law, fly from the wrath of the king, fly from the anger of Yehosheba, the wife of Elkanah, that was next to the king." That lady vexed me sore when days of peace allowed her pride free rein. But the crown has fallen from her head, her husband, Elkanah, lies slain upon the lofty fields. And now she is desolate in widowhood and can understand the pain of Miriam, my wife, who weeps for me, her loved one, in his roamings like a wandering bird. But whither shall I fly? Shall Jerusalem cry freedom upon me to enter her gates? Behold, Ahaz has cried freedom there to let his people sin, to serve new gods which he has chosen—Darmesek, god of Aram, to whom he has built an altar in Jerusalem, saying: 'These are the gods of Aram's kings, who help them; to them shall I sacrifice, and they shall help me also.' And in every corner of Jerusalem and in all the cities of Judah he has raised high places. And the people walk in darkness and rebellion, sacrificing and burning incense to Darmesek, god of Aram, and to Milcom, the abomination of the Amnonites, and to their Baals and Ashtoreths, the idols of the nations. He it is, King Ahaz, who makes Judah sin, and in all the places where he reigns the land rises against me. And shall I choose to dwell in Ephraim? There too snares are set to trap me. For the prophets of Beth-El and the company of priests stand everywhere on guard, and woe upon me if my name become known to my enemies, for they will not be sated with my flesh. My heart breaks within me for Judah, and of Ephraim it shall be said: 'They kiss their calves and slaughter men.' For the blood of man is worthless in their sight, but they love their calves, their priests, their prophets and their Baals, and they have become as slaves nailed to the doorposts of a house of evil, eternal slaves to idols. Behold, the year of Jubilee has come to summon every man to return to his inheritance, yet Ephraim is joined to idols, still arrogant in foreign bonds, and refuses to return to the Lord, the inheritance of their fathers. Alas, there is no freedom for Judah, no Jubilee for

Ephraim, and no redemption for my soul. Wherefore the Lord has cried freedom to the sword, to lay the land of Judah waste; and the trumpet resounds in the house of evil, the trumpet of the Jubilee, and Ephraim shall be carried unto Assyria."

The lone figure ceased pouring out his heart to God, and his servant approached him trembling and impatient, saying: 'Think of some plan, Uzziel, my master, for danger is nigh. Behold, our mortal enemies surround us, encircling the hill below. And though I know our enemies will not attempt to climb this place, which even the wild beasts cannot reach, how can that save us? Here on this fastness we sit as though on scorpions, fearing to descend because of our pursuers who lie in ambush. You see now, Uzziel, my master, that my words have come to pass. For how many times, my master, have I said to you: 'Whom have you here, what have you here that you perch like an eagle on this tooth of rock, eating your bread in desolation and drinking your water in fear? Hasten and find yourself another refuge.' And you promised to tell me the name of your wife in Zion, and to send me there to reveal to her your hiding place, that she might give you counsel from afar. If you had only sent me when you promised, perhaps by now your wife might have found a place of refuge for you, if she remains as faithful to you as you to her. But words count nothing, if deeds will not bring salvation."

"This is indeed no time for words," Uzziel answered. "Go to the crag's edge and lie upon the ground, and listen closely to what our pursuers say. Then tell me what you hear, for I know what must be done."

The servant did his master's bidding and listened intently until the sound of voices rose to his ear. Then he returned to the lone man and said: "I heard the confused noise of many men, but one voice I heard, saying: 'We stand on guard in vain. It would appear that the lion of Armana has left his lair, and made his way to the valley. Wherefore let us disperse and seek him among the thickets.' Thus one spoke, but his fellow answered: 'See, our master comes riding on his mule, and armed with sword and bow.'"

Then Uzziel stood thinking for some moments, until rousing

himself he said to his servant: "Come, I will meet my enemies with cunning. Take the horn from my room, and blow a great blast, so that they who lie in ambush will say: The sound of the horn is to warn the hunter of his peril, that he may hurry away to safety. Meanwhile I shall arm myself with sword, bow and arrows ready for the fray, and descend upon my enemies and cry peace upon them, declaring myself innocent of harm. But if they believe me not and do battle with me, then shall I indeed be innocent before the Lord. And I shall hurl myself upon them, striking right and left, that those who pursue me without cause shall die with me. For what does it profit me to prolong my life?"

Obedient to his command, the servant took the horn and sounded a great blast, and then a second, and a third. And just as Uzziel had foreseen, so did it come to pass. For those in ambush scattered among the thickets, seeking the lion of Amana. And Uzziel waited till he could not bear it more, then ordering his servant to lower the ladder, he descended armed to the hilt like a man of war, prepared for evil or for good.

The Hypocrite

Plot Summary and Extract

Translated by David Patterson

The Plot of The Hypocrite

The story opens in the poverty-stricken setting of a way-side inn. The owner, Yeruham, was formerly a rich merchant who entrusted his affairs during his long business trips to an upstart manager, Gaal. The latter, the rejected lover of Yeruham's daughter, Sarah, now Joseph's widow, in consequence contrived to ruin Yeruham, who was stripped of all his possessions. Joseph, however, had a faithful friend, Saul, who advanced him money to acquire the inn, and secured a post for Joseph in the service of the local baron. Sarah bore three children, Naaman, Ruhamah, and Raphael, the youngest of whom was betrothed at birth to Saul's daughter. But Gaal so poisoned the baron's mind against Joseph that he was dismissed and died of a broken heart.

Saul keeps faith with his dead friend, and sends his son, Naaman, to study agriculture. Naaman is about to complete his studies, return to support his family and bring Gaal to justice, when the latter induces Naaman's friend, Zimon, to plant false documents in Naaman's room and denounce him as a spy. Naaman is arrested and disappears, while rumour reaches Yeruham that he has been drowned. Gaal uses the opportunity to spread slander against Yeruham, and ruin his trade in the inn. He plans to force the old man to surrender documents which could incriminate him, at the same time hoping to marry the widowed Sarah.

The burden of poverty compels Yeruham—via the agency of Nehemiah, a champion of enlightenment—to beg a former business colleague, Obadiah, to buy his inn. But the latter, too, is under Gaal's influence and returns only abuse. Gaal's villainy is supported and excelled by that of his son-in-law, Zadok, an arch-hypocrite. The latter, whose real name is Hophni, having already deserted two wives, has usurped the name and credentials of a famous Palestinian scholar and rabbi who had died on a journey from the Holy Land. His base schemes are furthered by his servant Levi, who plans to marry Joseph's daughter Ruhamah, who, as Zadok learns from a letter addressed to Yeruham which he has intercepted, is due to receive a large inheritance from her relative Michael in London. Zadok, accordingly, advises Levi to plant some incriminating jewellery in Yeruham's house, and have him arrested for theft. Without her grandfather's guardianship Ruhamah will fall an easy prey to Levi. This jewellery, which formerly belonged to Sarah, had been taken by Obadiah in part payment of his debt. Obadiah had given it to his granddaughter Elisheva, who, being deeply in love with Naaman, had wanted to return it to Ruhamah, his sister, but had been robbed of it while journeying home.

By the eve of Passover Yeruham's household is in such dire straits that even the necessities for the festival are wanting. Suddenly Naaman arrives, disguised as Zimon. He explains that he had, himself, spread the rumour of his death, the better to pursue his revenge on Gaal. He describes how he has rescued Eden, Obadiah's son, from a band of robbers, while he was conveying a large sum of money for the baron. He has returned home with rich gifts from the baron, as well as a present for Elisheva from her father Eden, and one for Eden's wife, Zibiah. He has also brought a letter from Eden to Obadiah, urging that Elisheva marry only a man of her own choosing, and warning Obadiah against Gaal. Saul arrives the same day to swell the happiness of Yeruham's family, and intimates that, as a widower, he is ready to marry Sarah.

Their joy is shattered, however, by the arrest of Yeruham and Sarah, who are charged with stealing the jewellery which Levi had concealed in their home. Obadiah finally takes pity on them and offers bail, but he is preceded by the baron's wife. But Naaman, now known as Zimon, can make no progress in winning Obadiah's consent to his marrying Elisheva. The matter is complicated by Gaal's desire that she should wed his own son Zerah, while Zadok, whose wife has just died, is also angling for her. Moreover Elisheva is prejudiced against the supposed Zimon, being in love with Naaman. She is also suspicious of Zimon's relationship with Ruhamah.

Meanwhile Zaphnath, the proprietress of a neighbouring inn, who is the principal agent behind the campaign of slander directed against Yeruham's family, is conducting an illicit affair with Levi. Her husband, Yerachme'el, is a pious but impractical man who has been wandering through many lands for seven years, and has now returned in search of the wicked Hophni, alias Zadok, who is wanted for murder, theft, forgery, and bigamy. At Zaphnath's instigation, Yerachme'el is arrested and thrown into prison. Levi contracts a fever, and before his death reveals something of Zadok's past. Simultaneously Zadok and Gaal become estranged, while Zaphnath, whose adultery is exposed, flees to London with Emil, a worthless rake who is anxious to conceal his Jewish origin. They are accompanied by Zerah, Gaal's son, who has fled the country after stealing some money deposited with Zadok for safekeeping.

On the ship bound for London they meet Naaman and Ruhamah, as well as Azriel, a young scholar returning from the Holy Land with Shiphrah, whom he had saved from drowning in the Sea of Galilee. They are on their way to collect an inheritance bequeathed to them by Michael. They are accompanied by Heman, a native of Italy, but who has lived in Turkey and Palestine, where he befriended Azriel. He is travelling with his sister in search of Alkum, alias Hophni, alias Zadok, who has deserted her. The party is completed by Shlomiel, who is also seeking Hophni. Suddenly a dreadful storm springs up, and Zaphnath and Emil are washed overboard, but not before Zerah has revealed their secret and Levi's disclosures about Zadok.

Even before they return from London, enough of Zadok's duplicity has leaked out to alienate even the stubborn and bigoted Gaddiel; while for his part Zadok reveals something of Gaal's wickedness. Yet Obadiah still pins his faith to Zadok's integrity and exerts pressure on Elisheva to marry him. Elisheva is very distressed, for she cannot return Naaman's affection as long as she believes him to be Zimon. Meanwhile Eden's death is reported, and Gaal makes overtures to his widow, Zibiah.

After many adventures the party from London returns with the inheritance, and Naaman reveals his real identity to Elisheva, informing her also that her father Eden is still alive. Even Obadiah is reconciled to their marriage, and on the wedding-day Eden himself appears. For the celebrations the baron's castle is turned into a theatre to enact the play "Joseph and his Brothers." Zadok and Gaal are among the guests, the latter deliberately sitting next to Zibiah and urging her to forget the "dead" Eden, and become his own wife. His proposal is meanwhile overheard by Eden. The baron advances, and declares the time has come to put an end to strife. That the affair may be properly investigated he calls upon the contending parties, namely Gaal on the one hand, and on the other Obadiah and Yeruham, to submit their case to his judgement. Gaal comes forward and announces that as a gesture of reconciliation, he is willing to wed Zibiah, Eden's widow. At that moment Eden comes forth, takes off his disguise and denounces Gaal. Simultaneously Zadok's many accusers denounce him, so that even Obadiah's eyes are opened to his real nature. The final victory over the villains is complete, and their erstwhile victims handsomely avenged.

Part Three

Chapter twelve

The guests were assembled around the table, seated each according to his station. The old man was clad in a shroud-like linen garment white as snow, whose upper edge—an embroidered garland of beaten silver threads—encircled his neck like a crown. His girdle was fastened with a silver brooch, while his head was covered with a pure, white shawl, flecked with sparkling silver, so that he sat upon his couch like a king amid his courtiers. He first pronounced the benediction, which the guests repeated; then raising the dish on high they were reading in Aramaic the passage dealing with the bread of affliction, when lo, a sound of lamentation was heard from the room in which sat Zibiah with Elisheva. And the old man trembled and sent Shemariah to see what was the matter. And when Shemariah returned he related that the women were weeping for Eden, for no news had arrived of what had befallen him, and that was the cause of their distress.

"If that is so," Zimon replied, "I must read to them a letter which I doubt if even Elisheva could make out alone, for Eden himself wrote only a few lines at the end to testify that the contents are true and dictated at his command."

"Please go then," the old man answered without enthusiasm, "and read it to them to calm their spirits. But show me first if it really is his hand."

And Zimon took the letter from his pocket and showed it to the old man, who said: "This is indeed my son's writing in the margin."

So Zimon rose and went from the room carrying his stick. And Zibiah and Elisheva said to him: "You have already shown us your kindness and good faith. Now give us words of comfort to calm our spirits, for we are much distressed."

"Look, gentle Elisheva," Zimon replied, "I shall address myself to you, not to your step-mother, for she is vexed with me. The letter in my possession was dictated by your dear father, but written by a soldier who, although of our people, had so little skill with a pen that the characters are scarcely recognizable. Why should you strain your lovely eyes on them? So I will read it to you and to the esteemed Zibiah, who may regard me with more favour in a little while. At the end of the letter there are a few lines written in Eden's hand to confirm all it contains. Now, good ladies, listen to the letter."

"To Elisheva, my darling daughter, and to my beloved wife.

"May the Lord grant me life and peace, and protect me whether I dwell at home or travel abroad or walk in the valley of the shadow of death. May he carry me back safely to my father's house to bring joy to you all. That is my heart's desire and my prayer to God. There are times when a man forgets his Creator, dwelling in tranquillity and peace; but when danger threatens he repents, and remembers him constantly. Such has been my case, and now let me relate what has befallen me.

"Eight days ago the baron entrusted me with a hundred thousand pieces of silver to pay the various officers who supply the troops with bread, meat, and wine, and the horses with fodder. I set off on my way together with a servant lad to drive the horses. Towards evening the paths became slippery with rain and ice, and one of the horses caught his hoof on the treacherous path and was lamed, so that the carriage moved forward with difficulty. As the sun went down behind the mountains, we entered a vast forest, and very soon night descended upon us, plunging the path in darkness. As it was the first of the month there was no moon, while thick cloud blotted out the stars. Moreover, to my consternation, I perceived that we had wandered off the path and were lost in the pitch darkness. In my terror the curse of the holy Psalmist welled up in my heart: 'Let their way be dark and slippery and the angel of the Lord pursuing them.' And the cause of my fears was that the forest swarmed with desperate brigands, deserters from the army."

"Alas! I feel dark terror stealing over me," cried Elisheva. And Zibiah moaned: "Alas! I am distraught!"

"Be calm and fear not," Zimon replied. "Hear me out, for all was well in the end:

"Before we had continued much further our way led us among closely interwoven trees. When suddenly I heard the sound of whispering, and the noise of twigs breaking and footsteps in the undergrowth. Just then the boy who was driving the horses called out in a low, thin voice, which floated back to me: 'May God on high protect us! The path has run out, and a gaping chasm yawns before us.'

"The words of the lad terrified me. My stomach turned over as a wave of fear passed through me, and the dread of the Lord fell upon me. Had these three things combined against me, the blackness of the night, the treacherous path, and even spirits of evil pursuing us? But though my heart melted in fear, I encouraged the lad and said: 'Have we not two pistols? If trouble comes we can defend ourselves, and the Lord will protect us with his shadow.' Yet even as I spoke my teeth chattered and my hands shook, and the best plan seemed to remain where we were in absolute silence until the terror passed. But as though to terrify us more our horses whinnied. And suddenly I heard a voice crying: 'Where are you leading us, you wretch? Can't you hear the horses neighing? Hurry, comrades, there's spoil here!'"

"My heart cries out for my father," Elisheva exclaimed.

"My heart melts like wax within me," Zibiah wailed.

And from the next room a voice could be heard reading: "And we cried out to the Lord, the God of our fathers, and the Lord heard our cry, and perceived our sorrow, and our burden and our toil."

"Do you hear, dear ladies?" said Zimon. "The Lord listens to the voice of him that calls upon Him from the depths. Thus did He listen to Eden's cry."

Then he continued reading:

"As I heard those dreadful cries the fear of God took hold of me. The blood froze in my veins, my heart turned to stone. I put my finger on the trigger of my pistol, but my flesh crept with fear and my hands went limp. I determined to seek refuge in flight, but my legs seemed turned to lead. Therefore I entrusted my soul to my Creator, seeing that escape there was none, and death confronted me. Then before my eyes a terrible spectacle materialized—a wild man like an evil spirit or some offspring of death, his face covered with hair, a look of murder in his eyes, and every fibre of him tensed for slaughter. And in a hoarse voice he shouted to his comrades in evil: 'Didn't I tell you we would find our quarry here?' Then he roared at me like a lion: 'You there, all wrapped up in your shawl! Throw that armour off and bring out the money for us!' My strength ebbed away and my feet felt so weighed down with lead that I could not move. My eyes went black and my tongue clove to the roof of my mouth. I saw myself facing an untimely end, and as the murderer held my arm in a powerful grip I cried out: 'Finish me off quickly then, and don't prolong the agony.' But he merely shook me violently and handed me over to his four murderous companions, saying: 'Let no one dare harm him. He may have hidden the money, or thrown it into some secret hiding place. So don't touch him till I search the carriage, even if I have to rip it to pieces.'

"By then my soul was wearied of the murderers, and my body was damp with the fear of death. I broke out in a cold sweat, with the thought of murder numbing my spirit. My mind went blank and lost all power of cohesive thought. But from my heart's sorrow there welled up the memory of my old father, and your memory, my lovely daughter, and yours, too, my dear wife. I prayed to God for those beloved souls as long as I had strength. I wept from the depths of my heart and groaned in silence."

At that point Elisheva and Zibiah could contain themselves no longer, and wept bitterly. But their lament was not heard in the other room above the reading of the guests. And Zimon said to Elisheva: "Dry your pretty eyes, dear lady, for your lament need not continue long, and these tears will soon turn into boundless joy."
Then he continued to read:

"But when my servant saw that the end was nigh, he shouted aloud with all the strength of despair. Then one of the scoundrels said to the leader of the gang: 'This bird is chirping. Give me leave to nip off his head, for why prolong his life? We will learn nothing of the money from him. Just say the word, master!' At that my servant summoned his remaining strength in one last desperate cry, and I did likewise. I cried for help, although I knew not whence my help would come. But hope springs eternal in the human breast.

"Nor was my hope in vain. For just as I prepared to surrender my life to these murderers, and entrust my soul to the God of all flesh, a rifle-shot rang out, followed by a lusty voice that cried: 'Hurry up, men, with weapons at the ready! You heard that bitter cry for help, and our hands are against all accursed robbers. Hurry, and we'll take them alive!' And now a different tumult shattered the silence of the night. The robbers, five in number, returned the fire once or twice. But without time to reload their guns, their shots soon ceased. Their leader, however, hastily searched through my baggage, and snatching the bundle of notes equal in value to a hundred thousand pieces of silver fled for his life to some secret lair. Now the strange thing is that so long as death confronted me I withstood the darkness, yet as soon as I perceived that the mortal danger had passed, my spirit fainted and I know not what befell me. Therefore I can only repeat what my servant told me later. His account is as follows: When I saw that death had passed, I summoned all my strength and fled away, running and jumping like a stag. Then suddenly a fine young man rushed to the scene of slaughter like a fleet hind shouting: 'This way, men!' I told him that five bandits had held my master up to ransom, and he girded his loins and pursued them headlong, his five friends at his heels. And he caught up with one of the robbers fleeing between the trees and smote the back of his neck with an iron-loaded stick. Nor was a second blow needed, for he dropped senseless in his tracks."

Then Elisheva and Zibiah brightened and both looked at the handsome youth, and a smile appeared on Elisheva's lips as her gaze fastened on the stick and she saw through his disguise. Even Zibiah was reconciled, while Elisheva rejoiced to feel her love increase a thousand times. But Zimon continued his reading:

"When I regained my senses I was lying quietly and safely in bed. Sitting at its head I saw a fine young man silently tending to my wants, as an attentive son would tend a beloved father. And when he saw me rouse myself, his eyes filled with tears of joy. But as soon as I perceived the light of day, I cried aloud as I remembered the hundred thousand pieces of silver which had fallen booty to the robber, without hope of return. And even the baron, who had hastened to come to me and waited eagerly till I regained consciousness, shuddered as he heard of my loss. But the handsome youth, who had already shown his courage, now demonstrated his trustworthiness even more. For without a word he drew from his bosom the bundle of notes and laid them down before the baron's eyes. In short, not a farthing was missing, and everyone was overjoyed. Even my servant did not know that the youth had recovered the robber's spoil, for he had done so secretly. Yet with this immense sum he could have become a great man in the land. His behaviour has been wonderful. Can I describe the honour which the baron showed him? Words are superfluous, but the promise of the baroness herself to be his patroness will give you some idea. And the name of this youth is Zimon. All this has been written at Eden's command."

In the margin of the letter a few lines were added in Eden's hand:

My dear ones, I write these lines as testimony that everything in this letter has been written at my dictation. The noble Zimon stands before you, therefore give him your blessing for his kindness and for saving my life. Zibiah, my dear wife, please accept from him the birthday gift which I have bought as a token of my undying love. And you, my dearest daughter, Elisheva, you have already met the good Zimon in the town of Amon at the theatre. And even there he told you of his readiness to make henceforth a pact of friendship with

Yeruham, and espouse his cause. Therefore please accept these ornaments, which I send to you by his hand; and in return give your own jewellery to his friend Ruhamah, Sarah's daughter. And peace, prosperity and joy upon you, to Zibiah from your husband, and to Elisheva from your father, Eden.

> Written from the army-camp of the Baron,
> On this day of my salvation, the eighth day of Shevat,
1854.

Elisheva was astounded at the coincidence, remembering that on the eighth day of Shevat she too had made a vow to return the jewellery to Ruhamah. And now she perceived that the same generous impulse had stirred her father's heart. But for the moment her mind was full of the wonderful deeds which her dear friend had done for her father. So she turned to Zibiah and said: "What do you say now, mother, to all these marvels?"

"What can I say?" Zibiah answered delightedly. "I can only repeat the remark our friend Zimon made to you. I would like to take them all in my arms, and embrace them. But how can we express our thanks to Zimon, who is responsible for this great salvation? Forgive me, dear youth, for my unkindness to you when first you entered my house. But now my feelings are quite changed, for the Lord sent you like an angel of salvation to my husband in his hour of need."

"Indeed," Elisheva answered, giving her hand to Zimon. "It is not your stick, but my father's words that tell me that you are the angel that saved him."

As she was speaking, the words of the readers from the next room could be heard recounting the mercies of the Lord in Egypt:

"If he had slain their first-born, without giving us their wealth, it would have been sufficient."

And listening to the recitation Elisheva smiled charmingly and said: "You too have shown us much wonderful kindness. You have saved my father's life, defeated the angel of death, recovered the stolen money, and poured it out at the baron's feet. You really have performed miracles, and I can in no way recompense you. We shall be ever in your debt."

"You say you cannot recompense me?" Zimon repeated with a laugh. "But you hold the key to my reward!"

And Elisheva understood his meaning and said: "Please rejoin the guests, dear friend, and complete the reading with them. For we shall have the opportunity again to talk together."

"I shall always respect your wishes," replied Zimon, and with a winning smile he gave her his hand, then turned and left the room.

And Zibiah said to Elisheva: "You see, my daughter, how completely my feelings have changed in a few moments, because of what this youth has done. I shall no longer scold you or rebuke you on his account, for he has done wonders for us."

"He has indeed," Elisheva answered. "With his strong right arm he has preserved a beloved son for his father, a loving husband for his wife, and a merciful father for his daughter. And not only has he done all this, but to add joy to joy he has so changed your feelings towards me, that I know you will no longer vex me. Is not my father precious to us both? Then why should we be estranged without cause? Henceforth show me a mother's compassion, and I will show compassion in return."

As she spoke Elisheva embraced Zibiah and kissed her, and continued: "Do what I beg of you, and I shall call you mother."

"For my part I welcome the reconciliation and I shall carry out your wishes," Zibiah replied. "And if you desire Zimon, as it appears you do, you have only to say the word and I shall try to win over your grandfather as soon as he has learned of Zimon's wonderful exploits. For the matter will depend on him, and Eden, his son, will not run counter to his wishes. So tell me what you desire."

"What I desire!" Elisheva repeated thoughtfully. "But leave me a while, mother, for my desires and thoughts are all confused. My mind is still so full that I cannot yet calm my spirit. So let us talk of it again at a better opportunity."

Meanwhile Zimon had joined the guests in their reading, and they completed the Hallel prayer and drank the second cup of wine according to custom. Then, having washed their hands, they ate the unleavened bread and bitter herbs, and partook of the rich and tasty fish which was set before them. Then Zimon read out the letter before all the assembled guests, and they were all astounded—even more so when they perceived the stout stick in his hand, with which he had cracked the robber-leader's head, and they kept glancing at him in wonder. The old man blessed him effusively, and all the guests sang his praises and lauded his deeds to the skies, that he had fought the robbers and prevailed. But the whole episode sorely distressed the old man, and his heart was full of dark foreboding that this Zimon might become an obstacle and stumbling-block to his plans. Meanwhile Reb Zadok sat silently as if in mourning, wearing an inscrutable expression. His face remained pale even though fire consumed his frame. Nor was his fear of Zimon groundless, for the latter was a thorn in his side, piercing him to the quick. Yet he kept silent, for what could he do? Should he praise Zimon's deeds? That would only hinder his own schemes. Should he belittle the praise? But then the guests would realize that he spoke from envy, and that while still in mourning for his dead wife, he had already fixed his eye on Elisheva. That evening too he must be on his guard, for the evening augured evil. Zimon he regarded as an angel of destruction who had come hither to wreck all the schemes which he had laid. But as he looked at the old man the latter's expression gave him hope. Zadok brightened and felt better, while a flicker of joy passed across his face, as though every fibre of his body were crying out: "Elisheva shall yet be mine!"

Then Zimon said to the old man: "I have still another message from your son, but it is addressed to you alone and no one else. His message was but short, and whenever you are ready, I will repeat his words in full."

"Both a written and a verbal message," replied the old man testily, looking at his watch. "There is still time before we eat the last piece of unleavened bread. First trouble with a son, then with a daughter, and I have to worry about them all. But what can be done?"

With a sigh he rose from his couch and beckoned Zimon to follow him to his room, where Zimon gave him the letter, saying:

"This is not the time for me to speak, for I see you are in no mood for it; so read your son's letter."

And Obadiah took the letter somewhat unwillingly and read as follows:

> My honoured and revered father!
>
> From the letter which I wrote to my wife and daughter you will realize what the noble youth Zimon has done for me. He is regarded as one of our younger men who are winning respect for Israel in high circles. But the actions of your trusted Gaal are quite the reverse. His poisonous tongue, which is like the bite of an adder, plotted to destroy me, and God alone be praised that I escaped his snares. You will not understand this secret now, but I shall hasten to enlighten you when the time comes. Then your eyes will be opened to the wicked Gaal's designs and you will take pity on Yeruham's house which Zimon, too, has taken under his wing.
>
> One more request I make of you, my honoured father. The time is drawing nigh for my beloved daughter Elisheva to marry; and I know that she is dear to you, and that you are anxious about her future. Be so good, therefore, as to decide nothing without consulting her wishes and mine. For as long as I am on the battle-front, my position is like that of a dangerously sick man, and my requests must be regarded as a testament. My life is in constant danger, but blessed be the Lord of my salvation, who will shelter me with his shadow, just as he sent the good angel, Zimon, to save me and my servant when death faced us. Soon we return to barracks, so expect no word from me until we leave again. After that your son, who is entirely devoted to you, looks forward eagerly to seeing you.
>
> Eden.

"You have read it, sir, and you understand its meaning," Zimon remarked, as the old man finished reading the letter.

"I understand it right enough," the old man answered. 'The spirit of understanding comes with age. So leave me for a few moments, my friend, to commune with myself. In a little while I shall return, for it is time to pray to God, and that alone is true wisdom. We shall speak again about my son, who calls upon God for help in time of need, but forgets the great call which God makes to him. But leave me a little."

And Zimon recognized the old man's confusion of mind, and left him to join the others at the festive table. There he found Elisheva, to whom Hogeh was just giving a letter and saying: "Please read this letter written by my friend Azriel, with whom, I think, you are acquainted. This letter is both precious in itself and opportune, for it was composed on Mount Zion at the festival of Passover. So read it and see how great are his descriptive powers."

So Elisheva took the missive from Hogeh and read as follows:

In the year five thousand six hundred and thirteen according to the Jewish calendar, on the evening of the fourteenth day of the month of Aviv, the season of the ancient festival of Passover, I sit here on Mount Zion, a hill on the south side of Jerusalem, and make this solemn declaration with deep emotion. Peace upon you, mountains of Zion, Mount Moriah and the Mount of Olives, you sacred mountains that stand eternal as God's righteousness. Peace upon you, precious relics of antiquity, in whose name I made this journey, and whose remembrance fills my soul. Peace upon you, most precious of all dust, the dust of our fathers, whom I cherish.

On the fourteenth day of the first month, the season of joy and gladness for our fathers in ancient times, the season of praise and thanksgiving to the Lord, who brought them forth from Egypt to settle upon this lovely land, the inheritance of their father Jacob—on this pleasant festival I sit upon Mount

Zion, pencil in hand, to set down my inmost thoughts upon the page. And the mourning and desolate city of God looks down upon me from the north, through the veil of widowhood. Just as I had pictured her, so do I see her in all her holiness, as though mourning for her sacred desolation. My spirit aches to see her mounds forsaken, the forlornness of ancient times, and the desolation of each generation. Can this be Zion, so celebrated by the prophets who sprang from her? Enemies have destroyed her foundations, and fools have dispersed the words of her holy sons. But Mount Zion shall never crumble, nor shall the holy words be lost to Zion's sons. For these are the words of the living God, fixed in the heavens, lighting up the darkness like the stars. And even when heavy clouds conceal the stars, the spirit of wisdom shall shine forth, and pierce the blackness. The night shall vanish, and the light of God shine even as of old. Yea, a new light shall shine on Zion, which now lies desolate and mourning. The sons, which she bore in bewilderment, shall flock to her sacred ruins. They shall come streaming in from all the lands of the dispersion, for they are all her children, who bear her name upon their lips with every outpouring of prayer. They shall come to her and say that through all their sorrows and afflictions they have remembered her, and the love of Zion shall never be erased from their hearts. It is the love that springs from the delightful hope that hovers over her ruins, and whispers in our ears the consolation of Isaiah: 'For the Lord shall comfort Zion: He will comfort all her waste places; and he will make her wilderness like Eden, and her desert like the garden of the Lord; joy and gladness shall be found therein, thanksgiving and the voice of melody.'

But the word of the Lord has not yet come, and so I stand on the appointed mountain and meditate on ancient times when the Passover was prepared for those that came to celebrate it, and I among them in imagination. And the magic of my dream conjures up a vision of great crowds thronging the streets and market-places of Jerusalem. The shadows lengthen, the day ebbs away and the sun, that faithful witness in heaven, announces that the time has come to serve the Lord. And a voice cries out in the gates: 'Hurry, you people of the God of Abraham, and all who fear the word of the Lord both near and far, hurry to celebrate the Passover at the appointed season.' And at the sound vast crowds emerge from the city of God, the princes of Judah from their marble palaces, and the poor of the land from their tents. At such a time both rich and poor are equal, for the spirit of the Lord gathers them all. Together they bring their paschal lamb to their families and their fathers' houses, and together they stream into the courtyards of the Lord to the sound of drums, viols, and cymbals. Come, you that celebrate, and let us ascend the mountain to God's Temple, to give thanks to him that is sanctified in glory, who singled us out to be his people. How delightful is this mighty voice of Israel, chanting the hymn of praise in the holy Temple! And in the city's streets I hear the sound of voices crying: 'Eat, friends, of the Passover, with all your hearts. Eat of the roasted meat with the unleavened bread and bitter herbs, but break not the bone thereof.' And I, who had eaten nothing since morning, devoured the holy flesh with relish. The poor ate thereof and were sated; and my soul, too, was sated with joy, to mingle with this holy congregation, and to sing the stirring songs of valour amidst young and old.

This is the heavenly vision which my imagination conjured up concerning Mount Zion and her assemblies. All the delights of ancient times welled up and lived before my eyes. Hurrah! I thought—wake up, my soul, and awaken the love of the eternal people. Remember the days of old, that they may bring comfort at the present time. And you too, O sacred Hebrew tongue, don your holy garb and your spirit of noble grace, and sing to your lover, the youth of Israel, borne on the arms of God since the days of Egypt. Make your voice resound, that your words be heard to the very ends of the earth, wherever the sound shall reach. But sing your song only for him that loves you, for the people that has chosen you, for they are all your delight. Hurrah! my spirit marches proudly, walking the eternal paths of old. And with the power of imagination I hear a rustling from the grave, a cry from out the rock, the voice of the world's dead that sleep in the dust of the ground, rising rejuvenated from the ashes of death, and living before me in my sight. This is the great cry, which breaks forth from the Hebrew tongue to her people, resounding as in the days of her youth.

I plan to remain in Zion throughout the Spring. Then I shall travel the road of God to the Jordan and Hermon, to celebrate the Feast of Weeks in Tiberias. And when the festival has passed I shall make my way to Damascus, God willing. For the heart of man may plan his course, but God alone directs his steps to wheresoever he wishes.

May God be with me in all my paths, that my way be smooth. And you, dear friend of my youth, accept my best wishes, and my blessing be upon you and upon our friend, the learned doctor Hogeh, wherever he may be. I shall remember you from the land of Jordan, so think kindly of me, for I am your devoted friend, Azriel.

After finishing the letter, Elisheva handed it back to Hogeh and gracefully added: "Would that letters such as this might appear more often in our literature! For only such refinement of language will teach the youth of Israel good taste and fine understanding, and inspire their minds. But not so the harsh style which ruins the taste of the learned, and robs the language of its beauty. Azriel writes in an exalted style, and the words of his letter might well be counted among the holy things of Israel."

"The holy things of Israel?" replied Shubal indignantly. "It is not for women to declare what is good or what is holy. Such judgements can be given only by the pious men of the community, and they pour out their wrath against these refined and polished writings, condemning both the literary gems and their noisy authors equally to perdition. Yet you, Elisheva, declare that they may be counted among the holy things of Israel. Who then is destroying holiness with worthless phrases?"

"What is all this quarrelling?" the old man asked.

"It is no quarrel," Shubal replied. "But a slip of the tongue. Your daughter erred in thinking that fine language might be counted among the holy things of Israel, while I condemned all such authors and everything to do with them out of hand."

"Why do you persecute them so relentlessly?" replied Yair. "Once you defended them. Have you changed so much that you can cruelly assign them all to hell? Do you not hear their bitter cries?"

"Even from the depths of hell they would still cry out in elegant phrases!" Shubal retorted caustically. "Nor will they be there alone, for those who honour them, will accompany them down. But why should I joke about things which are so serious? In my youth I toyed with their glowing coals, and so scorched my fingers that even today I feel the scars. All who look for righteousness in them are deluded; for their fine words are like deadly flies that hover boldly about the flowers of paradise, daring even to penetrate the sanctuary and pollute the fragrant oil. They are saturated with lies, they shoot out their lips against both God and man, and tear out holy ideas root and branch, leaving not a shred, and rejecting them utterly. But what I always say to these slanderers is this: Do not malign in secret, but bring forth your arguments, and show them squarely to our brethren who remain faithful to Israel. Put them before us naked, without shrouding their faces in a mantle of righteousness, as Azriel has done in this letter. Then they can see their nakedness and be ashamed. For even Azriel covers himself with fig leaves which he has sewn together in this letter, and the secrets of ancient days he has moulded into a healing salve to hide the truth."

"You are a bigot, my dear Shubal," answered Yair, "and you wrap yourself in zeal for God like a cloak. But your zeal for God is really zeal against your fellow men. What harm do you find in Azriel that you deride him and despise his fine words?"

"Listen to me, Yair, my friend though my opponent," Shubal answered, 'you know that I, too, once trumpeted the praise of fine words and elegant language. But once my eyes were opened by experience to see the world clearly, I so learned to disdain them, and despise their honeyed sweetness, that they became anathema to me. For they are destroying Israel. And as for Azriel, Hogeh's friend, I am angry with him because he is a youth to whom God has given understanding and material advantages. I told him time and again: 'Stay here and hold fast to your faith.' But he was foolish and wandered off abroad. Now he is in the Holy Land, with the result that he transmits his visions from Mount Zion to Othniel, his friend, and sets him a fine example! But what is the good of making speeches? Take away the roses, I say, before the thorns begin to prick our young!"

"You are one of us indeed," replied the old man. "Would that there were more zealots like you in Israel. All these fancy phrases are woman's wisdom, and quite suitable for my daughter Elisheva; but the Lord did not intend it for men. If only Azriel had sent us some new legal decision, then I might have praised him."

"Would you have Azriel send us some new decision from across the sea?" asked Hogeh. "Do we lack them here? Does not Zadok give us them by the hundred and Gaddiel by the thousand, so that they spring up all over the town like grass? But if the Lord has not granted such a faculty to Azriel, let him at least keep what he has; for he has been blessed with a princely share of refinement and understanding."

"My dear doctor Hogeh," the old man answered disapprovingly, "I had not thought to hear such sentiments from you. But let us discuss the matter no longer, for sinful talk only leads to mischief."

"And the tongue that speaks it will be rewarded with coals of fire," Shubal added. "I am distressed for you, Hogeh, especially as you are so excellent a physician."

"Then you should heap coals of fire on your own lips," Yair answered with a smile, "for fire drives out fire! Or roll in the snow to cool the jealous ardour that burns in you. But in any case this is not the time for conversation."

"Just so," Zadok added. "This is not the time to argue, but to complete the Passover."

And as the old man supported him, they broke off the discussion until the Passover had been completed in every detail. Then they arose, and Naaman, still in the guise of Zimon, betook himself to the room to which Zibiah and Elisheva had retired, and addressed Elisheva in French: "You know, dear lady, what I have done for your father, and that he could find no way of rewarding me. But your love is all the reward I want. So tell me whether I have the right to hope."

Elisheva was confused, but also answered him in French: "This is neither the place nor the time to speak about such matters. Meet me tomorrow at the home of the baroness, and then I shall give you a proper answer."

"Hurrah," answered Zimon still in French. "I have listened most attentively, for to know your mind is what matters most for me now. I do hope that you will tell me plainly then that all my efforts have not been in vain."

"Tomorrow and not now," Elisheva repeated. "And now you must retire."

Just then the old man, who regarded Zimon as a thorn in his side, entered the room and said: "Night was created for sleep or study only—as the sages say. All other talking is unnecessary."

"Quite right, sir," Zimon replied. "But I was talking of your son, and so my words bring his daughter fresh life. Is that sinful?"

The old man laughed and quoted the psalmist: "'Show forth thy loving-kindness in the morning and thy faithfulness every night.' But now, my young friend, I have given orders that your couch be prepared in the loft. So take yourself up there now and retire to sleep."

With that the old man called to his servant Shemariah and bade him conduct Zimon to the place which had been prepared for him in the loft. So Shemariah put a candle in a silver candlestick to light the way for Naaman, took him up to the room prepared for him and arranged his couch, but sighing all the time. And when Naaman asked him why he sighed, he answered not a word, but taking the candle in his hand he tiptoed to the door, and opened it suddenly to find Zipporah!

"What do you want, Zipporah?" Shemariah asked her.

"Oh, nothing!" the girl answered. "Only that I slept here yesterday with my mistress Elisheva, and left a white handkerchief here."

"Then why are you so anxious about it?" Shemariah continued. "Surely you can find it tomorrow."

"I hope so," Zipporah replied, and went downstairs.

After she had gone Shemariah said to Zimon: "You see, yourself, that you are regarded as a pest in this house, and that Zadok alone commands respect here. I'm sure Zipporah was sent to listen behind the door to what I say to you. So I had better not linger here or Zibiah will box my ears again, as she has already done once today because I was praising you in the presence of Elisheva, who is always glad to listen to me. So consider your plans well, sir, and do what must be done for your own good and for her good too—for you need Elisheva. If God answers my request, I shall be more than ready to become your servant this time next year."

"How good of you!" Naaman replied, putting his hand on the servant's shoulder. "Then say a prayer for us. Perhaps the Lord will listen to your plan and bring it to pass."

"Would that he may," Shemariah sighed. 'This very day I promised Meir the Wonder-Worker eighteen pence if he would intercede to bring it about. So we'll see just how powerful he is. And if he deceives me this time, I shall tell everybody that it is useless to bring him gifts. And many people will listen to me, so that his losses will be great.'

Naaman could scarcely suppress a smile at the servant's credulity, but he said: "Don't worry about Meir the Wonder-Worker, for I'm sure your gift will not be in vain. It will certainly bring me what you asked from him. Then many people will hear of the miracle which he has performed and hasten to bring him gifts, so that faith in him will grow daily."

He had scarcely finished when Zibiah's maid came to summon Shemariah, saying: "You know how grumpy the old man is. You had better hurry down to him."

"Yes, hurry down to him," Naaman added in his turn.

And Shemariah answered angrily: "There's no peace and quiet for an old man." And turning away, he went downstairs.

Selected Further Reading

Auerbach, E., *Mimesis,* English version, New York, 1953.

Brainin, R., *Abraham Mapu,* Piotrokow, 1900.

Braudes, R. A., *Ha-Dat we-ha-Hayyim,* Lemberg, 1885. (First published 1876-7.)

Chase, M. E., *Life and Language in the Old Testament,* London, 1956.

Cohen, I., *History of the Jews in Vilna,* Philadelphia, 1913.

Davidson, D., *The Social Background of the Old Testament,* Hebrew Union College Press, 1942.

Davidson, I., *Parody in Jewish Literature,* New York, 1907.

Dolitsky, M., *Shebet Sofer,* Vienna, 1883.

Driver, S. R., *An Introduction to the Literature of the Old Testament,* 9th ed., Edinburgh, 1920.

Dubnow, S. M., *History of the Jews in Russia and Poland,* Philadelphia, Vol. I, 1916; Vol. II, 1918.

Eissfeldt, O., *Einleitung in das Alte Testament,* Tübingen, 1934.

Erter, I., *Ha-Zofeh le-Beit-Yisrael,* Vienna, 1858.

Fichman, J., *Anshei Besorah,* Tel Aviv, 1938.

    Allufei ha-Haskalah, Tel Aviv, 1952.

Forster, E. M., *Aspects of the Novel,* London, 1927.

Fowler, H. T., *A History of the Literature of Ancient Israel*, New York, 1912.

Frank, J., "Le-Toledotaw Shel Mapu," in *Ha-Shiloah*, XXXIV, 1918.

Friedberg, A., *Sefer ha-Zikronot*, Warsaw, 1899.

Ginsburg, S., *The Life and Works of Moses Hayyim Luzzatto*, Philadelphia, 1931.

Goitein, S. D., *Omanut ha-Sippur ba-Mikra*, Jerusalem, 1956.

Gordon, J. L., *Kol Shirei J. L. Gordon*, Tel Aviv, 1929.

Grabo, C. H., *The Technique of the Novel*, Scribner's, U.S.A., 1928.

Graetz, H., *Geschichte der Juden, Leipzig*, Vol. V, 1895; Vol. XI, 1900. English revised edition, *History of the Jews*, London, 1891-2.

Gray, G. B., *The Forms of Hebrew Poetry*, London, 1915.

Greenberg, L., *The Jews in Russia*, Vol. I, New Haven, 1944.

Halkin, S., *Modern Hebrew Literature*, New York, 1950.

Von Herder, J. G., *Vom Geist der Ebräischen Poesie*, 2 vols., Dessau, 1782-3.

James, H., *The Art of Fiction*, New York, 1948.

Kaplan, A., *Hayyei Abraham Mapu*, Vienna, 1870.

Klausner, J., *Yozerim u-Bonim*, Vol. I, Tel Aviv, 1925. *Historiah Shel ha-Sifrut ha-'Ivrit ha-Hadashah*, Vol. III, 2nd revised ed., Jerusalem, 1953.

Klausner, J. A., *Ha-Novelah ba-Sifrut ha-'Ivrit*, Tel Aviv, 1947.

Kleinman, M., "Abraham Mapu ve-Hashpa'ato," in *Demuyot we-Komot*, 2nd ed., London, 1928.

König, E., "Style of Scripture," in Hastings, *Dictionary of the Bible*, extra vol., 1904, pp. 156-69.

Lahower, P., *Mehkarim ve-Nisyonot*, Warsaw, 1925. *Toledot ha-Sifrut ha-'Ivrit ha-Hadashah*, 6th ed., Tel Aviv, 1946.

Leavis, F. R., *The Great Tradition*, London, 1948.

Lepin, J., in *Keset ha-Sofer*, Berlin, 1857.

Levin, S., *Childhood in Exile*, London, 1929.

Liddell, R., *A Treatise on the Novel*, London, 1949.

Lilienblum, M. L., "Olam ha-Tohu," in *Ha-Shahar*, IV, 1874.

Lods, A., *The Prophets and the Rise of Judaism*, New York, 1937.

Luzzatto, M. H., *Migdal 'Oz*, Leipzig, 1837.

La-Yesharim Tehillah, Amsterdam, 1743.

Macdonald, D. B., *The Hebrew Literary Genius*, Princeton, 1933.

Maimon, S., *The Autobiography of Solomon Maimon*, English ed., London, 1954.

Mapu, A., *Kol Kitevei Abraham Mapu*, Tel Aviv, 1950.

Matthews, I. G., *Old Testament Life and Literature*, New York, 1934.

Meisl, J., *Haskalah*, Berlin, 1919.

Moore, G. F., *The Literature of the Old Testament* (Home University Library), London and New York, 1913.

Muir, E., *The Structure of the Novel*, London, 1949.

Oesterley, W. O. E. and Robinson, T. H., *An Introduction to the Books of the Old Testament*, London, 1934.

Palmer, J., *Ben Jonson*, London, 1934.

Patterson, D., "The Use of Songs in the Novels of Abraham Mapu," in *The Journal of Semitic Studies*, Vol. I, No. 4, October, 1956.

"Moses Mendelssohn's Concept of Tolerance," in *Between East and West*, London, 1958.

"Israel Weisbrem: A Forgotten Hebrew Novelist of the Nineteenth Century," in *The Journal of Semitic Studies*, Vol. IV, No. I, January, 1959.

"Some Religious Attitudes Reflected in the Hebrew Novels of the Period of Enlightenment," in *The Bulletin of the John Rylands Library*, Vol. XLII, No. 2, March, 1960.

"The Portrait of Hasidism in the Nineteenth-Century Hebrew Novel," in the *Journal of Semitic Studies*, Vol. V, No. 4, October, 1960.

"Hebrew Drama," in the *Bulletin of the John Rylands Library*, Vol. XLIII, No. I, September, 1960.

The Foundations of Modern Hebrew Literature, London, 1961.

"Some Linguistic Aspects of the Nineteenth-Century Hebrew Novel," in The *Journal of Semitic Studies*, Vol. VII, No. 2, Autumn, 1962.

"The Portrait of the 'Zaddik' in the Nineteenth-Century

Hebrew Novel," in *The Journal of Semitic Studies,* Vol. VIII, No. 2, Autumn, 1963.

The Hebrew Novel in Czarist Russia, Edinburgh University Press, 1964.

"Epistolary Elements in the Novels of Abraham Mapu," in *The Annual of Leeds University Oriental Society,* Vol. IV, 1964.

Perl, J., *Megalleh Temirin,* Vienna, 1819
   Bohan Zaddik, Prague, 1838.

Pfeiffer, R. H., *Introduction to the Old Testament,* New York, 1948.

Rabin, C., "Olelot le-Toledot ha-Dramah ba-Haskalah ha-Germanit," in *Melilah,* Vol. V, 1955.
   Ivrit Medubberet Lifenei 125 Shanah, in the series *Leshonenu la-'Am,* Jerusalem, 1963.

Raisin, J. S., *The Haskalah Movement in Russia,* Philadelphia, 1913.

Ruppin, A., *The Jews in the Modern World,* London, 1934.

Sachs, S., "Toledot Abraham Mapu," in supplement to the 30th year of *Ha-Zefirah,* Warsaw, 1903.

Scholem, G. G., *Major Trends in Jewish Mysticism,* Jerusalem, 1941.
   Shabbetai Zevi, Tel Aviv, 1957.

Sha'anan, A., *Iyyunim be-Sifrut ha-Haskalah,* Merhavia, 1952.

Slouschz, N., "Miktab Mapu le-Ahiv," in *Ha-Zeman,* 1908.
   The Renascence of Hebrew Literature (translated from the French), Philadelphia, 1909.

Smolenskin, P., *Ha-To'eh be-Darekei ha-Hayyitn,* Warsaw, 1905. (First published 1868-70.)

Spiegel, S., *Hebrew Reborn,* New York, 1930.

St. John, R., *Tongue of the Prophets,* New York, 1952.

Streit, S., *Ba-Alot ha-Shahar,* Tel Aviv, 1927.

Waldstein, A. S., *The Evolution of Modern Hebrew Literature,* New York, 1916.

Waxman, M., *A History of Jewish Literature,* New York, Vol. I, 2nd ed., 1938; Vol. II, 2nd ed., 1943; Vol. III, 2nd ed., 1945.

Werses, S., "Iyyunim ba-Mibneh shel *Megalleh Temirin Zaddik*" in *Tarbiz,* Vol. XXXI, No. 4, 1962.

Wessely, N. H., *Shirei Tif'eret,* Prague, 1829

Diverei Shalom ve-Emet, 1782-4.

Ya'ari, A., "Abraham Mapu Bein Yehudei Arezot ha-Mizrah," in *Mo'zenayim,* III, 1931/2, part 48.

Zinberg, I., *Toledot Sifrut Yisrael,* Vol. VI, Tel Aviv, 1960.

Zitron, S. L., *Mapu u-Smolenskin ve-Sippureihem,* Krakow, 1889. *Yozerei ha-Sifrut ha-'Ivrit ha-Hadashah,* Vilna, 1922.

For bibliographical information on Mapu's letters see J. Klausner, *Historiah shel ha-Sifrut ha-'Ivrit ha-Hadashah,* in the bibliography to his article on Mapu.

Acknowledgements

The editor wishes to express his sincere gratitude to the many persons from whom he has obtained encouragement and advice, and particularly to Dr M. Wildenstein and Emeritus Professor H. H. Rowley of the University of Manchester, Professors C. Rabin and S. Halkin of The Hebrew University of Jerusalem, Mr R. May and the directors of the East and West Library, for their sympathetic interest and their many helpful suggestions. Not least, his sincere thanks are due to his wife, Josie Patterson, for her constant encouragement and help at all stages of the work.

David Patterson

About the Editor and Translator

David Patterson

David Patterson, CBE was founder President Emeritus of the Oxford Centre for Hebrew and Jewish Studies. He was an Emeritus Founder Fellow of St Cross College, Oxford and was the Cowley Lecturer in post-Biblical Hebrew at Oxford University from 1956-1989. He has published widely and made a tremendous contribution to the field of modern Hebrew literature and modern Jewish history. He passed away in December 2005, as this volume was in preparation.

The fonts used in this book are from the Garamond family